NO PLACE OF ANGELS

Also by Meg Hutchinson

Abel's Daughter
For the Sake of her Child
A Handful of Silver

NO PLACE OF ANGELS

Meg Hutchinson

Hodder & Stoughton

Copyright © Meg Hutchinson 1997

First published in 1997 by Hodder and Stoughton
A division of Hodder Headline PLC

The right of Meg Hutchinson to be identified as the Author of
the Work has been asserted by her in accordance with the
Copyright, Designs and Patents Act 1988.

10 9 8 7 6 5 4 3 2 1

A CIP catalogue record for this title is available
from the British Library

ISBN 0 340 67519 5

Typeset by Palimpsest Book Production Limited,
Polmont, Stirlingshire
Printed and bound in Great Britain by
Clays Ltd, St Ives plc

Hodder and Stoughton
A division of Hodder Headline PLC
338 Euston Road
London NW1 3BH

For my daughters, Lindsey and Kim,
who as children listened so patiently to
'Mother's stories', and who still listen with the
same loving patience

Chapter One

'I put you out of my way four years ago.'

Maria Beddows glared at the figure seated on the narrow wooden bench which ran around the walls of the third-class waiting room of Birmingham Snow Hill railway station.

'I put you where you could be no temptation and that is the way I intend matters shall remain. You thought to come out of that school and return to Holyhead House, to take up where you left off, but that is one thing you will never do.'

'But Holyhead House is my home!'

Maria's look was cold and hard as the brown-painted brickwork of the drab room. 'Holyhead House *was* your home, but not any longer. It ceased to be that the day you entered school.'

Her thin nostrils dilated, drawing in a deep draught of the room's cold air. 'Did you honestly think I would allow you to return, to enter my house again? Did you in truth believe you were sent away merely to finish your education?'

'But Father said . . .'

'It does not matter what your father said!' Maria snapped. 'Your father will not go against my decision when he hears what I have to tell him, and I say you shall not return home. You wanted to be out of that school, you were twenty-one

1

and of an age to please yourself, to do what *you* wanted to do. You wanted your freedom. Well, now you have it.'

Maria glanced quickly around the dim room but the sharpness of her voice had elicited no reaction from the people seated around the damp walls, huddled into their coats, heads down against the cold that filtered its way inside them. Smoothing her grey corded skirts as if to brush away any possible contact with the shabbily dressed travellers she stood up, her cold eyes sweeping the girl who posed a threat to the life she had so long desired, waited so long to enjoy – a life she had no intention of losing. Bending, she brought her face close to the thin pale cheek of the girl, seeming to any onlooker to be bestowing a farewell kiss.

'Take your freedom,' she hissed. 'But use it wisely. Stay away from Moxley, and stay away from me!'

'But I must come home to Holyhead House!' The girl reached out, clutching at Maria's skirts, her eyes wide and frightened. 'Where else would I go?'

Maria twitched her skirts free, her own eyes cold as the walls that surrounded them.

'I don't care where you go so long as you stay clear of Moxley.'

'But I have no money.'

'You should have thought of that sooner!' Maria's tone was acid. 'You had the opportunity to stay in that school, to become a teacher there. But you said no, turned up your nose at that. As a job and a place to live they were not good enough for you, were they? Not fitting for Meshac Beddows's daughter!'

'But I did not want to become a teacher, I wanted to come home . . .'

'I know what you want!' Maria said viciously. 'The same as I knew what you wanted before you were sent away to school. Oh, I knew what you were about – the coy little smiles, the lowered lashes every time he looked at you. Yes, I was on to your game and I put a stop to it. You can forget what is in your mind, forget all thoughts of returning to Holyhead House and taking up where you left off – forget Ryder Tempal, you will never have him!'

'You are wrong!' The carpet bag that held her few pos-sessions clutched in her hand, Carys ran after the older woman, already half way out of the door of the waiting room. 'I do not want Ryder Tempal, I never wanted him.'

'Oh, no?' Maria's brown eyes gleamed with menace. 'If you never wanted him, why is it that each time you came home for the holidays you hung on to him like a limpet, clung to him every moment he was in the house? Why, if you didn't want him, did you follow wherever he went, hanging on to his coat tails, embarrassing him with your attentions?'

It had not been like that. Carys followed her along the platform, aware of the watchful eyes of the uniformed station master. She had not followed on Ryder Tempal's heels; the reverse was true. He had dogged her footsteps wherever she went with his fawning smiles and lingering hands, followed her until she was forced to withdraw to her bedroom, the only place she could escape his unwanted attentions – her bedroom or her secret place.

'Please, I have no interest in Ryder Tempal.' She looked at the other woman but the face was cold and closed against her.

'Then that is as well for you, and it would be well to keep things that way. For should you try to return to Holyhead House or contact him in any way, I will see you dead!'

'Be you wanting this train, miss?'

Carys looked at the railway porter who touched his peaked cap to her despite the glare of the station master watching them from the doorway to his office. He had kept an eye on this girl dressed in a faded blue coat that had obviously been made to serve more years than it should. From midday she had stood at the end of the platform, an old carpet bag clutched in her hand, making no attempt to board any of the trains that had passed through. Now this was the last of the day. 'Get rid of her,' the station master had ordered the porter, 'tell her she has to leave. We can't have folk in the station overnight, much less a woman on her own.'

'Be you wanting this train, miss?' the porter asked again.

'I . . . I . . .' Carys turned to him, her amber eyes blank.

'Where do you be wanting to go?'

'Moxley, but . . .'

'You want this train then,' the porter said, relieved. The station master having taken several steps along a platform now almost empty of travellers, stared a silent command to the porter who added nervously 'C'mon, let's get you on board, train'll be pulling out in a little while.'

'No!' Carys hung back as the man made to take her bag. 'I can't – I can't go to Moxley.'

'But you said that was where you was wanting to get?' The porter cast a wary eye towards his superior.

'I know, that is where I thought to go, but now . . . now I can't.'

'Look, miss, this is the last train. There'll be no more till mornin' so it be this one or none at all, an' you can't go stopping on the station all night. So come on, there's a good wench, let's get you aboard.'

'But . . .' she said.

Carys's protests broke off as the station master, resplendent in brass-buttoned uniform, strode importantly up to where she stood with the porter whose eyes already spoke of his fear of the sack.

'Now then, young woman.' He did not touch his peaked cap; this was a third-class passenger and one who seemed barely able to afford that. 'If this be the train you be waiting on then you best be getting on now. It'll be pulling out in a few minutes.'

'No, I can't . . . it isn't.'

''Er said as 'er wanted Moxley an' I told 'er this was the train to be getting an' there'd be none other tonight,' the

4

porter almost gabbled as the station master's irate gaze settled on him.

'Was it Moxley you was a-wanting?'

A respectful 'miss' glaringly absent, the station master turned his stare to Carys. He was having nobody, young or old, male or otherwise, on his station overnight. It was the train or the street and no messing about on the way.

'Yes, it was,' Carys answered quietly, feeling the man's antagonism almost touching her. She shivered. She knew that touch well enough, had lived with it for the past four years.

'Well then!'

The station master fingered his well-waxed moustache, aware of the inquisitive stares of passengers already seated on the train.

'I . . . I find I can no longer go to Moxley.' Carys saw the impatience in the man's eyes and almost cringed in expectation of the blow that usually followed such a look.

'Well, you'll not be going anywheres else tonight.' Stubby fingers worried one end of the stiffened moustache. 'Least not on a train, that is, so you best be getting along. Take your ticket to the ticket office an' change it when you makes up your mind where you wants to be.'

He glanced at the porter hovering nervously at his elbow and gave a slight hitch of his head, which clearly said, 'That's if a woman can ever make up her mind about anything.'

'I do not have a ticket to change.'

Carys watched the man's look of incredulity turn to one of anger.

'You don't 'ave no ticket!' he burst out. 'Then what the 'ell be you playing at? You've been standin' on this platform nigh on seven hours an' all that time you ain't had no ticket? That means you either had no intention of going anywheres or else you 'oped to slip on to a train without paying and . . .'

'I had no such intention!' Beneath the anaemic flare of the

gas lights that punctured the shadows of the platform Carys's cheeks flushed hotly.

'Then why stand 'ere all day? Hollings, see 'er off.'

The station master strode away, his hand coming up smartly to his bottle green cap as he scurried to open the door of a first-class carriage for a late arrival.

Along the platform Carys shrank against the wall, seeking the protection of the gloom. She recognised the man climbing into the train: the tall muscular build even under the dark velour overcoat, the sure confident step. Yes, she recognised him as she would anywhere, but he must not see her.

'You best be getting along, miss,' the porter said kindly. 'You don't want no trouble and the gaffer there, well, 'e will send for the bobbies if you don't go.'

'I . . . I'm sorry, I did not mean to cause you bother.'

Lowering her head against the yellow gleam of the gas lamps and the possibility that the man who had just boarded the train might see and recognise her, Carys began to follow the porter towards the arched entrance that gave on to the street. A possible confrontation with the police would be more than she could take right now.

'Eh up, you mad-brained bugger!'

Knocked almost off his feet by the figure hurtling into the station, the porter reeled and automatically reached out for something to arrest his fall. His hand fastening on Carys's arm, she stumbled on to her knees, the shabby carpet bag flying off across the platform.

'What the bloody hell d'you think you be about!'

Scrambling to his feet, the porter glared at the young woman who had cannoned into him, at the same time helping Carys to her feet.

'Ain't you got no more sense than to go running wild around a railway station?'

'Eh, I be right sorry, truly, but that there be my train and if I don't catch it then missis will be on to me summat rotten.'

'Being sorry don't butter no parsnips.' The porter glared. 'You young uns think you can go round doing just as you like an' sod the rest of we . . .'

'I said I be sorry.' The girl turned to Carys. 'Eh, luv, I hope as you ain't hurt none?'

'No, no, I am not hurt.' Carys dusted her shabby coat with both hands.

'That be as it might.' The porter glanced behind in the direction of the first-class carriages and visibly wilted as he saw the station master hurrying across to them.

'What be all the to do?' The station master's moustache bristled at his underling.

'It be nothing, Mr Robins, sir.' The porter retrieved the carpet bag, shoving it into Carys's hand. 'This young woman bumped into we, that's all.'

'But that ain't all!' The station master sucked in his cheeks importantly. There had been an accident on his station and that was something he did not like, something he did not like at all. His moustache, so stiff with wax it stood out from each side of his face like a couple of malacca canes, bobbed up and down with the angry workings of his mouth. 'That ain't all at all! This 'ere young woman has been knocked down. In short, there has been a haccident . . .'

'Nobody ain't hurt.' The girl who had raced into the station threw an anxious glance towards the steaming train.

'Nevertheless a haccident is a haccident and must be reported,' said the station master, bristling anew.

'There is really no need for that.' Carys took the bag, her back to the train, aware of faces turned towards the little drama being played out on the platform.

'There be every need.' The moustache rose and fell importantly. 'It be the policy of the L.M.S. railway to report every haccident caused to a passenger, no matter how trivial. An' this has been a haccident.'

'But I'll miss my train if you keeps me hanging about while you writes out whatever it is you haves to write out. Tell him

7

you ain't hurt, miss?' The girl looked pleadingly at Carys. 'Tell 'im you don't want him making no report?'

'It don't matter what 'er says,' the station master returned pompously. 'There has been a haccident involving a passenger and as station master I haves to report it.'

'But there has not been an accident involving a passenger.'

Carys gave a last flick to her coat as she met the station master's intimidating glare.

'Of course there has!' he rapped at her. 'This here young 'ooligan knocked you down.'

'No, she did not.' Carys met the angry stare full on. 'She bumped into the porter who, as he lost his balance, accidentally caused me to stumble.'

'As I said, a haccident!' The station master wore his triumph like a medal.

'As you said, an accident,' Carys concurred quietly. 'But not an accident caused to a passenger. If you recall, I told you I had not purchased a ticket and that I was not intending to take a journey on any train. To be a passenger one must have a ticket and I do not have one, therefore I cannot be said to be a passenger, so it follows there is no need for you to write out a report.'

The station master's mouth worked fiercely, jerking the moustache up and down as he tried to come to terms with what he knew to be logical yet loath to relinquish his authority, seeing the girl's argument as in some way challenging the power he wielded.

''Er be right.' The second girl grinned. 'If 'er ain't bought a ticket then 'er ain't no passenger – so you can clear off out of my way afore I reports you for hobstructing the travelling of a young lady who has got a ticket, bought and paid for.'

'Just you makes sure as you have . . .'

'Oh, I have a ticket all right.' She fished in the pocket of her coat, drawing out a slip of white card. The black lettering and the neat hole punched in one corner showed clearly in the sickly yellow gas light as she waved it only inches below the dancing moustache.

A few yards away the engine belched noisily as a guard somewhere in the shadows blew his whistle.

'Blimey, I'm gonna miss me train!'

Grabbing Carys by her free hand, she ran for the train, oblivious to the calls of both porter and station master.

'Hold it, hold it!' she screeched, sprinting along to where the third-class carriages stood at the far end of the platform. 'Give a girl a chance to get on.'

Dragging Carys behind her, she jumped into a carriage, its door swung open by a passenger seeing them charge along the platform, and sank laughing on to the wooden seat as the guard blew three short blasts and the train steamed slowly forward.

'That was close.' The girl touched a hand to the bonnet that had come slightly askew in their race for the train. 'The missis would have my guts for garters if I didn't get back tonight.' She sank against the wooden back rest, her eyes closed. 'Eh, that was clever, the way you handled that la-di-dah station master. I would never have thought to pretend I hadn't got a ticket.'

'I was not pretending. I do not have a ticket.'

'Eh!' The girl's eyes opened and even in the dim light of the single candle enclosed in a glass shade held by a wall bracket, Carys could see consternation fill them. 'But you have to have a ticket! You can be prosecuted for tryin' to diddle the railway company.'

'I was not trying to cheat the railway company. In fact, I was not about to travel on this train.'

'Eh!' The girl's eyes widened still further. 'But . . . but you was on the platform.'

'Yes, but I was not about to board the train. I was just about to leave the station.'

'Oh, lor'!' The girl slumped back in her seat again. 'Oh, lor'. Now what do we do?'

Carys glanced across the carriage to the opposite seat where a woman fumbled her breast into the mouth of a screaming infant. What could she do? The best thing would be to get off at the first station and try to explain to the attendants there what had happened. And then what? Would the police be called and she arrested?

'Had you just got off this train at Snow Hill?' The girl shifted in her seat to look at Carys, ignoring the grumbles of a man wedged into the seat beside her as he pulled his flat cap over his eyes and settled to sleep.

'No,' Carys answered, seeing the woman feeding the baby look at her with interest.

'Well, if you wasn't getting on and you hadn't got off, what was you doing? I mean, it don't make no sense you being on the station if you wasn't coming or going.'

'Might be 'er was meeting somebody off the train.' The woman suckling the child eased her nipple from its mouth allowing it to burp noisily before pushing it back.

'Was that what you was there for, to meet somebody?' the girl asked. 'Lor', what will they do when they finds there you be, gone?'

In the narrow, half-dark compartment Carys smiled to herself. It had been four years since she had heard the peculiarly contradictory manner of speech that was the nearest Black Country people came to the King's English, a manner of speech that warmed her with memories.

They had spoken that way, the men and women employed in her father's enamelling works, but for all the roughness of their speech they had been kind to a small child lonely for companionship, unlike some of the teachers at that place her mother still referred to as a school who, for all their correct usage and polite speech, had made her life there a hell.

'Well, don't matter 'ow much they looks for 'er, they won't find 'er cos 'er be on this train.' The woman fastened her blouse across the breast she took from the now sleeping baby, adjusting the heavy woollen shawl about the child, then proceeded to peer across the narrow gap between the wooden seats.

'Eh, what we going to do?'

'Well, whatever it be, you better do it quick.' This time it was the man with the cap over his eyes who spoke. 'The conductor'll be here afore long and if 'e cops 'er without a ticket, it'll be the bobbies fer sure.'

'P'raps if we tell him what happened, he might turn a blind eye?' the girl suggested hopefully. 'If we tell him what with rushing for the last train, we hadn't time to go to the ticket office, he might let you off.'

'Arrh, and pigs might fly – only don't go holdin' your breath till you sees 'em go over,' the man answered drily. 'From what I hear, the railway be clamping down on fare dodgers. They be prosecutin' everyone they gets 'old of and that means six months down the line.'

Prison! Carys felt her heart leap in her chest. Would they really send a woman to prison for the sake of a few pence? She didn't ask the question aloud for she already knew the answer.

'P'raps if whoever you was supposed to meet said what you was at Snow Hill for, it would be all right?'

Carys heard the hope in the voice of the girl who had dragged her on to the train and hesitated, hating to destroy it.

'I was not there to meet anyone.' She had to say it at last.

'This is getting to be like one o' them there Sherlock Holmes stories.' The man sat up, pushing his flat cap back from his eyes. ''Er wasn't at the station to be going anywhere an' 'er wasn't there to be coming back, neither was 'er there to be meeting anybody – so what the 'ell *was* 'er there for? Best get your answer ready, wench, 'cos that magistrate is going to want to hear it.'

''E might not have to.' The woman lifted the hiccuping baby to her shoulder, patting it none too gently on the back. 'You could just pay the price of a ticket to the conductor when 'e comes round.'

''Course, that's right.' The girl heaved a long sigh of relief. 'I hadn't thought of that. Just pay to where you want to get off an' there'll be no trouble, that's the answer.'

Across from her the baby burped again and, crooning her approval, the woman rocked it in her arms. It would be the answer, Carys thought, except for the fact she had been left without a single farthing.

'No trouble?' The man shifted in his seat, a surly disgruntled movement as if this apparent solving of the problem had stolen his limelight. 'You drag 'er on to a train 'er didn't want to be on in the first place then tell 'er, all airy-fairy like, to cough up 'er own fare to pay for a journey 'er 'ad no need of – *then* you tell 'er it's no trouble! Huh! I know what I'd be telling you if it was me.'

'Well, it ain't you, is it?' the girl replied tartly. 'And I don't remember nobody asking you to stick your big nose into a private conversation.'

'Like that, is it?' The man slouched back in his seat, once more pulling the cap low over his eyes. 'Well, don't ask me to stick it in when that conductor asks for 'er ticket 'cos you'll ask in vain.'

'We won't have to ask.' The girl pushed herself more squarely on to the slatted wooden seat, shoving the man farther into the corner as a token of her annoyance. ''Er will pay for a ticket and there'll be no bother. That be right, don't it?'

Carys felt rather than saw the smile in the girl's eyes and had to force out the words that would drive it away. It had been done in the spirit of kindness, her being hauled on to this train; the girl had obviously thought she had intended boarding it.

'I can't pay for a ticket,' she said, 'I have no money.'

For a long minute the silence was broken only by the regular click of the train wheels passing over the points in the track, then from beneath the cap came a satisfied grunt.

'Like I said, best have an answer ready for the magistrate, 'cos sure as hell be hot 'e is going to want to hear it.'

'You mean, you ain't got no money at all?'

'Not so much as a penny,' Carys answered the other girl's question.

'Look, I don't understand this.' It took several seconds for her to speak. 'You was on a railway station but you had no intention of getting on a train, and you had no money to pay for a journey you didn't intend to take?'

'I told you it was like a Sherlock Holmes story,' came the voice from beneath the cap.

'Arrh, you did,' the girl replied acidly, 'but you ain't no Doctor Watson judging by the help you've come up with so far, so do we all a favour and keep quiet.' She turned to Carys, squinting at her by the dim light of the candle. 'Well, whatever you were about on that station it be my fault you find yourself on this train, so least I can do is pay your fare.' She hesitated, realising she had no idea where the other girl was headed. 'Where do you be going?' she asked. 'Where do you live?'

The answer was simple enough. Carys felt a tug in her chest. She was going nowhere, she had nowhere to live.

'My home is in Moxley,' she said, knowing she had to reply.

The girl rummaged in her bag then held out her hand, running a finger over the coins gleaming in her palm.

'I'm sorry but I've only got enough to get you to the station at Wednesbury,' she apologised. 'I ain't got the price of the cab you will need to take you on up to Moxley.'

'Wednesbury will do, I can walk from there.'

She would not walk to Moxley, Carys thought, she would not walk anywhere tonight except maybe a shop doorway somewhere. Then tomorrow . . . but what of tomorrow? It would bring no answer to her problem. Tomorrow would not bring her a home.

Chapter Two

Without a word to the maid who opened the door to her, Maria passed quickly up the broad staircase of Holyhead House, closing the door of her bedroom behind her.

Removing her feathered bonnet, she threw it on the bed, at the same time drawing a long slow breath. She had done it! She had prevented the girl's return to this house, prevented her from taking up with Ryder Tempal. There would be no more coy smiles and whispers, no more walks alone with him in the garden, and she, Maria, need no longer fear competition from a girl more than twenty years her junior.

'She shall not have him!'

Crossing the room, Maria Beddows stared with satisfaction at her own reflection in the long cheval mirror. At almost forty she still made an imposing picture. Her figure was good and set off to advantage in tasteful claret-coloured velvet, the dark hair dressed high on her head crowning a face that was almost beautiful.

Almost beautiful . . . Anger flared like fresh-lit coals in her brown eyes, drawing down her brows and marring her good looks. She had been aware of the girl's growing beauty, aware of the interest she commanded whenever guests were in the house, aware of the competition.

'But I put a stop to that,' she whispered to the image staring back at her. 'I have waited too long to let her take him from me, let her take what should be mine – what *will* be mine. She will not have him, she will *never* have him.'

Touching one hand to her head, she patted a non-existent stray hair into place, her well-shaped mouth curving into a triumphant smile. Her little trip to Birmingham had been successful; she had got rid of one thorn from her side and there would be no argument from the other. Meshac would make no effort to bring the girl home once he had heard what his wife had to tell him.

Meshac!

Dropping her hand to her breast, she smoothed it down to her tightly corseted waist, her mind busily weaving the threads of imagination. If only Meshac were to die, the rest would be so easy. If he were to die she would be free. The barrier to her happiness with Ryder Tempal finally removed, she would be free to lead the life she wanted, with the man she wanted.

A tap at her door interrupting the thought, Maria turned impatiently, calling her permission for the maid to enter.

'A messenger from the Bilston works, mum.' The girl bobbed a curtsy.

Message? Maria's mind whirled for a moment. Could it be that Meshac had met with an accident? Could he be dead? Seeing the girl look at her, knowing that for one unguarded moment she had let the light of hope shine in her eyes, Maria turned towards the bed, picking up her bonnet.

'Yes, Mary, what is it?' she asked, her voice more controlled than her thoughts.

'A message from the master, mum. He sent a man from the works to say as 'ow 'e will be bringing a guest to supper and to tell you they would be 'ome around eight.'

'Did the master say who his guest was?'

'No, mum, just that 'e was bringin' somebody to supper. Shall I tell Mrs Coates to come up, mum?'

16

'No.' Maria tossed the bonnet aside once more and turned back to face the maid. 'Mrs Coates will manage very well as she always does. Tell her I leave everything in her capable hands.'

Maria unbuttoned the claret velvet as the maid withdrew. Having a guest this particular evening suited her; it would delay any explanation of the girl's absence and give her more time to plan just what she would say as the reason for Carys's not returning home. Catching sight of herself in the mirror, Maria smiled.

Things were working out better than she could have hoped. Tonight with a guest to entertain Meshac would be certain to take more than a little of the wine and more than one glass of the brandy his doctor had advised against. Tonight he would have more than alcohol to lull him to sleep; tonight she would take steps to bring about her dream.

'It be a fair walk to Moxley . . .'

The girl who had paid Carys's fare to the none-too-pleasant conductor on the train turned to look at her as they left the L.M.S. station at Wednesbury.

'. . . and I don't feel too easy about your headin' off there all by yourself. It'll be black as pitch when you come to cross the 'eath.'

'I will be all right.' Carys clutched the carpet bag closer to her as though the paltry contents somehow gave her comfort. 'I am sorry to have taken the last of your money to pay my fare here.'

'Couldn't do no other seeing as it were my fault you was on that train in the first place.'

'But having no money left means you also will have to walk home,' Carys said as they trudged away from the dimly lit station.

'That won't hurt me none.' The other girl grinned. 'I'm used to walking home, ain't nothing new for me. But it is fer you, ain't it?' Her grin gone, the girl looked at Carys more shrewdly. The shabby, seen-better-days coat did not hide the girl's innate look of gentility though the hands that clutched the carpet bag were those of someone used to manual labour. Wherever this girl had come from she had been worked hard, but even more puzzling was where she was headed and how she had planned to get there without money.

'You ain't never walked to Moxley afore, have you?' she asked again.

Carys shook her head, turning her face away so the other girl would not see the tears that suddenly threatened to spill.

'I thought not.' The girl stopped abruptly. 'What's more, it be my guess you ain't going to walk there tonight neither. You ain't got a home in Moxley, 'ave you? In fact, it strikes me you ain't got a place nowhere.'

Across the street the last few women hurried homeward from the street market. They had waited for the nine o'clock bargains from Tedd's fish stall and Harry Stokes's meat stall, sold off cheap as the day's business came to an end. Soon the town centre would be deserted except for men coming and going between Wednesbury's many public houses.

'Well, I knows one thing for sure.' The girl tucked her arm through that of Carys. 'You ain't sleeping under no hedge. You best come with me. Mrs B. ain't so hard as to see a young wench out of a place to spend the night.'

'Mrs B.? Is she your mother?'

The girl's laughter rippled through the gathering night. 'Lor', that 'er ain't! Mrs Bates be the cook and housekeeper up at Ridge House – that be where I'm in service. I be the parlour maid-cum-everything else. Chief cook an' bottle washer me mom calls it, but it be better than nowt.'

Carys hung back as the girl made to pull her along. 'I can't just turn up there, whatever would they think?'

'Well, you can't stop out on the streets all night neither. What if the bobbies sees you and takes you in for vagrancy? That would mean three months down the line. I tell you, it be better you come to Ridge House with me for tonight and you can sort yourself out in the morning.'

She was right, of course. It was not wise to stay the night under a hedge. Though she knew it would be no different tomorrow, Carys allowed herself to be pulled along.

'Say, I don't know your name? I can't very well introduce you to Mrs Bates as the girl I pulled on to the train, can I?'

'It would not sound very good.' Carys gave an uncertain smile. She still wasn't sure that turning up on a stranger's doorstep and asking for a night's shelter was the right thing to do.

'So what shall I call you?' The girl elbowed her way past a group of women, their baskets about their feet as they waited for the tram that would take them up Holloway Bank.

'Carys – my name is Carys Beddows.'

The name obviously meant nothing to the girl leading the way along Bridge Street and Carys added no more as she followed.

'Was that where you had your last place then, in Brummagem?'

'Where?'

'Brummagem. You was on the station there and you says you wasn't goin' anywheres nor comin' from nowheres so strikes me you must have been there from the start.'

'Yes . . . my last place was in Birmingham.'

It was the truth, Carys told herself. The only home she had known for the past four years had been that convent in Birmingham.

'And they give you the push, did they, the nobs you worked for? Hey!' The girl stopped suddenly, peering at Carys through the gathering darkness. 'You wasn't kicked out for nicking, was you? 'Cos I ain't taking nobody to Ridge House whose fingers be too light for their hands. The missis there be a good employer and I ain't repaying 'er by taking a thief into 'er house.'

'I am not a thief!' Carys flashed, indignation at the accusation flooding her with heat. 'I . . . I left my last place of my own accord. I no longer felt any satisfaction in . . . in being there.'

'I knows what you means.' The girl carried on walking. 'I feels that way meself sometimes. I feels I'd like to up and get meself off to pastures new, but I ain't never quite had the nerve.'

Behind them a tram rattled and shook as it came on, already groaning at the prospect of climbing the steeply rising ground. Carys watched as it passed, hearing the conductor calling out the next stopping point.

'So, Miss Carys Beddows, may I hintroduce Miss Alice Withers?' The girl giggled as she dropped an exaggerated curtsey.

'I am honoured to make your acquaintance, Miss Withers.'

Carys returned an equally affected curtsey, causing both of them to break into laughter.

'Well now, ladies, how would it be if a fine handsome strapping bloke was to join in the joke?'

A candle in a jar suspended from a hook cast a weak glow over a wooden sign announcing the building the man was leaving to be The Globe public house.

Instinctively clutching her carpet bag, Carys stepped closer to Alice as the man swayed forward, the stink of his breath carried before him.

'Well, I'd say as how that would be a fair treat.' Alice faced him squarely. 'If there *was* a fine handsome fellow in the vicinity, which there ain't. There be only you, and you ain't so much strapping as strapped, I'd say, and the only joke you can be joining is the one on you if you thinks otherwise!'

'I bet you thinks that be clever?'

The man's hands went to the leather belt about his waist, its buckle gleaming in the dim light of the candle, and Carys felt her heart jolt sickeningly as he began to ease it loose.

'I think it be a lot cleverer than your taking that off.' Alice stood her ground, staring at the whiskered face just a yard from her own. 'The men in there be hot from ale, and the waters of the Tame be cold. Both can be foul, as you will find out when we scream, mister. Men hereabouts don't take kindly to wenches being apprehended on their way home o' nights. One squeal from me and you be like not to see morning.'

For several moments the man's hands fingered the buckle then dropped to his sides, his shoulder deliberately driving into Alice as he lurched away. 'Bugger off!' he called thickly, voice mingling with a burst of laughter coming from the public house. 'Anyway, who wants to put their 'ands on shit?'

'I doubt 'e would have said no, given half a chance,' said Alice. But relief he had given up so easily told in her voice. She turned to where Carys had slumped against the wall. 'Don't you pay no thought to that little performance.'

'But he . . . he was about to strike you!' Carys had lived seventeen of her years in Moxley and well knew what it meant when a man unbuckled his belt. Though it had never happened to her she had seen the marks of the buckle on many a lad's back when visiting the Bilston enamelling works with her father.

''E would have got more than 'e bargained for if 'e had.' Alice caught her arm, tucking it beneath her own as she set off again, following the road that now began to rise fairly steeply. 'Thank God 'e had the sense to realise it.'

'Does that sort of thing happen often?' Carys flinched as a figure scuttled from the darkness only to disappear fast, swallowed up by the blackness of an alleyway that separated one row of small mean houses from the next. They had been built close to the edge of the cutting made to lay the road and tram rails.

'Not to me it don't,' Alice chuckled. 'Seeing as I'm usually with me brothers if I have to be out at night. And woe betide any bloke who tries any funny business with them around!'

'But your brothers are not with you tonight?'

'No, and don't you never tell 'em I've been out on me own at night. That would give me mother a heart attack. It only be that the mistress had this brooch 'er wanted special to wear at some do 'er has been invited to and the pin broke so 'er asked me to take it to be mended.'

Along the dark ribbon of houses a dog barked, the short staccato sounds raking Carys's nerves. Her arm tensed beneath that of the girl walking beside her. 'Is that why you were in Birmingham today?'

In the darkness Alice nodded. 'What a grand day it's been an' all! I ain't never been there afore. It were quite flummoxin' findin' me way among all them streets – it were like a maze. But you'll know that from living in the place. I enjoyed the visiting of it but I don't know as how I would like to live there.'

'But why go all the way to Birmingham just to get a new pin put on a brooch? There is surely a jeweller closer?'

Alice puffed from the effort of the long climb, dragging air into her lungs only to force it out between her teeth. 'Mr Josephs along Hydes Road be a watchmaker, I don't know whether you would call that being a jeweller, but the mistress always gets 'er trinkets seen to by them in the jewellery quarter and that be in Brummagem.'

Carys remembered her one visit to that part of Birmingham some called 'the jewellery quarter', while others referred to the narrow twisting streets and warren of tiny workshops as 'the gold quarter'. Her father had told her, when taking her with him to deliver a specially commissioned set of enamelled cameos she herself had designed, that the men who worked here in these small cramped rooms handled some of the rarest gems in the world and produced the most fabulous pieces of gold jewellery.

'Phew!' Alice stood for a moment, catching her breath, as they crested the rise. 'Not much further now. Ridge House be just across the 'eath to the left there.'

She pointed into the darkness but Carys did not follow the direction with her eyes. She had turned to look back the way they had come. There at the foot of the hill Wednesbury spread a carpet of tiny pinpricks of light; the flames of candles set in jars and the odd gas lamp all danced like the Jack-o'-Lanterns her father used to take her to watch, flitting in and out of the branches of the trees growing around the pool in a flooded mine shaft. And beyond those pinpricks of light, in the outer ring of darkness, lay Moxley and her home.

Her home! Carys felt hurt and despair sear through her. From now on she had no home. She had thought earlier, standing on the station platform, that her father would not believe what was told him of her not wanting to return home, wanting instead to lead her life away from him, but even as she had thought it, she'd known her father would believe anything his wife told him.

'C'mon.' Alice took her arm again. 'Mrs B. will be getting nervous at me being out so long. And watch your step – the ground be pretty bumpy this way, but by cutting across the 'eath we save time. We would follow the road on to Hill Top and branch off there to go along the drive straight up to the house, but like I says, that puts another ten minutes on the journey. Me, I always cuts across the 'eath.'

Feeling the heels of her side-buttoned boots sink into the soft earth, Carys stumbled in the wake of a hurrying Alice, expecting every step to throw her flat on her face so that it was with decided relief that she eventually saw the great solid black mass of Ridge House loom out of the darkness.

'Stranded, you says?'

Martha Bates's eyes took in the figure standing just inside the door to the kitchen. The coat she wore had seen better days but her face was well-scrubbed and her boots were polished; the carpet bag was shabby but the fingernails of the hands that clenched it held no line of dirt beneath them. This girl, whoever she was, kept herself clean though her clothes were old and she didn't have gloves.

'Yes, mam.' Carys bobbed a polite curtsey.

And she had manners, Martha noted, her anxiety that Alice

23

had brought some undesirable back with her fading a little more. And the girl's manner of speech was pleasant, not the usual careless dialect of the Black Country.

'Well, get you in by the fire, wench, there be time to tell all about that after supper. And you . . .' She turned to where Alice sat beside the range, unbuttoning her boots. 'Did you do the mistress's errand?'

'Yes, Mrs Bates.'

In the warm light of the kitchen the girl smiled as she eased her feet from her boots, stretching her stockinged toes to the fire glowing behind the steel bars of the grate.

'And the brooch, you 'ave it safe?'

'Safe as houses.' Alice nodded.

'Well, let's be having it, wench?' The housekeeper held out an impatient hand.

Standing up from the chair she had taken beside the range, Alice gathered up her skirts and petticoats, bundling them beneath her chin then pushing her bloomers several inches down from her waist and beginning to unhook her corset.

'Alice!' Martha Bates's eyes rounded. 'What in the world be you doing, wench?'

'It's the mistress's brooch. I put it under me corset for safe-keeping.' The smile became a grin as she fished beneath the half-open corset, coming out with a small brown suede bag.

'Well, I never!' Martha took it, her mouth widening into a surprised smile. 'Whoever would think of putting it there?'

'That's what I thought.' Letting her skirts fall, Alice plonked herself back on her chair, wriggling her toes against the heat of the fire. 'You did keep tellin' me to take care and keep it safe, and you did keep going' on about them pocket pickers, so I put it in the safest place I could think of . . . weren't no pocket pickers going to get their hands under my stays!'

'Mistress will have herself a good laugh when I tells 'er where 'er brooch has been this last few hours. And speaking of hours, what took you so long gettin' back here?'

'Ooh, Mrs Bates, you wouldn't ask that if you had seen that

there jewellery quarter. Talk about finding your way out of a maze! I reckon that would be child's play compared to getting yourself out of that place. You no sooner finds your way out of one back alley than you be in another. Them narrow little streets all weave in and out of each other like threads on a loom. I got meself lost a time or two an' by the time I did get to Snow Hill station I'd missed the afternoon train and the evening one was just about to pull out. I was lucky to catch it, what with that bloomin' station master.'

'Well, you be home now, and seeing as you am, you best get that girl out of her coat and then see to making a pot of tea. I think we could all do with a drink and a bite of supper.'

Slipping the suede bag into the pocket of her starched white apron, Martha glanced at Carys still standing uncertainly by the door. 'Take off your coat, girl, and get you to the fire. I know the mistress would not have you turned out into the night. Though comes the morning . . .'

Slipping out of her coat, Carys watched while Alice hung it in a tall wooden cupboard set at the farthest end of the large kitchen then accepted the chair the girl had vacated.

'What will you do tomorrow?' Alice busied herself with cups and plates. 'I mean, you ain't got no money, so you says, an' you can't live off air so you have to get yourself a place somewheres.'

'It's true I have no money, none at all.' Carys felt the warmth of the fire sink into her bones. She had not realised she had been so cold. 'But don't worry that I will impose upon your mistress's hospitality, I will leave first thing in the morning.'

'And go where?' Alice fetched bread and a haunch of cold beef from the larder, returning to bring out butter, cheese, and a large jar of pickled onions which she set on the table.

'And do what?' The second question was asked as she poured boiling water into an enamel tea pot.

'I . . .' Carys hesitated, trying to judge whether her next words were such a terrible lie. They were not the truth, she had not thought of finding a job or a place to live, she had thought only of those words she had heard on the station platform: '*Stay away from Moxley . . . try to return to Holyhead House . . . I will see you dead . . .*'

'I thought perhaps I might find something in Wednesbury.'

'You might find work.' Taking a large knife from a drawer set in the wooden table that occupied the centre of the kitchen, Alice proceeded to slice several pieces of bread then went on to carve thick slices of the cold beef. 'Though I doubt very much it will be the sort of work you be used to. Your hands be red but I'd say you ain't never done no really hard work – well, scrubbing floors ain't what I would call work, and they only have my sort in Wednesbury. Try down there an' you're like to finish up gleaning coal from the pit heaps to sell for a tanner a hundredweight. Lor', you'd be better off in the workhouse!'

'I told you the mistress would laugh when 'er heard where you had gone and put 'er brooch.' Martha Bates bustled back into the kitchen, immediately taking charge of filling each of the plates with slices of beef.

'Was 'er brooch mended suitable?'

''Er was very pleased with it, Alice, though 'er was concerned when 'er heard you had been and gone and got yourself lost in that there jewellery quarter.'

'No need for the mistress to go worrying.' Relieved of carving the beef, Alice fetched the enamel pot from the hob, filling each of the three cups with hot strong tea. 'I did get lost but I soon found meself again.'

'Arrh, you be a sensible wench when you uses your head.' Martha smiled benignly before turning her glance to Carys, beckoning her to take a seat at the table.

'I told 'er about you and how you have no place you can be getting to tonight, and as I said 'er gives permission for you to stay here.'

'Thank you, it's very kind of you all.'

'Yes, well, they says kindness is a virtue. Besides, there might be a time we shall all need a bit of the same.' Martha glanced at Alice, the teapot still in her hands. 'Don't stand there nursing the pot wench, come along and eat your supper.

'Mistress says, if you have no objection, 'er would like a word with you afore you leaves in the morning.'

'Oh!' Carys looked up from her plate, concern adding to the shadows already underlining her eyes.

'There be nothing for you to fret over.' Martha noted the fear rising like a tide on the girl's face. 'Mistress is just wanting reassurance that you will be all right travelling about on your own like, but 'er said as if you don't have no wish to talk with 'er then we was to see you well fed afore you left.'

'Carys thinks 'er will p'raps find a job and a place to stay in Wednesbury.' Alice sliced a piece of beef, placing it in her mouth, and continued shortly, 'but I told 'er there be nothing likely to suit 'er in that town. It's nobbut iron and steel mills, and 'er wouldn't last two minutes in that lot.'

'Don't speak with your mouth full!' Martha reprimanded then. 'So Carys be your name, eh? I told the mistress you'd not spoken it.'

'I beg your pardon.' A faint touch of pink blending with the pallor of her cheeks, Carys immediately apologised. 'I am afraid the events of the day have driven all the manners from me. My name is Carys Beddows and I live . . . used to live . . . at Moxley.'

Used to live at Moxley. Again Martha Bates saw the shadow of pain flit across that pale face. So what had happened to take away that home? How had this girl come to be stranded in a railway station, and who was responsible?

One by one the questions rose in Martha's mind but they would remain unasked, at least until morning. This girl had taken all she could for one day. Much more and she would break.

'We all forget our manners once in a while.' She smiled. 'Now you finish your meal and then Alice can take you upstairs. There be a room next to hers you can have. It be only small but it will serve, and there be sheets and blankets in the linen cupboard.'

'Mrs B. likes you,' Alice said later as she finished helping Carys make up the small bed in a room on the top floor of the house. 'I think 'er would take you on as kitchen maid like a shot with the mistress's say so. If you decides to go and talk to 'er in the morning, why not ask if 'er will give you a position here in this house? You'd be better off here than down in the town. And besides, I likes you an' all.'

'And I like you too, Alice.' Carys smiled across the width of the narrow bed. 'And I am very grateful to you for helping me. I shall of course speak to Mrs . . .'

'Mountford,' Alice said as Carys hesitated. 'The mistress be Mrs Virginia Mountford.'

'. . . to Mrs Mountford,' Carys went on, 'but as for asking for a position in her household, I couldn't. I wouldn't feel . . . I've never . . .'

'. . . You have done the work of a kitchen maid before.' Alice finished the sentence for her. 'I can see that, and this place ain't too bad once you learns the routine and I could help with the heavier chores. Mrs B. ain't too much of a slave driver, neither. Believe me, girl, you could do a damn' sight worse than take a post at Ridge House.'

Yes, she could do worse than take a post at Ridge House. Carys washed her hands and face with cold water from a jug set on a wooden wash stand. Taking one of the two cambric night gowns that had had to serve her since entering that convent from her carpet bag, she slipped it over her head, smoothing the cold fabric over her body.

She could do worse than take a post at Ridge House – like going home to Moxley.

Chapter Three

The evening had gone much as Maria had thought it would. Meshac had eaten a great deal and drunk more while talking endlessly of enamelling. For once she had not allowed this to irritate her; it served her purpose to have him absorbed in talking business which kept his thoughts from the daughter he had expected to see home. He had asked about her once when their visitor had remarked upon the beautiful designs of the boxes and caskets he had ordered. Meshac had told him proudly of his daughter's skills as a designer and her proficiency with a pencil.

'Quite a good little artist, my wench,' he had proclaimed. 'Could have been an asset to the business had her been a lad, but a wench . . .' He'd shrugged, drinking deeply from his favourite Madeira. 'Wenches be good for naught but the marriage bed.'

That had been when he'd glanced along the exquisitely furnished dinner table to Maria sitting at its foot and asked why Carys was not present. But she had been prepared for the question. Smiling directly at her husband, she had spoken the lie without flickering an eyelash.

'She asked if she might have a few days with a friend who will be returning to her parents in India at the end of next week, after which the girls will probably never meet again. My dear, how could I say no? She looked so tragic at the prospect of losing her friend, and it will be only for a few days.'

Her lovely mouth drooping becomingly, Maria listened with satisfaction as her husband reassured her that allowing Carys to remain with her friend had been the right thing to do. Meshac . . . She watched him now, smiling at her with those faded eyes. He loved his child but he loved his wife more. She almost laughed. It was so easy! Each time he had asked why the girl did not visit her home, the touch of Maria's mouth on his had wiped the questions away. Poor Meshac, he was besotted, so much so he believed her every word, and that was all to the good . . . her good.

In the darkness of her soul, Maria smiled. But when she turned that smile upon their visitor it had been all grace and charm.

'Young girls do so enjoy tragedy, do you not think, Mr Fereday?'

Maria remembered the look he had given her from eyes so dark they might be chippings of the coal Moxley was built on; eyes that held none of the admiration she was accustomed to encountering in men.

Tying the ribbons that fastened her lace-edged silk night-gown about her throat, she crossed her bedroom, taking up a hair brush from a dressing table liberally strewn with creams and cosmetics. No, the eyes of Reuben Fereday had not glinted with the desire she loved to evoke.

It made him more interesting.

Stepping to the cheval mirror, she stared at her reflection. Beneath the silken nightgown her body was firm and slender. Dark hair released from the constraint of pins fell around her shoulders, framing a face that was beautiful – almost as beautiful as that of Meshac's child.

Meshac's child! Maria pulled the brush through her hair savagely. Born to be beautiful and raised in every comfort, the only child of a wealthy industrialist, she had claimed everyone's heart with her gentle ways and happy laughter. She had claimed the attention of Ryder Tempal. Maria wielded the brush with long angry strokes. But Carys would not finally claim that man, she herself had made certain of that today. The girl would not return to Moxley, would not be here to tempt Ryder Tempal, to draw his attention where Maria could not allow it to stray.

In the six months since she had first met the tall fair-haired handsome nephew of Colly Moreton she had come to realise he was everything she wanted, to realise it with a cold conviction. She was more certain about this than she had ever been about anything in her life before. He was everything she had dreamed of in a husband, in all the long dreary years she had been tied to Meshac Beddows, and somehow or other that was what he would become: her husband.

Meanwhile . . . Maria ceased to drag at her hair, holding the brush in her hand, her eyes glittering back at her from the mirror like bronze pools, her well-shaped mouth touched by the merest smile. Meanwhile . . . it might be interesting to test the seeming indifference of Reuben Fereday!

Alone in the small room set under the eaves of Ridge House, Carys lay staring into the darkness. Had the events of today really happened or were they simply a nightmare that had not yet ended? Had it been only this morning she had left that school; only hours since she had been abandoned penniless at that railway station? But her nightmare had begun long before that. It had begun over four years ago, when she first met Ryder Tempal.

Maria had known him for several weeks before his first visit to Holyhead House, having met him at the home of Colly Moreton, a friend and business associate of Carys's father.

She had just been to her secret place.

Carys stared at the shadows painting the walls of the tiny room. It had been the summer of her seventeenth year. Outside her window a cloud passed in front of the moon,

31

leaving a wake of darkness, as that summer had left a wake of darkness – four years of darkness that had seemed like four lifetimes.

Ryder Tempal had been in the drawing room when Carys had arrived home and from their first meeting his eyes had devoured her. Tall and broad-shouldered beneath aubergine coloured topcoat, he had taken her hand, holding it too long while he gazed at her with eyes the colour of a cat's.

Carys turned her head on the pillow as if in some way the movement would dispel the image of the handsome fair-haired man who'd stared at her from strange feline eyes. But the image persisted as the man had persisted, calling so often at Holyhead House as to be almost impolite.

That had been when Maria's attitude to her had deteriorated. Theirs had never been a close relationship, not one of real friendship or love, more a matter of mutual toleration. But that had given way the night Maria had come upon them in the garden.

The Moretons had been visiting for dinner when Zelda Moreton had suggested her nephew take Carys for a turn about the garden. It had been an exceptionally warm night and her father had supported the idea, claiming the air would do her good.

They had been in the garden only a few minutes when Ryder had grabbed her arm, almost dragging her into the summerhouse. Swinging her into his arms, he kissed her violently.

'Carys.' He whispered her name as his mouth left hers. 'Carys.'

Shock robbing her limbs of strength, she had stood limply in his arms as he rained kiss after kiss on her mouth.

'We will be married in a month.'

She remembered hearing the words but they had passed over her head, floating about her like motes in a sunbeam.

'Your father will agree, I am sure. I shall tell him of our

intentions when we return to the house and in one month you will be Mrs Ryder Tempal.'

Carys squeezed her lids hard down over her eyes, trying to dispel the memory as she had tried to so often over the past four years. But as always it remained, playing out its lurid drama in her mind.

'We will be man and wife and I will have more than your delectable mouth to kiss. This lovely body will be mine to admire, to enjoy . . .'

His hand had closed over her breast, squeezing the soft flesh, his wet lips searching for her mouth again.

'And I will enjoy it, so many times, and so will you . . .'

Her eyes open wide, Carys pressed the back of one hand to her mouth and sickness rose in her as she seemed to feel again his hands on her body.

His voice, hoarse and strained as his fingers kneaded her breast, at last penetrated the cocoon of shock that had enveloped her at the first touch of his mouth. She pushed against him but his arms held her.

'I . . . I don't want to be your wife . . .'

The feline eyes glittered down at her. His grip tightened as she struggled to free herself.

'I know this might seem a little sudden to you, but you knew from that first meeting I intended you to be my wife.'

'No, I don't wish to marry you. I will never marry you!'

In the darkness of her room at Ridge House Carys heard again his soft mocking laughter.

'Your intentions and mine may be different, but it is mine alone that matter. To fulfil those intentions I need money, and if the only way of getting it is to marry it then I shall do so. You have no say in the matter.'

'My father has!' She had twisted free from his arms but he stood in front of the door to the summerhouse, barring her escape. 'He will not agree to a marriage for which he can see I have no desire. He would never force me to marry you.'

'He will when he finds out his daughter has enjoyed the bed without the marriage!'

Ryder had launched himself at her then, the weight of him tumbling her to the ground, knocking the breath from her body. She had heard the tearing sound as he had snatched at her bloomers and the sound of her own cry muffled by the pressure of his mouth as he rolled on top of her.

That had been when Maria had lashed her foot hard into his ribs.

Carys had heard nothing of what she had said to Ryder. Scrambling to her feet, she had run for the house, entering through a side door and gaining her room via the back stairs.

The following day Maria had dropped her bombshell.

'Mrs Bates said you wished to see me, ma'am?' Carys bobbed a curtsey to the woman seated beneath a high rectangular window.

Virginia Mountford, iron grey hair complemented by the deep plum-purple shade of her gown, looked at the girl who had sought shelter beneath her roof. Her dress of brown calico was shaded in patches, the paler colour a testament to its long service, but though old it was brushed and well-pressed, and the boots that peeped from beneath it bore no evidence of clay, though having come here with Alice, she would have arrived by way of the heath.

'Sit down, my dear.'

Virginia watched as Carys took the chair placed opposite her own. The girl did not stare open-mouthed at the quiet elegance of the room which meant she was accustomed to such surroundings, or at least had been.

'My name is Virginia Mountford, but no doubt Alice has already told you that?'

'Yes, she did, ma'am,' Carys replied as the woman smiled.

'And do you have a name?'

'I beg your pardon.' Carys blushed at this repetition of the

34

night before when she had forgotten to introduce herself. 'My name is Carys Beddows.'

'Of where?'

The woman's keen eyes on her face, Carys hesitated. Hill Top was only a few miles from Moxley. Would this woman know Meshac Beddows? Would she guess the girl in her house was his daughter?

'I . . . I come from Birmingham.'

The grey head nodded. 'The wise men came to Bethlehem from the palace of Herod, my dear, but that was not their home.'

The tinge of pink in Carys's cheeks deepened. Virginia Mountford was a shrewd woman.

'I came here from Birmingham where I have been at school for four years.' Carys swallowed hard on the word. 'Before that I . . . I lived at Moxley.'

'Moxley!' The grey head bobbed again. 'I have been there on occasions – a small place with a few houses and a church. Much like here at Hill Top except we have no church. We have to go into Wednesbury for that.'

She had visited Moxley! Carys let her glance rest on her own hands, clenched together in her lap. Chances were she knew of Meshac Beddows's child, but did they know of her mother's lies?

'Alice bull rushed you on to a train last evening, so I hear?'

If this woman knew of her history it seemed she was not about to refer to it. Carys felt weak with relief.

'It was not meant, ma'am. Alice did rush me into the train but thought she was doing me a kindness.'

'That is the one fault with Alice.' A quick smile curved the older woman's mouth. 'She does not think. She acts first, leaving the thinking until later. But she is a good girl and one I can trust. What she did, she did from the best of intentions so you must allow me to see you get where you wanted to go before meeting her.'

'There is no need! I . . . I can manage alone, thank you.'

Like she had managed yesterday? So lost and confused she had been, capable of going nowhere. Virginia thought over the scanty bits of information her housekeeper had gleaned from Alice whilst this girl had been dressing.

'My dear.' She spoke gently but there was a firmness in her voice. 'It is not easy managing alone, especially when you are young and straight out of school. Take the advice of one older than yourself and accept help when you know it to be offered in true friendship.'

Carys looked at the woman who had taken her unquestioningly into her house, sheltered her when there had been no need for her to do so, fed her, and was now offering yet more help. And suddenly she knew that help *was* indeed being offered out of a sense of friendship, and one that deserved to meet with the truth. Slowly, her fingers clenched together against the pain of it, she told of the events on the platform of Snow Hill railway station.

'Did you not think of returning to your school? They would surely have given you shelter until you had time to sort yourself out,' Virginia said when Carys finished speaking.

'To be honest, I did not think of that. I was so dumbfounded my brain did not seem to function.'

'That is not surprising! You were left there without money and without a home, but there must be a reason for such an action?' Virginia Mountford's eyes, grey as her hair, were fixed on Carys. 'Though I do not ask you to tell me of it.'

Carys did not want to tell this woman of the unreasonable and totally unfounded jealousy that had led her to be interned for four years in a hell only the cynical would call a school, and which had now robbed her of the home she loved. But she felt that the kindness already shown to her deserved a full answer.

'There is a reason, though it was no more than an imaginary one,' she answered softly. 'Maria thought the attentions Ryder Tempal paid me were welcomed by me, when in reality I

36

found them detestable. Whenever I knew he was to be a guest at Holyhead House, I would try to invent some reason to be absent, the more so as his visits increased, but my attempts to avoid meeting him were not always successful. Then one night he came as a dinner guest with his aunt and uncle, the Moretons of Mesty Croft, and when he suggested a turn in the garden my father agreed. It . . . it was while we were there that he pulled me into the summerhouse and when I refused to marry him, he tried . . . he tried . . .'

'To rape you?' Virginia asked. 'Is that what he tried to do to you?'

'Maria must have known he was forcing himself upon me but she refused to accept it. So far as she is concerned, I was the one to blame,' Carys said against the tightness of her throat.

'That, I presume, is when you were sent away to school?'

'Yes.' It was a whisper redolent with the misery of four years. 'Except it was not a school, it was a convent – Maria entered me as a novice in the Convent of the Holy Child. As such I was to undergo three years' training then take the vows that would keep me there forever.'

'You had no idea what she had planned?'

'No, and neither had my father, of that I am sure. She must have told him some dreadful lie to keep him from searching for me.'

'I doubt he would have found you, incarcerated as you were in a nunnery. Many poor girls are lost that way.'

'It was my fourth year, the year of my final vows, when I became twenty-one. Sister Mary Immaculata, the Mother Superior, sent for me and asked if becoming a nun was my true vocation. Was I ready to give my life in the honour and service of God? I told her I hoped always to honour God and to serve him but not in the ways of a nun. She then told me I was free to leave if that was what I wanted. That she had only agreed to my entering the convent on condition the final decision of whether or not to take the veil should be mine alone.'

'Obviously Maria thought that after three years you would no longer wish to leave?'

Carys nodded. 'Mother Superior also returned my sketches.'

'Sketches?' Virginia Mountford's brows rose questioningly.

'It seems Maria had shown them to her as proof of my lasciviousness, of the danger I was in of becoming a woman of loose virtue. They apparently showed I was a child in need of strict moral training, for my own good, and I have no doubt she told the same to my father. She had brought the sketches with her so that Mother Superior could judge for herself the truth of what she had been told and then counteract such wickedness.'

'But Mother Superior did not destroy them?'

'No.' Carys shook her head. 'She said that such work could only be a gift from God, that great artists like Michelangelo and Raphael had made such sketches, and that I should use my talent to His glory and to enrich the lives of others.'

'These sketches, did Maria destroy them when she came to collect you from the convent?'

'I . . . I did not tell her I had them, nor did Mother Superior.'

'So you have them still?'

'They are in my carpet bag.'

'May I see them?'

Virginia watched the girl as she asked the question. There was no swift rush of colour to that beautiful face, no guilty lowering of the eyelids, yet there was something: a slight set to that fine mouth, a tilt to the head. Whatever she had sketched there'd been no intention of wickedness, no evil except in the minds of those who wished to see it.

'My bag is in the kitchen. I will fetch it.'

'No.' The older woman pulled a bell rope beside the fireplace. 'Alice can bring it.'

'My dear,' she began again, having instructed Alice to bring the carpet bag to the drawing room, 'I am going to claim the privilege of an old woman and use your given name, which by the way is a very pretty one.'

'It was my father's grandmother's name.' Carys smiled.

'Ah, the old names. So much nicer than the airy-fairy ones young parents seem so fond of these days. Well, Carys, to continue with what it was I intended to say! In short, child, you have nowhere to go and I have no one to talk to. If you will consent to stay here in Ridge House, I shall be pleased to have you.'

She had not waited to see the sketches first, to judge from them the girl's suitability to be in her house; she would not base her judgement on a few pencil lines scratched over a piece of paper. Virginia Mountford had accepted Carys at face value, accepted the girl on her own judgement and not that of others. Feeling the tears begin to trickle, Carys spoke softly.

'I thank you for your kind offer, ma'am, but perhaps you should see my sketches before offering me a place in your home?'

'I don't need to see any sketches to know you, child.' Virginia waited as Alice entered the room, handing Carys the carpet bag and bobbing a curtsey to her mistress before leaving. 'I asked to see the sketches merely from an interest in art. My husband, God rest him, had quite a passion for paintings. He collected many throughout the years and I too enjoy them, though I have to guard them from my nephew who would have them in a public gallery.'

'Your nephew is an artist?'

'No, though he seems to have inherited his uncle's passion for works of art. But Reuben is one of the new breed. "Art belongs to the public" is his motto. The beauty of it should not be a privilege held only by the wealthy few . . .'

'I think I agree with him, ma'am.' Carys's face coloured slightly as she voiced her opinion.

'Maybe I do too.' The old face wrinkled in a conspiratorial smile. 'But I will not give the young rogue the pleasure of knowing it. He can do what he will with this house and all it contains after I am gone, but in the meantime he will continue to think whatever it is he thinks of his old aunt. Now, Carys girl.' She held out her hands. 'Let us see these oh-so-terrible sketches of yours.'

'Sister Mary Immaculata was a wise woman!' Virginia Mount-ford held the last of the sketches in her hand. 'There is more than beauty in this work, there is strength – the strength of man glorying in life, praising the God who created him. They are hymns whose words cannot be written; songs in which only the true artist may join.'

Carefully rolling the parchment, she handed it back to Carys. 'You have a great talent, child. I hope you use it well.'

Taking the rolled up sketch, Carys replaced it in the carpet bag, covering it with her one extra petticoat and pair of bloomers.

'Well now, girl.' The older woman leaned back, her grey hair glinting with the sheen of gunmetal caught in the sun. 'I have seen what it was Maria thought the work of the devil. Now I await your answer to my proposal: will you stay here at Ridge House?'

'*Stay away from Moxley!*' Carys heard the words in her mind. Would Ridge House be far enough away? Hill Top was some four, maybe five, miles from Moxley and Wednesbury lay between. Would that span be enough to separate her from Maria or was the danger of their meeting too great a risk to take? But where would refusing this woman's offer lead her? 'You could do a damn' sight worse than take a post at Ridge House,' Alice had said. Remembering the convent and that awful interlude at Snow Hill station, Carys knew she was right. Ridge House, even with the possibility of meeting Maria, was the safest place to be.

'Thank you, ma'am.' Carys met Virginia's grey eyes frankly. 'I should be grateful for a position in this house. I can scrub and clean, and am well acquainted with the laundry room and the preparation and cooking of food. I can use a needle and was taught the skills of using herbs for healing. I was also taught to keep household accounts.'

'All this by the convent?'

Carys nodded, a thousand memories screaming in her silence.

'They did well, the Convent of the Holy Child, but did their teaching include none of the arts?'

'None apart from the music required for services. Not dance or drama and certainly not drawing. Even though Mother Superior acknowledged the skills of the artists of the past, she did not encourage their practices in any of the sisters or novices.'

'Well, that will not be the case at Ridge House,' Virginia smiled. 'You must take up sketching again, though I doubt you will find much of beauty beyond the garden. This Black Country of ours is well named for its feet stand in coal and its head is crowned with the chimney stacks of iron and steel foundries. In truth, a depressing picture. But its people have hearts as strong as the steel they work, they are among the finest and hardest working people this country has. Treat them fairly and they will treat you the same. And, remember, they are not all Marias!'

No, they were not all Marias. First Alice and now her mistress had proved that. Carys stood up, the carpet bag in her hand. 'Will I tell Mrs Bates that you have given me a position here or would you have me tell her to come and see you?'

'We have not yet decided upon what you are to do.' Virginia Mountford's eyes took in every aspect of the girl facing her though they never once strayed from her face. 'As I said, I have no one here I can really talk to and could do with a companion. But you look uncomfortable with the idea. Does it not suit you?'

A flush of warm blood rising to her cheeks, Carys lifted the gaze that had fallen to her feet at this proposal. To appear to be throwing the offer back in her face was the last thing she wanted, but to become companion to Virginia Mountford would be to come into contact with her friends . . . friends who would talk, friends who might also be acquaintances of Maria.

'Forgive me if I seem rude, ma'am.' She swallowed hard. The answer she was about to give could dash the offer of a home, it could put her back on the streets without money or hope, yet it had to be said. 'I . . . I would rather be in the kitchen with Alice and Mrs Bates. It . . . it isn't that I have no wish to be a companion to you, believe me, but . . .'

'But you see that as possibly bringing you to the attention of Maria?' Virginia pulled the embroidered bell cord. 'I should have thought of that. Hill Top is a small hamlet but gossip travels far. You are right, my dear, a housemaid will raise less speculation than a companion, though perhaps we two might chat together from time to time?'

'That would give me a great deal of pleasure.' Carys smiled, relieved that her refusal had caused no animosity.

'My dear . . .' Virginia Mountford hesitated slightly then went on, 'Forgive an old woman's curiosity, and of course you must not answer my question if you feel it intrudes upon your privacy, but this Maria you speak of – is she perhaps an elder sister or maybe your step-mother?'

'No.' Carys felt the room close about her. 'She is neither of those. Maria is my mother.'

Maria slipped off the jacket of her cerise velvet travelling suit and sent her feathered bonnet swinging across the hotel room. The journey to Birmingham had long ceased to be a pleasure; the train was far quicker and less obvious than her own carriage but the fear of being seen by someone who knew her increased with each trip. Not that there would be many more. She loosened the buttons of her skirt, letting it fall in heavy folds about her feet. Soon there would be no need for her to come to this dreary hotel hidden away in a maze of streets behind the Bull Ring; soon she would have the life she yearned – a life that did not include Meshac or Meshac's child.

She had never thought of the girl as her own. There had been no rush of mother love twenty-one years ago when she had given birth to her and no depth of love had developed in her as the years had passed.

She had kept their relationship more on what could be construed as sisterly terms, though in her case the elder sister felt nothing for the younger; in fact she had felt no emotion at all until Ryder Tempal had made an appearance, bringing in his wake something Maria had not experienced before, bringing jealousy, jealousy of a girl whose beauty was fast approaching her own . . .

Maria kicked away the froth of petticoats with an impatient thrust of her foot; pushed off her frilled bloomers. She had not seen him for a month, one which she had tried to pass in gaining the attention of Reuben Fereday – but his response to her advances had been so restrained as barely to be polite.

Snatching off her lace-edged chemise, she twisted it viciously in her fingers. Reuben Fereday had been to the house several times and on each occasion had enquired after the girl, eliciting fresh queries from Meshac too. Fereday showed no interest in Maria. But he *would* show an interest! She threw the chemise from her. He would show an interest as all of Meshac's friends showed an interest in his attractive wife.

Attractive! Crossing to the square mirror set above a small dressing table, Maria stared into it, seeing the dark hair fashionably dressed in thick glistening coils, the cool alabaster swell of her breasts, the trim waist and the face men found so appealing. Yes, she was attractive, but not beautiful. Not as her daughter was beautiful!

And how much longer would it last, this attractiveness? Not long enough. Maria loosened the pins from her hair, letting it tumble over her creamy shoulders as she stared into the mirror. Not long enough to waste further time married to Meshac Beddows.

'Now that is the way a woman *should* wait for a man!'

Maria looked to the door reflected in the mirror then turned, holding out her arms to the man standing just inside.

'Isn't this the way you would want your wife to wait for you?'

He smiled, walking into her arms and drawing her naked-ness hard against him while pressing his face to her throat.

'Just this way,' he breathed thickly. 'And when you are my wife this is the way you will always wait for me.'

'Which is what I have been doing for a month now!'

Pushing him from her, Maria stared at him, an accusatory light in her brown eyes.

'A month and not a single word from you! Where have you been? Or, more to the point, what girl have you been chasing this time?'

'I have been with no girl,' Ryder Tempal said easily. What Maria did not know would not hurt her. 'I have been to Liverpool on business for my uncle.'

Maria allowed herself to be drawn back into his arms. Colly Moreton had talked of having business in Liverpool.

'But now I am back here with you.' He bent his head, kissing the tip of her breast. 'The only place I want to be, with the only woman I want.' Dropping to his knees, he drew his hands over the lines of her body, following with his tongue from her navel down over her stomach. 'Maria.' He pressed his mouth against the dark mound between her thighs. 'Oh, Maria, my love! If only you were my wife.'

She would be soon. Maria watched him from the bed as he threw off his clothes; watched the muscles ripple in his strong body and felt the blood quicken in her veins, felt the desire for him surge through her like a rip tide and knew it was just as dangerous. He was like a drug to her, robbing her of any sense but that of wanting him, and she had waited long enough for what she wanted. Her daughter was gone out of her life for good. Soon it would be the turn of her husband.

Chapter Four

'I bet you be fagged out?' Alice poked the fire in the kitchen range, clearing dead ash from between the bars.

'Of course 'er be tired, 'er as worked like a good one all day.' Martha Bates smiled at the girl her mistress had taken in out of the night. She had not said much of where she had come from or to whom she belonged, but so long as she worked well and kept her tongue civil then Martha reckoned her business was her own. Spooning liberal amounts of sugar into the large cups of cocoa she had just made, she handed one to Carys then turned to Alice, still working ash from beneath the embers of the fire. 'Just throw a bucket of sleck on that then come and drink your cocoa afore it be cold.'

'I'll get it.' Carys rose quickly, bringing the bucket filled with small fragments of coal from the scullery.

'It don't go on like that.'

Alice took the bucket as Carys prepared to empty it on to the fire.

'You have to damp it down first otherwise it will burn through afore morning and that'll mean havin' to light the range all over again. Here, let me show you.'

Filling a small pan with water from the pump over the sink,

47

she tipped it a little at a time into the bucket, mixing the chippings and coal dust into a thick paste.

'That be the way to damp a fire for the night.'

She grinned as the last of the paste was scraped from the bucket and on to the quietly hissing fire.

'Last all night, will that, and still be alight in the morning.'

'Arrh, that will keep the kitchen warm enough through the night, and you will be glad of that come winter mornings.' Martha nodded as Alice disappeared to wash her hands in the scullery. 'This house can get cold as a barn, stuck up here atop of the hill. I often wonders why the mistress don't go some place else. I know for a fact 'er as a fine house in Evesham 'cos I've been there with 'er a time or two.'

'Ee, I wish I'd been to Evesham . . .'

Alice returned to the kitchen, her hands red from their scrubbing in cold water. She knew that one hint of coal dust left on them would have her back in the scullery scrubbing them over again.

'I ain't never been nowhere 'ceptin' Wednesbury . . . oh, an' Brummagem.' Alice tilted her head to one side, remembering. 'But I don't like Brummagem. Did you like living in Brummagem, Carys?'

Had she liked living in Birmingham? Carys stared into her cup. Truth was she knew almost nothing of the place. One visit to the jewellery quarter with her father had afforded her very little insight, and on that journey to the convent she had seen nothing but a blur of tall buildings set so close together along the streets they seemed melded into one other. And once inside the convent she had seen nothing beyond its high curtain wall.

'You won't like getting up in the morning, Alice Withers, so cut the cackle and get yourself off to bed. And don't go chattering once you be upstairs. Carys be near tired out, 'er won't want to be listening to you prattling all night.'

*   *   *

'When I be wed I shall have my husband take me to Evesham and to . . . to lots of places.'

White calico nightgown tucked over her feet, knees drawn up to her chin, Alice perched on the end of Carys's bed, her eyes as dreamy as her thoughts.

Pulling a brush through her hair, Carys smiled to herself. Mrs Bates's intervention downstairs had cut short Alice's questions but had not dispensed with them. Tying her plaits with pieces of ribbon she turned to the girl, who was momentarily lost in a pink cloud of imagination. Carys liked Alice and knew her questions were just a young girl's harmless curiosity.

'Wouldn't you like to travel, to see places, ride in a carriage with your husband?' Alice asked dreamily.

'I would have to get a husband first.'

'Have you got anybody . . . I mean, was you walking out with a lad when you was at Brummagem?'

'No.' Carys's smile faded as thoughts of the convent returned. 'I was not being called upon by a man . . . in fact, I had not one visitor during the whole time I was there.'

'What, never!' Alice's eyes rounded. 'Not even your mam or your dad?'

Carys shook her head and when she answered her voice trembled. 'It . . . it was not allowed.'

'Ee, I don't rightly see as how a school can stop your parents coming to see you.' Alice frowned. 'Specially if they be paying a deal o' money for the teaching.'

'It was not a school,' Carys said, her trembling still visible. 'It was a convent, the Convent of the Holy Child, and I was entered as a novice.'

'A nunnery!' Alice breathed. 'They put you in a nunnery?'

'My mother did. I believe my father thought I was in some exclusive finishing school, possibly even on the Continent somewhere. That can be the only reason why he accepted my not going home for holidays.'

'But why should your mam stick you in a nunnery? I mean,

49

what had you done . . . you didn't go in 'cos you wanted to, did you?'

'No, I did not enter the convent from choice. As for my mother's reasons, she must have had them though I don't know what they were.'

Maybe no words of Maria's had told her the reason she was to be locked away from the world but her actions had spoken loudly enough, especially that night in the summerhouse.

'Anyway, you be out now and of an age where 'er can't push you anywheres you ain't of a mind to be, so forget about 'er. But truly, ain't you never had a fancy for a boy?'

Carys climbed on to the bed too, her own knees tucked beneath her chin, and smiled at the girl whose questions flitted from one subject to another with the ease of a butterfly exchanging one resting place for another. She had never had a fancy, as Alice put it, not for a boy, but would the same be true of a man? She felt traces of warmth steal into her face. Would it be true of the man she had seen in her secret place?

'There must have been somebody?' Alice warmed to her theme. 'You said you was seventeen when you was put into that nunnery. You must have had an eye to some lad in that time. Ain't no wench reaches seventeen years without some bloke taking her fancy.'

'Well, I did.' And Carys laughed, glad the light of the one candle was not strong enough to show the bloom of pink on her cheeks.

'Lor'!' Alice looked almost stricken. 'What on earth did you do with your time?'

'Sketched.'

'Sketched!' Alice's face lost none of its stricken look. 'You mean, drawring? With a pencil and paper?'

'Yes, drawing with a pencil and paper. Or sometimes with charcoal.'

'Lor', how boring!' Alice threw herself flat across the narrow bed. 'Catch me with a pencil and paper.'

'It wasn't boring.' Carys glimpsed the sun on water, caught

a breath of the perfume of wild flowers and heard the faint hum of insects in the grass. Her secret place had never been boring.

'These sketches what you drawed, have you still got them?' Alice sat up once more, her curiosity rekindled.

'A few.' Carys admitted. 'Just the ones Maria . . . my mother . . . took to show to Sister Mary Immaculata.'

'Sister Mary who?' Alice blew out her cheeks, letting the breath escape her mouth expressively. 'That be a mouthful of a name. Fancy landing a babby with a label like that! Immac . . . Immac . . . Lor', I can't even say it.'

'Immaculata.' Carys laughed again as Alice pulled a face. 'It was the name she took when she entered the convent.'

'Did you have to have another name?'

'Yes.' Carys's smile faded. 'I was known as Sister Michaela.'

'Michaela.' Alice rolled the name over her tongue. 'Michaela . . . hmm, I like it. It sounds better than that Immac . . . whatever it was. It be more real, if you knows what I mean. Who chose it, you or your mother?'

'Neither.' Her mother had already left when the name had been allotted to her. In the dimness she recalled the gentleness of the old nun who had given her her name in Christ – so different from the Mistress of Novices whose voice was hard and whose hand was harder. 'The name was chosen by Sister Mary Immaculata. She said my drawings held some of the beauty of those of Michelangelo, so perhaps it would be fitting to bear a form of his name.'

'You've lost me.' Alice drew up her knees, closing her arms about them. 'I ain't got a clue who this Michael Angelo bloke is.'

'Never mind.' Carys stood up. 'It's time you were off to your own room. If Mrs Bates hears us still talking she won't be any too pleased.'

'Give us a look at them there sketches first, the ones you copied off that Michael bloke?'

'I did not copy his work, nor anyone else's for that matter.'

'All right, so you didn't copy nobody.' Alice grinned. 'So let's be having a look.'

Carys guessed the easiest way to get Alice away to her own bed would be to show her the sketches. Taking her carpet bag from beneath the bed, she drew out the several rolls of stiff yellowy parchment.

'Hey!' Holding them one by one, Alice stared at them by the waxy light of the candle. 'These be bostin', they am, they be real good. Stick these in a fancy frame and they could hang in a posh house. You should show these to somebody who knows about drawrings and such.'

She twisted the sheet of paper, trying to angle the light more fully on to the charcoal lines drawn across it. 'This one be *great*, Carys. No coddin', I thinks it's lovely.'

She meant it, Carys realised, watching the appreciation on the other girl's face, she really wasn't pretending.

'Who is he?' Alice peered at her, screwing up her eyes to pierce the semi-gloom beyond the reach of the candlelight. 'Do you know him, did he pose for you?'

'No, I do not know him.' Carys retrieved the sketch and, rolling it, replaced it with the others in the carpet bag. 'And no, he did not pose for me.'

'But he is real? I mean, he ain't somebody you just made up. He ain't no wotsit of the imagination?'

Carys pushed the carpet bag back under the bed. 'No, he is not a figment of my imagination, Miss Alice Withers, he is real as . . . as Mrs Bates's anger will be if she finds you still here when she comes upstairs. Now go to bed!'

'I'm going.' Alice slid from the bed, padding on bare feet to the door. 'Lor', I wish I'd met a bloke like the one in that drawring.' She giggled impishly before opening the door a crack and checking the corridor for the housekeeper. 'You can bet your birthday five bob piece we wouldn't have parted strangers!'

Climbing into bed Carys blew out the candle but the image of the man she had drawn still blazed vividly in her mind.

She had been in her secret place, in the hollow set into the rising ground that surrounded the Cracker – the name given by the folk of Moxley to a flooded cavern in the earth that had once been a mine shaft. She remembered the light breeze that had blown across the open heath, how it had touched a fern to her cheek. Sketching had been the one real interest in her life, and this pool with its surround of softly rising ground was a favourite location. In the darkness of her room she saw it now in her mind: the sun glinting like a million golden sequins on the dark surface of the water. She remembered thinking how cross they would have been at home had they known where she was but she had told no one of her secret: of the hollow just deep enough to seat her, allowing the ferns to camouflage her presence, and keep her safe from prying eyes. It had been so peaceful there.

She had closed her eyes, lying back among the cool greenery. So quiet. Here she could be alone, shut away in her own tiny kingdom. Warm and comfortable, she lay cradled in her green world until an inquisitive insect landed on her nose. Brushing it away, she sat up, surprised to see the sun was considerably lower in the sky. She must have been asleep. There might be concern over her long absence.

Gathering the sketch pad and pencil she had laid beside her among the ferns, she made to stand up then fell back as a movement in the water, near the far bank, caught her eye.

She had not seen what it was that had caused the widening ring of ripples now spreading over its glassy surface but it was not a fish, of that she was certain.

Hidden by the curtain of ferns she had watched the water, waiting for whatever it was to break the surface.

Then it came. In one glorious surge, arms lifted to the sky, tiny drops of water showering like a cloud of diamonds from dark hair, the man's figure rose from the black depths.

Below her the crash of water echoed on the still summer air and Carys sucked in her breath, watching, as the figure launched itself into the air, landing almost flat on the surface and momentarily displaying a long muscular body before it was lost again beneath the water.

Warmth touched her cheeks with pink. Carys turned her head on the pillow, embarrassed to remember the way she didn't turn away. Instead she had sat transfixed, waiting for the figure to rise again like Neptune from the deep.

For several minutes she sat watching him sport, churning the silken water as he dived and rose then dived again.

She knew very well she should not be there, much less watching a man bathe. But the thought did not spur her to leave. Aware of the pencil gripped tightly in her hand, she began instead to sketch – marking every line with movements as fluid as the bather below her; capturing the litheness of his movements, the sheer joy of his communion with the water, the perfect beauty of his body as it emerged, arms raised, head slightly turned towards her.

Carys felt again that catch in her throat as the head stayed turned to her for a long second, and the ripple of fear that sang along her nerves at the thought of being discovered.

But he had dived again, pushing himself upward then curving that strong body into a surface dive that carried him from her sight down into the black satiny waters.

Held almost as in some unseen trap she had waited for the figure to rise once more.

But it did not.

Carys turned her face to the window, seeing the moon hanging like a great yellow lantern in a sky as dark as those waters, and her eyes probed its blackness as she had the depths of the Cracker.

But still the figure did not rise.

Anxiety stifling her breath, she had stared at the still dark water, its glassy surface unbroken by even the tiniest ripple.

She remembered how moments had ticked into seconds and seconds into eternity and still the air had remained in her lungs, held there almost as if, by sheer will-power, her suspended breath had filled the man's body, holding him safe from the encroaching waters.

'Hey!'

The remembered shout caused her to release her breath, as it had then, forcing it from between her tight lips, leaving her head reeling and her lungs aching as on that day.

'Hey, you!'

The second shout, angry this time, had cleared her head instantly. Without realising, she had risen to her feet while watching for him to surface and now from the opposite side of the pool he watched her. Before she could prevent it her eyes had swept the length of him, standing naked as Adam must have stood at his creation. Then, embarrassment flooding her, she grabbed her bonnet and fled.

Regaining the path that would lead her home, she pushed her drawing pad between her knees, holding it secure, while with her pencil between her teeth she tied on her bonnet, smoothing the curls that had blown awry in her mad dash from the pool.

Who was he? Who was the man who had swum the width of the Cracker underwater? Alone on the narrow path that led from the village across the open stretch of countryside to Holyhead House, Carys released her sketch pad and pencil then hitched her skirts calf-high. He could be any one of the Moxley men. Many of them used the flooded mine shaft as a place to wash and swim during summer. But, more importantly, did *he* know her? The Cracker was wide and the sun had been behind her, casting her face into shadow, but had light and distance been enough . . . or in spite of both had he recognised her for Meshac Beddows's daughter?

The dull thud of a horse's hoofs on the grass broke in on her thoughts: her father coming from the workshops. He used this path whenever he went there on horseback. She had hitched her skirts a little higher, breaking into a run towards the sound – that at least would furnish an excuse for her unusually red cheeks. Then she had stopped. The sight of the huge black horse, its rider sitting easily in the saddle, pulled her up sharply. The rider was most definitely not her father.

'So.' Tall even in the saddle, the man had brought down his crop against his gloved hand, eyes insolently roving over her. 'You didn't stay to thank me.'

'Thank you?' Carys answered, letting her skirts drop. 'I am unaware of any need to thank you for anything, sir.'

'No?' His glance had lifted to meet hers. Carys turned her face from the window, suddenly remembering the feeling his eyes had aroused in her.

'Do you always take what you want then leave without thanks or payment?'

'Payment?' She had looked up at the face way above her own, a face without a trace of friendship, as hard as it was handsome. 'I am at a loss to understand you. Now, if you will excuse me, I am expected at Holyhead House.' If the mention of Meshac Beddows's large red-brick house sprawled along the top of Moxley Hill was meant to make him move aside and allow her to pass, it failed miserably. The great black horse had stood like a living wall in her way.

'So you work at the House, do you?' The rays of the sinking sun touched his dark hair with a ring of red-gold. 'And your afternoon off is spent watching naked men swim. Then you run away without thanking them for entertaining you – or do you pay for your amusement?'

Something in those dark eyes had warned of danger. Carys remembered looking quickly across the rough uneven landscape. Even if her father were already home, surely some of the pitmen would be making their way to the cottages on the far side of the heath? But as she looked she knew it was too far for any shout of hers to be heard. She had stepped aside then, beginning to run, leaving the path to cut across the heath towards home, her skirts flattened against her legs. But she had gone only yards before the horse once again cut across her path.

'So you do leave without payment!' In her memory she saw

again the huge black horse and heard its whinny of complaint as its rider jerked the reins. 'Has no one ever told you that is bad manners?'

Lifting a hand to her throat, Carys rubbed at it. Fear seemed once more to hold her in its grip.

'And . . . has no one ever told you that to harass a woman is more than bad manners? It . . . it's criminal.'

'Harass!' He had laughed low in his throat. 'Is requiring payment for one's services harassment?'

'I . . . I was not watching you.' A fleck of foam from the horse's mouth drifted on to Carys's cheek. 'Not in the way you appear to think,' she added, brushing away the spittle.

Her sudden movement had caused the horse to shy but the man had it back under control before she could take advantage of the diversion.

'And in what way do I appear to be thinking?'

Beneath the shadowed eaves of the room Carys's face flamed as the man's slightly cynical smile had caused it to flame there on Moxley Heath.

'I . . . not . . . not in a manner becoming to a gentleman!' She had been angry at the insolent way he stared at her.

'Maybe I am not a gentleman, and you are no lady. After all, clothes do not make the man, if I have remembered the saying correctly.'

In her mind Carys saw again the slight curve of his mouth, the proud set of his body as with one hand he held the huge horse to his will. The fine lawn shirt thrown on with too much haste to fasten across the chest, the corded fawn trousers and coffee-coloured coat, masking him with the trappings of civility, masking yet not hiding man.

'You remember correctly.' Her answer had been sharp, made to cover the fear that had risen in her as he barred her way. 'The clothes you wear have quality and refinement. The man, I think, has none.'

She had seen amusement gleam in eyes black as night as he leaned towards her, his short riding crop lifting the collar of her dress.

'And these trappings?' His voice was low, with the texture of velvet. 'Does not their quality belie the woman beneath them? A woman who hides herself in the grass to watch a man bathe naked in a pool?'

Carys closed her eyes against the picture in her mind but it refused to fade. He had let the crop trail from her throat down to her breast, halting there as his devil's eyes had stared into her own.

'I was not hiding.' She had slapped the crop away at the same time, stepping backward on the rough uneven path that skirted the pool.

'No!' He straightened in the saddle but his eyes still held hers. 'But you were not exactly proclaiming your presence on the hillside. Not, that is, as long as you thought you might be seen. If not hiding, what am I supposed to think you were doing?'

'I don't care what you think!'

She had turned then, determined to go back the way she had come; she could skirt the Cracker and come out of the hollow on the opposite side. From there it was just a short way to Bull Lane. There were sure to be people about the Fever Hospital or the few houses grouped around the old coal mines at Cock Heath.

But quick as she had been, he had been quicker, guiding the horse to cut off her escape.

'Then I think you *were* watching me.' The black eyes swept over her from her head to her feet then rose again with slow insolence to her face. 'And what is sauce for your goose must equally be sauce for my gander. You have seen me naked, now I must see you in that same delightful state . . . so, miss, off with these.'

He had reached forward with the crop, hooking it in her skirts and lifting them above her knees. Stepping back and slapping at the crop all at the same time, she lost her balance and fell sprawling on to her back.

'Now that is most enticing to any man.' His smile had faded as he stared down at her, sprawled open-legged, her petticoats bunched about her waist. 'And with any other man you may not escape so lightly next time, young miss, so my advice is: stay away from that pool!'

Then he had gone. Carys opened her eyes. Beyond her window the moon slipped behind a bank of cloud, hiding its image in grey softness, disappearing as he had disappeared. But his image had refused to be hidden; it had stayed, stubbornly clear, in her heart.

For four years those coal black eyes had stared at her from the depths of her soul.

'So you be in the business of selling enamels? Then you could do no better than come to Bilston. Make the finest enamels in the world do the folk of Bilston, and the ones that work for Meshac Beddows makes the finest of them all. You'll do no better, and you can take that from me.'

Reuben Fereday looked at the faces of the guests seated about the dining table at Holyhead House. Each time he came to Bilston, Meshac invited him back here to this house, and each time he accepted the invitation. But why did he come so often? He could place larger orders with Meshac Beddows's works, orders that would reduce the need for his visits to one a year instead of one a month. So why didn't he? He smiled at a pale-faced guest whose yellow hair hung like tallow candles about her neck, and from the corner of his eye saw her mother beam from her to Meshac's wife. But there was no answering smile on that woman's attractive face. So why did he come? He felt brown eyes fix on him. Maria Beddows would think it was for her. She had tried hard enough to gather him into her net, as he supposed she gathered every man who came into her circle. The woman had looks, in fact most would call her beautiful, but for him that fine-boned face and those inviting eyes held no attraction other than as the wife of a friend.

No, it was not this woman who caused him to return to Bilston so regularly or to haunt Moxley Heath with every visit. It was the memory of a young girl with the wind in her hair and defiance in her eyes. A girl he guessed to be no more than twenty who had watched him as he swam in that pool, and then denied it. It was to find her, to see her again, that he came with such regularity. She had said she was returning to Holyhead House, this house, yet on no visit here had he seen her. That in itself would not be surprising if the girl were one of the lesser maids, but her bearing, the way she had carried herself, the way she had stared boldly into his face, the answers she'd snapped out with no trace of the hesitation or servility that could be expected in a servant, all made him doubt it. Besides which she'd carried pencil and sketching block and Meshac Beddows had spoken proudly of a daughter whose drawings he had adapted for use on many of the boxes he manufactured. But if the girl was his daughter, and if he did have the pride in her he seemed to have, why was she never present in this house? And even more of a mystery, why had Maria never spoken of having a daughter?

'Like I says, Fereday, you won't never buy finer work than can be got from Meshac Beddows.'

'I know that, Mr Turner.' Reuben drew his mind back to the conversation. 'I have only the best in my gallery in Birmingham. That is why I buy Bilston enamels, Meshac Beddows's enamels in particular.'

'You makes a good choice and all. Be a shame you don't deal in iron and steel, we could have done business happen you did.'

'What *do* you have in that gallery of yours, Mr Fereday?' Reuben felt the delicate probing of Amy Turner's question. She wanted to know the depth of the pockets of the man she saw as a husband for her daughter, a man she seemed to prefer above the one seated beside the girl, the one introduced to him as Ryder Tempal.

'I have many beautiful things, Mrs Turner, mine is a gallery of fine art. I have paintings, wonderful glassware, fine jewellery . . . but they are all insignificant against the beauty of the ladies seated at this table. I would deem it an honour were you to pay a visit there.'

'Well said, lad.'

Maria watched her husband drain his glass of Madeira then sign for it to be refilled. Let him drink, despite the doctor's warning. The more he drank, the easier would be the task she had set herself.

'You should go, Maria.' Meshac picked up his refilled glass. 'You could buy yourself a trinket, only make sure it don't be no enamel. I can get them doo-dads for free.'

Maria allowed herself to smile with her guests but her eyes were as calculating as her thoughts. This could be a perfect excuse for going to Birmingham. God knows, she found it hard enough to think them up any more.

'I should like nothing more.' Maria deliberately kept her gaze on her husband. 'But you so rarely seem to have the time to spare, my dear, you are kept so busy at the works and I could not go alone. I would be terrified at the thought. Why, I fear going alone to my dressmaker and she is only on the borders of the city.'

'Then perhaps you would allow me to escort you, Mrs Beddows?'

'Arrh, that be it, you take 'er for me, Ryder lad. Only make sure 'er don't give all my money to young Fereday.'

He had taken her bait as she'd known he would. Maria felt a warm glow of satisfaction. Meshac had given her the opportunity to be with Ryder, an opportunity she would not waste on visiting any fine art gallery for more than an hour, though that much would have to be spent there to avoid questions.

'And you, Miss Turner?' Ryder smiled at the girl beside him. 'Will you come with us?'

'I will take my daughter with me,' Amy Turner answered quickly. 'I too shall be accepting Mr Fereday's invitation . . . before very long, I hope.'

Reuben smiled inwardly. An inventory of his assets? It was as clear a signal to him as her rejection of his offer should be to Ryder Tempal. But why was she averse to the man paying attention to her daughter? Unless . . . He caught the glance that passed between Maria and her guest. He need ponder that question no longer, the answer was clear. Ryder Tempal was Maria Beddows's preserve.

'I look forward to it,' Reuben answered. 'I look forward to both of you visiting the gallery, but for now I must ask you to excuse me? I promised my aunt I would be back for ten. She retires early these days and it is not often I get to see her.'

'Your aunt be the widow of Oliver Mountford? Had the making of nails and screws along Carters Green and a house up at Hill Top, if I remembers.'

'There is nothing amiss with your memory, Mr Turner.' Reuben placed his napkin alongside his untouched glass. 'My uncle was Oliver Mountford and my aunt still has the running of Mountford Nail and Screw at Carters Green, and still lives at Hill Top.'

'Ee, lad, I clean forgot!' Meshac tipped Madeira into his mouth before rising from the table. 'Noah, get yourself a cigar and a brandy while I show Fereday the paintings he come to look at.'

'Why don't you relax with Noah and our guests, my dear?' Maria rose as quickly as her husband. 'I can show Mr Fereday the paintings, and I am certain Mr Tempal would take Edwina for a turn in the garden though he must not keep her too long in the summerhouse.' Maria's eyes gleamed as they met those of Ryder Tempal. He would not try his tricks on Noah Turner's daughter; his sights were set on other quarry.

'I'll do that if you have no objection, Fereday? The wife can show you all you wish to see.' Meshac shuffled from the table.

And that I hold no wish to see. Reuben followed the others from the dining room then turned towards the library as Maria led the way.

'Meshac had the paintings brought in here.' She opened the doors that gave on to a large room, its walls lined with books. 'He thought it would be more practical for you to view them in one room rather than trail through several.'

Reuben crossed to a long mahogany side table set in the one windowed alcove of the room where a dozen or so miniature oil paintings, each mounted in matching frames, had been set out for his inspection.

'These are exquisite!' He picked up one that was obviously a portrait of Maria, hair and eyes dark against the cream of her shoulders, the line of her amber gown just showing at the base of the frame. 'Who was the artist? A member of the Royal Academy?'

'No, no one of such distinction.' Maria picked up another of the miniatures, this of a woman with a flat straw bonnet over greying hair that escaped the hat in straggly tendrils, while the eyes retained a thousand secrets. 'This one is the flower seller that sits at the gate of St Leonard's church in Bilston.'

She handed him the miniature, taking the first one from him and replacing it on the table.

'Whoever painted these deserves that distinction.' Reuben held the miniature closer to the light of the gasolier. 'I swear Turner himself has no more delicate touch or finer appreciation of colour.' He glanced along the table, hungry to see the beauty of each small picture. 'Just look at this one!' He took up a painting of a pool set in a hollow below rising ground thick with ferns. He had seen that pool, bathed in its waters the day he had returned hot and dusty from Meshac Beddows's workshops. This was the pool where the girl he was searching for had sat watching him, and where he had caught up with her. Suddenly everything seemed to fall into place in his mind. The girl was returning to Holyhead House, the home of Meshac Beddows. She carried a sketch pad and pencils. Meshac had once boasted of his daughter's skills as an artist. These paintings had not been done by an accredited artist. It all pointed one way . . . Reuben's hand shook slightly as he replaced the painting with the others. The artist had to be the daughter Meshac spoke of, she had to be Meshac's child.

Forcing his voice to remain easy, he looked at Maria. 'These are exactly what I am looking for. They will make beautiful cameos mounted in a gold setting – that is, if your husband's enamellers are capable of reproducing the same quality as the originals? I take it the artist will have no objection to his work being so reproduced?'

'She won't have . . .' Maria stopped herself quickly. She had not meant to give any clue as to the painter's identity. 'The . . . the designs belong to my husband. They were done by one of the men in the workshop, I don't remember which one.'

She could be referring to any of the buildings referred to as workshops. Reuben thought of the warren of tumbledown dwellings whose outhouses had all become workshops complete with bellows and furnace; the women hammering lumps of metal-bearing rock into powder, hour after soul-destroying hour; their children sitting on the floor cleaning plates of tin or bronze before carrying them to their father who applied the powdered oxides mixed with water as a paste to the metal, then placed them in the furnace where oxide and metal would fuse. Maria was trying to tell him this work came from one of the dark, vermin-infested places those people called home and workshop, but Reuben knew it did not. The painter of these miniatures was not one of Meshac Beddows's workmen, it was Meshac Beddows's daughter.

He faced the woman who had brought him into the library, seeing apprehension in her deep brown eyes, and knew his suppositions to be correct.

'Meshac told me his daughter was a very talented artist. In fact, he said she was responsible for several of the designs I have bought from him, and you say this artist is female?'

Reuben saw the flicker of alarm shadow Maria's eyes and the slight tightening of her mouth before she turned to the table holding the miniatures. He was right. These paintings were the work of her daughter, so why deny it? And why had she not once, during any of his visits here, mentioned the existence of the girl?

'Could these also be her work?'

'Possibly.' Maria turned towards the door. It would be a mistake to deny what he asked, he would simply go to Meshac and that would spark off more of her husband's doubts and queries as to why the girl had never returned home after being sent away to school. School . . . Maria felt a twinge of guilt then pushed it away. It had to be a convent, it had to be a place of no return. Though the girl *had* left, she *had* returned to the world. But she would never return to Moxley, that much at least Maria had achieved.

'But you are not sure?' Reuben's glance followed her.

'No, Mr Fereday, I am not sure.' Maria's cool voice was a warning for him to question her no further.

'Then might I perhaps meet your daughter, ask her myself if this is her work?' He ignored the message in her voice.

The door already open, Maria turned to look back at him, a triumphant smile touching her mouth. 'I am afraid that will not be possible, Mr Fereday. Our daughter has taken Holy Orders.'

Chapter Five

'Be sure you be back here by the time it be six o'clock, my wench, or you will be hearing from me. And be sure to keep an eye on Carys. That Portway Road be hardly a fit place for young women to walk on their own, what with Irish navvies and Gypsy Fields none too far off.'

'We'll be fine, Mrs Bates.'

'Arrh, I knows *you* will, Alice Withers,' Martha Bates murmured, watching the two young women run across the yard and past the carriage house towards the heath. 'Ain't you I be so concerned for. A bevy of brothers taught you to look out for yourself, but the other one . . . that wench don't have the appearance of being able to fight off unwelcome hands.'

'You'll like me mother.' Clear of the grounds of Ridge House, Alice slowed to a walk. 'Her rattles on a bit, and her tongue gets the better of her at times, like Mrs B. reckons mine do.' Alice grinned, showing strong even teeth. 'But her don't mean no harm by her gossip, and after all, that be the only thing women in these parts can indulge theirselves in. Ain't never money to spare for anything else.'

'That is the very reason I think I ought not to visit your home.' Carys had been unsure from the first about imposing upon Alice's mother. Money in the Withers household was

67

too hard come by to spend any of it on entertaining her. 'I do not want to put your mother to any trouble.' It was not really what she wanted to say but to put it more bluntly could give offence to Alice and that was the last thing she wanted.

'You won't be puttin' her to no trouble.' Alice bent to pick a daisy, twisting the fragile stem between her fingers as she walked. 'But you will put her out good and proper if her hears you talk like that. We ain't got much but what we do have me mother gives willing. Her likes having folk to call, 'specially somebody posh like yourself.'

'But I'm not posh!' Carys laughed, something that came more easily as the days at Ridge House went by, giving her a sense of being wanted, a sense she had not known for so long.

'Oh, but you am,' Alice insisted. 'You talks so lah-di-dah. But in a nice way,' she hastened to add. 'I wishes I could talk like you do.'

'There is nothing wrong with the way you speak.'

'Suppose not.' Alice twirled the tiny flower. 'Be strange if I talked any different, coming from the Black Country, but I still thinks it would be nice if I could talk all pound-noteish now and again.'

'Pound-noteish?' Carys laughed again. 'What on earth does that mean?'

'You knows. Pound-noteish . . . bay-windowed . . . lah-di-. . . posh . . . like gentry. Fancy being able to talk to a lad like that!' Stopping, she turned to Carys, the daisy held in an affected pose, her mouth pulled into a prim line. 'Ho, thah you be, my deah. Do come and sit dahn. Take the weight orff while I rings the maid for tea.' She paused. 'What do you think?'

'I think perhaps not.' Carys's laugh floated over the silent heath. 'I much prefer the Alice Withers we have. Besides, talking as posh as that would have the lads thinking you too grand for them to come courting.'

'Ain't none come yet, posh talk or not.' Her smile fading, Alice walked on. 'Seems I don't have any lad's eye.'

'I wouldn't see that as being the truth.' Carys caught the other girl's arm, tucking her own beneath it. 'More like there are several just waiting for the right moment to approach you.'

'Well, I wish one of them would shift his shins. I already be more'n one an' twenty. That would be an old maid in me mother's times.'

'But these are not her times.' Carys squeezed the girl's arm. 'In a few months it will be nineteen hundred, a new century, a new beginning, that will bring more for women than marriage following on the cradle. Twenty-one will not be the end for a woman still unmarried.'

'Try telling me mother that.' Alice sounded gloomy. 'Every time I goes home her asks if there be a lad calling on me yet, and her face gets as long as a fourpenny hock when I says there be nobody.'

'Then don't tell her that.'

'What! Tell me mother a lie?' Alice dropped the flower, her brown skirts brushing it aside as it fell to the earth. 'Ee, Carys, I couldn't! Her would know the minute I tried it. You can't pull the wool over me mother's eyes. Well, not for long you can't.'

'I did not say lie to her.'

Ahead of them a skylark rose from the ground, the sound of its call spreading over the stillness, and Carys followed its ascent towards the soft powder-puff clouds.

'I just said, do not tell her there is no one calling on you . . . yet.'

'Yet?' Alice turned a puzzled look on the girl walking beside her. 'But that be meaning there is somebody wanting to, and that be a lie.'

'It is only a lie if you say it,' Carys answered. 'But you would not be saying it, you would merely be implying it and therefore you would not be telling your mother a lie.'

'Well, if her starts on me today, might be as I'll just try that what you said . . . imp . . . imp . . .'

'Implying.' Carys smiled.

'Arrh, that!' Alice scooped up a fresh daisy. 'Might be it'll bring me a lad an' all.' Her smile returning, she plucked a petal from the flower, watching it float gently downward as she released it. 'He loves me . . . he loves me not . . .'

Their arms interlocked, they walked on, laughter echoing behind them.

'We won't 'ave long to spend at me mother's,' Alice said as they left Holloway Bank, following a left fork that took them into Potters Lane. 'It be a fair step to Brick Kiln Lane an' we be only halfway yet.'

Carys kept up with her friend's quickened pace as they passed the somewhat dilapidated Railway Hotel then picked their way gingerly over the tram rails before branching into Portway Road.

'I never comes back along here on me own, specially if it be dark,' Alice confided, glancing covertly at the long rows of small houses separated at intervals by uninviting alleys. 'This be a rough area, mostly Irish brought in when the Birmingham Navigation was being built. It was thought they would take theirselves back off to their own country once the canal was finished, but they still be here an' that has led to more than one lot of trouble in the town. The men here see the navvies as taking jobs that should rightly go to them, and when they don't there's trouble.'

A woman with a shawl pulled tight about her head stepped from the shadow of an alley, flinging a bowl of greasy water on to the narrow street. She stood, one hand on her hip, staring after the hurrying girls.

'That be one o' their women,' Alice said, pulling Carys closer to her. 'They be handy with their fists just like their men, it wouldn't pay to argue with the like o' that one.'

'If you never go home this way alone, how will we return to Hill Top?' Carys asked, hoping Alice would have an answer that would not include the Portway Road.

'Well, none of me brothers will be home, they'll be working

till seven, but not to fret. For a halfpenny we can ride the tram up from the market place to Hill Top.'

'Ride the tram!' Carys would have stood still but Alice pulled her on. 'Then why didn't we take it coming down?'

Alice giggled. 'What, and have you miss the thrill of walking the Portway!'

'Alice.' Carys followed her friend, taking the right-hand turning that led them past the black looming mass that was the church of Saint James, bringing them into Brick Kiln Lane. 'Next time, will you ask whether I want thrilling?'

'I knowed me mother would like you.'

Later they sat side by side, the wooden slatted seats of the steam tram jarring their bones as it grumbled its way up the slope.

Alice's mother had welcomed her, Carys thought, and had talked endlessly as Alice said she would, but her eyes had been sharp enough, taking in Carys's shabby coat and worn boots though she had asked no question as to her background. No, she had asked nothing. Carys watched the line of houses break off, giving way to open heath. But that did not mean she had none to ask.

''Tis a pity me dad and brothers were still at the brick yard,' Alice went on. 'But p'raps Mrs B. will give we a Sunday afternoon afore long and then you can meet the whole bloomin' family of Witherses.'

'Tickets, please!'

Carys glanced at the blue-uniformed conductor, his generous moustache twitching as he smiled down at them. She was glad his interruption had put a timely end to her need to reply.

'So where do you two pretty young ladies be goin' then?'

'Hill Top.' Alice fumbled in her pocket, taking out a small purse. 'Two halfpennies to Hill Top.'

Taking the penny from her, the conductor dropped it into the leather bag at his waist. Then giving the handle of his ticket machine two brisk turns, he punched out their tickets.

'There you be, me wench.' He handed both tickets to Alice, his moustache wiggling as he smiled. 'It be a pity you wasn't riding on further, give we a chance to get us selves acquainted.'

'You'll be getting yourself acquainted all right,' a woman almost buried beneath her hessian shopping bag and a large wicker basket covered with a blue cloth, called from the rear. 'Acquainted with your missis's foot if 'er catches you chattin' to the wenches!'

'You wouldn't tell 'er though, would you, Dolly?' Beneath the shiny peak of his cap the man's eyebrows were raised. 'Not with you an' me being lovers all these years.'

'Lovers!' The woman's jowls shook as her laughter rang out. 'I'd rather go to bed with a half pint of old ale any day.'

'Is that right?' The conductor raised a hand, fastening his fingers on the leather cord that ran the length of the tram. 'And here's me thinkin' you rode this tram every day all on account of my charm.'

'That bloomin' hill be the reason I rides this tram every day.' The woman gathered the bag from the seat beside her. 'Charm I can get without the paying of a penny.'

'Go on with you, Dolly!' He pulled the cord and at the front of the tram a bell jangled. 'You know you wouldn't miss my smile for a shilling, let alone a penny.'

At the touch of the brakes the tram shuddered to a halt and the woman hauled herself along the confined space between its double row of benches, dragging the well-filled hessian bag behind her.

'I wouldn't pay a shilling to ride with the King himself,' she puffed, easing herself and her bag from the tram to the roadway, 'and he could smile all the way from here to Buckingham Palace.'

Handing both girls from the tram in the wake of the woman and her bags, the smiling conductor hopped back on to the platform, giving the cord a double pull and holding on to the handrail as the driver released the brake and the tram lurched forward. He raised his free hand in a wave as the tram pulled away.

'Was the conductors as friendly as that on them Birmingham trams?' Alice asked, returning the wave with a grin before she began to follow the faint track across the heath that would lead them to Ridge House.

Carys glanced to the left, seeing the ground slope away to where the town lay, its grimed buildings smothered beneath the pall of black smoke that seemed to issue from every part of it. She carried her glance further to where Moxley lay beyond the limits of her vision. 'Keep away,' Maria had told her, and she had done so, not daring to defy the mother who had locked her away for four long years, a mother who in all that time had not once come to see her.

'I don't know.' She turned away, feeling the pull of her home across the dividing heath and knowing she could not yield to it. 'I never rode on any of them. That day we met on the railway station was my first day out of the convent and I came there with my mother in a horse cab.'

'Of course, I was forgetting about you being in a convent.' Stubbing her toe on a stone protruding from the ground, Alice stumbled, laughing as she regained her footing only to frown when she looked at the scuff mark the stone had scratched across the toe cap of her boot.

'Bugger it!' Spitting on her fingers, she bent and rubbed them across the offending mark. 'These be my best boots an' all!' Catching the look on Carys's face, she burst into laughter. 'Ee, they wouldn't have me in no nunnery, not if they heard me choice of language!'

'Mrs Bates will have you in the coal cellar if *she* hears it.' Carys smiled, finding the other girl's grin too infectious to resist.

'Oh, I minds my Ps and Qs when I knows Mrs B. is around. But, seriously, what was it like never getting outside that convent? I mean, didn't it drive you mad?'

'I thought at first it would,' Carys answered. 'But after a while I got used to it.'

'Lor', I'm sure I never could.' Satisfied she had done the best she could to cover the damage to her boot, Alice continued to walk in the direction of the house. 'They must all be saints who live in them places?'

Not all of them. In her mind Carys saw those eyes . . . the passion in them changing instantly to fear and then more slowly to hatred, a hatred that had turned four years of Carys's life into a living nightmare.

It had been only the second month after her entry to the Convent of the Holy Child. One of the nuns had sent her from the infirmary, where she had been set to scrubbing floors, to bring the Mistress of Novices to the bed of one of the sisters who had contracted tuberculosis and was on the point of death.

'Oh, this is the time it would choose to happen, with Sister Mary Immaculata away to the Mother House for three days.' The harassed nun had looked up from tending the sick woman, her eye falling on Carys. 'Leave that, child,' she ordered. 'Go you to the room of Sister Veronica. Father Hawthorne from Saint Saviour's church will be with her arranging the service in the chapel. Tell them Sister Thérèse is making to leave this world and ask the Father if he will come and give her the Last Rites. Quick, child, don't gawp like an idiot . . . go!'

And she had gone, running through the silent corridors breaking the rule that forbade it, ignoring the admonitions of the nuns she passed until she came to the room the Mistress of Novices used as an office and without thinking to knock, opened the door.

Sister Veronica was there as she had been told but she was not seated at the large plain oak desk. Instead she stood against the far wall, both arms stretched in a wide angle over her head, naked except for the wimple that still covered her hair. Eyes closed, her head arched slightly backward, she moaned with each thrust of her body, thrusts that matched those of the priest, naked as herself, who lunged into her.

Carys remembered the catch of her own breath, loud in her throat, and over the priest's shoulder saw that Sister Veronica's eyes had opened.

That had been the start of the torment. A constant hounding that had kept at her from the beginning to the end of every long day, days of work almost without cease from getting up at four in the morning until the evening meditation when she was allowed to sit for an hour to read the Bible before Compline, the last service of the day. As it ended at ten she was released to drop exhausted into her bed.

It had only been on leaving the convent that she had come to understand Sister Veronica's hatred of her, or rather to realise it was not so much hatred as fear; fear that Carys would speak of what she had witnessed, that the life the woman had forged for herself within the security of those walls would be snatched away. That fear had eaten away at her until she could think of nothing other than reducing Carys's own life to a state where she could no longer endure it; she had known only that to be utterly safe she must drive away the girl who had seen her fornication, seen the breaking of her vows.

'Well, I'm no saint.' Alice caught her hand, pulling Carys after her as she broke into a run. 'And if you have to live in one of them places to qualify for a halo, then you can keep it.'

If only she were free they would marry. Those had been Ryder Tempal's words to her as they had lain in that hotel bed together just a week ago. He loved her, he had said as he rolled her beneath him, and had kept on saying it as they made love again and again.

Ryder loved her.

But did he? Wouldn't it be nearer the truth to say Ryder loved money, any man's money, and would take any man's wife or daughter to get it?

She had been right to suppose there had been more to the attentions he had paid Meshac's child than simple flattery, and the same could be said of his performance tonight; he had played the game right up to his armpits, almost charming the bloomers off that mealy-faced girl of the Turners right there at the dinner table.

Maria pulled the pins from her hair, letting the silken weight of it tumble about her shoulders.

Ryder Tempal was looking for a wife, one who would bring him money. But that girl on whom he had danced attendance tonight would not be that wife, nor would the one he had tried to rape four years ago. He had set his sights on Meshac Beddows's money and that he could have, but not Meshac Beddows's daughter. The money would come only with Meshac Beddows's wife.

Behind Maria her husband coughed the lung-rattling cough of a man who had spent too many years in the dust of frit being pounded into powder for the painting of enamels, breathing in the oxides and silica until his lungs were half filled with the noxious black dust.

Twenty years she had listened to that cough; twenty years in which every moment she had wanted to silence it forever, to rid herself of the man almost twice her age to whom her parents had married her, despite the fact they knew she had no love for him.

Maria watched him now in the mirror of her dressing table, his domed head balanced like a huge pink egg on a stumpy neck. His shoulders were stooped from endless hours spent bent over a table carefully mixing the precise balance of powdered frit and metallic oxides or poring over designs for enamelled boxes and caskets. He had given her all the comfort his wealth could buy but still she had not loved him. And her daughter? Maria's hand closed over the beautifully enamelled hairbrush but she did not pick it up.

Did she love the child this man had fathered on her? Had she ever loved her? The answer, if she had to make it, was no. There had never been any love in her for the child she had felt had been forced upon her, a child expected of the union, her side of the bargain! Maria's gaze moved from the man standing behind her, coming again to her own face and body. She had never wanted a child, never wanted anything that would threaten the beauty of her body. Motherhood! Eyes on eyes, Maria smiled at herself. They could keep it!

But the child had been pretty, right from birth she had held the promise of beauty, and now that promise was being fulfilled. Day by day the girl came nearer to being a beautiful woman, a beautiful chestnut-haired, amber-eyed woman. One to rival Maria herself.

Her hand tightened on the hairbrush. That was the thought that had consumed her like fire each time Ryder Tempal had smiled at her daughter, each time he took her arm or suggested a turn about the garden. A beauty that would rival her own, detract from the attention that had always been hers. That was what would happen should her daughter return to this house. In the mirror Maria watched the shadows take her eyes, watched the rise of that emotion that bit into her with the strength of a ravening beast . . .

Behind her Meshac coughed again and Maria's hand tightened about the hairbrush.

She knew what that emotion was. If she were honest with herself she could put a name to the feeling which flared each time Ryder Tempal looked at another woman, any woman, the feeling that made her wish them dead.

Was that what she wanted for her own daughter? To see her dead! Maria's eyes shifted, fastening on the slim column of darkness in the gap between the heavy drapes pulled across the windows, the thought hammering in her mind, demanding an answer. Was that the measure of her love for Ryder Tempal? Did she desire him so much she would be prepared to kill for him?

Her glance sliding back to her own mirrored reflection,

Maria lifted the brush to her hair, the answer already stamped on her brain.

Yes, she would kill for him . . . if she had to.

'I'll be away to my room.'

Maria watched her husband weave uncertainly through the door that connected her bedroom with his.

'I will come to say goodnight, dear.'

In the mirror her reflection smiled. Meshac had taken to sleeping in a separate bedroom since that evening some two months ago when he and Reuben Fereday had sat for several hours discussing enamels, during which time Meshac had paid a great deal of attention to the brandy decanter. That night she had taken a step toward achieving her dream.

Meshac's heart was not strong. They had known that for some time but it had not stopped Maria; in fact that weakness was the weapon she had used, that and Meshac's other weakness.

She had waited until she guessed he would be undressed and then had gone into his room. He had been standing with his nightshirt in his hand and she had apologised sweetly for coming upon him that way, but at the same time had released the strings of her silk négligée, letting it slip from her shoulders to display her own nakedness.

'I just wanted to say goodnight, dear,' she had murmured, standing still as his eyes had fixed on her. 'But I will leave if you wish?'

'No, I don't bloody wish!' Meshac's voice had been thick with his desire for her, a desire he could never deny himself.

Gathering up the silken folds she had held them across her breasts, eyelids lowered in a supposed shyness that even after more than twenty years could still hoodwink Meshac.

Dropping the nightshirt he had lumbered forward, catching her in his arms and bringing his mouth down hard against her own.

Maria lifted a hand to her mouth, wiping her fingers across the fullness of her lips as if to wipe away the memory.

She had stood there while one hand had squeezed her breast, the other kneading her naked bottom, and then she had taken his hands, drawing each slowly over her body before placing them at his sides. Then, with a quiet shushing of his protests, she leaned into him, her body brushing against his as she slid slowly to her knees.

Passing a hand about each of his thighs she had brought her mouth to a point just below his navel. She could hear the noise of his breathing, a ragged gasping that each kiss accentuated. Sliding her hands to the front of his thighs she moved them slowly, intimately, matching the movement to each kiss. upward toward the flesh jerking below her mouth.

She had felt him trembling, the noise of his breathing gradually becoming a fight for air. Then he had fallen, crashing heavily against the bed.

Snatching up her fallen robe, she had run back to her room then, being careful to close the door that connected it to Meshac's. Pulling repeatedly on the cord that rang for the housekeeper, she waited, using the minutes to fasten her night clothes, hiding the nakedness beneath.

Now, taking her hand from the hairbrush, Maria stood up. Releasing the ties of her turquoise silk night coat she stared at her body in the mirror. Two months ago the touch of that body had almost finished Meshac. He must not get excited, the doctor had said when he had been summoned. It was fortunate for her husband she had been awake and heard him fall and understandable that she had been too afraid of what she might find to go into his room herself. There must be no exertion, the doctor had explained tactfully, his heart would not stand up to any stress. Rest and quiet must be the order of the day for Meshac Beddows.

Touching a hand to her breast, Maria watched it slide slowly over her shapely waist – but the hand she felt was Ryder Tempal's.

Ryder! Maria's eyes lifted to their own reflection. Had tonight's performance with the Turner girl been a way of showing her he would not wait much longer? Was he showing her that if she were not free soon he would play elsewhere?

But there was Meshac!

Maria slid her hand sensually over her flat stomach.

He stood between her and Ryder.

The soft light of the oil lamp beside her bed bathed the room in mauve shadows and in the shadows Maria's eyes gleamed.

But Meshac had a weak heart. Meshac would not stand there much longer.

Chapter Six

'Eh, Mrs Bates, is he handsome?' Alice's eyes gleamed with interest across the supper table.

'Handsome as he ever was,' the older woman answered, a touch of affection in her voice. 'But then, he always was a nice-looking lad, right from being a babby, and always knew his manners. There was always a "thank you, Mrs Bates" from him whenever he was here, just the same as today. Popped his head round that door he did just afore he left this afternoon. "Thank you for tea, Mrs Bates," he said, just the same as always, arrh! A right well-mannered lad be the mistress's nephew, there be no airs and graces about him. Not like some as has been to this house.'

'Oh, I wish I'd been here!' Alice breathed.

'Would have made no odds if you had. Be no use you setting your sights on the like of Reuben Fereday, my wench, he be far above we. But like I says, he don't have no bob on hisself.'

'Don't you wish you had seen him?' Alice turned a dreamy look on Carys.

'Why would I want to see the mistress's nephew?' Carys sliced her cold beef into squares, popping one into her mouth.

'Why not?' Alice returned. 'You never knows? Might be he would take a shine to you. Lord knows you be pretty enough for any man to take his hat off for.'

'I doubt that, but it is nice of you to say so.'

'Now then, Alice Withers, don't you go putting ideas where they have no call to be.' Martha Bates set her knife and fork noisily on her plate. 'Don't do for young wenches to go around with their heads full of nonsense, and your head be fuller than most. Reuben Fereday won't have no interest in either of you two except for the interest any lad has for a pretty face and a trim waist, and that sort of interest brings nothing but trouble. So mark my words and no more talk of catching his eye. That way you will catch the mistress's eye and be out of a position. Think on that when you be dreaming your dreams!'

'All the same,' Alice whispered, grinning at Carys as they carried plates to the scullery sink, 'I still wishes I'd been here when he was. Ee, right good-looking is Reuben Fereday.'

'Don't be talking all night over the washing of them plates, there be the mistress's tray to bring down from her room.'

'Mrs Mountford is not unwell, is she?' Carys asked, returning to the kitchen, concern furrowing her brow. Virginia Mountford took each of her meals in the dining room despite living alone; this was the first time Carys had known the routine to be broken.

Untying her voluminous white apron and folding it ready for laundering, Martha settled herself into her favourite chair to the left of the kitchen range.

'No, the mistress be herself. Just said as she wanted nothing more to eat tonight. Now, Alice,' she glanced at the girl coming in from the scullery, drying the last of the water from her hands on her own apron, 'you bank up the fire while Carys fetches that tray downstairs, then you can tell me all about your afternoon.'

Carys had not remembered Virginia Mountford had a nephew. She skipped lightly up the imposing staircase of Ridge House, her steps soundless on the thick carpeting. But then, why should she? There had been no reason for her to do so. But even so, she wondered, was he handsome, this Reuben Fereday? And would he perhaps have 'taken a shine to her', as Alice had said?

Stepping along the landing, by the dim glow of the gas lamps that burned at each end, Carys glanced at the portrait that hung on the wall: a face framed with dark hair, and eyes of almost the same shade gazing out with a strong piercing stare that seemed alive. Virginia Mountford's father had had a strong handsome face, as strong and handsome as the man she had met that day on Moxley Heath. Carys had never seen him after that day but had not forgotten even the smallest line of his body as it broke from the water, or the exasperating curve of his mouth as he had lifted the collar of her gown with his whip; she had not forgotten the man whose similarity to the portrait hanging in this corridor was so striking. Could they be from the same family? Carys lifted her eyes, almost expecting to see the same faint line of a scar above the right eyebrow that the man on the heath had borne. Had the man she had spoken to been Reuben Fereday, nephew to Virginia Mountford? Surely no mere accident of nature could account for such a striking similarity of feature?

Moving on towards the door to her mistress's room, Carys's thoughts raced. If the man who had been to Ridge House this afternoon were the man she had sketched, would he have recognised her? Did he remember as she did? And if he did, what then? She had told him she was returning to Holyhead House so would he want to know how she came to be here? Lifting her hand, Carys tapped on the door.

It was as well she had not been present at Ridge House this afternoon.

In the soft shadowy light of her bedroom Maria stood listening to the silence. She had dismissed the staff, giving them permission to retire as soon as the last of the guests had left, the Turner girl simpering up at Ryder as he fawned over her.

But he would not fawn so much after tonight. After tonight his attention would be all for her.

She listened again. There was no sound of movement. She would not be disturbed.

Almost on tiptoe she crossed the room, her hand fastening on the door that separated her from Meshac. He had almost died that night two months ago when she had pretended her need of him – almost died of the lust she could so easily rouse in him. Tonight there would be no almost, tonight would see her freed.

Turning the handle, she pushed open the door. Beside the huge oak bed burned a single lamp, casting a pool of sallow light over the face of the man who lay there.

'Meshac,' she called, her voice husky with promise. 'Are you asleep, my dear?'

On the white pillow his head turned, and across the dimness of the space that separated them Maria saw the leap of desire in his eyes. He had courted the wine and brandy decanter all evening yet still the urge to make love to her sprang readily, and as on that other occasion this suited Maria's purpose to perfection; the stronger his desire for her, the easier it would be to achieve her objective.

Crossing slowly to the bed, she stood with the pale light playing across the ivory swell of her breasts beneath the parted turquoise silk.

'I could not sleep.' She bent over him, brushing his mouth with her own. 'Did I do wrong to come to you, Meshac?'

'You never do wrong for me.' He threw off the covers, his speech slurred as he made to rise from the bed.

'Don't get up, dear.' Maria touched her fingers to the remaining fasteners on her night coat, pulling the ribbons with excruciating slowness, eyes watching the changing emotions play across her husband's face, seeing his fingers open and close with the promise of stroking the nakedness revealed as her gown fell fully open.

'Maria, you be so beautiful.' Meshac's mouth hung open,

his stare devouring her from head to toe as he held out his arms to her.

'Is this what you want, Meshac?' She cupped both breasts in her hands, lifting their fullness as she smiled again. 'Do you want them in your mouth? Do you want to pull on the nipples like you used to?'

His breathing sharp and ragged, Meshac reached up but she stepped back, just clear of his hands.

'Or do you prefer this?' She let her hands slide down over the slender column of her body, touching her fingertips to the mound of dark silken hair at the base of her stomach. 'This is what you wanted every night, remember, Meshac? Remember how you pushed yourself into me, night after night?'

Air rasping in his throat Meshac pushed himself to his feet, eyes bulging from the passion surging through him. 'Yeah,' he slurred, 'that be what I want, Maria.'

'Are you sure, Meshac?' Her fingertips playing among the dark bush, she laughed throatily. 'Are you sure you can still do it? Are you the man you think yourself to be? Remember last time, the heart attack you suffered? But don't worry, my dear, Ryder Tempal can do all you cannot. He sucks my breasts as you once did. He pushes between my legs just as often as you used to do.'

A low gurgle rising in his throat, Meshac swayed as he stared at her.

'Oh, yes, he has been carrying out your husbandly duties for some time now.' Maria trailed her hands back along her stomach to her breasts. 'He enjoys doing it.' She let her head tilt back slightly on her neck. 'He enjoys stroking my breasts, enjoys lying naked on top of me, pushing deep inside, and I enjoy it too, Meshac, as I enjoyed it tonight.'

The cry that came as he fell across the bed, his hand clutching convulsively at his chest, gave way to a rattle, a terrible rasping sound that splintered the silence of the room.

Crossing to the bedside, Maria looked down at the face twisted with the strain of breathing but whose eyes were not yet glazed with death. They stared back at her, unreadable in their pain.

She had thought her tormenting of him would surely kill him, but Meshac was alive. Maria felt the cold touch of fear. She had told him about herself and Ryder, he knew now they were lovers, and tomorrow . . . She thought quickly. There must be no tomorrow for Meshac.

'Yes, I enjoyed it, Meshac.' Despite her fear she bent slightly towards him, cupping one full breast to his mouth. 'Just as your daughter enjoyed it.'

Beneath her a hand clawed weakly at her arm but Maria slapped it away.

'Oh, yes, my dear,' she murmured, watching the changing emotions on his twisted face. 'Did you think I put her in some distinguished academy to finish her education? Oh, no, Meshac, I only told you that so you would raise no objection to her being sent away. The truth is I sent our daughter from this house to put an end to the education Ryder Tempal found so much pleasure in giving her. For one lesson I found them engaged upon in the summerhouse, they were both naked, Meshac.' She brushed her nipple across his mouth. 'Naked as I am now. Picture it, my dear, your child and Ryder Tempal. Her soft little moans as he drove into her, her hard little nipple in his mouth . . .'

Beneath her the rattle gave way to a long shuddering moan. Straightening Maria took the lamp in her hand, holding it close to the man sprawled backward across the bed. His eyes were still open but no sight remained in their glazed depths. Maria bent close, holding her free hand against the slack lips, feeling for breath on her fingertips, watching for any lifting of the chest.

For several long seconds she remained bent over the unmoving body then straightened up. Replacing the lamp on the bedside table, she made to ease the clawing hand away from the chest then hesitated. It would look more natural left there; a man suffering a massive heart attack would naturally claw at his chest. Lifting Meshac's legs back into the bed, she pulled the covers across him, leaving them awry about his waist as though he had pushed them down in his fight for life.

Satisfied that nothing looked out of place or suspicious, she picked up the turquoise gown. 'It was true what I said about Ryder and me, Meshac.' She laughed softly, looking into those sightless eyes. 'We *are* lovers and I do enjoy it, but it was not true what I told you about your daughter. Your precious child and he were not lovers, though that was no fault of his. I arrived at the summerhouse in time to prevent his seducing her, and it was no exclusive finishing school I entered her in, it was a convent. I put your daughter in a nunnery, which was why she made no visits home. But you would never have agreed to her going to such a place had I not told you her carryings on with Tempal were not the first I had caught her at, told you she was too free with her favours, that she required a hand stronger than ours if her morals were to be saved. And you believed me, Meshac, oh how easily you believed me! But then you believed anything I told you when I came to you like this!' She spread her arms wide, displaying her magnificent body, the smile widening on her lips. 'You always *were* a fool, Meshac!' She dropped her arms but the smile remained fixed to her mouth. 'You believed me each time I told you I was visiting her, yet each time I was making love with Ryder Tempal . . . But Carys renounced the convent life six months ago, she is no longer locked away behind its walls. She could be anywhere, doing anything, perhaps whoring to make a living. But you will never know that now, will you, Meshac? You will never know that.'

'I told me brother I would ask you, Mrs Bates. He will be outside now, waiting on your answer.'

'The Wakes, you say?'

'Yes, they be setting up on the heath across from St John's church yard.'

'Well, that be the quickest twelve month . . . where be that year gone to?'

'It is that long since the Wakes was here last. They only comes once in a twelve month, Mrs Bates.'

'Arrh, wench, I knows that.' Martha Bates looked at the housemaid, her plain face almost pretty with the excitement that lit it. Martha had loved the Wakes in her turn; going there had been an excuse to preen before the lads of the town and she had preened along with the rest of the village girls. The yearly visit to the Wakes had brought many of them a husband, her own dear dead Samuel among them. 'Right you are then, Alice.' She nodded. 'Go tell your brother he can come for you at six tomorrow night.'

'Mrs Bates . . .' Alice hesitated, glancing quickly to where Carys sat, a cloth spread across her lap as she cleaned the downstairs cutlery with a mixture of salt and vinegar. 'Mrs Bates, me mother said to ask, will you be allowing Carys to go an' all?'

'Oh, did 'er!' Martha looked sharply from one girl to the other. 'You be sure it was your mother said to ask that question, Alice Withers, and not that brother of yours waiting out there in the yard?'

'No, Mrs Bates, it weren't me brother, it were me mother, honest it were. Her said if two wenches was to be going then it needed two lads to look after them. Me mother said that going to the Wakes wasn't like a Sunday stroll in Brunswick Park. Her said a wench could get shoved and pushed unless a strong lad was there to see her didn't.'

That was right enough, Martha thought, once more remembering her girlhood days, and many a young man would take advantage.

'Your mother has the truth of it.' She nodded again. 'But I can't be letting you two girls out together. What if the mistress should have callers? I couldn't be answering the door and seeing to things in the kitchen, now could I? Stands to reason a body can't be in two places together.'

'There would be no need, Mrs Bates.' Carys looked up from the fork she was cleaning. 'I have no wish to go to the Wakes.'

'Ee, Carys!' Alice's eyes widened. 'You don't know what you'll be missing. The Wakes be a fair treat – all them side shows and hoop-la stalls.'

'Have you ever been to the Wakes, Carys?' Martha Bates turned her attention to the girl who had been at Ridge House these six months and of whom she knew little more than she had on that first night. There was something about her, a sadness deep inside that clouded her lovely eyes and showed occasionally on that pretty face.

'Have you, Carys . . . did your brother take you to the Wakes, or your parents?'

Dropping her glance to the cloth in her hand, she rubbed it across the fork but the action did not register in her mind.

'I have no brother, and no, my parents never took me to visit the Wakes.' The words were soft, suffered with silent tears. 'My father was always busy with his work, and my mother . . .' She swallowed hard as cloth and fork blurred together in her vision. 'My mother . . .'

'Well then, young woman, I think it be high time you took your first look at Mr Pat Collins's Wakes,' said, Martha sensing the unhappiness that stole the last of Carys's words. 'And this seems to be the perfect opportunity.' She glanced back to Alice, still standing just inside the kitchen door. 'You go tell that brother of yours we will be needing two escorts tomorrow night . . . Oh, and tell him . . .' she called as Alice whirled away before she might change her mind '. . . tell him to give my regards to your mother.'

'I would really rather stay here.' Carys swallowed the hurt speaking of her parents had caused, though her throat still felt tight with tears.

'You stay tied to the house too much altogether.' Martha rose from her chair. Balancing on one foot, she lifted the catch that held the door of the lower oven with the toe of her boot. Bending to peer at the pie inside, she murmured her approval of the golden-brown pastry crust before swinging the oven door closed again. 'A trip out once in a while will do you no harm.' She straightened up. What she really wanted to say was that whatever was troubling Carys needed to be faced; hiding herself away would provide no cure. Instead she smiled. 'For once in her life young Alice be right, a trip to the Wakes *do* be a fair treat. And who knows? You might even win a coconut.'

'Ee, I would rather save my pennies for a ride on the King and Queen boats!' Alice joined in as she came back into the kitchen. 'They fair bring your heart to a stop when they swings right over.'

'I don't go along with them newfangled contraptions.' Martha reached for the apron she had folded over the airing line strung above the range, tying it about her ample figure. 'What be wrong with the old swing boats?'

'There be nothing wrong with them,' Alice said, wriggling out of her coat. 'That is, if you have a lad with you to pull on the ropes enough to keep them swinging. But with the new King and Queen boats you don't have to do no pulling, they be worked by a steam engine.'

'I still says the old ways be best.' Martha smoothed the apron over her black skirts. 'Where there be steam there be noise, just like that there railway station down there in the town – great noisy engines! They be like something the devil dreamed up.'

'It's progress, Mrs Bates.' Alice winked at Carys. 'You don't never have progress without noise.'

'We will in *my* kitchen.' Martha placed her hands on her plump hips. 'Starting with you, Alice Withers, so stop your noise and start progressing with laying the table in the dining room. There be less than an hour to the mistress's suppertime and nothing done towards the making of it. And you, Carys, you get that cutlery swilled and put away then come and give me a hand with the salad.'

'What were the Wakes like when you was a young girl, Mrs Bates?' Her work in the dining room finished, Alice slipped off her frilly white cap and apron, folding them ready for the laundry woman who came in every Monday to do the washing and Tuesday to see to the ironing.

'You don't have to make it sound like that was a hundred years ago. I might not be as young as you but I ain't no fossil neither. First off, like I said earlier, there were not the racket that you young uns seem to think absolutely necessary to have a good time. We enjoyed ourselves without all the din of music you hears coming from that there steam organ. You could hear folk talk when I were a girl. There would be stalls selling pies of every kind, sweet sellers walking round with great trays hanging from their shoulders, every kind of sweet you could think of laid out on them. Ee! When I think of them great fat lollipops me dad would buy for us kids to take home, and me sat up on his shoulders sucking mine, dribbling sugar juice all down me chin . . .'

'What else was there, Mrs Bates, apart from hawkers, I mean?' Alice settled herself, drawing a stool closer to the range.

'Oh, there was all sorts of wonders.' Martha stared into the red heart of the fire, seeing her yesterdays in its flickering glow. 'And didn't us kids think they were wonders, even when we knew what we were shown were nowt but fakes? But the pretence didn't matter, it were the Wakes and the Wakes were magic.'

'It sounds wonderful even now,' said Carys, seeing the reminiscent smile playing about the older woman's mouth.

'It *were* wonderful, me wench,' Martha went on, seeing once more the childhood spent and lost. 'Least to we children it were. There was a roundabout with little wooden horses to ride, I remember. That were worked by two men turning a sort of double handle. Then there was swingle boats – least, that's what we called them. You sat one at each end and worked them by each pulling on a rope.'

'Them be much the same as now.' Alice looked up from her seat at Martha's feet.

'I dare say they be.' She nodded. 'Mr Pat Collins ain't fool enough to throw 'em out. Could be they'll still be working long after them steam-driven rides be gone to the knacker's yard. Arrh, the rides was a delight, not to mention the cake walk. Many a lad found the excuse to put his arm around a girl as her was shook off her feet on that thing.'

'Did you have a lad put his arm around your waist, Mrs Bates?'

'Arrh, Carys, I did.' Martha laughed. 'But it were a sight smaller in them days. That were where I met my Samuel. I were on the cake walk and I got shook right off my feet, accidentally on a purpose.' She laughed again, savouring the memory. 'Sam, he were right behind me. I'd noticed he seemed to turn up wherever me and my sister happened to be. Well, like I said, he was right behind me and catched me as I lost me balance and kept his arm round me all the while till we got off at the other end. We was married three years later. I was just eighteen.'

'Me mother seems to doubt I'll ever be married,' Alice said gloomily. 'Her be forever asking if there be a lad calling on me.'

'You sets too much store by not being courted yet. I've told you often enough, a man don't pick gold from the surface, my wench, he has to dig for it. Sooner or later one will dig down to you and you'll be wed right enough.'

'Hey, p'raps I'll find my true love on the cake walk!'

'As long as you don't find him in the two-headed man's tent!' Martha's laughter rang out again. 'A fella with one mouth be enough for any woman.'

'*Was* there a two-headed man?' Alice asked, forgetting her problem of having no sweetheart.

'Oh, arrh, Alice. Well, that's what the sign above the booth said, though whether both heads were real was something else again. That were where the wonder was, though, in them side shows. There was the bearded lady and the strong man ... He sat me and my sister on his one arm and lifted us both up high, and we weren't little babbies neither. Then there was the snake woman. Her sat in a glass cage with at least a dozen of them horrors sliding all over her. Or for a halfpenny you could visit the world's tiniest man – ee, that were something to see! He was perfectly formed, hands, feet ... and handsome! He had a face would charm ducks out of the water, but he were no more than thirty inches high. Then there were jugglers and tumblers, dancing bears and performing dogs, and of course there was always a woman to tell your fortune. Nearly every young wench paid her tuppence to hear what the future held for her. Ee!' Martha sighed. 'I tell you, the Wakes was really something then.'

'Did you pay your tuppence to hear your future, Mrs Bates?' Carys asked, thoroughly enjoying hearing of days past. Her own mother had never talked to her this way, never told her of her childhood, never shared with her a memory of the past. But then, Maria had never had much time for her daughter, leaving the care of her to a nanny then a tutor, and the loving of her to her father.

'Arrh, I was no different from the rest.' Martha returned her gaze to the fire but her eyes were fixed on a world where she was young. 'I paid my pennies, wanting to be told I would be swept up by a man rich as a prince, who would marry me then take me to live in a house as big as the one Queen Victoria has up there in London.'

'So you wasted your money?'

'I wouldn't go so far as to say that, Alice.' Martha smiled, her eyes still on her long-gone world. 'I lived on that dream many a month – at least I did till I realised Sam Bates were the only man I wanted. The fact that he had neither riches nor a house that would cover a couple of hundred football pitches didn't happen to worry me after that.'

'Ee, I hopes there'll be a fortune teller with the Wakes this year,' breathed Alice, 'I'd love to know what my future be holding.'

'I can tell you that.' Martha stirred in her chair, the memories of her youth sliding away. 'It holds a tired head and a slow hand unless you get yourself up to bed, and *that* means the sharp edge of my tongue. Now get that fire stoked up and off you go, the pair of you.'

'I hope the fortune teller tells me of a tall handsome fella who be coming to sweep me off me feet.' Alice heaved the heavy bucket of coal chippings on to the fire then damped it down with water from the kettle.

'You'd far better be hoping the mistress don't go having any unexpected callers.' Martha's eyes followed as Carys took the kettle to the scullery to refill it. 'If her does then it will be no Wakes for either of you.'

Did *she* want to know the future? In her own small bedroom Carys slipped the calico nightgown over her head, shivering against its cold touch. Did she want to be told of a future that could only hold more of the same? Her mother had held little love for her as a child, but from finding her being almost ravaged by Ryder Tempal had seemed to hold none at all. Why? She sat down on the edge of the iron-framed bed, staring into the light of the candle on the small chest beside it. Why had her mother blamed her, why had the blame been put squarely on her shoulders and none on his? Maria had not even wanted to listen to any explanation. *She* was the one in the wrong, Maria had told her. *She* had been responsible for what had happened. *She* had teased and flirted with Tempal, leading him on until he didn't know what he was doing. *She*, Carys, had acted the trollop.

But she had not. Carys stared into the candle flame. She had repeatedly done her best to avoid being in Ryder Tempal's company, making any excuse that would take her out of a room he was in. And why had she? Carys sat bolt upright as for the first time the question asked itself.

Why *had* she gone to such pains to avoid Ryder Tempal?

Was he ill-mannered? Was his manner of speech rough and uncultivated? Was he a braggart? Was his appearance or mode of dress not all it should have been? Carys knew the answer to each of these questions to be no. So why had she held such an aversion to the man?

With the last question came the answer.

Her body trembling with the force of her realisation, she let it flood into her mind, let the whole horrid truth of it flare like a beacon.

Maria was in love with Ryder Tempal!

Held there by the enormity of what had stared her in the face so often when she had come across them unexpectedly, Carys thought back across the twelve months before she had been sent away from Holyhead House.

His arm so often about Maria's waist, her hand pressed a moment too long to his mouth. Then had come the intimate whispering and sidelong glances across the dinner table, the invitations to the house that had grown more numerous with every month, the visits always timed to take place when her father would be at the enamelling works.

And her supposed trips to the dressmaker!

Carys swallowed the sickness that threatened, clenching her fingers, driving nails into palms in an effort to use one pain to drive out another. But the thought came on, driving into her consciousness, subduing any resistance until it was uppermost in her mind.

Were those visits purely what they were supposed to be? Had her mother really gone so many times to a dressmaker she had visited so rarely before knowing Ryder Tempal? Or were they an excuse to cover meetings of a very different kind? Lovers' meetings?

Maria and Ryder Tempal lovers!

Carys's fingernails cut deeper into her palms but the sharp sting was not enough to stem the flow of her thoughts.

Was it true? Was Maria that man's lover? Was that the reason she had incarcerated her own daughter in a nunnery, and why she had decried her as a virtual prostitute to the Mother Superior there? Was it the same reason that had caused her to label that sketch as lewd?

Almost without realising it, Carys slipped to the floor, drawing the carpet bag from beneath the bed. Opening it, she drew out the sketches Sister Mary Immaculata had returned to her. Climbing back on to the bed, she spread the sheets of paper around her. A likeness of her father at a work-bench, the light from a small window centring on an enamelled box held in his hand; one of the foundry men, sweat glistening on bare arms and shoulders as he bent before a furnace; and the sketch of the man rising up out of the waters.

'All men, only men!' Maria had told the Mother Superior, as if emphasising Carys's need to be cleansed of some disease. But these were the only sketches Maria had chosen to take with them to the convent, the rest she had ordered to be burned.

Carys remembered the look on the young maid's face as the sketches had been thrust into her arms, a look that said she would keep them safe. But for what? Carys's glance rested on her father's face, the charcoal lines of the sketch seeming to move in the flickering candlelight. Did the maid intend to give them to him? If she had it had not succeeded in softening his heart towards Carys, it had not moved him into recalling her from the convent.

'Why?' Tears clouding her vision, she touched a finger to the charcoal face. 'What did Maria tell you, Father? Was it something so dreadful you could not bring yourself to see me? Was it so awful to you that it made you want me out of your life for good? But I did none of the things she accused me of.'

A tear fell on to a corner of the sketch and Carys wiped it away, her finger smudging the black charcoal line into a softer grey shadow.

'I did none of them, Father,' she whispered brokenly. 'I did none of them.'

Gathering the sketches together, she paused, letting her

gaze rest on the one of the unknown man. Maria had called it obscene, Sister Mary Immaculata had likened it to Michelangelo's David, and Virginia Mountford had pronounced it worthy of the Royal Academy.

And she herself? Why had she kept it? Why, even now, did she not destroy it? Why, in the one sketch she had made since leaving the convent, had she drawn the remembered face of this man, a face so like that of Virginia Mountford's father?

Taking up the last of the drawings she held it for a moment, the light of the candle imbuing it with life, seeming to bring a taunting curve to the lips, a sensuous gleam to the black velvet eyes, and almost to lift the eyebrow topped by the faint line of a scar.

She should tear them up and in the morning put them on the kitchen fire, rid herself of these sketches, then perhaps she would be rid of the memories they invoked, of the unhappiness they recalled, of the pain that stirred afresh each time she looked at them. But already her hands had rolled them together and she was reaching for the carpet bag.

Settled beneath the sheets, the candle blown out, plunging the room into blackness, Carys closed her eyes. She had not answered her own questions. She had not told herself why she did not destroy her sketches. She had not told herself the reason behind her drawing of that handsome face.

Behind her closed eyes a strong athletic body leaned down from the saddle of a great horse, a man whose mouth curved in a mocking smile as he lifted the collar of her dress with a riding crop.

No, she had not told herself why. She turned into the pillow, pressing her face into its softness. But she knew the answer.

Chapter Seven

Caine Lazic paused in his task of filling the wooden water bucket, stretching his tall spare frame, easing away the strain of scooping water from the dark slow-moving brook. It was well named, he thought, staring down into its black depths. The Tame, the name the Saxons had given it, meant Dark River. The water, not much wider than a brook here as it cut its way across the flat plateau of ground, was dark but did not deserve the filth sent to despoil it from the numerous iron and steel works that disfigured the landscape, from every tiny back alley workshop that scarred the land like the marks of the pox leaving it little more than heaving sludge.

He glanced towards the wagon standing only yards away, then to the horse tethered to a nearby gorse bush, its yellow blossom defying the touch of the soot-laden air that hung over this town, marring plant and building alike with its black fingers.

Why bring the wagon here? his mother grumbled every year. And in reality there was no reason, no reason to return to this place that seemed to carry the curse of his name, no need to come, year upon year, to a part of the country that gasped in the fumes of smoke and dust of furnaces when he could as easily have driven the wagon to places of such beauty it seemed the Lord must have made them as homes for his angels.

But this was no place of angels. He turned his gaze, letting it wander over the jagged black scars of surface mining, the great grey slag heaps rising like weeping pustules from their edges, at the pitted holes that were gin pits: shafts stabbed into the earth, the coal ripped from its belly and the wound left open and gaping while another was sunk beside it.

No, this was no place of angels. This place held the devil. His devil. The one that brought him back here every year. The devil whose pitchfork of hatred and revenge prodded until he returned to the place where he had been blinded, to the place where he must seek recompense.

Every year they had come, he and his mother. Always at the same time of the year, always in the early spring, keeping faith with the time it had happened, when that one blow had torn out the eye of a ten-year-old gypsy boy.

Every year for sixteen years they had come.

Caine glanced over to where his mother sat on the steps of the painted bow-topped caravan. She was old, too old to face many more winters. And when she was gone? He let his gaze travel across the heath to where the road sliced through it. When she was gone, how would he travel? How then would he follow the gypsy ways? The ways that decreed his mother's wagon and all she owned would be burned at her death. He should take a wife, she was forever telling him, take a wife and build a wagon for himself. But Caine knew there could be no wife for him, no bringing children into the world, no family that would need his caring, until the devil he carried inside him was gone; until the need that brought him to this town was assuaged, that same need which for sixteen years had drawn him, guiding the wagon to this spot as though unseen hands held the old piebald's reins.

Every year they had come and every year that same inner voice had told him this was not the time, an innate knowledge that was the true legacy of his Romany blood telling him the moment was not yet come; that same inborn certainty that was telling him now, telling him this year he would taste revenge.

Picking up the water bucket, he carried it across to the wagon, emptying it into the large wooden barrel roped to its side.

This year . . . next year, whichever it was, he would be here. And be it with the help of God or devil, Caine Lazic would take his revenge.

'You two be minding yourselves!' Martha Bates tugged at the side of her all-enveloping white apron, smoothing away imaginary creases in the way she always did when wanting to emphasise a word or a feeling. 'And you lads,' she called to Alice's brothers, waiting over against the corner of the stables and carriage house, 'make sure and keep your eyes on these wenches and not go staring after others.'

'We'll watch them, Mrs Bates.' The taller of the two, a man well into his mid-twenties, stepped forward, flat cap held in his hand.

'Arrh, well, you makes sure as you do. And, mind, I want them back here at nine on the dot. Ain't no call for young folk to be out later than that!' Martha called, feeling the last word should be hers.

'Nine o'clock, huh! Her must think you two still be babbies!' Alice's second eldest brother, Edward, shoved his own flat cap back on short-cropped fair curls.

'No more a babby than you, our Eddie.' She tossed him a sharp look. 'You grumbles about everything you be asked to do lessen it be asked by that Peggy Rogers you be sweet on. If her was to ask for the moon, you'd be daft enough to go looking for a pair of sky hooks to haul yourself after it.'

'I ain't sweet on Peggy Rogers.' But Eddie's face flushed a deep plum red.

'Then if you ain't, you don't have the sense you was born

with,' his elder brother replied, 'cos that girl be taken with you, though for the life of me I can't see why.'

'Davey be right.' Alice fell into step beside her brother, tucking her arm into his. 'Peggy Rogers be a real nice wench, and if you don't have sense enough to say something to her soon then you can be sure some other fella will.'

'I'm sorry if having to escort two of us to the Wakes has meant your brother giving up time he wished to spend with someone else.' Carys looked up at the face of the man who now fell into step beside her. 'We are not very far from Ridge House. If I return now he could leave Alice with you and go wherever it was he wished to be.'

'That be a right nice way of thinking on your part, Miss Beddows.' Davey's smile curled the side of his mouth, giving his face a boyish appearance. 'But Eddie Withers has to learn there are others in this world beside himself; he must learn that once given a promise is to be kept.'

'A promise?'

'Arrh, miss, a promise. He told our mother he would look out for Alice and yourself and that is what he be going to do.'

'Mind!' He glanced ahead to where brother and sister, arms still linked, skipped across the heath like two children let loose to play. 'He don't never take no forcing into keeping his word, he's a great chap really, it's just a habit of his to grumble. I think it's a leftover from when we was kids and I was forever telling him what he could or couldn't do. Ordering him about, was what he called it. But seeing the size of him now, I wouldn't like to risk doing it again.'

Carys caught the smile that accompanied the words and heard the affection in the tone of Davey's voice. There was a strong bond between the brothers, a family feeling that she had witnessed on her visits to Alice's home, a love that bound them together and which had been painfully absent from her own life.

'I missed you when you didn't come with Alice on Sunday,' he said, breaking the small silence that had begun to build between them.

'Mrs Bates cannot easily manage with both Alice and myself gone from the house,' she answered. 'And seeing I have no family, it makes sense for Alice to have Sunday afternoon to go home.'

'But that leaves you no time at all for yourself!'

'Not quite.' Carys widened her stride, stepping over a small hollow in the path. 'I get an afternoon once a week.'

'And that be all?' Davey pointed to a stone jutting from the ground, alerting Carys to the danger of stubbing her toe against it.

'It's enough.' She skirted the obstruction. 'And Alice tells me we are fortunate in our free time. She says she knows several girls who get only one afternoon free a month.'

'Still it be little enough, though my father be always saying how well off we be compared to his father's time. He often tells of how me granddad, an eight-year-old lad, was woken for his shift in the coal pits at three in the morning, walking three miles over the heath in bare feet, come hail, rain or snow; and how, with only a couple of slices of bread and cheese and a can of water, he worked till seven at night then fell asleep, still underground, till his father finished his own shift at nine and they walked the three miles home. Compared to that my own shift of six in the morning to seven at night be not so bad.'

'And you have to work that number of hours every day?' Carys asked. She had known the workers employed by her father had worked many hours but had they really been as long as the ones these brothers of Alice worked?

'I know what you be thinking.' Davey laughed. 'You be thinking that if I works till seven every night, barring Sundays, of course, then how come I could be up at Ridge House for six o'clock?'

'Well, I had not thought that.' Carys answered his laugh with a smile that lit a twinkle of dancing lights in her lovely amber eyes. 'But since you mention it . . .'

'Since I've mentioned it . . .' Davey glanced down at her then quickly looked away, feeling his heart lurch at the beauty of the girl beside him.

'Since you have mentioned it?' Carys urged, unaware of the effect her smiling mouth was having on the man beside her.

'Arrh, well now!' He tried to keep his voice steady, to curb the flow of emotion that had his pulse going like the Great Western Railway's 'Zulu' express train that passed through Wednesbury station twice a week. 'Things be different this week.'

A squeal from ahead drew Carys's glance to where Eddie had his sister by the waist, lifting her off her feet and swinging her round.

'Why this week?' she asked, smiling as Alice squealed again, demanding to be set down.

Davey watched the antics of his brother and sister, taking advantage of the few moments their cavorting gave him to calm himself. Carys Beddows had had this effect on him from his first setting eyes on her seated at his mother's table. Since that time a few weeks ago he had thought of little save the girl with hair the colour of ripe chestnuts and amber eyes that glowed like the evening sky in summer.

''Cos this be Wakes week.' He forced himself to look ahead when all he wanted to look at was the sweet loveliness of her face. 'And Wakes week be special. The men at the brick yard be allowed to knock off one hour early during that week so as to visit the Wakes. That be one up on me granddad's time, eh?'

'Is it just the brick yard allows its workers an hour off their shift, or does everyone get it?'

'I reckon just about every man in Wednesbury will be treated the same. Them as works in the iron and steel foundries do, I knows that 'cos I've got mates as works there, and I reckon any other employer would follow suit. Could be he would have trouble should he try to put a stop to the Wakes hour.'

'So the people set great store by the Wakes?' Carys said as Alice broke free from her brother's grasp, swinging a friendly punch at his shoulder as he danced away from her.

'It be the highlight of the year, that and Christmas. They be the only times folk here seem to forget work, though I reckon most of them work just as hard at play.'

'That is a very deep piece of philosophy, Davey Withers.'

'I don't know about philosophy.' He caught her hand as her boot tangled in a clump of gorse, steadying her as she pitched forward. 'But I do know you and Alice would walk a lot easier if we left the heath and followed the road.'

Calling for Eddie and his sister to do just that, he released Carys's hand, embarrassed at the grin that flashed across his brother's face as he turned.

'Ee, Carys, we be going to have such a grand evening!' Alice's excitement shone in her eyes. 'I am going to have a go at everything there be on that fairground.'

'You'll need a shilling or two to do that!' Eddie laughed as his sister caught the other girl's arm, skipping her off. 'Have you suddenly been left a fortune by some rich lord as has been secretly in love with you for years?'

'Could be I have.' Alice tossed her head at her brother's teasing. 'And maybe I married him, secret like, and maybe now I be a very rich widow.'

'And maybe water don't run out of a bucket with a hole in the bottom of it!' Eddie laughed again. 'But somehow I don't think so.'

'You'll see,' Alice retorted. 'You might sing your song to a different tune when you sees how much I'll be spending.' Lowering her voice to a whisper, she squeezed Carys's arm. 'He don't know I've been saving every penny since Christmas turned.'

'But that can't be much?' She whispered back. 'Mrs Bates says you take your wages home to your mother every week.'

'Arrh, I do.' Alice glanced at the tram rumbling past as they left the heath to follow the road down to Bridge Street. 'But her gives me two shillings pocket money back and I don't have to spend much on clothes. Wearing me uniform every day saves a deal of wear on me own things, and I ain't keeping a bottom drawer, so what with me birthday five bob piece I have enough to see the both of us has a lovely time.'

'Alice, what is this birthday five bob piece?' Carys glanced to the opposite side of the road to where a man and a woman followed two children from a dark alleyway set between the long oppressive ribbon of houses.

'You'll be getting one on your birthday. The mistress gives each of the staff a gift of five shillings on their birthday. I told you she was a good sort.'

Yes, Alice had told her that. Carys watched the small girl on the far side of the road, pink ribbons trailing from a straw boater set on blonde ringlets, flounced pink skirts touching the top of shiny button boots, a maroon coat reaching just below the knee. The boy, taller and obviously older, also dressed in Sunday best, caught her hand as excitement sent her running in front of her parents. That child could have been her. She could have danced along, caught in the joy of an outing to the Wakes with her parents. But she never had. She had never known the kind of happiness that bubbled in that child. She had never been given the mother love that showed now on that woman's face.

'When is your birthday?'

'It is in August, the fourth of August.' Carys's mind flew back to the last birthday she had spent at Holyhead House – a birthday made special by her father's gift of an amethyst pendant, and even more so by the pride in his voice when he had said her designs were accounting for many sales of his enamels. There had been no more birthday gifts after that. But it was not the lack of gifts that brought the swell of tears to her throat, it was the loss of her father's love.

'That be still nearly six months.' Alice flicked her fingers as she counted the weeks. 'So you will have to wait before you will be getting your five bob. Still, not to mind, you will get it . . . if you live that long!'

She grasped Carys with both hands, dragging her away from the wheels of a carriage that had swept from the yard of the White Horse Hotel, careering around the corner into Mounts Road at the very moment Carys made to cross.

'Bloody mad-brained bugger!' Davey stepped quickly up to the girls, his eyes blazing fury as he looked after the carriage, turning now on to the heath where torches flared, lighting up the fairground. 'I'd like to kick his arse into his earholes!'

'That could prove quite painful . . . for both of you,' Carys smiled, hoping to relieve Davey's obvious concern for her.

'I bet it would bring tears to his eyes afore it would fetch them to mine, just the same,' he growled.

'Well, there's been no harm done,' Alice said, her enthusiasm for the evening ahead quenching the anger she would normally have displayed. 'C'mon, I don't want to waste a single minute.'

Her brothers close behind, they walked to where the flaring torches beckoned and Alice squealed her delight as the steam organ began to boom its strident music across the heath.

'Ee, Carys, do you think her will be here?' Alice shouted over the noise of the organ, the wooden figures adorning it clashing cymbals and beating drums.

'Who?' Carys called, feeling herself deafened by the blasts of music. 'Will who be here?'

'Her.' Eyes sparkling, Alice plunged into the crowds already milling about the sideshows, children's eyes feasting on the promised wonders. 'The fortune teller.'

Blushing as a ball was shoved into Davey's hands, with the stall holder inviting him to win his pretty sweetheart a fairing, Carys moved on.

'Ee, I hopes her is!' Alice said, as they paused before a booth boasting it housed: 'The living Cyclops, the only genuine three-eyed man'.

'Well, if she is not, we could always come back here,' Carys giggled. 'He is bound to see more with three eyes than we can with two.'

'Ee, you be getting a right cheeky monkey, Carys Beddows!'

Grasping Carys's arm more firmly beneath her own, Alice led the way between coconut shies and sideshows, breathing her delight and wonder as they came upon the majestic steam boats. Set a little apart from the rest, giving clearance for their boat-shaped bulk, sides painted with a central crown from which red, white and blue garlands stretched in loops and swirls from fore to aft, encircling the names William and Mary, they swung to and fro, gathering height with every swing, halting for seconds at the apex of each ascent before falling back to climb the other way.

'Watch!' Alice quivered as the riders, locked inside the metal restraints, screamed in delighted fear as the great boats rose and fell. 'Watch, they'll go right over . . . there, I told you!'

Carys felt the other girl tremble as the huge steam-driven boats reached the critical point, their occupants screaming as they swung right over in a complete arc.

'C'mon!' Alice fumbled two coins from a purse tucked inside her coat. 'Let's go on them first.'

'Mother said not to let you go on anything that might be dangerous.' Eddie stepped in front of her, barring her way to the tiny wooden platform on which a man stood selling tickets.

'That ain't dangerous!' Alice snapped, seeing the promise of a ride being snatched away.

'You don't think so.' Eddie refused to move. 'But then that be you all over, you never did see danger in nothing.'

'Well, there ain't none in them there boats,' she returned sharply. 'The folk be fastened in tighter than a pea in its pod. How can you reckon it be dangerous?'

'Be you takin' a ride or ain't you?' The man on the platform called, jingling coins in his hand. ''Cos if you ain't, then shift outta the way so other folk can get on.'

''Cos it'll be me and Davey will get Mother's tongue and Father's boot if you gets yourself hurt.'

Seeing the disappointment on her friend's face, Carys turned to Davey. 'It would not be *so* dangerous if you and Eddie were there to hold her, would it?'

'Reckon not.' Davey smiled down at her. 'But then, one of us would be holding *you*.'

'No,' Carys lied quickly. 'I have never been able to stomach being swung back and forth, please don't ask me to ride on one of those things. And please,' she turned her sweetest smile on him, 'don't let Alice be disappointed.'

He could not refuse her. Looking into her glowing amber eyes, Davey knew he would never be able to refuse this girl anything.

'C'mon then.' He swung away, taking his sister by the arm. 'Let's you, me and Eddie ride the King and Queen boats.'

From the edge of a crowd intent on the blood-spattered challenger being beaten senseless in a bare-knuckle contest a man stared at Carys, her head thrown back as she watched the giant boats ride the air.

Tall, his body muscular beneath a fashionable three-quarter-cut coat, his blond hair free of a hat, his yellow cat like eyes were fixed on her face. Across the ground separating them he could not be sure. The flickering light of the flaring torches cast shadows across the features that seemed so like . . . but that was all it could be, a similarity to a girl he had last seen four years ago.

Ignoring the demand they should move on from the woman clinging on to his arm, he watched the girl who clapped delightedly as she was joined by two men and another girl of about her own age.

It could not be her. Maria had said her daughter had chosen to remain in that convent. Carys Beddows had taken Holy Orders. All the same, Ryder Tempal's glance followed the slender young woman as she moved off.

*　　*　　*

'You've been on just about every ride there be to ride on and seen every sideshow that be decent. It be time we got you back home. No doubt it be getting well past eight,' Davey warned as Alice danced towards the bare-knuckle fighters. 'And there be no way you be going to watch men beat the life out of one another, so you can come along . . . and no arguing.'

'I don't want to watch no fighting,' she called over her shoulder, her step quickening. The crowds were thinning as families began to wend their way home.

'It must be getting late,' Carys said as Alice pulled her along. 'Mrs Bates said we must be back by nine.'

'We will.' Alice was almost running now. 'But I just have to get me fortune told first. There be a booth over against the one that holds the "Wolf Boy". There! There it is!'

Dragging Carys behind her, her brothers trailing in their wake, Alice dashed up to the small booth, dashing inside before Davey could grab her.

'I should have known her wouldn't go home without going in there.' He shook his head despairingly. 'And I suppose you will want your fortune told besides?'

'Of course.' Carys had held no intention of consulting the fortune teller but neither did she intend to let Alice take all the blame should they be late back to Ridge House.

'I give up!' Davey shook his head. 'But at least I have the consolation of being able to make a quick escape from Mrs Bates's tongue. You two will have to bear it . . . on your own heads be it.'

'But I thought your mother's instructions were to keep your sister free from anything you thought dangerous?'

'That they were, but there be dangers a man shouldn't be called upon to face, and a furious Martha Bates be one of them!'

One foot on the step of a horse-drawn carriage, Ryder Tempal watched a girl laughing up into the face of the man beside her, a girl he was almost certain he knew well. A girl Maria thought locked away in a convent.

*   *   *

'Ee, her was great!' Seated on Carys's bed, her feet tucked in her nightgown, Alice's face took on a dreamy look. 'Madam Rosa, Fortune Teller to Royalty.'

'So you keep saying,' Carys answered, her voice low so as not to be heard by Mrs Bates. She was cross enough at their arriving home ten minutes late without adding fuel to the flames by letting her know they were still not in bed.

'No, but her was, Carys. Her told me all about me family: about me dad hurting his arm that time in the brick yard, and her said me mother thought that when our Eddie were a babby he had got the TB from somewhere and how her pinched a orange every day from Gascoyn's fruit stall in the market 'cos the doctor said fruit were good for him and me mother hadn't the money to buy it. Ee!' Her eyes registering surprise and concern, Alice looked across the cramped room to where Carys was tying her hair with a ribbon. 'Do you think that were true, Carys? Do you really think me mother would steal oranges?'

'Do you think so?'

'I don't know what to think.' Alice frowned. 'I've never known me mother do anything down in her life, her's always been too open-handed, too ready to give to anybody what asked. I've never known her take even a farthing that wasn't due to her.'

'Then why think so now?'

''Cos Madam Rosa . . .'

Carys threw the long rope of her hair back across her shoulder. 'Alice, if Madam Rosa told you the moon was made of green cheese, would you believe it?'

The concern in Alice's eyes faded and they took on a look of wide-eyed innocence. 'But it is, isn't it?'

'Alice Withers, you . . . !' Holding a hand over her mouth, Carys stifled the laughter bubbling in her throat.

'Well, if me mother did pinch them oranges, I reckon as her has more than paid for them since, what with the price old Solly Gascoyn charges for his stuff!'

Their laughter subsiding Alice sat up, bedcovers tangled about her where she had rolled like a puppy, her face solemn once more.

'What do you reckon as to what Madam Rosa said about me brothers?'

Trying to straighten her covers, Carys sighed. 'Why not go to bed? We can talk about Madam Rosa's predictions tomorrow if Mrs Bates . . .'

'Her said as our Eddie will be married within a twelve month and that the girl would make him a good, sensible wife.' Alice ignored both plea and warning. 'I guess that'll be Peggy Rogers, and a good thing an' all. Our Eddie needs a wench that'll keep his head out of the clouds. But what her said about our Davey didn't sound too good.'

One thing Carys had learned since coming to Ridge House was that once Alice got started on something it was best to let her get it out of her system. Only along that path lay the promise of peace. So Carys climbed up on to the bed, hunching her knees under her chin and wrapping both arms around them.

'Her said our Davey wouldn't know a smooth life,' Alice went on as Carys settled herself on the narrow bed. 'Seems how he will love a woman, but that same woman will love another. Our Davey will watch her wed and his heart will break. He will not take a wife till he be near enough forty and by that time will have made money. But that money will not mend his heart nor take his thoughts from his one true love.'

'Alice Withers, you are making this up!'

Grabbing a pillow in her arms, Alice held it to her face, laughing into it.

'I know,' she gurgled, 'but it sounds good.'

'It does *not* sound good.' Carys smiled despite her determination not to. 'It sounds like those penny dreadfuls you have in the box under your bed.'

Alice pretended to drop the pillow, striking a melodramatic

pose, holding the back of one hand to her forehead and the other with palm flat against her heart. 'I am undone,' she sobbed, 'you know my wicked secret.'

'I know you should be on the halls!' Carys laughed, then clapped a hand across her mouth, glancing towards the door.

'Don't worry,' Alice whispered, dropping her pose. 'Mrs B. went to her bed half an hour ago.'

'And you should be in yours!' Carys whispered back. 'We will both be too tired for anything in the morning.'

'I did make up the bit about the money, but the rest, that about our Davey not getting the woman he really loved and not being wed till he be nigh on forty, that were just as Madam Rosa told it to me.' Alice chose not to hear Carys's whisper. 'Ee, poor Davey! I wonder who the wench is he be sweet on?'

'I am sure you will know sooner or later,' Carys answered, hoping deep inside the foretelling would not come true. She had met Davey Withers only twice but that was enough to tell her he was a gentle, caring man, one too good and kind to be hurt.

'So what did her tell you?' Alice switched easily from one question to another. 'You said you would tell when we got back.'

'It's too late . . .'

'No, it ain't.' Alice shuffled into a more comfortable position, tucking her night-gown over her feet. 'I told you my fortune. I told you her said there was a man in the shadows: a tall, well-built man with hair golden as sunlight, a man whose clothing spoke of wealth, and that he was looking at me, and giving a love token to a young lad and pointing to me. Then her said the token would be in my hand before the spring of the new year. You said p'raps things would change come the turning of the century, *you* said that an' all, so that bit must be true.'

Carys shook her head. 'I am not a teller of fortunes, Alice, I don't know what your future holds.'

'No, but you knows what *yours* holds,' she retorted. 'Or leastways what Madam Rosa says it holds. So come on, Carys, a promise is a promise.'

'I think the woman invented a future for me, just as you have invented wealth for Davey . . .'

'It ain't impossible our Davey could come to be rich,' Alice interrupted.

'No, it is not impossible, and I sincerely hope he may . . .'

'Look, forget what was said about him.' Alice fidgeted, wriggling the covers of the bed into an even more crumpled pile. 'I want to know what was said to you.'

Knowing it would be useless to resist, Carys rested her chin on her hands, eyes gazing into the shadows of the room. 'She said a woman had done me great harm though the cause of it was not of my doing. She had struck at me from a jealous heart in the hope of keeping a man, one who would play her false. She said this woman was well known to me and would strike again after the year had turned. That due to her I would know great fear, and that she would try to take my life but would take another's instead.'

'Go on!' Alice urged as she stopped speaking.

'She said that soon I would learn of the death of someone dear to me.'

'And?' said Alice, squirming.

'She said that in the distance a man stands beside a brook, a man whose face bears a mark of Cain, a man who holds a heart in his hand and vengeance in his soul.'

'My God!' Alice loosed a long pent-up breath. 'Didn't her have anything good at all to say? What you tell me sounds too awful for my worst nightmare. Be you sure that was all?'

Drawing her gaze back from the shadowed corner, Carys drew a steadying breath. 'She said that the efforts of the woman who wished me harm would come to nothing, and also the one who had found me a home would remain close for the rest of my life.'

'That be the mistress,' Alice murmured. 'I did say you

would be best off staying at Ridge House. I did say that, Carys.'

'You did, and that at least was a sensible prediction.' She jumped from the bed. 'And now I am going to make another, and that is you get off my bed and leave me to get to sleep or you will find yourself on the floor.'

'All right, I'm going!' Alice scrambled from the bed as Carys made a determined grab at the rumpled quilt. 'Carys,' she called softly, the bedroom door ajar, 'this time I don't hold no truth to that fortune teller. I reckon her was making the whole thing up, so don't you go worrying over what her said.'

The bed straightened, Carys settled beneath the sheets. One short breath had extinguished the candle, plunging the room into darkness. Alice held that no truth was contained in the words Carys had heard in that booth at the fairground.

Gradually the darkness retreated before the moonlight from the room's small window, collecting itself into shadows that hovered about the walls.

But Alice had not been told all Madam Rosa's words, she had not heard everything.

In the blackness Carys heard again the words she had chosen not to tell her friend.

'I see a man whose hair and eyes be black, black as the inside of the devil's mouth. A man who searches beside a pond, searches for a woman, one who carries pencil and paper in her hands. He has searched this long time, and though he be far, still he be near. There be long months to go before he finds what he be seeking but find it he surely will, for his will be the claiming of you, 'tis him will have the taking of you.'

Searches beside a pond . . . Carys covered her eyes with her hand, shutting out the limpid light of the moon. But though she dismissed the light she could not rid her inner eye of the image of a strong handsome face, one whose hell-dark eyes mocked her, the face from the sketch which lay beneath her bed.

Chapter Eight

'Mistress says her wants to see Carys. Says to ask you to send her to the drawing room at eleven.'

Alice placed the last of the dining-room crockery on the large table that occupied the centre of the kitchen at Ridge House, her gaze troubled.

'Do you think the mistress be annoyed at Carys and me for being late back last night?'

'Did her say to send you upstairs as well?' Martha Bates looked up from the pastry she was mixing in a large earthenware bowl.

'No.' Alice rested the tray on the table but her hands kept hold of it. 'Her just said to ask you to send Carys to her at eleven.'

'Well, if her doesn't want to see the pair of you then it isn't you coming in ten minutes late that be the trouble. And in any case the mistress would not be seeing you for that unless I had complained to her about you, and I haven't done that.'

'Then what do you think it is, Mrs Bates? Could it be Carys don't be doing her job proper?'

'Mistress wouldn't be sending to see her about that neither, least not until I'd been spoken to first. Truth be I don't know what her's being sent for.'

'Ee, I hope her won't be given the sack!' Alice turned as Carys came from the scullery. 'Mistress wants to see you in the drawing room, Carys. I hope you don't be in no trouble.'

Halfway into the kitchen she stopped dead. Around her the familiar range and dresser merged with whitewashed walls before dissolving into spindrift mists that melted into emptiness.

In a fraction of time one world had faded and she stood in another, a world of silently moving figures robed in black, a world of cold, high-ceilinged rooms and closed doors. 'The Mistress of Novices wishes to see you. You will go to her room at eleven.' In the shrouded, fear-ridden mists of her mind the words became twisted. She was to go again to that room where she had seen . . . the room where she was beaten.

'Carys!'

'Yes, Sister . . .'

It was a low, frightened reply as memory carried her down a long soundless corridor lined with closed doors that each gave on to a tiny cell holding a narrow iron bed and single cupboard. One by one they slid past until she came to one bearing the sign 'Mistress of Novices'. Tapping at this door, she entered, head bent and eyes on the floor.

'Your work is unsatisfactory.' The voice ringing in her mind did not even give her her name. 'You dawdled over scrubbing the floors in the Chapel of Our Lady.' A thin cane whistled through the air, slicing across her arms and hands, stinging through the thin cloth of her novice's robe. 'And you were talking while working in the vegetable garden.' The cane rose again, the force of its blow almost knocking her off her feet. 'What were you talking about?' The voice became a hiss. 'Perhaps you were talking about what you saw here, were you?' The cane sliced close to her face, striking hard on her shoulder. 'Were you? Were you!'

'No, Sister Veronica. No, I was not . . . no . . . no . . .'

'Carys . . . Carys wench, it's all right, it's all right. You be here with Alice and Mrs Bates. Shh . . . shh . . . there ain't no Sister Veronica here.'

Grabbing the tray of freshly washed dishes from Carys's trembling hands, Alice set them beside the dining-room crockery she had brought from upstairs.

'Ee, Carys!' she said, as Martha led the girl to a chair. 'I didn't mean to scare you.'

'You have a mouth as big as a parish oven, Alice Withers,' the housekeeper snapped, 'and you don't know when to close the door.'

'I'm sorry, Mrs Bates, I didn't think Carys would take on like that.'

'That be another of your faults, you don't think!' Martha's plump face was wreathed in anger. 'You come barging into the kitchen, talking about trouble and folk getting the sack, with never a thought for the consequences.'

'Ee, I am sorry.' Alice's mouth drooped. 'Last thing I would want would be to give Carys cause for worry.'

'I know, me wench.' Martha's anger faded as rapidly as it had risen. 'You wasn't to know the girl would take on. Go brew a pot of tea, a cup will help pull her together.'

Yes, it might, thought Martha, holding Carys, feeling her tremble. But it would not banish fear which could drain a face to the colour of milk and reduce the girl to a quivering wreck, nor heal a pain that went deeper still. That would take time and love, both of which, God in His mercy, she would have at Ridge House.

Carrying the enamel tea pot to the table, Alice looked towards Martha and at her nod filled three cups.

'Here you be, Carys.' Martha pushed a cup into the girl's hands, noting the tremors that still shook her fingers. 'And you sit yourself down an' all, Alice. Five minutes will do no harm, we can all catch up later.

'Come on, Carys, drink up.' Martha smiled, though it was forced. She was concerned for this girl who had turned up out of nowhere with no place to go. Surely the mistress had no complaint? Surely she was not about to dismiss her? It was true they had been told almost nothing of her background and less of her parentage but her very demeanour told she could not be from the slums.

'Carys, I be real sorry for mouthing off. I didn't mean . . . I wouldn't . . .'

'It was not your fault, Alice.' Carys looked across at the girl seated on the opposite side of the table.

'Weren't nobody else's.' Alice's eyes brimmed with tears. 'Me and my big mouth.'

'You are not to blame.' Reaching out, Carys pressed a hand to her friend's arm. 'It was just a memory.'

'Some memory!' Alice blurted out the very words Martha Bates was thinking. If what they had just witnessed was due to a memory then just what were the memories locked in this young girl's mind, and who or what was responsible for them?

Pulling back her hand, Carys cradled both of them about her cup.

'I don't think it be anything serious the mistress wants to see you about,' Martha said, as Alice drew a handkerchief from beneath her apron and wiped her eyes. 'So both of you be putting your fears away. Were anything amiss, Martha Bates would have heard of it first.'

'You thought it was somebody called Sister Veronica was sending for you.' Alice held the handkerchief to her mouth as Martha's glance told her once more her mouth was running ahead of her brain.

'Sister Veronica was the Mistress of Novices,' Carys said, knowing the time had come for explanations and suddenly feeling relief on realising she could tell these two kind people what had happened to her. 'I was placed under her supervision when my mother enrolled me in the Convent of the Holy Child. She was strict but not unkind. Not at first. It seemed she understood the loneliness of newcomers to the convent. Then one afternoon it was just before Exposition of the Blessed Sacrament, I was scrubbing the floor of the infirmary when one of the Sisters sent me to fetch the visiting priest to an old nun dying of tuberculosis. I ran all the way to the office of the Mistress of Novices, though I knew running was forbidden. When I got there I knocked and rushed right in, without waiting to be given leave to enter.' Carys paused, a flush of colour staining cheeks that had been chalk white. 'Sister Veronica was there.' She forced herself to go on. 'And so was the priest. They were . . . they were . . .'

She hesitated, finding the words painful to say, feeling that to speak of what she had seen was a betrayal of trust, a breaking of her word, a promise made in her heart long before the nun's cane had beaten it from her mouth.

'Carys, wench.' Understanding her hesitation yet knowing too that there would be no healing until she spoke what was in her mind, Martha softly encouraged her. 'Carys, there is that inside you that would be best shared with others. It may be you have promised not to speak of it and don't care to break your promise. So maybe it's best if I speak the words for you. Your promise will not be violated but p'raps your heart will be eased.'

Taking the cup from Carys, she laid it on the table then folded the girl's hand in both her own. 'It be my belief,' she went on as softly as before, 'that you came on that priest and that nun doing what should be done only between man and wife.'

For fully half a minute silence hung like a stifling shroud over the kitchen. Alice, holding her breath in the prison of her lungs, stared at the housekeeper. What she had just said . . . it couldn't be the truth. Nuns and priests, they didn't do such things . . . Beside the long dresser the clock on the wall ticked away the seconds but Alice would not breathe, would not fracture the silence by proclaiming the truth.

'That be it then.' Giving Carys's hand a final comforting pat Martha pushed back her chair. 'There will be no more said on that subject in this kitchen, or beyond it.' She cast a meaningful glance at Alice who only now was releasing her breath. 'You, Alice, get them crocks put away then see to the dusting of the front parlour.' She glanced over at the clock which showed ten minutes to eleven. 'And you, Carys girl, get yourself up to your bedroom. Wash your hands and face and put on a fresh apron before you go to the mistress. And remember,' she added as Carys walked to the door that gave on to the back stairs, 'you can't be in no trouble 'cos if you was I would know about it. And anyway, you know yourself by now the mistress be no ogre.'

But why should Virginia Mountford want to see her?

Carys tied on a freshly laundered apron, smoothing its starched expanse over her skirts.

Was she to be dismissed? She felt her heart thud in her chest. Would she have to return to that convent?

Virginia Mountford sat in a high-backed brocade chair beneath a wide window overlooking a part of the garden that was filled with roses – ones that had been bred and named for her. Her husband had been a keen gardener while he lived, and developing a new strain of rose each year had been his delight. Shifting her glance to a beautiful long-legged table she smiled wistfully at the huge bowl of 'Ginny's Beauty' at its centre, the wonderful golden-bronze of the petals of her favourite rose reflected in a huge oblong silver-framed mirror.

Oliver had never once spoken of his sadness at their having no child but she knew that the sadness was there. How she had wanted to give him a son, but the years had passed and none had come to them. She swept her glance over the rest of the room: the walls panelled in oak, the beautiful French tapestries, graceful Regency chairs and sofa. They had been given wealth in plenty, she thought, but the richest gift of all had been denied.

A tap at the door pulled her back from the realm of memory. Touching one hand to the single rope of pearls about her throat then smoothing her deep blue skirts, before folding both hands together in her lap she called permission to enter.

Carys, face still pale from the episode in the kitchen, bobbed a brief curtsey.

'You asked to see me, ma'am?'

Virginia looked at the girl. If she and Oliver had been given a daughter she would have been about this age and she too would have been lovely, she would have had her father's laughing eyes and . . . Pushing the thought away, she tightened her mouth with the effort and for several seconds found it too difficult to speak.

'Yes.' She spoke at last but the words were thick with tears. 'There is a matter I wish to speak to you about.'

Carys felt her stomach muscles twist but lifted her head proudly. If she was to be dismissed, then whatever the reason she would face it full on.

'Sit down, Carys.'

The chair nearest her was a few feet to her right and on moving across to it she caught sight of a box, its beautiful enamelled sides and lid edged with a delicate filigree of silver. Without thinking what she was doing, she picked it up, turning it in her hands, knowing each of the lovely scenes painted on it before even looking at them.

'It is very beautiful, do you not think so?'

At Virginia's softly spoken question Carys looked up, sadness and longing stirring the depths of her amber eyes.

'Yes, it is very beautiful. Forgive me, ma'am, I should not have touched it.'

'Bring it to me.'

Taking the box Carys handed to her, Virginia touched one finger to its smooth surface.

'My husband bought me this box many years ago,' she said, her voice taking on the tone only a cherished memory can bring. 'It was an anniversary gift, the tenth year we had spent together. I remember he said he had bought it while on a business trip to Bilston. I have never been there but I imagine it must be a very pretty place to produce such beautiful objects as my box.'

Pretty? Carys remembered the times her father had taken her there with him. The cramped, huddled together houses, each of them giving part of their tiny space over to a workshop where every member of the family old enough or strong enough to work pounded metal ores into frit, or sat in the sallow light of tiny smoke-filmed windows coating tin and brass with white lead. Above all she recalled the fierce heat of the coal-fired kilns.

'You seemed surprised when you saw this, almost as if you knew it?' Virginia Mountford looked up. 'Is that so, Carys? Do you know this box?'

'I,' she answered softly. 'I have seen something like it before. 'I . . . I am familiar with the design.'

'Hmm!' Placing it on a rosewood table set near her chair, Virginia nodded. 'Bring your chair over here to the window and sit beside me.' Then with Carys seated, she went on: 'Would you tell me how you come to recognise the design on my box?'

'Only my father's enamels have that depth of brilliant blue. He . . .' Carys hesitated. She had not meant to speak of her father, the words had just tumbled from her out of pride in his work.

'It is a wonderful blue, so very vibrant.' Virginia ignored her hesitation. 'I have often wondered what gives it such a magnificent depth. It always reminds me of the blue of the Madonna's robes in the religious paintings of Raphael and Botticelli.'

'That is because my father shared their secrets. He added a tiny amount of powdered lapis lazuli to the oxide, then fired at over eight hundred degrees centigrade.'

'Lapis lazuli.' Virginia nodded again. 'The favoured stone of the Pharaohs of Ancient Egypt.'

'My father thought them among the greatest artists the world has known. He said they understood colour better than any Renaissance painter.'

'Your father sounds a very perceptive man?'

Was he perceptive enough to see what his wife had done to his daughter? Virginia watched the girl who sat looking at the box. Perceptive enough to realise that to face his wife with the truth was to lose her. Was that too much for him? Was living without his child preferable to living without his wife? Was that the real reason he had not found her?

'Was it only by the depth of blue you recognised that box as your father's work?' Virginia probed gently.

She had already told this woman of Maria and her jealousy; it could do no harm now to tell her the rest. Carys drew a long breath.

'That box is one of a set of six. Their design and painting I recognise from my childhood. My father encouraged me to draw, he used many of my designs in his products and often took me on visits to his enamelling works in Bilston. He preferred his employees to give up the practice of using their homes as workshops and gave them every encouragement to do so by building foundries that were roomy and light, though not everyone would give up their old ways. But my father treated his workers fairly. He paid them a decent wage, unlike some others in his trade, even though this caused him to be ostracised by some of the masters.'

'So you are familiar with the trade of enamelling?'

Carys nodded. 'Yes, ma'am.'

'One more question,' Virginia said as the girl looked from the box to her. 'Is your father's name Meshac Beddows?'

For a moment Carys did not answer. How had her mistress come by that information? She had told her of Maria, the morning after being brought to Ridge House, but she had not mentioned her father's name. But she *had* mentioned Moxley and Holyhead House. It would be simple for Virginia Mountford to discover the name of its owner.

From her chair beneath the spacious window Virginia

waited for the answer to her question and felt pity well in her when it came, a simple yes.

'Forgive my bluntness, my dear, but I think you will soon understand the reason for it. I had to be sure, you see. I had to be positive there could be no mistake. Now that I am, I feel I should show you this.'

Reaching for the newspaper, she handed it to Carys.

Puzzled, her eyes scanned the page. What could there be in a newspaper that Virginia Mountford felt she should see? It was then, halfway down the third column, that she saw the blacker, bolder print of a headline:

TRAGIC DEMISE OF PROMINENT INDUSTRIALIST.

A sudden awful fear squeezing her heart, she read the underlying report, the cold impersonality of it ripping at her heart.

Meshac Beddows, proprietor of Beddows Enamels of Bilston, who died of a heart attack one week ago, was today laid to rest in the cemetery of the Church of All Saints, Moxley. Mr Beddows, whose home was Holyhead House, was a great benefactor to Bilston and to Moxley. He will be greatly missed by family, associates and employees.

Bethesda Lazic sat on the small wooden stool set close to the wood fire over which swung a smoke-blackened pot. She had come here to this same spot with her son for sixteen years. Sixteen years in which he had searched in vain for the only cure for the trouble that ailed him: revenge.

Would that cure be found this year, or would his hope fade as the summer would fade? Yet if it did, it would flourish once more as surely as the buds of spring would break, and with it the journey would begin all over again.

Did she resent their coming? She stared into the fire, seeing among its dancing flames a tall boy, trousers ragged below the knee, a laughing, handsome, black-haired boy whose strong limbs and sparkling eyes seemed fashioned by the gods.

No! She pulled hard on the yellowed stem of a clay pipe breathing out smoke from between teeth equally discoloured. If Caine were to die she would come alone; she would come until she took the life of the woman who had blinded her son, or the Lord took Bethesda Lazic from the earth.

True she grumbled at their returning here every year, but that was a shield, a pretence, to keep her son from knowing the depth of her own pain, and the longing in her heart to see that woman die.

She watched him through the smoke of her pipe. He was tall as his youth had foretold he would be and strength rippled through every cord and sinew of his body, but the pride had gone from him, marring him as that whip had marred his face. He should have had a wife by now, and children to carry his Romany blood, children she could sing the old songs to as she had sung them to him. But the blood that ran in his veins ran also in hers and with it the same desire that burned away all others. Bethesda Lazic would nurse no child of her son and that struck her to her heart but as surely as the sun rose in the heavens she would see that woman pay.

'Take what you be wanting from the pot.' Caine came up to the fire. 'Then see that all is ready in the wagon, I want to be away within the hour.'

'Be it Bromwich you be heading to?' Bethesda removed the pipe from her mouth, tapping out the remains of burned tobacco against the stool.

Caine glanced across the wide emptiness of the heath. They had spent sixteen of the springs and summers of his life up along West Bromwich. They had taken the wagon across the lyng fields scattered about with tiny purple flowers, massive oak trees spreading branches so wide they seemed to cover the earth, then down into the wooded hollow of the pretty Sandwell Valley which, long ago, had sheltered a Benedictine monastery but now held a beautiful mansion owned by a lord.

Each year they had been given permission to set the wagon at the edge of a copse of sycamore trees that bordered Swan Pool. There the estate workers, and even some of the people of the town, would come seeking his mother's herbal cures, and many a woman asking for her palm to be read while she was there. It brought money to keep them in food, the money he himself earned from odd jobs being kept against the winter months.

But this year he would not go to the Sandwell Valley. This year he would turn to the north.

'I was thinking to go in the opposite direction.' He looked back at his mother. 'I thought to go along of Bilston then on to Wolverhampton, making up into Shropshire for the winter.'

Bethesda made no reply, showed no surprise at this change to the route they had followed so many years, accepting the inner knowledge that was telling her son the time was now.

'I'll make we both some tay then put the fire out.' Placing the empty pipe in her mouth, she rose from her stool and went into the wagon.

Would it be this year? Was the quickening in his veins a sign that the reckoning had come at last? Murmuring softly to the old piebald mare, he fastened the harness to the collar about her neck then slipped a halter and lead reins over her head. Guiding the horse the few yards to where the caravan rested, he gently and slowly backed it between the shafts. Then, his movements quickening, he fastened straps and buckles, securing the harness about her back and tying the traces to the shafts of the wagon.

'Tay be ready,' Bethesda called from the fire, as yet still burning. 'Come drink it while it be hot. 'Twill be some hours afore you get the next.'

His hand resting a moment on the mare's soft flank, Caine glanced to where the Holyhead Road cut a narrow trail across the heath, letting his eyes follow the figure of a woman dressed in a coat that had once been blue but was now faded almost to grey. She was bareheaded but the spring sun glowing on her hair seemed to turn it into a cap of bronze. She walked slowly, head held low to her chest, hiding her face, but around one arm he saw a velvet band, the circlet of black that spoke of bereavement.

Bethesda too had seen the woman, and as she watched her pass the nerves in her own body jangled and a sixth sense, passed from mother to daughter in her family for as long as could be remembered, and so strong in herself as never to have played her false, told her that in some way the path of that woman would cross with her own; that in the future their lives would intertwine. Watching the figure slowly following the line of the road, Bethesda felt that here was a woman who would be the key to the revenge her son had sought so long, though that revenge would ultimately come through Bethesda Lazic.

The two tin cups washed and stored in the cupboard inside the wagon and her stool safely wedged beside the stove, Bethesda emptied the last of the water from the pot, dousing the small cooking fire before kicking earth over it. The woman had passed from her sight along the road but deep inside her every nerve still sang. This was the reason her son had changed their route of sixteen years. Whether he knew it or not, the fates were ready to play their part.

Chapter Nine

. . . Was laid to rest . . . died a week ago . . .

The words she had read in the newspaper danced in Carys's mind.

Her father was dead!

The numbness that had overtaken her in the drawing room of Ridge House gripped her still.

Her father was dead. She would not see him again. She would never be able to put her arms about him, to tell him the truth he would never know she was not what her mother had surely claimed. That she had done none of the things that had been told to the Mother Superior of the convent.

Behind her on the road a horse clopped loud on the rough surface, the rumble of a wagon's wheels rumbling in the quiet afternoon, but Carys heard no sound other than the crying of her own heart.

'You were not to know,' Virginia Mountford had told her kindly. 'And heart attacks happen so quickly, they can take a life and give no warning of their coming. The Lord took your father swiftly and that was a blessing. Accept it as such, my dear. Forget now about the past, forget Holyhead House, there is nothing for you there.'

There was nothing for her there.

The cold chill of truth added to the numbness that held her. There was nothing for her in her father's house, nothing except trouble and perhaps danger should Maria find her there.

'Stay away from Moxley, and stay away from me!'

Those had been her words that day on Snow Hill railway station. Well, she would stay away from Maria, and as for her father's house, there was nothing she wished for there, but she would not stay away from Moxley, away from the churchyard that held her father's body. She would pay her respects from love for him, a last service Maria would deny if consulted.

'Could you be doing with a ride, missy?'

Alongside her a gypsy wagon came to a halt.

'The road be rough, missy, and you have a look of weariness about you.'

Carys looked up at the wagon painted with bright flowers, its window hung with yellow curtains.

'The offer be kindly meant, you need have no fear.'

Carys's glance switched to the woman on the driving seat sitting beside a man who held his head turned slightly away. The woman's face was heavily lined, bearing the marks of her years. Her hair, grey as morning mist, escaped in straggling wisps from beneath a red head kerchief fastened at the nape of her neck. A black shawl, splashed liberally with a pattern of full-blown roses, was draped about her shoulders, the knot which held it resting where breasts had once jutted firm and proud, though they were now indistinguishable beneath layers of clothing that ended in dark layered skirts sweeping to her boots.

'Or be it you have no liking for gypsies? In that case, we will be on our way.'

'I have no dislike of gypsies.' The woman's voice clearing some of the fog from her brain, Carys realised the rudeness her failure to answer had implied.

'Then think on the length of the road that lies ahead. Your feet be aching now, if I be not mistaken, and they will ache a deal more before you get where you be heading. I know this way well, there be no dwelling atwixt here and Moxley and that be a step of two miles or more.'

Already the air was cooling, the sun losing the weak warmth of spring. Carys realised the sense of accepting a lift. The horse hardly looked capable of speed but its pace would still outmatch her own and her strength would be saved for the homeward journey. Squinting up at the old woman, back resting against the closed bottom half of the wagon's stable-type door, her shoulder touching that of the man beside her, Carys thanked her, catching hold of the hand held out to help her on to the wagon.

'You be telling us where it is you want to be set down?' The woman hitched herself along the wooden seat, allowing Carys to sit without their bodies touching. 'We be bound for Bilston though we might not get the whole way before the light goes. The days still fade quickly this early in the year. Mayhap my son will camp up for the night some way from that town, but we will take you as far as we go.'

'I am going to Moxley,' Carys answered. 'I want to visit the church there.'

'That be the church of All Saints.' The gypsy woman nodded, her gold hoop earrings glinting in the pale sunlight. 'I know it, though I have never been inside.'

Bethesda waited for the girl to respond, wondering, if an answer came, if it would be the same as that her sixth sense had already placed in her mind. This girl's home had been in Moxley, though it was there no longer. She had been taken from it while still little more than a girl by Gorgio reckoning, and put in a place that had brought fear to her heart and labour to her back. The girl would not know, for Bethesda guessed she did not have the gift of the sight, but this day would bring a new fear.

'Moxley was once my home . . .'

Bethesda listened to what she knew.

' . . . but I . . . I left when I was seventeen and have

133

not been back since then. I am going to visit my father's grave.'

'It is good to see respect for the old given by the young. Your father has been long gone?'

'Last week.' Carys felt the tears catch in her throat. 'He died last week.'

And he was placed in the ground but yesterday. Bethesda could have added but did not. The girl was grieving and had no kin of her own to share her pain. Suddenly feeling the familiar surge in her stomach, the old gypsy clamped her lips tight together. It always came to her like this, almost as if her veins had widened, allowing a rush of blood that was followed by a fierce heat, a burning that seemed to reach from her very soul into her mind, searing away her thoughts, clearing her brain, removing all else in preparation for the coming of the sight. Then it was with her. Clearly as watching actors upon a stage she saw a woman rolling naked beneath a golden-haired man, then the same woman handing a younger woman to a nun. The picture in her mind changed to a large house, to a bedroom in that house, a bedroom where that same woman flaunted her body before a different, much older man, a man who grasped his chest before falling dead across the bed. The woman turned and Bethesda saw her face. It was the face of the woman she and her son had searched for these sixteen years.

'I'll pull off the road here and take to the heath.'

Caine spoke for the first time as he guided the piebald left on to the rough surface of untilled ground. Over to the right fields of corn waved their shoots like small green flags. 'I tell you so you will have no worry that we don't be going where my mother said. I know the tales Gorgios tell about gypsy folk making off with their children.'

At Carys's side Bethesda relaxed as the sight left her, but the uneasiness that remained puzzled her. This was not how it usually was. Once the sight had revealed itself, shown her what it was she had to know, then it cleared, leaving no trace of having been. But this time . . . this time she felt its purpose unfulfilled, unfinished. This time she had not been given the whole of it. Sometime in the future it would come again, and she must watch and wait.

'Arrh.' Bethesda nodded. 'Lies told to frighten young uns into behaving, filling little hearts with fear and little heads with untruths. Gorgios call that love . . . pah! I wouldn't give that sort of love to a pig in the wild.'

'We leave the road here 'cos beyond that rise lies the toll house.'

Caine resumed his explanation and Carys turned to look at him, past the figure of his mother, but still he kept his face turned slightly away.

'We pay no toll to travel God's good earth.' Bethesda again took the conversation to herself. 'It was given to all men, for all to walk freely. It was given to Adam who was father to us all, and the Almighty did not tell him to parcel it up and give parts to some, telling them to make others pay to cross it. No, that was the idea of graspers, men who batten on the backs of others. But they'll not batten on the gypsy folk, they won't take our money for things that be the God-given right of every man.'

Cresting the rise, Caine pointed ahead to where a double-storied octagonal building, an added gable to one side giving a lop-sided effect, stood close to the side of the road.

'Carts have to pay threepence to pass that,' he said, 'and a packman pays a penny.'

'I have threepence.' Carys reached a hand to her pocket. 'I will pay for you to pass the toll.'

Catching her hand as Carys made to pass the coins to Caine, Bethesda almost gasped. With an intensity that threatened to spill her from her seat, the feeling came that this girl and the woman who had blinded her son were close kin.

'We'll take nothing from you, missy.' The words were said slowly, giving time for the feeling to fade away. 'It be a kindness you offer and we be grateful for it, but we won't take it. A Romany takes no reward from those he offers his wagon to, but we will remember all the same.'

And she would remember, Bethesda thought, as the wagon skirted past the toll house, its keeper standing beside the crudely built dry stone wall that sheltered a vegetable patch from the gorse and grass of the heath. She would remember, and would return a kindness with a kindness.

They drove on in silence, the landscape beginning to grow more familiar to Carys. Over in the distance a curtain of trees she knew shielded the hospital where fever patients were cared for, the thread of Bull Lane leading to it across the heath, and moments later she caught the glint of light reflecting from the waters of the Cracker.

'That be where we'll set the wagon.' Caine pointed a brown finger towards the pool. 'There be shelter and water enough and none so close as to be troubled by the presence of a gypsy.'

Calling a soft 'whoah' to the mare, he let the reins fall slack across her back.

'This be where you will be leaving, miss.' He jumped from the driving seat, coming to where Carys was beginning to climb down. Putting his hands to her waist, he steadied her.

'Thank you.' Turning quickly as he released her, Carys caught her breath. One side of his face was drawn together in a long puckered scar, and the socket of one eye was empty.

Without reply he returned to the wagon, swinging himself up into his seat and taking the reins into his hands. With a quiet word to the horse, he set off for the pool.

Watching as the caravan dipped into the hollow that held the swimming hole, Carys remembered a different scene. One where a young girl sat among screening ferns, pencil and paper forgotten as she watched the figure of a man rise from glistening black water, the gem-like droplets showering into the sun as he shook water from his dark hair.

It had been a lifetime ago.

Turning away, she pressed on over the heath, slanting

her steps towards the road she must cross to get to the church.

Glad that it was Wednesday, and the middle of the week would almost certainly mean the churchyard would be empty of people, Carys crossed the road, pausing by the gate beyond which headstones loomed like skeletal fingers, the Sunday flowers shedding the last of their colour over the grass-topped graves. Sunday afternoon was the time the village folk brought their tokens of love and remembrance to their departed loved ones, this being their only free time. Even their burials were usually made as late in the day as could be arranged, she knew from hearing his workers talk with her father. That way they lost less time from their work and less of the money they needed to feed the living.

But she had brought no token of her own love. Carys looked at the flowers, mostly yellow gorse cut from the bushes that littered the heath, with a sprinkling of blue periwinkle and the pinkish-mauve of lungwort found among the hedgerows. She had not thought even to bring these wild flowers, she had nothing to lay on her father's grave. For a moment she thought to turn back, to come again when she would have flowers. But it was not flowers she wanted to give her father, it was her love. To tell him, though he could not hear, of the love that had never faltered in her, the love of him that she would hold in her heart forever.

Keeping to the path of scree stones she walked around the side of the church, its red sandstone colour already veiled by soot drifting from the foundry chimneys of Bilston and Wednesbury. She came to where other headstones, more generously spaced than the rest, were enclosed by a boundary wall. In one corner, beneath a large oak, a mound of flowers more colourful and plentiful than the rest was heaped beneath a stone of blue-grey marble.

Slowly, Carys walked up to it, her eyes blurring at the words carved in the headstone:

Sacred to the memory of Meshac Beddows
Born sixth day of June 1840
Died fourth day of April 1899
Husband of Maria Ann Beddows
Father of Carys Margaret Beddows
He rests with God

'Father! Oh, Father!' Tears blinding her, she sank to her knees on the damp earth. 'I'm sorry,' she sobbed, 'I'm sorry for the hurt I must have caused you, I'm sorry for the pain I must have given you.'

'Was on no account of you the master suffered pain, and you was not the one gave him worry.'

Tears still blurring her vision, Carys saw that a woman was on her knees beside her, a posy of wild flowers in her hands.

'Mary?' Carys brushed a hand across her eyes, clearing the tears from them. 'It is Mary, isn't it?'

'Arrh, miss, it is me, Mary Bartlett. But what brings you here?'

'I came to visit my father's grave.'

'I could guess that for meself, miss. What I means is, how come you could get leave to come here today and not yesterday when your father was buried? I mean to say, it be a bit strange them letting you out after the service was done with.'

'Them?' Carys's voice held a question.

'Arrh, miss, you know, them nuns in that convent you have joined. I know it don't be often they'll let you out after the taking of Holy Orders, but for the burying of your father . . .'

So that was what Maria had told them, and her father too no doubt: that she had chosen to take the veil, that it was her own decision not to return home.

'I am here now,' Carys answered, choosing not to deny what had obviously been said.

'Arrh, here you be, and in the clothes you went away in four years since.' Mary Bartlett looked squarely at the girl beside her. 'Truth is you be no nun, you have taken no Holy Orders, you have given no vow. That be the truth of it, don't it, miss? Permission to go outside a convent might be given and given late, but a nun would not change her habit for any other clothes. The mistress has told us one thing but your presence here tells another. You were left behind all right, but it weren't in no convent, you tell me if I be wrong?'

Mary laid the flowers among the others.

'I was in the room when that lie were told to your father. It was his wife caused his pain, not you, and I can guess why it was done. The mistress isn't one to lose what her sees to be her own, and Ryder Tempal comes in to that category.'

'Does . . . does he still come to the house?'

'That he does, miss.' Mary pushed herself to her feet, brushing moss from the skirts of her green coat. 'He's been a regular visitor, mostly during the day when the master was away at the works. We below stairs used to wonder how he made his living, always gadding about like he does, but then we reckon as we know how. His sort lives off the women they dance attendance on, and Ryder Tempal isn't one to dish out flattery and get nothing in return.'

'Was Mr Tempal present when . . . when my father suffered his heart attack?' Carys touched a hand to the soft earth that covered her father's coffin.

'No, miss.' Mary watched the caress, the last tiny gesture of love. 'It happened sometime after your father had gone to bed. The doctor didn't say exactly when, or if he did we got no word of it below stairs. It were Mr Wilkins, you know, the butler, who found him when he took his hot shaving water to his dressing room and the master was not there. Mr Wilkins says he went into the bedroom and the master was lying in bed, all peaceful like, with the covers pulled over him. He must have died in his sleep and you can be sure that way he would have no pain.'

'I didn't even bring him flowers,' Carys whispered.

'C'mon, miss.' Maria's housemaid lifted Carys to her feet and held her while she sobbed. 'Try not to take on. Your father wouldn't want you to shed tears, though we all know it be best at times. Come sit in the church for a while, just till you feel more eased.'

Sitting in a pew at the back of the dimly lit church, the maid waited until Carys's tears abated.

'Where do you be living, miss?' Quiet as the whisper was, it seemed loud in the silence of the church. 'You're not on the streets, are you?'

Carys twisted her damp handkerchief in her fingers.

'No, Mary, I am not on the streets. I have a position with Virginia Mountford. She owns Ridge House at Hill Top.'

'A position!' Mary was dumbfounded. 'You mean, you are a servant?'

'A housemaid.' Carys smiled fleetingly. 'Like yourself, Mary. There is nothing wrong in being a housemaid.'

'No, miss, no, there isn't, for the likes of me that is. But you – you be the daughter of Meshac Beddows. You shouldn't be housemaid to anybody. Why not come home, miss? Come home with me.'

'I don't think that would be wise, Mary.'

'Why, miss? On account of your mother? I don't see how her could do you mischief once everybody in the house knows you be back.'

'*Come back to Moxley and I'll see you dead!*'

Mary had not heard those words, she had not heard all that Maria Beddows had said.

'I do not think my mother would want to do me mischief, but I prefer to stay at Ridge House, at least . . . at least until the shock of my father's death has worn off a little.'

Mary watched the afternoon light strike the stained glass windows and burst into a glory of colour, showering the altar standing at the end of the long aisle. She knew the girl was defending her mother when she said the woman would not want to do her mischief: Maria would do any woman mischief if she thought Ryder Tempal were paying them a mite too much attention. Or was her daughter waiting for Tempal to disappear from the scene? Mary felt a cynical laugh in her throat. Much chance there was of that while Maria Beddows had a penny left! And even should he take himself off there would be another to take his place; the mistress was too fond of a young man's company to remain alone for long.

'You know your own way best, miss,' she said, deciding to say no more on the subject. 'But you knows you have friends at the house, so if ever you feel . . .'

'I know, Mary.' Carys touched the other girl's hand. 'Thank you.'

'Ee, Miss Carys.' Mary folded the hand between both her own. 'I hates to think of you being a housemaid.'

For several moments they sat together, hands entwined, their figures almost lost among the heavy shadows at the rear of the church, hiding from the light.

'I have to be going.' It was Mary who spoke, standing as she did so. 'I only get an hour off today and that be almost spent.'

Leaving the pew, they both curtsied acknowledgement towards the altar before leaving the church.

'You sure you will be all right, going back on your own, miss?' Mary squinted against the bright light. 'I don't rightly know where this Hill Top be that you spoke of. P'raps you should wait here and I'll get Mr Wilkins to send one of the men to take you there?'

'That will not be necessary, Mary, I shall be perfectly all right.' Carys hesitated, wanting to return to her father's grave.

'Then let me see you on your way.' Mary guessed at the reason for her hesitation, but further grieving would do no good. 'I don't want to think of you here all day by yourself.'

Allowing herself to be steered down the pebble path and beyond the gate, Carys returned Mary's friendly hug, fresh tears rising to her throat as the girl waved her along the road.

She had said goodbye to her father. And her mother? Her mother had said her own goodbyes four years ago.

'I tell you, it was her!'

Coming from her bedroom, Maria paused as voices drifted up to her from the hallway below.

'Couldn't have been.'

The answer came clearly. Whoever it was had not thought to lower their voice.

'I tell you, it was!'

Recognising the voice as that of the housemaid, Mary, Maria waited. It was surprising how much could be learned from servants who did not know you were listening.

'But it couldn't have been, the mistress said . . .'

'Oh, we know what the mistress said!' Mary's voice became tart. 'And we all know what a liar her can be when it suits her.'

Maria allowed a cold smile to curve her mouth. Mary Bartlett could speak of her as she wished . . . until Maria had heard all she had to say.

'I tell you, it was her I was talking to. There her was, kneeling by that grave and sobbing something awful. It fair pulled me to pieces hearing it. And when I spoke to her, I was recognised straight off. Ee, poor wench! Her clothes were that shabby – they were the very same ones as her left the house in. I tell you, Amy, my heart fair bled for her.'

'But if it *were* who you say it were, why hasn't her come back here?'

'I asked that,' Mary replied. 'Her told me her preferred to be with that woman, said her wanted to stay in her house till her was over the shock of her father's passing.'

'But a servant? That wench never ought to be no servant, Mary.'

Mary's voice carried clearly to Maria. 'I told her that an'

142

all and her answered that there be nothing wrong in being a housemaid. Nor there isn't, I said, not for such as meself, but you should be grafting for nobody.'

'Ee, it ain't right, Mary. That girl should be in her own home.'

'Reckon her should, and I also reckons we all know why her isn't.'

Above them Maria waited. Fear was telling her who the subject of the two maids' conversation was, but her brain was telling her to hold back, hear everything before moving.

'It be jealousy,' Mary went on after a moment of silence. 'The mistress be jealous of her own child. It be that and nothing else caused her to say that girl had taken the veil.'

'Her child!' Amy's voice was suddenly scornful. 'More like Meshac's child. He had far more feeling for that girl than ever her mother had . . .'

It *was* Carys! Maria felt her brain swirl. The maids were talking of Carys, of seeing her beside a grave. That could only mean her father's grave. Maria's hands tightened. That meant Carys was here, in Moxley.

'. . . but I never thought a mother could be jealous of her own.'

'That one could if her thought to lose her playmate. Maria Beddows would scratch the eyes from any woman's head if her thought Ryder Tempal had looked at them with a passing fancy.'

'Ee, Mary, do you think the mistress has been playing away?'

'Don't you?' Mary laughed. 'I not only think it, I be willing to wager a year's pay I'm not wrong. That one be mad about Tempal, anybody but a blind man could see that. And you ain't blind, Amy Fletcher.'

'So who be this woman the girl be housemaid to?'

Maria caught her breath, every part of her focused on the answer.

'Said her name was Virginia Mountford.'

143

'Don't ring no bell, can't say I've heard that name before.'

'It's not surprising . . .'

Mary's voice was fainter now, as if she had moved across to the far side of the hall. Maria took a careful step nearer to the head of the stairs, mindful to remain out of sight should either of the girls glance upward.

'. . . seems her don't live in Moxley but somewhere called Hill Top.'

'Where do that be?'

Amy's voice was even fainter than Mary's. They were moving away. Maria clenched her teeth, willing herself to listen. She must hear the rest.

'Blowed if I know.' Mary was only just within hearing range. 'All I know is what I was told. Miss Carys said her was housemaid to a Virginia Mountford who had a place called Ridge House and that it were somewhere along a place called Hill Top.'

Slowly, quietly, Maria released her breath. Carys had not taken her warning. She was living only a few miles away. She turned to her bedroom and pulled the cord that would summon her maid.

It had been a week since she had learned where her daughter was living; a week in which Mary Bartlett had been dismissed from her post as housemaid.

Leaning against the upholstery of her carriage, Maria gazed at the passing heath, at its interchange between tilled field and fallow, between hedged corn and wheat field, then the giving way to gaping black stretches of worked out surface mining and high heaps of shale and spoil that erupted like huge grey boils on the skin of the earth.

But she was not interested in the beauty or the deformity. Her mind was engaged only upon her own errand. She had waited a week, not wanting to return the calls of condolence to Holyhead House nor to reply to those arriving by post without leaving a suitable time between.

A widow must not be seen to be making the effort too soon.

Opening the bag that hung about her wrist she drew out a card, the edges of which were black. A card that bore the name 'Virginia Mountford' and a message of sympathy in her loss. Maria smiled. How fortunate that the woman's husband and Meshac had sometimes done business together.

'If you would wait in here, ma'am, I will tell the mistress you be calling.'

Opening the door to the library, Alice bobbed a curtsey as the woman, dressed entirely in black, a fine tulle veil covering her face and shoulders, passed inside.

Maria glanced around the room. Bookcases of light elm-wood lined the walls on three sides, each filled with expensively bound books, while the fourth was taken up by an elegant fireplace, its carved lines clean and tasteful. It seemed Virginia Mountford's preferences were much the same as her own, with none of the heavy ornate furniture so beloved of forty years ago and still markedly present in many of the houses Maria visited.

'Mrs Mountford asks if you will join her in her sitting room, ma'am.' Alice bobbed a second curtsey as she returned, then led the way upstairs to a room adjoining Virginia's bedroom, one which she kept as her private sitting room.

'My sympathies, Mrs Beddows. How very kind of you to call.'

Accepting the chair Virginia indicated, Maria swept a rapid glance around the room, again noting the graceful Regency furniture, the tapestries and carpet that spoke so strongly of France. In taste at least she and the grey-haired woman seated opposite her had a lot in common, it seemed.

'I wished to return your own kindness.' Maria folded the delicate black tulle back over her head, revealing her face. 'It was very thoughtful of you to send your condolences on my bereavement.'

'Will you take some tea?' Virginia's hand went out to a tapestry bell pull beside the fireplace.

'Thank you, but no.' Maria gave a faint smile. 'I still am not ready for social calls.'

'I understand.' Virginia withdrew her hand.

'However, I felt I must call on you right away upon hearing . . .'

'Upon hearing?' Virginia looked at her visitor, not liking what she saw. But no, that was not so. It was more what she felt, a feeling she could not define, yet one she most definitely did not like. 'What is it that you heard, Mrs Beddows? And now think I should hear?'

Maria dropped her glance to the black velvet bag resting in her lap, hoping it would give the impression she was not entirely happy with what she was doing.

'It was something I overheard two of my housemaids talking about. That was a week ago and I have wrestled with my conscience all that time as to whether to speak of it to you or whether to forget the whole thing.'

'But in the end you thought you should speak?' Virginia's eyes stayed on her face. Maria Beddows was a very attractive woman but Virginia felt it was an attraction that existed only on the surface; that the woman had no trace of inner beauty, a beauty of the spirit that could shine through even the plainest individual, and knew she would have had much the same feeling had she not known what the woman had done to her daughter.

'Yes.' Maria took her time raising her eyes. 'I was afraid that not to speak would be to do you a disservice.'

'I appreciate your thought for me. Perhaps you will tell me what it is you have to say?'

Maria drew a deep breath, holding it for a few seconds before letting it sigh slowly from her parted lips, making it seem as if what she was about to say was causing her grief.

'As I explained, I overheard my maids talking. They were discussing a meeting one of them had had with a young woman they said was a housemaid in your employ – a young woman named Carys.'

'I do have a housemaid of that name.' Virginia nodded.

'May I ask, did she come with references?'

Virginia felt her dislike of this woman increasing but stilled a desire to ask her to leave. 'No, Mrs Beddows, she did not. In point of fact she came with another of my housemaids. They met in Birmingham.'

'And, forgive my asking, do you know her background?'

'Only the little she told me.'

'I see.' Maria paused again then quickly, and for effect added, 'Of course, there is every possibility I may be wrong and that the girl you employ is not the one I dismissed four years ago.'

'I agree the possibility exists,' Virginia said coldly. 'But tell me, if you will, the reason for that dismissal?'

Maria allowed her glance to falter and her fingers to twitch nervously on the bag in her lap.

'It . . . it was a rather delicate matter. I spoke to her one day as she returned from her afternoon off. She had what appeared to be a sketch pad in her hand. She said she had been drawing, and was most reticent when I asked to see her work. She became rather agitated when I repeated my request, and when she eventually showed the sketches to me I saw why. Some were quite pretty, good depictions of the area, but others . . .' Maria drew another long breath. 'Well . . . others were obscene.'

'Obscene?' Virginia repeated the description. 'That is a serious, not to say distressing, statement.'

'It was my fear that, given those drawings, she might be engaged in doings of an even more unwholesome nature during her time away from the house, therefore I dismissed her.'

'As I shall myself most certainly do if I arrive at the same conclusion.' Virginia reached for the bell pull, this time giving it a sharp tug.

'Alice,' she said when the girl presented herself. 'Has Carys returned from her errand?'

'No, ma'am.' Alice darted a glance at the woman in black.

'Alice,' Virginia asked again, 'has Carys ever shown you any sketches?'

'If you mean drawrings, ma'am, yes, her has.'

'Does she still have them, do you know?'

'They be in her room, under her bed.'

'I want you to bring them here.' Virginia caught the girl's look. 'It will be all right, Alice. I will speak to Carys when she returns.'

'Very good, ma'am.'

Turning to her visitor as Alice left to fetch the sketches, Virginia's face showed none of her feelings. This woman had not come here out of solicitude but from spite. She wanted only to do more harm to a girl who had done her none, and that girl her own daughter!

'Take out what is inside,' Virginia instructed, when Alice returned with the carpet bag belonging to Carys. 'And, Alice, I want you to tell me truthfully if those are the sketches that were shown to you.'

Unrolling the sheets of paper, Alice looked at each one. 'Yes, ma'am, these be the same.'

Virginia nodded. 'Try to remember, Alice. Were there any shown to you that are not here now?'

'No.' Alice looked again at the sheaf of drawings. 'This be all of them. I remember 'cos I counted them when they was spread out on the bed. Well, I say all of them, but there be one new one – Carys drawed it two or three weeks since. I know, ma'am, 'cos I kcpt a listen out in case Mrs Bates took it into her head to come upstairs to bed early like. Her would have got mad to find we was not in our beds.'

'Will you show us the one you mean?'

Fumbling nervously, the maid drew out one paper from among the rest, handing it to her mistress. Looking at it, Virginia Mountford felt a wave of pleasure spread through her. The sketch was a likeness of her father, taken no doubt from the portrait in the corridor, though the girl had shown him as much younger. Handing it to Maria, she indicated that Alice should do the same with the remainder.

'Are those the drawings to which you refer?'

Maria's nostrils widened, evincing disapproval. 'They are. It would appear the girl I dismissed has found her way into your house, Mrs Mountford.'

Taking back the sketches, Virginia glanced again at the drawing of a man, his powerful body surging up out of a pool of water, every charcoal stroke shouting his pleasure at the feel of it, every line perfect. But it was the face that held her breath. Half turned away, it was shown only in profile. The sketch drawn long before being brought into this house and the one so recently drawn had the same face, she realised, a face almost identical with her father's portrait though in fact it was a face she had seen much more recently: the face of her nephew.

Forcing herself to hand the drawings to Alice, she dismissed the girl, telling her to return the bag to Carys's room.

'I am sorry if the reason for my call has distressed you.'

'On the contrary, Mrs Beddows.' Virginia's back was ramrod straight and her eyes icy, but her voice was steady as she answered, 'It has afforded me the pleasure of seeing those drawings once again. Oh, yes,' she saw the surprise spring to Maria's eyes, 'I have seen them before. They were shown to me the morning after the girl came to this house.'

'But how does she . . .'

'How does she still come to have them? Is that what you were going to ask? She has them because the woman who was asked to destroy them saw them not as obscene but, as I do, as things of beauty. That woman was Sister Mary Immaculata, Mother Superior of the Convent of the Holy Child, and it was you who handed those sketches to her, you who told her the same lies you have just told me. You did not turn a housemaid out of your home, Mrs Beddows, you turned away your own daughter!'

Virginia's knuckles whitened as she pulled the cord beside the fireplace and her top lip turned inward with suppressed anger. 'Was attempting to confine a girl to a life behind walls your way of showing concern for her moral welfare, or was it rather your way of disposing of a threat to your own sordid affair? Yes, Mrs Beddows, I know a little of Ryder Tempal's part in all of this. And as for the rest, I can guess. It is my opinion you got rid of that girl because you were afraid – afraid he would come to prefer her over you. Just what sort of a mother do you call yourself? I call you none at all!'

'How dare you!' Maria's face blanched with temper. 'How dare you speak to me like that? I will . . .'

'What?' Virginia did not blink an eyelid. 'What will you do? Take me to court for slander? Do it, Mrs Beddows. I am too old for that to worry me but not too old to enjoy it – enjoy hearing what you have to say to a magistrate regarding your entering your daughter into a convent then abandoning her, penniless, on a railway station when she refused to take the vows that would keep her locked away for life. And certainly not too old to enjoy hearing what your friends will say afterwards.'

Virginia smiled. A light tap on the door brought Maria to her feet.

'You will no doubt have your solicitor contact me? I look forward to it.'

Watching Maria sweep out of the room followed by an obviously curious Alice, Virginia Mountford felt a cold touch in her stomach, a feeling that warned she had not seen the last of Maria Beddows.

Chapter Ten

Reuben Fereday looked at the beautifully enamelled boxes laid out for his inspection. In the dim light of the tiny workroom the colours seemed to glow, vibrant and alive, and he found himself marvelling, as he always did on his visits here, that so drab and smoke-heavy a town as Bilston, with its narrow streets and viciously cramped houses, could produce something so exquisite.

'These are excellent.' Taking one of the boxes in his hands, he turned to the man at his side whose shoulders were hunched from bending over a workbench almost every waking hour.

'Thank you, sir.'

'Who is responsible for the designs?' He turned the box in his hand, a memory stirring in the back of his mind.

'I don't rightly be knowin' that, sir.' The workman pushed his flat cap back on his head. 'They be some the master brought along of 'isself.'

Reuben continued to examine the box. The garden he saw painted there, a summerhouse boxed in by a hedge of white roses . . . He had seen that same summerhouse, admired those same roses.

'Do you have more like these?'

'Arrh, sir, but I ain't got them 'ere.' The man pulled his cap back on to the front of his head, drawing the peak low over his brow.

'Where are they?' Reuben replaced the box on the bench that ran the length of the narrow ten-foot-long room.

'They be along of the master's room. 'E kept them there, said as 'ow they was not to be sold, but since . . . well, mistress 'as the running of the business now and 'er says to sell. That be 'ow I comes to have put that one out with the others, though it come 'ard, having to go against master's wishes.'

'Did Mr Beddows give you any reason for not wanting this particular box to be sold?'

'No, sir.' The man touched a finger to the box, its jewel-bright colours aflame against his dirt-streaked skin. 'But they was special to 'im, that much I does know. Though just between me and yourself sir, begging your pardon, it be my guess that there box, and the five others in the master's room, were drawed by his little wench. 'Er were mighty fond of drawring, as I remembers.'

Drawn by his daughter! Reuben felt his heartbeat quicken. The design on that box seemed likely to have been drawn by the daughter of Meshac Beddows as it was a picture of the garden at Holyhead House. And the girl . . . the girl he had confronted that day above the pool at Moxley, she had carried a sketch pad, and had claimed she was returning to that same house. The girl he had looked for each time he passed through. The girl who had taken Holy Orders and was now lost to him forever.

'The others . . . I would like to see them. Take me along to Mr Beddows's room.'

'Don't know as I can do that, Mr Fereday, sir.' The man pushed at his cap again. 'Mr Beddows, 'e didn't like nobody goin' into his room lessen 'e was there.'

Taking out his watch, Reuben glanced at it then replaced it in his waistcoat pocket. He had several more calls to make in Bilston. He could return here later in the day.

'What time will Mr Beddows be here?' he asked.

''E won't be comin', sir.' The man shook his head. 'Not no more 'e won't.'

Reuben glanced at the man, noticing for the first time the look of sadness and worry on his face.

'You said a moment ago that the mistress now has the running of the business. Is that mistress Mrs Beddows?'

'Arrh, that be 'er, sir.'

Reuben's brows drew together. 'Has Mr Beddows sustained some accident?'

'No, sir, 'e ain't had no accident.'

'Then why will he not be coming here again? You *did* say he would not be coming any more, did you not?'

'Arrh, I did, sir.'

Reuben glanced the length of the confined workroom. At the far end a woman hammered a large lump of frit, pounding the metal-bearing stone into powder. Her dust-covered skirts were held about by an apron of rough dark cloth, her hair beneath a scrap of the same material. Nearer to him, two boys of about eight years old each painted metal boxes with a coating of white paste-like substance, before placing them beside a brick-built furnace that belched the heat of hell into the room whenever it was opened. Lastly a young girl of around fourteen held a box to the grimy light of a window set high in the wall, then dipped a fine paintbrush into liquid oxides mixed in a cracked saucer, painting each with a steady hand on to the white-glazed metal. Reuben glanced again at the selection of beautifully decorated boxes set out along the bench. The skills of these people were astounding, their artistry and knowledge of oxides producing artefacts of a beauty that could match any in the world. And mostly, he knew from his visits, not all from workshops such as this, but from tiny, dark back to back places that were part of a family's living quarters.

Glancing toward him, the girl halted in her task, her eyes enquiring.

'Perhaps I should call to see Mr Beddows on my next visit.' Reuben returned his attention to the stoop-shouldered man hovering beside him.

'Won't do no good.' The man turned as the door to the furnace was raised and the two boys began to fill its red hot interior with freshly glazed boxes. 'You won't see no more of Meshac Beddows 'cept you goes to Moxley cemetery. That be where the master is now, six feet under.'

'Mr Beddows is dead?' The slow rise of irritation that had sharpened Reuben's last words gave way to surprise.

'Arrh, sir.' The man's eyes followed the loading of the furnace. 'Been gone this last month or more. Mistress be the one has the running of this and all the rest of the master's interests in the town. But how long before . . .'

'How long before . . . ? Go on, man, say it. How long before what?'

Pushing his cap completely back from his head, the work-man ran a hand through his thinning hair.

'I knows I shouldn't be saying so, sir, but the worry of it all has me and the missis there awake nights. Y'see, since the master was took there ain't been much come our way. No orders, I means. The mistress, 'er says to sell whatever be asked for, but 'er didn't say anything about customers' orders. And the master, 'e always seen to it we 'ad fresh supplies of frit to work with, but there's been none of that since his wife took over. We be wonderin', the missis and me, what be going to 'appen. Does the mistress's intention be to close down the enamellin'?'

Reuben could see now the cause of the worry on the man's face. Should that happen, this and many another family in Bilston would know the misery of empty stomachs.

'The five other boxes you spoke of, can you fetch them from Mr Beddows's room? I am interested in purchasing the set.'

Reuben watched the crestfallen way the tired-looking man pulled his cap back over his head. It must seem that his own response was heartless but Reuben could give no answer to

154

the man's question. He had no knowledge of Maria Beddows's intent.

'If you'll pardon the sayin' of it, sir, I don't know as I can. The master, 'e never let nobody into that room 'less 'e was with them.' He nodded to where a small, low-windowed brick building stood across the yard from the workroom, a building Reuben knew had served as Meshac's office. 'That box there, one of them six, that was fetched out by the mistress 'erself, and 'er 'olds the key.'

'I see. Thank you.' Reuben made his way to the door, the eyes of the man's family following him. 'Will you see to it my boxes are dispatched to Birmingham on the morning train?' he asked as they stepped into the yard. 'As for the others we spoke of, I will contact Mrs Beddows, today if possible. Should it happen that anyone else enquires after their purchase, then do not sell them until you hear from her or myself.'

Closing his hand over the florin Reuben dropped into his palm following every visit to the workshop, the man touched his cap with a lead-stained forefinger.

'I'll do that, Mr Fereday. Won't nobody see them boxes, least not with my showing of 'em they won't.'

Why did he want those boxes so much?

Reuben glanced sideways as the driver of his hired carriage shouted a loud uncomplimentary caution to the carter cutting across the path of the hansom, causing the horse to veer too close to a passing dray, then fell back into the dark well of the thoughts that had plagued him throughout the rest of the day. He had visited each of the enamelling firms with which he did business. The articles they produced were of a surpassing degree of workmanship, the colours being of a clear brilliance or a muted softness that seemed to whisper, their beautifully executed designs sometimes breathtaking.

But it was more than that. He did not want those boxes purely for the beauty he was sure each would have.

Passing along Pipes Meadow, Reuben watched the sad little

buildings that clung to the edge of the road as though to a lifeline, watched them string into Temple Street, cluster round the Mission Hall. Such a dreary, work-laden maze of narrow streets. So many tiny houses that had half the living space given over to a workshop where women and small children must help with tasks that hardly paid for their bread.

The cab driver called softly to the horse as he guided it left into Lester Street, then half turning to Reuben called, 'We be coming up to The First and the Last. It be a decent ale house, sir, if you be feelin' in need of something to wash the smell of the enamellin' from your throat.'

'The First and the Last?' Reuben glanced at the man.

'Arrh.' He nodded. 'It be first ale house in Bilston if you be coming in from Moxley end, and last one when you be coming out again.'

Reuben smiled, admitting to himself the logic of the name, though guessing from his knowledge of the humour of this town that it bore little resemblance to the original.

''Course that don't be its proper name,' the driver added, as though divining Reuben's thoughts. 'Proper name be The Bush, but it's always gone as The First and the Last to the folk round about.'

Consulting his pocket watch, Reuben saw he had more than enough time until the last train to Birmingham. A stop might be welcome, if only to clear his head of thoughts he knew to be hopeless.

Across from the inn a smithy rang to the sound of hammer on anvil, while away behind it Bradley Heath lay like a grey-green carpet, spreading away to the black hill mounds of waste from the Fiery Holes and Bradley Rowe coal pits. All around the loveliness of nature was being scarred by coal mining and the making of iron and steel.

But that was the burden of these little towns that had been so aptly named the Black Country. He turned, glancing back the way they had just driven. Overhead the sky was dark with the smoke of a thousand tall chimneys, while from the ground as many black drifts spiralled upward, adding their tribute.

'There be a fire in the snug, sir.' The cab driver hitched a feed bag over the horse's head, his tone hopeful.

Reuben gave a brief nod. 'Thank you. But I will take a glass here in the open. I have had more than enough of being indoors today.'

'I'll send Caggy out to you then, sir, and if you have no objection to me having a mug of the best meself . . .'

'No objection.' Reuben walked several steps in the direction of the smithy, somehow finding the tiny green that fronted the ale house a peaceful spot despite the noise of hammer on iron.

'Afternoon to you, sir.'

Returning the inn keeper's pleasant address, Reuben waited for the ale he ordered.

'There you be, sir.'

The landlord laid a tankard on a table constructed of roughly planed planks then, still using his left hand, took the coins held out to him.

Reuben smiled to himself. The man was left-handed; that explained his being called Caggy.

Taking up the tankard, he sipped the cool liquid, the smell of hops and barley pungent in his nostrils.

Why had he told Meshac Beddows's workman to sell those boxes to no one else? Gazing out over the bare heathland, the thoughts he had hoped to banish returned full strength. True, they were beautiful, but he could get boxes of equal beauty. The artistry rife within the smoke-filled confines of Bilston was nothing short of startling, so why insist on having these?

From the heath a light breeze fanned his face. In his mind he saw again tendrils of softly curling chestnut hair being lifted by that same breeze then falling gently about a lovely young face. The face of the girl on the heath. *She* was the reason he wanted those boxes, because *she* might have painted them. He wanted them because of her. He wanted her!

*   *   *

'Good afternoon, Mr Fereday.'

Maria Beddows, dressed entirely in black, held out her hand.

'My condolences, Mrs Beddows.' He touched her fingers briefly. 'I did not hear of your loss until today or I would have paid my respects sooner.'

'It . . . it was a very private funeral, I could not bear . . .' She touched a lace-edged handkerchief to her nose.

'Forgive me. I should not intrude upon your grief.' Reuben half turned to where a housemaid was placing his gloves and cane upon a side table.

'No, Mr Fereday. I must get used to seeing people again, accustom myself to life without Meshac. Please, stay.' Maria gave him a wan smile.

The silk of her skirts rustling, she led the way into her sitting room.

'Mrs Beddows.' Reuben had waited until the business of taking tea was over. 'I visited Meshac's workrooms today in order to ascertain if my order for caskets had been completed.' He paused, looking at the woman opposite him. Even in widow's weeds she made a striking picture. 'I beg your pardon for speaking so directly to you but I must ask – will the agreement I had with your husband still stand or do you consider a signed contract to be preferable?'

'I had not thought . . .' She made a suitable show of touching the handkerchief to her eyes again.

'Of course not,' he apologised. 'It was clumsy of me to speak of business so soon.'

'Yet it must be spoken of.' She raised long lashes touched with the silver of tears. 'But it is all so foreign to me. I have no idea where to begin. Meshac did not make a practice of discussing his business with me.'

That much he could believe, but as for her not having any idea what to do, that was something else. It was his bet Maria Beddows knew exactly what she was going to do. Watching her turn her glance to a photograph, its heavy silver frame draped with black tulle, then dab again at her eyes, he felt certain this was all a show put on for his benefit.

'If only Meshac had acquainted me with the running of his business.' She traced a finger over the sepia-coloured print of her husband. 'But he always maintained it was not for a woman to worry her head over such things. That being so I find myself unsure in which direction to proceed. Should I try to carry on with the enamelling business or should I sell it? One thing Meshac did tell me was that the trade was dying out. The call for enamelled products was almost gone. If that is so, then I think perhaps I should sell up while there is still a chance.'

Sell up while there is still a chance *of profit*, she meant. Reuben glanced away, to the elegant furniture and beautiful carpets. Enamelling had brought Meshac and his wife wealth and all that went with it; to the people who produced the wares it had brought little more than a bare living, and now even this was to be taken from them.

He brought his glance back to Maria. 'At the workroom I asked to buy a set of boxes, only one of which had been set out for my approval. I was told you had authorised the sale along with anything else a prospective buyer might wish to purchase. However, it turned out the other five boxes were locked in the office to which only you have the key. Would it be possible for you to arrange that I might see them? With a view to their purchase, of course.'

So that was why he was here. Maria glanced at the handkerchief held between her fingers. She had guessed Reuben had some other motive for calling at Holyhead House than to see her. But to ask specifically for a few boxes . . . Why? Why that particular set when there were so many others to choose from? What was it that set them apart? It was surely not the standard of the painting; all Meshac's workers were the best the town had, he had always been careful to select *only* the best. So what was it that lay behind Reuben Fereday's request?

'I think you must be referring to the workshop in Vine Street.

Meshac did his testing of new oxides there.' Maria looked up. 'He was quite strict about the room he used being kept locked. I believe he would allow no one but himself in there. He took me with him only once, just after our marriage, but I have to admit I understood nothing of his talk of metals and oxides. The man you spoke to will be . . .' Her voice tailed off as though she was searching her memory for a name. '. . . Blakeway, Thomas Blakeway. Yes, his family occupy the rest of the building.'

Reuben thought of the house-cum-workshop, one of many such he had seen in that town.

'I cannot say I know the boxes of which you speak, Mr Fereday.' Maria gave him the benefit of her practised smile. 'But I will send word to Blakeway to have them brought out for your inspection when next you are in Bilston. I trust he knows the ones in which you are interested?'

'Yes.' Reuben nodded. 'Though I am not sure when my next visit will be. It could be several months. Perhaps you might allow them to be sent to my gallery in Birmingham?'

'Of course. I will have word sent today.'

'That is most kind.' He got to his feet.

'It has meant your coming out of your way to visit me here. I hope that does not mean you will miss your train to Birmingham,' she continued.

'No.' Reuben consulted his pocket watch. 'I have ample time.'

Marie followed him towards the door of the sitting room, the few feet separating them allowing her to admire his broad shoulders and tight hips; to imagine them, as she had on several nights when sleep had evaded her, without the concealment of clothing.

'Your gallery,' she said as he opened the door, 'you once invited me to see it. Does the invitation still stand?'

'Certainly.' He stood aside, allowing her to pass in front of him. 'Whenever you feel you are ready to do so.'

'Then I shall visit you. I shall also endeavour to keep our

business relationship going. I only wish Meshac had prepared me for such a task . . .'

'Your husband did what he felt was right. He thought to protect you from such mundane matters.'

'Yes, of course you are right, Mr Fereday.' Maria's well-practised wan look was once more directed at Reuben. 'But I find it all so confusing without him.'

'Might I suggest, a relative . . . someone who could take on the management for you?'

She shook her head, the handkerchief once more in operation. 'There are none,' she murmured. 'I have no one on whom I can rely for advice or comfort.'

You have a daughter. The thought brought a sudden anger he could not explain. A daughter who had taken Holy Orders. She may have been unable to give advice on the running of the business but she could have given comfort. Why? He found himself wondering. Why had a girl so young and so beautiful given herself to a life of seclusion from the world? Was it truly a vocation, or had there been some other reason?

Trying to keep the sudden unreasonable coldness he felt from showing in his voice, he went on, 'Then I urge you to employ a manager, Mrs Beddows.'

Following him across the hall Maria waved away the housemaid coming to hand him his gloves and cane. 'I would find dealing with a manager a very daunting prospect, Mr Fereday.' She dropped her lashes appealingly. 'I would be much happier were a friend to help me.'

'Then perhaps you will allow me . . .' He smiled into the eyes lifted quickly to his own '. . . allow me to suggest Mr Ryder Tempal. He, I feel sure, would be very willing to assist.'

Closing the door behind him, Maria let her hand rest on it, anger hot inside her. She had hoped to draw him into acting as her manager, hoped in that way to bring him close to her, but he had not succumbed to her portrayal of a helpless widow.

She had thought this her chance to find just out to what extent Reuben Fereday's seeming indifference stretched.

She had failed today. But she had a great many tomorrows.

'Back to Bilston, sir?'

Behind him Reuben heard the thud of the door of Holyhead House as it closed. A thud that was just a little too loud. Almost smiling, he stepped into the hansom. Maria Beddows had thought to secure him as her manager . . . and what else? Settling into the seat, Reuben laid his cane across his knees. Whatever else it was the woman had planned, he wanted neither.

'No.' He glanced at the man awaiting an answer to his question. 'No, not Bilston. Take me to the railway station in Wednesbury.'

He wanted time to think, to decide whether to continue to buy from Beddows Enamels. He could buy anywhere in Bilston, there was no need for him to have any more to do with Meshac's widow, yet Reuben knew he had to maintain that link, however tenuous, however hopeless, the one link he had with the girl on the heath.

Picking up the road that ran past the gates of Holyhead House, the driver turned the horse to the left, taking the carriage in the direction of Wednesbury. Bilston had a railway station, and it was some two or three miles nearer than the one he had been told to go to. He gave a flick to the reins, calling encouragingly to the horse. It wasn't his place to point that out. Besides, it was all money in his pocket. He could ask at least twice what he would ask for the run back to Bilston.

Hands resting idly on his cane, Reuben watched the final scattering of poky buildings give way to the heath that separated them from the tall spired church that seemed to stand sentinel over the huddled village.

Maria Beddows had mentioned the probable selling of the business that now belonged to her. And his daughter? Had

Meshac made any provision for her should she forego the life of a nun, or had he written her out of his life completely?

The rumbling of a cart on the other side of the road drew his attention but as it passed by his eyes remained on the glint of water just visible in the hollow that fell away from the road. That was the pool where he had swum. The place where he had met a girl who had haunted his thoughts ever since.

Was she Meshac Beddows's daughter?

Yes. His mind and his reason told him that she was.

And had she taken Holy Orders?

His reason told him she had. So why did his heart tell him otherwise?

His gaze lifting from the expanse of water, he caught sight of the caravan nestled at the tree line. It had not been there that day, but then gypsies drifted in and out of places like mist on a morning sky.

Seated on her stool beside a fire of sticks, Bethesda puffed on her old pipe. This would be the year of her avenging. The taking of retribution would be hers alone, it would not fall to Caine. The sight had told her so and the sight never told her wrong. Her son had waited long to take revenge for the spoiling of his face. She had heard him many nights get up from his bed, and watched those same nights as he had walked round and about their camp in lonely torment. He deserved to take payment in kind, to take full toll for what had been done to him, to taste the sweet fruit of vengeance that he had yearned half a lifetime for. His would be the tasting. Bethesda sucked on the stem of the briar pipe. Hers would be the plucking.

Her eyes on the hansom, she let her gaze travel with it along the road that cut like a knife across the pitted heath. Within that cab sat a young woman's happiness. It would be long yet in reaching her, but the arrival was predestined, as it was ordained that her son Caine would be the instrument of the girl's salvation.

Chapter Eleven

'You say the mistress sent you to get the girl's things?'

'Just her bag.' Alice watched her mother peel potatoes. 'It was just the bag I 'ad to fetch.'

'Still don't seem right to me somehow. Mistress of Ridge 'Ouse 'er might be, but to go lookin' into a young woman's private effects behind 'er back! All I can say is that gentry should be better brought up than they seems to be. You wouldn't find no child of mine prying into folk's private things, no, by God you wouldn't! Try that and I'd 'ave the skin off their arse, no matter how old they be.'

'I didn't open the bag, Mother, not until I gave it to the mistress.'

'I should 'ope not neither.' Letty Withers looked up sharply. 'You've always been taught to respect other people, and their property an' all.'

Letty selected another potato and set to paring it thinly. 'Dressed in black, you say?'

Alice nodded. 'From head to foot, with a veil pulled down over her face so it couldn't be told who it were 'cept you heard her name.'

'Beddows, you says?' Letty sliced through the skin of the potato, letting it drop in one continuous coil into the enamelled

165

basin held on her lap. 'Maria Beddows . . . Can't say as that name rings a bell. Ain't nobody of that name in Wednesbury, not as I knows of anyway, and I knows most.'

'Her don't belong of Wednesbury.' The last of a pound of peas shelled, Alice gathered the empty pods and set them to one side. Her mother would use them later to make pea pod wine. 'Seems her comes from Moxley.'

'Moxley, is it?' Letty dropped the peeled potato into a large cast-iron pot before setting aside the knife. 'I ain't never been there so it don't be surprising I don't know the name.' She looked over to where Alice was now scalding tea in the tea pot. 'But it be a bit strange, 'er bein' called Beddows. That be the same name as that young wench you brought visitin', don't it?'

Taking the heavy pot of potatoes to the fire, Alice hung it on the hook from which she had taken the kettle moments before.

'Arrh,' she said, gathering the peelings from her mother and carrying them into the scullery where they would be boiled down for pig food. 'Carys be named Beddows.'

Letty followed her to the scullery carrying the basin of water in which she had rinsed each potato. Going out into the yard, she flung the contents into the shallow runnel that drained between the houses, mouth clamped tight against the smell that rose from it.

'What be even more strange,' Alice continued as her mother returned to the house, 'is Carys said as how her home was in Moxley afore her was taken to Birmingham.'

'And what did this woman in black want with the wench's bag?' Letty cleared a space on the table, setting two heavy platter cups beside the jug of milk her daughter had fetched in from the scullery.

'Seems as her asked to see the drawrings Carys had in it.' Alice filled the cups from the teapot. 'Anyroad up, when I fetches it from the bedroom the mistress tells me to open it and give them there drawrings to her visitor. Then her asked

166

me to say if they was the self-same ones as Carys had with her the night I brought her to Ridge House. And when I said they was, all saving the one her drawed since, well, then mistress said I was to put them back where I got them from. That was all I heard.'

'So the woman didn't take any of them drawrings?' Letty asked.

'No.' Alice handed her mother one of the teacups, taking the other herself and sitting beside the fireplace. 'Seems her just wanted to look at them. Her didn't find them much to her liking neither, not judging by the way her nose screwed up when her looked at them.'

'There ain't nothin' filthy about them, I 'opes, not with you lookin' at them an' all?'

Alice knew her mother's Chapel upbringing and her views on anything she thought unfit for the sight of God. 'No, there were nothing like that. They was pictures of an open heath, and a pool with ferns and trees all round.' She sipped at her tea. What her mother was not told about the figure of a man rising naked from the water of that same pool would not give her sleepless nights!

'So, if her didn't take any of them drawrings, why did her ask to see them? And if, as you said, the woman had not visited Ridge House in all the time you 'ave served there, why did her come that day?'

Alice continued to sip her tea. She had asked herself the same questions but had come up with no answers save one: Maria Beddows was up to no good. One way or another she meant to harm Carys.

'And what did the wench 'ave to say when you told her of this visit?' Letty refilled her cup.

'That was the strangest thing of all,' Alice answered. 'I told you of how Carys told Mrs Bates and meself about how her come to be in that convent and how her had been left on Snow Hill station without a penny piece? Well, it turns out that the woman who left her there and the mistress's visitor be one and the same!'

Letty Withers looked at her daughter, disbelief bright in her eyes. 'Be you telling me . . . ?'

'Arrh, Mother.' Alice nodded. 'I be telling you Maria Beddows be Carys's mother.'

'God love me!' Letty dropped her cup heavily on to the table. 'Her knows her own flesh and blood be servant to another when all the while it seems there be money enough to keep her at home?'

'That be the nub of it though, don't it, Mother? Carys ain't wanted at home, and though I can't be rightly explaining why, I feel that mother of hers don't want her to be at Ridge House neither. In fact, I sometimes think her would rather Carys was nowhere at all.'

'Ee, wench, don't be lettin' your imagination run wi'out a rein!'

'Well, if her meant Carys any good, why not take her home to Moxley?'

'And why not take her there if her intention was to do the wench more hurt?' Letty gathered the cups in one hand, the cream-coloured enamel tea pot in the other. 'Surely it would be easier to do in her own place with no outsiders lookin' on?'

Alice followed her to the scullery sink, drying the crockery her mother washed.

'Anyroad,' Letty enquired, 'why should her want that young wench out of the way?'

'I can only think that the man who tried it on with Carys in that summerhouse figures in it somewhere. I bet her mother be more than friends with that one, otherwise why not tell Carys's father what happened? But her didn't. And it seems he still visits the house from what was said to Carys in that church.'

'Do you mean that her mother and . . . who did you say he was?'

'Ryder Tempal,' Alice supplied the answer.

'Well, whoever he be, do you be saying that them two be great together?'

'I say there be the possibility.' Alice laid the drying cloth over the airing line strung across the black-leaded grate of the tiny sitting room-cum-kitchen. 'I can't think why else a mother would want her daughter out of the house.'

'Wouldn't be the first woman to lose her head over a younger man,' Letty mused.

'Then you think her mother be jealous of Carys as well?'

'I don't think nothing of the kind,' Letty snapped. 'And don't you go making presumptions either. You keep your thoughts to yourself, Alice Withers. What you don't say you can't be blamed for. A still tongue be a wise tongue, just you remember that.'

But what her daughter had said made some sense, Letty thought as Alice hugged her goodbye. There was nothing so quick as desire for a man to set one woman against another.

'Was it your daughter the maids were speaking of?'

Ryder Tempal sat in the drawing room of Holyhead House, legs stretched out comfortably in front of him, very much at home.

Maria glanced down the long sinuous length of him, feeling the twitch again in the base of her stomach. She wanted him. Wanted to feel the nakedness of him press against her. It had been a couple of weeks since that last quick visit to a hotel in the Bull Ring and as yet he had not suggested another.

'Yes, it was her,' she answered. 'I called on Virginia Mountford last week. It appears Carys is serving as a house-maid at Ridge House, just as I heard.'

'Then it *was* her I saw!'

'You saw her?' Maria asked sharply. 'You saw Carys?'

Pale sunlight danced on his fair hair as he nodded.

'When? When did you see her?' Maria's voice was harsh.

'Oh, a couple of weeks or so.' He smiled languidly but his yellow eyes were watchful. 'I saw her at the Wakes. At least at the time I merely thought it could have been her, but you said she had chosen to take her final vows, didn't you, my dear? And that she would spend the rest of her life behind the walls of that convent, so how could it have been Carys that I saw? Now, it seems, it was.'

'Why did you not mention this before?'

'For the same reason, Maria. How could I possibly be seeing a girl who was cloistered in a nunnery?'

'Well, she is not cloistered any more.' Maria moved about the room in her agitation.

'So it appears.' Ryder Tempal drew in his legs, straightening himself in his chair. 'So you, my dear, must bring her home.'

'Oh, must I?' Maria swung on him, her eyes glittering with temper. 'You would like that, wouldn't you? It would suit you just fine having her here under this roof. Perhaps this time you might succeed in tumbling her. That is it, isn't it, my darling? You could have your cake and eat it at the same time.'

Ryder glanced at the woman he knew wanted to be his wife, his languid smile hiding the thoughts firing his brain. If Carys were out of that nunnery, as it seemed she was, what were his chances of marrying her? Meshac must have made provision for just such a thing as her renouncing her vows; if Ryder had the daughter for a wife he would no longer have to pander to Maria. True, the woman was attractive, but she was also possessive, too possessive. Carys had not been responsive that night in the garden, but that had been his fault. He had rushed his fences and she had taken fright. Next time it would be different.

'Well, you can hardly leave her there as Virginia Mountford's paid help.'

'You're right.' Maria's anger seemed to melt into a dazzling smile. 'You are so very sensible, Ryder. Of course she must come home, though it will mean some very great changes in my own life, and maybe a few in yours.'

Ryder drew in his breath, holding it against what was still to come.

'You see, my dear . . .' Maria paused, letting her words hang on the silence. 'Under the terms of Meshac's will every last penny of his was to go to his daughter in the event of her leaving the religious life and re-entering the world. Every stick and stone of his business, together with this house, would revert to her.'

'But you?' Ryder's brow furrowed. 'What of you? Meshac could not have meant you to have nothing.'

'Oh, he didn't.' She laughed hollowly. 'He said he left me that same comfort he suspected I had enjoyed for the last two years before his death.'

'Comfort?' Ryder watched her sink gracefully into a chair, smoothing the folds of her black taffeta skirts. 'I don't understand.'

'Don't you, Ryder? Don't you really?' Maria's smile faded. 'He meant you. You were the comfort he was leaving me. Don't you see? He knew although he never admitted as much. Meshac knew about us! But to admit it would have meant losing me, and that my poor deluded husband could never bring himself to face.'

So everything he coveted belonged not to Maria but to her daughter. Ryder almost smiled. And it could still be his, and with it he would no longer have to hang on to the skirts of any woman who had more than ten shillings to her name, and thanks to the fates would not have to marry Meshac's widow to get it. He would marry Meshac's child.

Maria turned the key in the lock of the office door, closing it carefully behind her. Moving to the window, she stared through the dust-covered pane to the low-roofed workshop that stood opposite. Thomas Blakeway was not in the doorway.

Satisfied she was not being observed, Maria crossed to a locked cupboard against the far wall. She had seen inside that cupboard once only but had never forgotten the jar Meshac had pointed out to her.

Opening the cupboard, she ran her glance quickly over

the line of jars on its top shelf then across the brushes ranged below. These were Meshac's oxides, kept for his own experimentation. He'd had a real feel for colour and had often stayed late here, mixing and firing new blends.

Reaching into the very back of the shelf, she drew out a small glass jar, lid fastened down securely. She read the label written in her husband's flowing copperplate hand, then glancing towards the window, slipped it into her bag.

'Is everything all right, ma'am?'

Thomas Blakeway watched the wife of his late employer as she prepared to climb into her carriage.

'I am afraid I cannot truly say.' Maria smiled sweetly. 'You see, Mr Blakeway, I would not know, especially with regard to my husband's office, this being the only time I have ever been inside it.' She turned as if to return to that building. 'You must be familiar with it, however. Perhaps you can tell me something of its contents, of what use my husband had for it, for I can see no papers there that correspond with customers' requirements?'

'I be sorry, ma'am.' Thomas shook his head. 'I ain't never been in the place meself. Master, he let nobody in there. Place were kept locked and he held the only key.'

'Then I can only leave it to be sorted along with the rest of Mr Beddows's business interests.' She sighed affectedly. 'It is all so very difficult.'

'Arrh, ma'am, that I can understand.' Thomas twisted his flat cap nervously in hands stained black by the constant handling of metals. 'But, beggin' your pardon, I 'ave to ask if you be goin' to keep on with the enamelling?'

'Keep on?' Maria made a pretence of not knowing to what the man was referring.

'Yes, ma'am. Be you goin' to carry on with the making of enamels, boxes and such? I know I shouldn't be botherin' you with it, not with you having no knowledge of such, but the family . . .' he glanced behind him to where his wife and children were working on the last of the materials. 'We only has what we earns here and we be almost out of frit, and the last of the metal was used yesterday.'

'Do you know where Mr Beddows obtained his supplies?'

'Arrh, ma'am, I do.'

'Then order enough for another month of working.' Maria climbed into the carriage. 'That will last until I can install a manager.'

'An' what will we be making?' Thomas looked at the carriage, head jutting out from between stooping shoulders.

He looks like a tortoise, Maria thought, distaste for the man and the workshop thick in her throat.

'What sells best?'

'Jewellery boxes, ma'am,' he replied. 'Boxes and caskets be about all we 'ave call for these days.'

'Then you had best make boxes.'

'And the design?'

Maria felt irritation with the man seep into her. What did she care what he painted on them?

'Repeat the work of last month.' She gave a peremptory tap on the door of the carriage then as quickly called for it to halt. 'Speaking of boxes,' she said as Thomas drew level with the door, 'Mr Reuben Fereday enquired of me concerning five that, I understand, are in my husband's office?'

'Arrh, that be so. They be in there still, far as I knows. Least that's where the master put them.'

Reaching into her bag, Maria handed him a key. 'Fetch those boxes to me, I will have them sent on.'

The boxes lined up on the seat beside her, she watched the smoke-blackened houses thin away, replaced by open heath. She would see that the boxes reached Reuben Fereday, but would not dispatch them to his gallery in Birmingham. She would take them there herself. When it suited her.

Bethesda squatted beside the edge of the pool, her flounced skirts taking on a darker hue where they rested on the damp ground. Leaning out over the water she washed the rabbit she had just skinned and emptied of its innards. It would make a good meal with the onions and potatoes she had earned that morning.

They had soon learned of her potions, the folk of the village, and had begun to visit her in their twos and threes as did the folk of West Bromwich whenever they camped in that part of the country.

Why had they not gone there this spring?

She swished the rabbit carcass in the water, brown eddies of blood swirling away in circles.

Why had Caine broken with his usual practice and come to Moxley instead? He had said nothing to her, but she had seen him glance after the girl they had dropped off near to the church that was just a little way further on. Did he know what the sight had told her? Did her son feel, as she did, that the girl had a part to play in the vengeance that drew ever closer?

Pushing herself to her feet, Bethesda felt the pain that none of her herbal remedies eased shoot through her hips. Soon she would be unable to travel with her son. She would have to set up a camp that would not move with the seasons, would no longer see the finger of God move across the broad fields of England or see his wondrous mountains.

'But Bethesda Lazic will not stay tied to that camp for long,' she muttered, swinging the rabbit in the air shaking away droplets of water. 'When the time comes, I holds that which will end all pain and sorrow, that which brings freedom to the spirit and gives it licence to roam the stars.'

Her steps uneven with pain, she limped across the open ground to where the caravan rested beneath the fringing trees. Taking the stick Caine had sharpened to a point, she skewered the rabbit then placed it across the fire, resting each end on tripods of branches built to each side. Holding a hand to her hip, as though to charm away the pain, she gazed towards the pall of grey that lay like a blanket across the distant sky, knowing it was the darkness of smoke from the chimneys of the myriad workshops of Bilston. How could people live like that? she thought. Breathe that filth when they could breathe God's clean air? To live in a few feet of dark cramped space when they could roam the beautiful countryside . . . She smiled, showing gapped teeth stained brown from tobacco. And these were people who thought gypsies were fools!

Taking an iron pot that was strung along the side of the caravan, she half filled it from the barrel Caine had filled the night before. Settling it on the glowing heart of the fire, she dropped in the onions and potatoes she had cut into rough cubes, adding a handful of dried herbs she always gathered from the wayside.

The meal prepared, she fished out the briar pipe from a pocket deep in the folds of her skirts and lowered herself painfully to the stool set in the lee of the painted wagon. Tonight she might taste the juice of the poppy, but not now. The pain had not yet beaten Bethesda Lazic.

Squinting against the pallid sun, the pipe held unlit between her teeth, she watched the approach of a woman, a child swaddled beneath the chequered shawl that draped her thin shoulders, three more of less than five years holding to her skirts.

'Good day to you,' Bethesda said, the pipe still in her mouth.

Just beyond the fire the woman halted. From where she sat Bethesda could see the tiredness in her eyes, and lines she guessed to be premature coursing her face. Beside her the children pressed their faces to her patched skirts.

A mended skirt. The fact was not lost on the gypsy. And the children. Their clothes were worn and obviously passed down one to the other but they were clean. But while each of them was barefoot their faces were scrubbed. The woman was poorer than a church mouse but she cared for her children.

'Good day to you.'

The woman dropped a hand to the head of the small boy as he began to cough, holding it there, comforting him with her touch until he wheezed to a stop.

'That be a dreadful hack of a cough.' Bethesda removed the pipe, resisting the urge to spit tobacco-tainted saliva on to the ground. Children of the Gorgio were frightened enough of gypsies and these poor mites could do without the adding of more.

'It be getting worse.' The woman lifted her hand from the boy's head. 'Nothing I do seems to 'elp.'

'And why be you here?'

Her face threatening to crumple as the boy was once more siezed by a fit of coughing, the woman looked at Bethesda.

'I 'eard about your ointment healing the open wound on Joseph Bartrum's leg, and the mixture you gave Hannah Lacy for when 'er stomach be bad, and I thought as how you might have a potion that would help my lad?'

Replacing the pipe in her pocket, Bethesda looked towards the boy clinging to his mother's skirts and again felt the breath being snatched from her body and the blood tumbling through her veins like a torrent let loose from the hills. She sat unmoving as the sight claimed her. There would be naught she could give would save that child nor the woman who had given him life. The cough that wracked him was devil given, the sickness that had eaten her lungs eating his. With the eyes of her mind she watched two bodies wrapped in one winding sheet, the mother holding the son in her arms as they were lowered into the ground.

Stirring as the sight left her, Bethesda rose to her feet and mounted the steps of the caravan. Inside she pulled a battered wooden box from beneath her narrow bed. Lifting the lid, she smelled the sweet scent of herbs that had instilled itself into the wood. Selecting a linen bag, she loosed the drawstring and took out a handful of dried yellow flowers of meadowsweet. Then opening a cupboard she drew out a small jar, a snippet of cloth secured over its open top with a string.

'These will do the lad no harm.' Coming from the wagon she held out the jar and the herbs she had placed in a piece of cloth.

'Cover a pinch of the herb with water fresh boiled. The jar be honey from bees collecting their nectar from the sweet flowers of the fields. Take as much as would cover a farthing and add it to the cup then leave it to cool. When this be done, sieve the mix through a cloth and give it to the lad to drink, once at his rising, once at noon, and once with the setting of the sun.'

'Will it cure him?' The woman's tired eyes were lit with a beam of hope.

'Curing be with the Lord,' Bethesda replied as the cough now took the woman. 'I be just another of His instruments.' She would not add that if it were God's will the child would recover for she knew already that would not be, that the boy would not know health in his life.

Hitching the child she carried in her arms higher on to her breast, the woman fumbled in a pocket of her skirt then held out her hand to the gypsy woman.

'I'll not . . . take . . . all from you,' she said, her breathing shallow and ragged as the cough subsided. 'I don't be having the money to pay for that which you offer. If you would measure a portion of the herbs it will be enough.'

Bethesda looked at the coin lying in the woman's open palm. One bronze penny. It would buy the herbs if not the honey; it would also buy a pennorth of scrag end of mutton from any butcher and that would mean a meal of broth for them all.

Wincing at the pain catching her hips, she bent towards the lad, placing the jar of honey in his hand and giving the cloth-wrapped flowers of meadowsweet to the taller of the two girls.

'I will be taking no money for things the Almighty gives freely,' she said, straightening. 'The flowers of the field be His gifts along of the bees, as my knowledge of their benefits be also His gift.' She had needed no church or chapel, nor the teaching of any priest, to learn compassion and the idea of charity never entered her head. 'Help thy neighbour and the Lord will help thee.' That had been the all of her

Romany upbringing and she had followed it well through the years.

'Thank you.' The woman's hand closed over the coin but her dark-ringed eyes were wide with gratitude. 'The Lord bless you, as I do.'

Once more taking her pipe from her pocket, Bethesda placed it in her mouth then sat watching the woman lead her children away. A woman on whose shoulder the Angel of Death already rested his hand.

Chapter Twelve

'I told him, I told our Davey you wouldn't be wanting to walk with him.' Alice looked apologetically at Carys. 'But he would insist. Said he would call about three.'

'I really don't want to go out.' Carys picked up a china Staffordshire dog, dusting it carefully. 'Not that I don't like your brother, I do, I like them both, it's just that I don't feel I want to go walking.'

'It would do you good though, Carys.' Alice picked up the second dog of the pair, giving it a thorough rub with her duster. 'You hardly ever goes out. You might just as well still be in that convent for all you do with your spare time.'

'I go with you to your mother's house.' Replacing the ornament, Carys crossed the room and began carefully to dust the dainty porcelain figurines grouped on a graceful long-legged table.

'Huh!' Alice retorted, setting viciously about dusting the silver-framed photographs grouped along the mantel-shelf above the fireplace. 'Twice. You've been to me mother's twice. I 'ardly calls that visitin'.'

'What would you call it then?' Carys laughed.

'You knows what I mean.' Alice turned to look at her. 'Every time it be your turn for an afternoon off, you refuses,

179

and though I be grateful for the taking of it, it don't be right. You *should* get yourself out. Won't do no good living your life inside four walls. Ee! Be you worrying over that visit? The one your mother made to the mistress . . . you ain't frightened of her?'

Carys replaced a figurine, her hand resting on the delicate piece.

''Er won't hurt you.' Alice came to stand beside her. ''Er just tried to get you throwed out so as to make you leave Hill Top. 'Er still be jealous of you but 'er can't do anything, not now mistress knows everything.'

'No, I am not worrying over Maria's visit.' Carys picked up another ornament, feeling a need to avoid the other girl's eyes. 'And as for being afraid . . . Maria might prefer me not to live here but she would never harm me.'

'Well then!' Alice said firmly. 'If nothing be worrying you, why not go out for a couple of hours? Our Davey, well, I know he's not handsome, but he be a nice chap and he thinks the world of you.'

'Alice, I . . .'

'Look, don't say anything now,' she interrupted. 'Wait and see 'ow you feel come three o'clock.'

She would still feel the same, Carys thought as Alice went back to her dusting. David Withers had called at Ridge House several times, always with the excuse of a message for his sister but they both knew it was Carys he hoped to see. But though she liked him a lot there was no feeling deeper than that. She would always want him as a friend, but as a husband, a man to whom she could give her heart and her love . . .

Taking up the box that held dusting cloths and polish, Carys carried it out into the corridor that led to the kitchen and replaced it in the boot cupboard in the scullery.

She could not give her heart to Davey Withers. It was given already. Given to a man she had seen only once, a man who swam naked in a pool on Moxley Heath.

*   *   *

'I think as Alice be right.' Martha Bates relaxed into her usual chair. Sunday lunch served and cleared, she watched as Alice and Carys collected plates and dishes for washing. 'You should go out for a while, get some fresh air into your lungs, you be looking right pale.'

'You need only be out half an hour or so,' Alice whispered as they carried crockery into the scullery. 'Would keep Mrs B. quiet an' all.'

'Very well.' Carys gave in. She did not want to go over the whole argument again. She would walk with Davey but must make it plain to him there could not be anything between them. It would be unfair to allow him to think otherwise.

In her bedroom Carys removed her apron, folding it neatly and laying it on her bed against her return, doing the same with the dress provided as uniform. Noticing a spot on the hem of her petticoat, she fetched her only other one from the chest beside the door. Taking off the one that was marked from polishing the hall floor earlier, she slipped the fresh one over her head, feeling the cloth catch on the pins that held her hair. Glancing into the mirror as she lifted her hands to free it, she caught her breath sharply. Draped about her head, hiding her hair completely, the white petticoat fell like a wimple about her shoulders like the headdress she had worn for almost four years.

'You will not be so quick to spy again.' The voice of the Mistress of Novices whispered against her ears and she flinched as she seemed to feel again the sharp sting of the slap to her face. 'Remember who has charge of you here. So long as you wear the robe of a novice it is I who order your life.' Carys flinched again as memory brought another slap to her face. 'You will say nothing of what you saw in that room, do you hear? You will say nothing!' The slap had come again, hard and vicious, to her mouth. 'Remember why you are here. To cleanse you of the lust that drove you to draw a naked man, to set his body on paper so you could look at it in your room after you had fornicated with him in some field.

Don't deny it!' The voice in her mind cracked with an anger driven by something Carys had not then understood. 'I have seen the drawings Mother Superior thought hidden, I know what you are, and if you breathe a word about what you saw I will make sure the whole convent knows it too. They will not believe the word of a slut against that of their own sister!'

The weight of the petticoat pulling against a hairpin released it and the garment slid down over her shoulders, wiping the vision from her mind. Trembling, Carys fastened the cloth-covered buttons that held it to her waist. She had thought the memories of those years buried and as good as forgotten but she had been wrong; it had taken only the fall of a petticoat to bring them flooding back.

Her hands still shaking, she slipped on the same brown dress she had worn when her mother had taken her to the Convent of the Holy Child, and had worn again only when she had left it. She had thought, when at last that day had come, that she would be returning home to Holyhead House to be with her father again. But she had been wrong.

Would it have been so much worse for her, life behind the convent walls? The other sisters had been so kind; only the fear and shame of what she had done with the priest had driven the Mistress of Novices to treat her as she had. But for all her harsh treatment Carys had not sought the help of any of them; she had told no one of Sister Veronica's cruelty to her. Young as she had been, she'd sensed the woman's unhappiness and would not have added to it.

Doing up the last of the buttons that fastened the bodice of her dress, she turned from the mirror. Taking a ribbon from the same drawer that had held the petticoat, she tied it about her hair, catching the silken chestnut strands within its bright yellow.

Ready to go back downstairs, she bent to smooth the covers of her bed and as she did so, caught her foot against the bag pushed beneath it. Lifting it out, she sat with it beside her. Had Virginia Mountford noticed the similarity between the two faces she had drawn, one so long ago, the other recently? Had she wondered at the likeness of one man to another as Carys herself had done? Drawing out the sketches, Carys looked from one charcoal drawing to the other. It was remarkable: the same bone structure, the same colouring, the same eyes and mouth. They might be sketches of the same man save for the fact one had been young and virile, a man who had dived and swum in a pool on a heath, and the other was Virginia Mountford's father.

Staring down at the sketches Carys seemed to hear again the voice of the Mistress of Novices. '. . . You set it down on paper so you could lust over it . . .'

Was it true? Was that the reason she had kept the drawing Mother Superior had returned to her, the same drawing her mother had used to blacken her character?

Touching a finger to the paper she traced the lines of the face, remembering the mocking look the man on the heath had played over her, remembering his mouth, his dark slumbrous eyes that seemed even now to draw her down into their velvet depths. Was thinking of him each night as she lay in bed, lust? Was conjuring the memory of his words and the timbre of his voice, lust? Was wanting to see that handsome face just one more time, lust?

She should destroy these sketches, get rid of them, and then perhaps the phantom of memory would leave her. Her hand curling the edge of the paper, she felt her heart twist. To destroy her sketch would not destroy her memories. She would never forget. She had met him only once, but that would last forever. Rolling the sketches together she replaced them in her carpet bag, pushing it back beneath her bed. Halfway along the corridor that gave on to the stairs she glanced at the portrait of Virginia Mountford's father. Even should she destroy her drawing of an unknown man she would be faced with his likeness so long as she remained in this house. But here or anywhere, she would need no portrait to remind her. A far more enduring one was drawn upon her heart.

'Our Eddie and Peggy Rogers have put a date to their marriage.' Davey Withers plucked several bright yellow flowers from a clump of gorse.

'That's wonderful.' Carys smiled. 'When is their wedding to be?'

'In the summer. They asked the priest for July the sixteenth, that be our mother's birthday.'

'So it will be a double celebration?'

He nodded, breaking several more strands of the brilliant flowers from the bush.

'Does Alice know yet?'

'Not yet. I expect Mother will tell her when next she gets to come home.'

'Then I shall not tell her. To do so would spoil your mother's pleasure. She is pleased for them, isn't she, Davey?'

'Oh, arrh!' He stared at the flowers, twisting their tough stalks together to hold them into a bunch. 'It's what my mother has been wanting long since. Her would like to see all of her brood married and settled.'

'So Alice has told me.' Carys watched him twine the stems of the gorse. 'She says every time she visits, your mother asks if she is walking out with a man yet, and she does not seem too pleased with the answer always being no.'

'That I can believe.' He looked up from the flowers to stare out across the heath. 'Like I said, Mother will only be truly satisfied when each of her children be wed, but I reckon not all of us will go as easy as our Eddie has.'

Meaning himself, Carys thought, feeling almost guilty as she glanced at him. She ought not to have come walking with him, it would only serve to give him the wrong impression and that could well cause him pain when she had to tell him of her feelings, tell him she could only ever feel friendship for him.

'Alice would like to be married, I am sure of it,' she said, feeling the awkwardness of the silence that had settled between them. 'And I don't think it will be long before some man asks for her. Then your mother will have the pleasure of planning a second wedding.'

'Arrh, she will have the pleasure of them two . . .'

As he turned to face her, Carys saw the sadness in his eyes and knew she would not have to tell him of her own feelings. He already knew!

'. . . and that will have to be enough for her, for I have no notion of wedding any girl.'

In the quiet of her mind Carys heard the whispered words: *'Seems how he will love a woman, but that same woman will love another.'* Despite herself she had to acknowledge the truth. Whether spoken by Madam Rosa or invented by Alice, they had been right. Davey Withers was in love with her. And she? Was she in love with another, and if so was he the man on the heath?

'You may think that now, Davey.' She tried to sound light-hearted. 'But given a year or two you will feel differently.'

'I will never feel differently.' Savagely he threw the tiny knot of flowers to the ground. 'I love *you*, I will never feel the same for any woman.'

'Davey, I . . . I . . .' Carys looked at the broken posy lying like a pool of sunlight on the bare earth.

'You don't have to say anything.' He turned to look at her, his eyes swimming with misery. 'I know you don't return my feelings, but at least you have never pretended otherwise. You have never tried to lead me up the garden path.'

'I would never do that, Davey. I would not deceive you, in that or in anything else.'

'I don't know who the chap is as holds your heart,' he said softly, 'but I do know he be the luckiest man on God's earth. But *you* know this. Should I ever hear of his harming you in any way – in any way, Carys – then I'll break his back.'

Feeling his fingers tight on hers as he helped her over a

stile that separated heathland from tilled ground, Carys felt a surge of warmth towards the tall, gentle man, but at the same time a twinge of pain that twisted her heart. The man who held her heart was the luckiest on God's earth . . . What would Davey say if she told him she was in love with a man she had met only once, a man she would never meet again?

'It is so good to see you, Reuben, but should you leave your business to come calling on me?'

'Since when has business, or anything else, come before my favourite aunt?'

Reuben Fereday tossed the parcel he was carrying on to a wide-seated Hepplewhite chair, pulling Virginia Mountford into his arms and hugging her.

'Your only aunt, young man.' She freed herself, the look she gave her nephew as warm as his hug.

'Of course.' He grinned at her. 'But still my favourite nevertheless, the woman of my heart.'

'Sit down, you rogue,' Virginia laughed. 'And tell me all your news. What have you been doing with yourself?'

'Oh, the usual.' The grin remained, showing white even teeth. 'Drinking, debauching . . .'

Virginia laughed again. 'Your usual behaviour, as you say. Rape and pillage. It's a miracle you have time to visit your aunt.'

'I interrupt those fascinating activities only for you.' He took up the parcel he had thrown on to the chair and handed it to her. 'Happy birthday, Aunt.'

'It's almost too pretty to open,' she said, admiring the swathe of pale peach-coloured ribbon expertly ruched and tied into a bow.

'Then shall I place it on a table somewhere where you can admire its packaging?'

'Age has not improved you,' she returned, attempting to put a note of reproof into her voice yet failing dismally. 'You are still the cheeky imp you always were.'

Looking up as a tap on the door answered her earlier order for tea, Virginia watched Alice try to settle the tray on the table without taking her eyes from Reuben's face.

'Thank you, Alice,' she said as the maid hovered, a moon-struck look on her own face, then as the door closed behind her, asked, 'Rape?'

Reuben's wicked smile flashed. 'I think I will stick to pillage, if you don't mind?'

Her own smile mischievous, Virginia pulled the swathe of ribbon, releasing it from the package.

'Oh!' she breathed, lifting a pair of beautifully painted cameo portraits from a velvet-lined box. 'These are absolutely beautiful, Reuben. Thank you, my dear, thank you so very much.'

'I knew you would like them.'

'How could I not? They are truly exquisite. Who is the artist?'

'A fellow called Edward Emslie. He has already been noticed by the Royal Academy. I think he is set to become a great painter.'

Virginia tilted the miniatures in their oval frames, using the light from the window to release the depths of their colours. 'Well, if this is a sample of his work, then I agree with you.'

Placing the paintings on a table beyond the rays of sunlight, she returned to her chair and poured tea for them both.

'The library might be the place for my lovely present,' she said, handing Reuben his cup, 'but I don't go into that room very often so I would not be able to look at them as much as I would wish.'

'Then why not in your bedroom?'

'Such beautiful faces should not be hidden away in an old woman's bedroom. No, I shall have them here, in my sitting room.'

'The same as you have the charcoal sketch of Uncle Robert?' Reuben lifted his glance to where the black and white sketch in a plain lightwood frame hung over a small writing desk, moved to the private sitting room for his aunt's convenience. A dark-haired, somewhat heavy-browed face stared back at him, a half smile hovering at the back of his eyes, echoing the line of the mouth.

'It is an exceptionally good likeness.' He rose, crossing the room to where the portrait he had not seen before hung. 'Did the artist know Uncle Robert?'

Virginia sipped her tea, her eyes too on the sketch of her late husband. The artist had not known Robert, the startling accuracy had been caught from a treasured photograph and drawn by the same hand that had copied the oil painting of her father. Watching her nephew as he examined the sketch, she thought back to when Carys had brought the sketch to her, with a shy smile and half apologetic words. 'I hope you do not mind . . .' Virginia had not minded, but had cried out with pure pleasure as she had unrolled the paper and looked down into those smiling eyes.

'The artist and your uncle never met,' she said at last.

'You could almost swear they had not only met but had known each other for a long time.' He leaned across the desk, bringing his face closer to the sketch, examining the lines of it as though searching for some unseen signature. It had the same sureness, the same character, as the painting on the box he had bought from Beddows Enamels, and *she* had sketched with charcoal! But it could not be by the same hand, it could not be by the girl he had surprised on the heath so long ago; that girl had given her life to a convent.

He turned swiftly, refusing to let memory fill his mind, refusing to allow it to plague him as it had done so many times before. Why was it he thought so often of a slip of a girl he had met just once? Why couldn't he forget her?

'So, Aunt, what have you planned for your birthday?'

Virginia caught the look on his face as her nephew turned away from the sketch, caught the frustration and unhappiness before he banished the last vestiges to smile at her. Did he recognise the style of the artist? Had he and Carys Beddows met somewhere? Realisation dawned. The drawing of the younger man . . . the one she had thought to be her father in his earlier days . . . the faces that were so alike, one drawn years before the girl had set foot in this house. It was not a representation of Virginia's father that Carys had drawn, it was her nephew!

Virginia replaced the cup she was holding on to the silver tray, using the movement to shield her eyes from Reuben, not wanting him to see what she knew to be reflected there. Was the girl now working as a maid in her kitchen the cause of what she had seen on Reuben's face? Had he met her, and if so what had happened between them to produce such a look as she had caught in his eyes? Had he done something terrible to the girl, something so awful that even now he could not face up to the truth of it without pain? Had he forced himself upon her? No! Virginia thrust the thought away. She could not, would not think such a thing of him. Reuben would never treat any girl so.

'I shall spend it here at Ridge House, probably with a book and a cup of Mrs Bates's hot cinnamon milk,' Virginia answered his question, relieved that it had turned from the subject of who had drawn the sketch of her husband. She would not tell him of the presence of the artist in her house. If he had met Carys Beddows almost five years ago and that meeting was the cause of the worm eating away at his heart, or maybe his conscience, then she would not feed it. Best let the past lie.

'Do you honestly mean you prefer a book and cup of hot cinnamon milk to dinner and the theatre with a very eligible young man?'

Virginia answered the smile that now veiled the sadness she had seen a moment ago. Yet she knew it was merely below the surface. For a moment she thought to recant her decision not to speak of Carys, but to do so and be wrong in her assumptions would be to cause embarrassment to them both.

'I might reconsider if that eligible young man were quite handsome.'

'You are a flighty piece, Virginia Mountford.' Laughing, he pulled her into his arms. 'Lucky for you I am here to keep you on the straight and narrow. I shall be back for you at six tomorrow. And be sure, woman, I will take a shot-gun to any other young beau I see hovering around!'

'I will be sure to have them safely hidden in the cupboard by five minutes to six.'

Smiling, she held her face up for his kiss. Her brother's child had the looks and the charm of his grandfather, so why, at the age of thirty-two, was he still unmarried?

Guiding the horse he had hired from the stables in Great Western Street away across the heath towards Wednesbury, Reuben did not see the couple crest the rise that backed Ridge House, the late-afternoon sun glinting on the girl's chestnut hair.

Clutching the posy of wild flowers Davey had picked for her, Carys watched the horse and rider canter down the hill and into the distance. He had sat a horse with the same ease, tall in the saddle as the rider she watched, and with the same dark hair unfettered by a hat. She remembered the wide shoulders and strong body, one she had sketched rising from the diamond-strewn water, and the sensuous mouth that had mocked her on the heath. Perhaps . . . But she turned away. The man who had waylaid her on Moxley Heath was no more than a memory, a phantom who came to haunt her nights. For Carys Beddows he might never have been.

For her there could be no perhaps.

Chapter Thirteen

Eyes half closed, Maria watched the tall, agile figure come towards her where she lay on the bed, light from the window catching his fair hair in a halo of light.

A halo! Maria could have laughed at the thought. That was one thing Ryder Tempal would never wear. Nor would she! Lifting her arms to him, she felt the heat of desire flare through her, and as his body covered hers she felt she did not care. Having a halo came a poor second to having Ryder Tempal.

It had been too long. Maria moaned softly as he drove into her. It had been three months since Meshac's death, three months since she had tasted the pleasure now ripping through her almost painfully. Observing the rules of society she should not entertain for at least a year, more if she wished to be well thought of. But to hell with society! She gasped as he took her nipple in his mouth, teasing it with the tip of his tongue. It had been too long, too many nights spent lying awake thinking while her body yearned. She would not wait so long again. Regardless of what people thought, she would marry Ryder Tempal, and that marriage would be soon.

How many times had he done this? Maria turned her head on the pillow, watching the breath heaving in his chest. How

191

often in those three months had he lain with a woman, and which one?

Outside in the street the shouts of tradesmen mingled with the rumble of cart wheels. Maria glanced around the room they had taken for the afternoon and her nose wrinkled with distaste. It was not distaste solely for her surroundings but for the fact that they must meet here at all. But soon that need would be over.

Propping herself on one arm, she touched a hand to the fine golden hairs spread like mist across Ryder's chest. Soon they would lie like this in her own bed at Holyhead House. Meshac had left her the comfort she had enjoyed for two years before his death: the comfort of Ryder Tempal's body. It was one she meant to enjoy, and one she would not share. There would be no other women for him. He would enter Holyhead House as its master but she would be mistress of it, and of him!

'I think we should marry.'

The movement of his chest eased but his eyes remained closed.

'I want us to marry.'

She traced a finger down the line of his chest, losing its tip among the golden hair at the base of his stomach.

Slowly he breathed again, a measured sound that hid the sudden onset of apprehension. He wanted Maria Beddows's money, but not Maria herself.

'We will marry,' he answered, still not opening his eyes. 'As soon as is decently possible.'

'Decent!' She laughed softly. 'Since when did decency enter into your mode of thinking, my dear? You have always taken what you wanted, whether the taking were decent or not.'

'But we must think of your position.' His eyelids lifted.

'This is the only position I care about.'

Her fingers busy in his crotch, she leaned over him, breasts brushing his chest as she closed her mouth over his.

She had said she wanted to marry. Ryder's thoughts moved

quickly. Did that mean now, within a few weeks? He had planned on having at least a year in which to part her from her money, or at least enough of it to tide him over until the next rich widow came along, or a mother desperate enough to pay well for him to marry her daughter. But instinct told him Maria would not wait a year. If he did not give her what she wanted she would find someone who would. And where would he be then? There were precious few heiresses in Bilston.

'But perhaps you do not wish to marry me?'

Maria moved her fingers teasingly and smiled inwardly as his penis jerked.

'Maybe you have set your sights in another direction?' She trailed her tongue over his chest, tasting the salt tang of sweat, searching his navel with the moist tip. 'In which case . . .'

'There is no other direction.' Reacting to the warning of his brain, he grasped the hand that, despite the trend of his thoughts, had his body intoxicated. He lifted it above her head, pushing her on to her back. 'There is only you, my darling, I want no other woman but you.'

Parting her legs, feeling the hard fire of him inside her, Maria knew that what he said was a lie. He would take a woman tomorrow and not even bother to wave her goodbye, supposing the woman were young and wealthy. A woman like Carys.

Later, fastening a pale blue cravat at his throat, Ryder went over the thoughts that had troubled him since leaving the bed. What guarantee had he that Meshac's daughter would not claim her inheritance? She was no longer enclosed in a religious order, and Hill Top was just a few miles from Moxley. How long would it be before she enquired after her father's will, and could Maria prevent her from finding out about its terms? And if Carys did learn of the whole of her father's wealth belonging to her, where then would *he* stand? To be married to Maria Beddows was one thing; to be married to her without her money was another altogether, and one he definitely did not relish.

'What of your daughter?' His back to Maria, he felt the tension quicken in the room.

Taking her time, threading each button of her black jacket slowly through the relevant button hole, she watched her own reflection in the fly-spotted mirror. She had known the question would come, known the thoughts being so carefully analysed in his mind.

'What of her?' she asked, slipping the last of the buttons into place.

'You know perfectly well!' His desire sated, Ryder was in no mood for prevarication. 'What if she returns? What if she claims that which is hers once we are married?'

Reaching for her hat, Maria set it on her head, securing it with a pearl-topped hat pin before drawing the veil of black tulle over her face. 'Then you, my dear Ryder, will be married to the wrong woman, but married none the less.'

Taking up his gloves, he glanced across the room at the woman who only minutes before had lain moaning beneath him, the meaning implicit in her words rankling in his mind. Was it worth the risk? Could he marry her, knowing the threat of losing Meshac's money hung over them like a cloud?

Maria smoothed a black lace glove over her hand, easing it over each finger with separate, deliberate movements. Both gloves fitted to her satisfaction, she raised her glance to his. 'Of course,' she said softly, 'there could be no question of Meshac's child claiming her inheritance were she not here to claim it.'

'But she *is* here!' Ryder spoke irritably.

'Yes, she is here.' Behind the tulle Maria's mouth thinned. 'And so long as she is we are under threat. So, my dear, *we* must do something about it.'

'What do you mean?'

'I mean, if we are to enjoy our marriage, the girl must be got rid of.'

A shiver of unease touched Ryder's spine. Maria was a determined woman, there was no telling to what lengths she was prepared to go to get what she wanted.

'You tried that once before without success!'

The touch of sarcasm in his answer did nothing to endear him to her.

'Then this time we must have the benefit of a man's superior intellect.'

'Meaning?'

From behind the softness of her veil, Maria surveyed his handsome features. Ryder Tempal was a good-looking young man, both in face and body, but there his appeal ended; his morals and his backbone were neither of them worth a thought. But it wasn't his morals she was interested in, and this once at least she would see to it he found the backbone to do as she wanted. For her to be sure of him, he must be as much a part of getting rid of her daughter as she herself.

'You, my darling,' she answered his curtly spoken question, 'must help me dispose of our problem.'

Tracing his lips with the tip of his tongue, Ryder felt the same unease ride higher up his spine. 'How?' he asked.

'Tomorrow!' Maria swept to the door of the shabby room, the swish of her heavy silken skirts raising a cloud of dust from the worn carpet. 'Come to Holyhead House tomorrow afternoon. I will tell you then how we will make certain Meshac's money will never go to his child.'

'I have had a most enjoyable few days, Reuben. The theatre was a most refreshing change and I so enjoyed seeing your gallery. Thank you, my dear.'

Virginia Mountford smiled at her nephew. He was the last of her line and had always been dear both to her husband and herself, taking the place of the child they had never had.

'The more enjoyable for me, Aunt. Having the most beautiful woman in the room on his arm does wonders for a man's ego.'

'Yours needs little bolstering,' she laughed, 'but flattery lifts mine.'

'Who is flattering?' Reuben's dark eyes smiled beneath his finely marked brows. 'You were the most beautiful woman at the theatre, and at the hotel where we dined I could feel every man's envy.'

Virginia played a glance over his face. Apart from the small white scar high on his eyebrow he was the image of his grandfather. She remembered the accident that had resulted in that scar. He had played all morning in one of the outhouses behind Ridge House. Then, in the afternoon, she and Oliver had been taking tea in the rear garden when Reuben had called to them. They had not seen him at first, then when he called a second time they spotted him on the roof of the stables, standing with arms outstretched, a contraption of webbing and feathers strapped to his back and buckled about his wrists.

Virginia closed her eyes for a second as the fear of that moment returned to her. Oliver had shouted for Reuben to climb down but he had only laughed. 'I am going to fly.' His child's voice had rung with the confidence of ignorance. 'I shall fly like Daedalus.' Scrambling over the roof, his foot had dislodged a slate, sending it hurtling to the cobbled yard, the sound of its landing sickeningly loud in the hot afternoon.

'Reuben, stay where you are!' Oliver had risen to his feet and was already halfway to the stables. 'Don't move, we will get you down.'

'No need!' Reuben's laughter floated to her on the still air. 'I can fly down. Watch, Uncle Oliver, watch me fly!'

Virginia had stared, seeing the figure of her husband seem to move in slow motion, seeing her nephew raise his arms, and vaguely, as though it were simply a shadow moving along the base of the stable wall, seen the figure of Ned Jeavons, one of the stable hands.

'Stay still, Reuben!' Oliver's shouted command had mixed

with the child's delighted laughter – and then he had jumped!

Virginia never knew if the scream remained imprisoned in her throat. She remembered only the small body as it launched itself into the air, arms flailing wildly as it fell, tumbling head over heels, and Oliver coming to a standstill, unable to move as the child's figure hurtled towards the ground.

His boyish laughter turning into a frightened cry, the boy had called her name and Virginia's blood had turned to ice. Then he had landed, his head lost beneath a jumble of webbing and chicken feathers – landed in the arms of Ned Jeavons! Virginia released the breath in her throat. Ned had fallen from the weight of his catch and the boy's head had struck the cobbled yard. She had run to them as Oliver had taken their nephew into his own arms, thanking Ned profusely while she dabbed Reuben's bleeding face with her handkerchief.

'Reuben.' Virginia felt all the love she had for him surge upward. 'Reuben, are you happy . . . I mean, truly happy?'

His mouth moved as if to answer, then catching the look in her eyes, he hesitated. He had never been able to fool his aunt. Oh, sometimes as a child she had allowed him to think he had hoodwinked her but it had never been truly so. And now? He knew it was useless even to try.

'I am as happy as I ever expect to be, Aunt.'

He had told her the truth. Virginia climbed into the hansom. There was something in Reuben's life that was causing him pain, keeping him from happiness, and she could not ask what. He was no longer the child who confided his secrets in her, he was a man who would keep his own counsel. She leaned from the cab, touching a finger to the tiny scar white against the bronze of his skin.

'Take care, my dear.' Her caution was for more than his physical welfare. She could almost feel the pent-up emotions inside him, emotions that might tip him into the arms of a woman he did not love. 'Take care, Reuben, don't go flying in the wind.'

In the sitting room of Holyhead House Maria glared angrily at Ryder Tempal. He wanted to have jam on both sides of his bread. He wanted Meshac's money but wanted none of the risk that would accompany the getting of it.

'If you really think the girl will give you so much as a second look, you are sadly mistaken!' she rasped. 'You destroyed any chance you might have had with her when you attempted to treat her like one of your whores.'

'Like I treat you, you mean!' Ryder saw her flinch against the sting of his reply. The sight pleased him.

'Like I allow you to treat me . . . so long as it pleases me.' Maria's voice was soft, dangerous as a serpent, and her wide brown eyes sparked a warning. 'But then, my dear, I can pay for my little foibles, *I* have the money. Take care yours do not cost you what little you have!'

Ryder moved uncomfortably beneath that fixed stare. She could well be right when she said her daughter would not countenance him as a husband, and if so he would be out without a penny after servicing this bitch for over two years!

'It most probably would make very little difference to my life should she return and take what her father left her.' Maria could not resist driving the nail home. 'I am, after all, her mother. She would understand my sending her away – I was just trying to keep her from the likes of you until she had gained a little more experience of life.'

'And she was to get that experience in a convent?' His smile was acid but Maria let it slide over her; he was fighting a losing battle, she could allow him one small triumph.

'Do you really think I could not give a plausible reason for that?' She laughed. 'Meshac is dead, he cannot deny it was his doing together with the leaving of her on that railway station. A few tears, Ryder, a few tears and she will believe all I wish her to believe. Then I shall be in comfort for life. But *you*, my dear, where will you be? With Colly Moreton's daughter, perhaps? I don't think so. Nor with any other girl whose parents know about you. Face it, Ryder. You either do things my way or you have seen the last of Meshac Beddows's money.'

'What do you suggest?' He knew he was beaten.

'A love letter.'

'A love letter!' His eyebrows rose. 'How will a love letter dispose of your daughter?'

'We could call it a poison pen letter, if you prefer.'

'I would prefer to know what the hell you are talking about!' Irritation bubbled in him. 'Yesterday, in that hotel, you said to come here and you would outline your idea, but so far all you have done is talk about yourself, how you will come out of this. That, frankly, is highly irritating, so say what you have to say or I am leaving.'

'Frankly . . .' Maria's eyes burned with an almost intense savagery '. . . Your being highly irritated does not bother me one bit. As for your leaving, then do so . . . if you can afford to.'

Ryder clenched his jaw. She had won again. Always it came down to his having no money, and always that gave her the upper hand. But it would not be that way forever. One day he would have every halfpenny she now called hers, and that would not constitute the only change in Maria Beddows's life. When that day dawned, *his* would be the upper hand, and he would bring it down . . . hard!

'How do you propose a love letter will get her to leave Hill Top?' he asked, tasting the bitterness of new defeat with every word.

'Oh, I do not propose Carys should merely leave Hill Top.' Maria allowed her smile of triumph to remain just a shadow about her mouth. 'That would keep matters much as they are now. She could return whenever the mood took her. You, I am sure, my dear, do not want to live under such a constant threat. Therefore I propose she should depart permanently. In other words, I propose we kill her.'

'Kill her!' Ryder's face blanched. 'For God's sake!'

'No, not for God's sake, Ryder,' she returned smoothly, 'for yours.'

Silence settled over the room. Maria smoothed her black taffeta skirts and waited. He would agree. He would see the sense of what she had said. He would help her to get rid of Carys and of these trailing widow's weeds she hated so much. And he? He would become her husband . . . should she still want him.

'Could it be done?' he asked at last. 'Could it be done without our being found out?'

'Yes.' Maria felt her blood begin to race. She had gone over it in her mind again and again, testing her idea for faults, altering and refining until it was perfect. 'I have a way that will be totally undetectable.'

Drawing a linen bag from a pocket in her skirt, she held it in her hand. 'This is an oxide from Meshac's private supply. He showed it to me once just after our marriage. When I made to touch it he pulled it away, telling me it was quite deadly. It was kept locked in a cupboard in his room at one of the workshops, to which no one but himself held a key.'

'What did he use that stuff for?'

'In his experiments with enamelling colours, Meshac liked to try for unusual shades. I took it from his room when I paid the workshop a visit a couple of weeks ago.'

'Won't it be missed?'

'The man in charge told me he had never been in that room, nor had anyone other than Meshac, at least not in the time he had worked there. He said Meshac took great care to keep the place locked. He guarded his secrets well. If no other person goes in there then no one knows what the cupboard held.'

'Did he see you take it, the man in charge?'

'No.' Maria shook her head. 'I was careful to watch for

that. Rest assured, no one knows of the existence of this jar other than you and me.'

'But if that stuff is as lethal as you say, why did Meshac hold on to it?'

'How do I know?' Maria snapped. 'He did, that is all I need to know.'

'What exactly is it?'

Stretching the neck of the bag, she folded the linen back upon itself, disclosing a jar half filled with a white powder. Across the body of the jar a label read: 'Thallium'.

'I've never heard of it,' Ryder said, leaning forward to read the spidery copperplate scrawl.

'That is not surprising.' Maria replaced the cover, drawing the strings of the bag tight. 'Though I would be surprised if anyone in Biloton has. Meshac got it from a chemist in London. He told me his name was Crookes, and he had recommended the salts for use as a dye or in paint. But Meshac was warned that they were highly dangerous. They could be absorbed into the body by the mucous membranes in the mouth and also through the skin. Thallium was, he said, odourless, colourless and tasteless, one of the most toxic of all metal Mr Crookes had encountered, and once it has entered the system a man can be dead in twenty-four hours.'

'Phew!' Ryder eased back into his chair. 'Lethal is the word. But how can you get her to take it? She will hardly open her mouth while you spoon it in.'

'Agreed.' Maria half smiled. 'But then she will not have to open her mouth and I will not have to spoon it in. You, my love, will be the one to give it to her.'

'Me! But how? She will hardly take a spoonful of that or anything else from me.'

'But it will not be given from a spoon, it will be given in the letter I spoke of. Thallium dissolves in water. Paint that water on to an object and the water evaporates while the toxic salts remain. If that object is then handled before the oxides are burned in the furnace, they can kill. So you will mix the salts with water and soak a sheet of writing paper. When it dries it will show no trace of the powder. Then you can mix a little more in a bottle of ink and write a love note with it.' Maria's eyes took on a scathing gleam. 'For that you should not need my assistance. Then all you need do is address an envelope with an ink that does not contain thallium and deliver it to her at Hill Top.'

'Deliver it personally!' He frowned his displeasure. 'There is surely no need for that? It can go through the post.'

'And thus be the more traceable.' Maria scowled. 'The fewer people see or know of the letter, the better.'

'But it is bound to be seen by someone other than your daughter when I hand it in at Ridge House.'

In irritation Maria went on: 'That is exactly why I said you were to deliver it personally. It is to be given to no one but Carys. And, remember, no name is to appear on the letter or the envelope, not yours or hers. It must remain impossible to trace its sender.'

'But why must *I* write it?' he asked suspiciously. 'Why not you? She cannot be too familiar with your hand.'

'Perhaps not, but that is not my reason. You stand to share most handsomely in the profits, therefore you must share the risk. With you as deeply entrenched in this as I am, I can be more sure of your continued complicity.'

Rising to her feet, Maria handed the linen bag to Ryder. 'Be careful when you are handling that sheet of writing paper,' she said with acid sweetness. 'Wear gloves when you write on it and a fresh pair when you address the envelope. Remember how very lethal is the powder you are dealing with, I would hate to lose you under such circumstances.'

'I'm sure you would.' He matched her sarcasm with his own. Theirs was no love match. This marriage would be one of convenience, and the convenience would be all his.

'One more thing,' Maria said as his hand fastened on the handle of the sitting-room door. 'Once the letter is written, take everything you have used – gloves, ink, pen, everything – and bury them somewhere lonely and deep, *very* deep.'

As the door closed behind him Maria sank into her chair. He would do as she had instructed. He would deliver the letter to Meshac's child and the poison would enter her body through the skin of her fingers as she held it, then she, Maria, would have all she wanted. She would own Meshac's property. She would own Ryder Tempal.

Chapter Fourteen

Carys looked at the little heap of withered brown leaves and stalks, the colourless flower heads, all that was left of the floral tribute Mary Bartlett had laid on Meshac's grave. No one had been to tend it since that day.

Kneeling on the soft earth she felt the tears rise in her throat. He had loved her so much and she had loved him, always so happy to see him home, wildly delighted whenever he said she could accompany him to the workshops.

'What happened, Father?' she whispered. 'What went wrong? We were so happy until . . .'

Her words hung on the silence. She had been happy until *he* made an appearance; until day after day she found herself making excuses to be away from the house in case *he* should call, in case she had to meet Ryder Tempal.

But her mother had always been so ready to welcome the man into their home, and even when she had discovered him trying to rape her daughter, it had not been him she had blamed, not Ryder Tempal who had been sent away, enclosed in a religious order, not visited once in four years!

'You could not have known, Father.' She touched a hand to the moist earth warmed by the sun. 'I am sure you knew nothing of where I was. You would not have left me there, you would have come for me.'

Beyond the wall surrounding the church Bethesda Lazic watched the kneeling girl lay a posy of blue cornflowers and scarlet poppies on a grass-covered grave. She did not need to read the headstone to know who lay buried there, even had she the skill of letters, which she had not; nor did she need to see the face of the girl to know it was the same one who had ridden with her and her son on the wagon.

The girl had not spurned the hand of the gypsy, she had not turned her back on them as did most folk, she had not treated them worse than a man would treat his animals. Her own hand brown and gnarled as a dead twig, Bethesda gripped the shawl she had half filled with wild herbs and plants as the sight rushed in upon her, pushing the blood through her veins, pounding into her head, washing her mind clear until no other thought stood in its path and she was left staring at pictures no mortal eye could see.

A brick-built house stood tall and square atop a rise in the ground. To one side the heath was pocked with the marks of coal pits; to the other it fused with fields of waving corn, the gold rippling to the edge of a town sprawled at the foot of the hill. As she watched, a man with hair the colour of the corn called to a young ragged boy, taking something from his pocket, holding it towards the child, smiling as he enticed the lad to him. With her inner eyes Bethesda peered at the man's outstretched hand, at what he held towards the boy. It was a letter. She was looking at a letter. Then the boy was running away up the hill like a startled hare and Bethesda saw a girl, in the dress of a servant maid, come from the house towards him.

She leaned heavily against the curtain wall of the church, almost drained of strength as the sight left her. It had been stronger this season, stronger than at any time since the blinding of her son. The time was near and drawing ever nearer, the time of vengeance, and in her soul of souls she knew the girl kneeling at that graveside would play a part in it.

Taking the withered flowers, Carys carried them around to the back of the building, to where she knew from childhood the groundsman kept his compost heap. Returning, she stood a moment more beside her father's grave then turned for the gate. Seeing Bethesda, she smiled and quickened her step.

'You be paying your respects.' Bethesda nodded as Carys came to her. 'That be good. The young should respect the old, whether they be living or dead. That one there,' she flicked a sideways glance in the direction of Meshac's grave, 'be it the same one you spoke of when you rode the wagon?'

Carys glanced behind her to where the blue and scarlet posy nestled in the green grass. 'Yes,' she said softly, 'my father.' When she turned back her eyes were filmed with tears.

'It be 'ard.' Bethesda saw the grief in the girl's eyes and knew they must hold more yet. 'Losin' the ones you love never be easy, and them you love most hurts worst of all. But we gets over it, we lives on.'

But there were some griefs you never got over. Bethesda turned away from the church, crossing the road to reach the heath on the far side. There were some griefs too powerful to forget, too powerful to heal. Grief like the losing of an eye, like the losing of grandchildren who were never to be born.

'Is your son well, ma'am?'

Beneath her bony frame Bethesda's heart warmed. She had never been addressed as 'ma'am', not once in all her life. Not even by the villagers who came to her with their ailments of body or heart, asking for her cures and potions. They paid her in kind or with a penny but never with the word this young woman had chosen to speak.

''E be well.' She smiled, exposing a gapped line of tobacco-browned teeth. 'Be you tied to returning 'ome straightaways?'

'I have until six this evening, then I must be back at Ridge House.'

'Be that a tall square house atop the rise as you leaves Wednesbury, on t'other side from this?'

'Hill Top,' Carys answered. 'Ridge House stands just on the crest.'

'We ain't never camped thereabouts, but I knows it.'

Bethesda remembered the house the sight had shown her. 'I work as a housemaid there.'

The sight had not shown her wrong. Bethesda felt her pulse quicken. This was the girl she had seen, in white cap and apron over dark skirts: the uniform of a servant girl.

'And would a housemaid take a drink o' tay with a gypsy woman, or be 'er too grand for that?'

'I can't speak for any housemaid,' Carys smiled, 'but for myself I would enjoy a cup of tea.'

'Come you with me then, and welcome.' She looked sharply at Carys as the girl took the shawl from her but said no word. Theirs would be a binding, a coming together in a friendship that would need no words. Theirs were lives that had been linked together by powers stronger than theirs.

Reaching the caravan set beneath the fringe of trees, Bethesda saw the younger woman's eyes turn towards the pool of dark shining water. It held memories, she knew, and a promise she did not yet understand.

Taking the shawl from Carys, she carried it up the steps into the caravan, emerging with a small wooden box held in her hands. Setting it beside the stool, she reached for the tin kettle, black from the smoke of many fires.

'Settle yourself, girl.' She nodded towards a log Caine had placed beside the ring of ash that marked the cooking fire. 'I'll fill this from the barrel and set it to boil. Won't take not five minutes to brew a dish o' tay.'

'Let me do it.' Carys reached for the kettle.

'Nay, girl.' Bethesda shook her head. 'Though you can be fetching pots from the wagon, should you have a mind.'

She turned away, leaving Carys to climb the few steps into the caravan. Inside she stared at the neatness of it. At the far end was a narrow bed, the base of it a line of beautifully carved cupboards. The bed, covered with a quilt of bright yellow that was echoed by the curtains of the bowed window, its tiny alcove set around with deeply carved edge, folded back from which was a pair of painted wooden doors. From the wooden roof a candle lamp hung on a length of chain, while along the sides were more cupboards and a huge, heavily carved chest.

Carys stared around her, feeling herself almost clothed in warmth and light. The little room was sparkling clean and bathed in colour, a place that shouted a welcome.

'Cups be in the cupboard a'side of the stove,' Bethesda's voice floated in to her.

'I never dreamed a gypsy caravan would be so pretty. Are they all as beautiful as this?'

Bethesda took the cups from Carys, pursing her lips and blowing into each to chase away imaginary specks of dust. 'What thought you they would be like?'

'I really had no idea.' Carys's cheeks took on a pinkish tinge as she met the piercing gleam of the gypsy woman's eyes. 'I sometimes saw gypsy caravans pass across the heath when I went with my father to Bilston and I wondered what the insides were like, but I never imagined them to be as beautiful as this.'

'Arrh, they be beautiful.' Bethesda placed the cups on a flat stone. 'And every one be different.'

'Different, how?'

'They all be built each by their own man, and each man holds his own ideas as to the decorating of what he makes.'

'You mean every gypsy builds their own caravan!' Carys asked, surprised.

'Every gypsy man do, and it be painted by his own hand. Together with the making of the bed and all it holds, 'cept for curtains and bedding. That be the charge of the woman he takes to wife.'

'Did your husband build this one?'

''Ave I not said already that that be so?'

'But surely your son will have no need of doing so? Your caravan will be his after you.'

Spooning tea into the cups from the box beside the stool, Bethesda poured boiling water over it. Then from the caravan she fetched a china jug covered with a linen cover, and a tiny matching lidded dish.

'My son will not be taking the wagon when I die. No true Romany takes the wagon of another. When I pass from this world, the wagon and all that is mine will pass along of me.'

'Do you mean the caravan will be broken up and buried?'

Adding milk to the cups, the gypsy woman handed one to Carys, pointing to the lidded dish.

'There be sugar for the taking.' And as Carys spooned some into her own cup, added: 'The wagon will not be buried and nor will I. It will be burned to ashes with my body inside it.'

Carys looked at the prettily painted wagon. So much artistry and care, so many years of love, to be burned away. Finishing her tea, she thanked Bethesda for her hospitality then set off, following the line of the Holyhead Road where it led towards Hill Top.

Cramming tobacco into her briar pipe, Bethesda held a burning stick to the bowl, sucking hard on the stem, coaxing the cheap tobacco to burn. Throwing the stick back into the flames, she stared through the lavender haze of smoke, watching the young woman growing smaller with distance and feeling a knot of apprehension, almost of fear, tighten her stomach.

'You be in danger, child,' she whispered. 'You be in mortal danger.'

In the parlour of the little house he rented, Ryder Tempal fumed over having to write that letter. Why him? he had wondered as he rode from Holyhead House. Why could not Maria have written it? But he knew her insistence had been because to have him write it would increase her hold over him. Brandishing her money in his face at every opportunity was not enough for Maria; she wanted him bound to her with stronger fetters, wanted him tied by fear of the hangman's rope. Well, they would play things her way, but not forever. One day the tide would turn in his favour, then Maria Beddows would dance to his tune.

Laying the gloves he had fetched from his dressing room beside ink, pen and paper he had already arranged on the small writing desk, he turned and locked the door. His cleaning woman had left but he would take no risk of anyone walking in on him.

Next he took a small piece of newspaper and rolled it to a cone. Slipping on a pair of the gloves, he held the cone over the bottle and tipped a little of the white powder into it, watching it trickle into the ink. Laying the cone aside on a piece of cloth torn from a shirt, he recorked the ink, shaking the bottle to absorb the powder. Maria had been right when she said it left no trace. He had soaked some into a sheet of writing paper and it had dried without stain or odour.

Reaching now for the sheet of notepaper set aside on the cloth, he uncorked the ink and began to write. He had thought long over the wording. It would be better were it to appear to have been written by some boy overcome by infatuation, someone who lacked the finer skills of writing.

'*To the most beu . . .*'

He crossed the last word through with a thin line as though unsure of its spelling and carried on.

> *. . . lovely Girl I knOw,*
>
> *I see Your smile in the Morning sunlight and Hear Your sigh on the eVening breeze. I feel the touch of your hair in the Mists from the HeaTh and hear the sounD of Your voice in the Song of the skyLark. My heArt is happY when I see you but When you do not come it is a Stone, heavy in my Chest. I Watch for You in the Town and When you come Your smile fills mY daY with happiness.*
>
> *your adMirer*

211

Folding the letter, he removed the gloves, putting them aside on the cloth and slipping on the fresh pair. Looking at the folded note, he hesitated. Were this oxide as powerful as Maria seemed to think, then a little extra precaution would not go amiss. Tearing another small piece from the shirt, he used it to pick up the folded letter and place it in the envelope. Pressing the same scrap of shirt on to the wet sponge he used for sealing letters, he applied it to the envelope. Then using his usual pen and ink he wrote upon it:

To the Girl wiTh prEtty haiR

That would be enough. It must seem her admirer did not even know her name. Leaving his regular pen and ink in their usual place on the writing desk, he gathered all the rest into the torn shirt, glancing around several times in order to ensure that nothing had fallen to the floor or been forgotten in any way. Satisfied he had overlooked nothing, he placed the letter in his pocket. The rest would fit easily into a saddle-bag which would not give rise to speculation should anyone see him riding on the heath.

Clearing Paul Street, leaving behind the last of the straggle of cottages, he guided his mount past the Blue Fly coalmine, crossing over newly constructed Hydes Lane on to the heath. He kept to the trackways worn into the earth, knowing the fields about Mesty Croft to be riddled with worked out mines, not all of their shafts having the precaution of a cover.

The saddle-bag containing the deadly powder and materials he had used to write the letter jogged against his knee with the movement of the horse. Ryder glanced at it. He would feel more comfortable once he had disposed of it, but could not risk doing so here. To do so would be to risk being seen by men coming and going from the mine. He would wait. Five minutes further across the heath he would pass Burr's Cottage and beyond there the disused Traveller's Rest pit. He smiled at the irony of the name.

There would have been no rest for any man there, traveller or otherwise.

Urging the animal forward, he followed the way towards Ridge House. In a few months a new century, would begin and with it a new life for Ryder Tempal.

From the vantage point of horseback he stared across acres of flat heathland. Satisfied he was alone, he dismounted, taking the saddle-bag. The ground about him was littered with black patches marking the earth like open sores, the scars of endless numbers of gin pits each discarded for a new one when the coal seam ran too deep for a man to work alone.

Watching the ground carefully, he picked his way to where a hole gaped in the covering scrub. Peering into it, he could see no bottom. That would be sunk at least a hundred feet into the earth, and if he dropped a few clumps of gorse into it no one would guess a saddle-bag lay hidden underneath.

Giving a swift, cautionary glance all around, he dropped the bag into the shaft. Then pulling up several small bushes of gorse and fern he sent them following after.

The evidence was gone, lost altogether. Soon it would be the same for Carys Beddows.

Riding on, skirting the hedges where the heath gave way to fields of corn, he came to a hump-backed bridge that crossed the Tame Valley canal. A little way beyond a boy sat on the towpath dangling a stick with a string attached into the water. Halting the horse Ryder watched the boy for several moments before calling to him. The lad turned his head but did not move.

'Would you like to earn sixpence?' Ryder smiled pleasantly.

'Depends on what I 'aves to do for it?'

'Take a message to Hill Top. Do you know Hill Top?'

'Arrh, mister.' The boy watched Ryder through wide, intelligent eyes. 'I knows it.'

'Then perhaps you know Ridge House?'

The boy nodded. 'Big house. On the crest.'

'That is the one.' Ryder smiled again. 'I have a letter I wish to be delivered there but I find myself late for an appointment. Take it for me and I will pay you sixpence.'

Maria had said he was to take the letter personally, but then how was she to know he had not? If he were not the one to give it to Carys then there was even less chance of his being implicated in her death, should the cause ever be discovered.

'Do I get the tanner now, or do I 'ave to fetch it from you later?'

'I shall not be at home for several days.' Ryder congratulated himself on the ease with which the lies tripped from his tongue. But then, he had always been peculiarly well accomplished in that art. 'That being so, I shall pay you the sixpence now.'

Reaching into the pocket of his velvet waistcoat, he drew out a small silver coin, tossing it in the air, letting the sunlight glint enticingly on the metal before catching it in his palm.

'Well, lad, do you take my letter or not?'

'Arrh, mister.' The boy scrambled to his feet, stick and string forgotten. 'I'll take it for yer.'

Removing the letter from the side pocket of his coat, Ryder held it as the boy came up to him.

'I do not want this delivered to the front door. You are to ask for the housemaid and give this letter to her. It is very private and must be given to no one else, do you understand?'

''Course I does, mister, I ain't no fool. You wants that there letter given into the 'ands of the 'ousemaid and nobody else. Ain't nothing to understand in that.'

'Then see to it you give it to her and her only,' Ryder cautioned again.

'Be it for your lady friend?'

'That is none of your business.'

'I thought as much.' The lad grinned cheekily. 'A love letter. In that case, mister, I shall carry it next to my 'eart.'

'And my hand next to your ear, if you go on like that.' Ryder remained good-humoured; he did not want the boy to back out, leaving him with the distasteful task of carrying a letter to the servants' entrance of Ridge House.

'Only pulling your leg, mister.' The boy held out a hand for the letter.

'Now you are certain you know the house?'

'Ridge House,' the boy said, emphasising the words. 'A red-brick house. It stands on the crest of Hill Top. I am to give your letter to the 'ousemaid there and to 'er only. Satisfied, mister?'

Giving the boy the letter, Ryder watched as he stuffed it beneath a shirt that lacked several buttons.

'My tanner, mister.' The letter tucked away, the boy held out his hand for payment.

'I shall expect an answer to that letter tomorrow.' Tossing the sixpence, Ryder watched the boy's grubby fist close over it. 'So make sure you deliver it or it will be much the worse for you.'

'Billy Aston be no thief, mister.' The grin that had transformed the young face faded, replaced by a look as hard and challenging as any fully grown man might assume. 'If you ain't got no trust in me, then yer takes yer money back now.' He held his open palm towards Ryder, the sixpenny piece gleaming in the sunlight. 'A bargain be a bargain, and once made Billy Aston don't be the one to break it.'

'Then we have a bargain, Billy Aston.'

Touching his heels to the sides of the horse, Ryder turned in the direction he had come. How long? he thought spurring his mount to a canter. How long would it take that powder to do its work? How long before Meshac Beddows's child departed this earth and how long before her money became his?

Chapter Fifteen

'Carys.' Alice glanced behind her to where Mrs Bates sat reading yesterday's newspaper sent down from the mistress's sitting room. 'When you goes to that cemetery to visit your father's grave, you goes through Wednesbury, don't you?'

'Of course.' Carys selected another of the carrots she had washed in the scullery and began to slice it into thin narrow strips.

'Do you go straight up along the Holyhead Road or do you follow the old Bilston Road?'

'The Holyhead, it's more direct. Why do you ask?'

'No reason.' Alice shrugged.

'There be a basket of early potatoes beside the sink in the scullery.' Mrs Bates turned the page, shaking the newspaper into manageable folds. 'The mistress will enjoy them with a little parsley butter. You can scrape them when you be finished doin' them green beans.'

'I'll get them now. Beans be finished.'

''Ave you got all the strings off them?'

'Yes, Mrs Bates.'

'You certain, Alice? You knows how mistress detests gettin' a piece of it hanging from one of them.'

'I took good care, Mrs Bates.' Alice flicked a smiling glance to Carys. 'I told you 'er would ask,' she mouthed silently, then coughed to cover the laughter that bubbled in her throat.

'I will help you carry them.' Her own mouth twitching with a suppressed giggle, Carys followed her friend into the scullery.

'Shh!' She touched a finger to her mouth as Alice laughed aloud.

'I told you.' Words and laughter muffled together behind her hand, Alice made a charade of peering over a newspaper. ''Ave you got all the strings off them beans?' she mimicked.

'We had better take those potatoes into the kitchen before Mrs Bates comes and catches you impersonating her.' The smile still around her mouth, Carys caught one of the handles of a round wicker basket.

''Ang on.' Alice rested a hand on the other handle but did not lift. 'Carys, can I ask you something.' She paused, the laughter gone. 'It be something personal.'

Looking into her face, Carys saw the faint blush gathering in the other girl's cheeks.

'I have no secrets I would not want to share with you, Alice. Ask me whatever you wish.'

At the word 'secret', Alice's blush deepened. Carys would share any with her but she had kept one from Carys. Only for a few hours but the length of time did not matter. She had kept it to herself and now the guilt of it weighed heavy. She should have told her the minute she returned from the cemetery.

'Carys,' she whispered, 'when you goes down into Wednesbury, do . . . do you meet an admirer?'

'A what?' Carys's eyes widened with surprise.

'You know, a man. Be there a man you think be sweet on you?'

'Alice, what on earth makes you think that?'

'I ain't just being nosy, Carys, honest I ain't, but I just had to ask. Believe me, I 'ave me reason.'

Releasing the handle of the basket, Carys straightened. 'I hardly ever go into the town,' she whispered. 'Once a month I go to Moxley, to the cemetery, but as for going to Wednesbury town, well, I am always with you. If there were a man sweet on me, you would know it as well as I. There is no one.'

No one other than Davey. She kept the thought to herself.

'Then it had to be for me.' Alice let out a long breath of relief.

'What did?'

'The letter.' She grinned, her guilt suddenly alleviated. 'A young lad brought it while you was out, said it were from a man and that he had to give it to the 'ousemaid at Ridge 'Ouse and to her alone. Nobody else were to get it. Brought it the back way, he did. I seen him over by the line of bushes farthest end of the garden and went to find out what he was doin', trespassing where he weren't supposed to be. That was when he give me the letter.'

'Did he not say who it was sent it?'

Alice shook her head, her fair curls bobbing beneath her starched cap. 'Just said it were from a man, then legged it as fast as if his backside was on fire.'

'What makes you think it might have been meant for me? The name on the envelope . . .'

'That be it,' Alice interrupted, 'there were no name on the envelope.'

Carys's brows drew together, a puzzled look evident in her eyes. 'Then if the envelope bore no name, how could you know it was intended for either of us?'

'That takes no reasoning.' The grin returned, wide and cheeky, to Alice's face. 'There be only two women in this 'ouse beside you and me, and I wouldn't describe either of them as being a girl.'

'Be you two going to take all afternoon on the fetching of a basket of potatoes?' Martha Bates called from the kitchen.

'Coming now, Mrs Bates.' Alice grabbed one handle of the basket. 'Tell you later,' she whispered as Carys took the other.

*　　*　　*

Draped in black tulle, Maria ignored the polite 'good day, ma'am' of the station porter holding the carriage door open for her to alight from the train. She had thought not to make this journey again, not to frequent another of the seedy back-street hotels of Birmingham, but as yet there was no other way of meeting Ryder Tempal. It was too risky having him in her bed at Holyhead House, so for the present it was this or nothing, and she was definitely not ready to accept it be nothing.

Emerging from Snow Hill station she signalled a hansom, holding out a slip of paper to the driver.

'I knows where that be.' Alighting, the man held a hand to Maria's elbow, assisting her into the cab. 'Be no more'n a five-minute ride, ma'am.'

Maria nodded as the door closed on her and the man resumed his position, clucking to the horse to set away.

Following along the busy Colmore Row, Maria looked out at the imposing Regency buildings of the Great Western and the Union Hotels, with their uniformed doormen and chandeliered reception halls, and her resolve hardened. As soon as was possible she would frequent those places, do the things Meshac had never wanted to do. Meet as many young men as she liked, and have her pleasures wherever the fancy took her.

''Ere we be, ma'am. Queen's 'otel.' The cabman waited while Maria took a florin from her purse. 'Place be named for its keeper,' he grinned, showing grimy teeth. 'Queenie Meers. Ain't no palace 'er be runnin' 'ere, though. Be you sure it be this place you be wanting? A lady like yourself would be better off in the Great Western, if you don't mind me saying so like. There can be some unpleasant characters gets to Needless Alley.'

'I shall be here less than half an hour.' Maria held out the florin.

'Then p'raps you will be wanting me to wait?'

'No.' She turned towards the doorway of the rundown building. She had no wish to stand here where she might be seen, though the chance of anyone she knew being in this Godforsaken part of the city were thankfully slight. 'I shall not require you to wait.'

'Your change, ma'am.' The man selected a coin from a handful drawn from the pocket of his greasy coat. 'It be a shilling ride from Snow Hill.'

'You may keep it.' Gathering her skirts, Maria swept into the hotel. Needless Alley! She glanced at the drab walls and faded carpet. Only when a man was dead could he need less than this place furnished.

'Did you *have* to choose such a down and out dump!' She stared angrily about the room Ryder had booked.

'Perhaps you would prefer me to take a room at the Grand, or maybe the Excelsior?' He smiled scathingly. 'You would have stood an excellent chance of being recognised by any number of your late husband's acquaintances in either of those places, they are very popular with businessmen.'

Snatching off her hat and veil, Maria threw them on to a marble-topped dressing table. To stay here would only increase his hold over her but to leave would be to add to the frustration that nights spent alone had built in her. She would take what she wanted quickly and then go. At least, she thought, turning toward him, there would not be the awful smell drifting across from the fish market – a smell that had perfumed the hotel behind the Bull Ring.

'Why waste time talking about the hotel?' He came to her, his mouth descending on hers, fingers already loosening the buttons of her jacket. He had to make this good if he hoped to get the money he needed. 'There are many things I would rather do with you than talk.'

Shrugging out of her jacket, Maria parted her lips as it fell to the floor, her blood already rising as his tongue probed her mouth. One by one he removed her clothes, each movement of his hands accompanied by kisses to her lips and eyelids. Then, as she stood naked, he slipped agilely out of his own.

221

Maria let her eyes rove over his body: the tight thighs and waist rising to a well-muscled chest. Ryder Tempal kept himself in good condition.

Standing for a few moments he saw the approval flash in her eyes and her lips part in anticipation. Maria Beddows liked what he had so let her view the goods. He intended she should pay for them. Stepping close, he pulled the pins that held the thick swathes of her dark hair, letting it tumble like black velvet about her shoulders. Holding her face between his hands, he stared into eyes already smouldering with desire. Yes, Maria would pay.

'Soon we will spend every afternoon like this.'

Beneath him she sucked in her breath as he pushed into her. 'We will make love as often as we wish. And that will be often, my love, very often.'

Waves of desire riding high in her, Maria could only moan as she clamped both hands to his buttocks, drawing him further into her as she lifted her body to his, riding each thrust of his hips.

Twisting his hands in her hair, he dragged upward, forcing himself further into her. Then his breath became a long agonised gasp as desire spent itself. But her own body exploding with his, Maria was oblivious to the pain inflicted by him.

'Did you write that letter?'

Passion spent she lay beside him, her eyes on the smoke-stained ceiling.

Ryder kept his eyes closed. He could so easily prevent what he knew to be coming. He had only to roll his body on to hers and she would forget the letter. But what was not answered now would have to be answered later, and later he could give her his body to more effect, to satisfy both her need and his wants.

'Yes, I wrote it.'

'And you delivered it yourself?'

Reaching for his coat, Ryder took out a slim gold case, a

present from a former paramour. There would be others, he thought, extracting a slim brown cheroot, both presents and lovers. Maria was merely one of a line, and even when she became his wife that line would continue. Choosing a match from a box thoughtfully placed beside the bed, the one convenience other than the saucer presumably put to serve as an ashtray which the room offered, he lit the cigar, inhaling deeply before answering drily: 'I delivered it myself.'

Allowing smoke to trickle from between his lips, he folded one arm beneath his head.

'Did she say anything?'

'I gave her no time.' He drew on the cheroot, expelling the smoke in a grey stream that spread like a veil before floating upward.

'But she recognised you?' Maria propped herself on her elbow, looking down at his face. 'She must have done.'

'People change in four years,' he answered.

'You have not.' Maria thought of the possibility of his having been seen on his way to Hill Top. He was not unknown in Wednesbury, a number of people could have recognised him. One of them just might wonder what had taken him to the home of Virginia Mountford.

'I made pretence of wiping my face with my handkerchief. I threw the letter to the ground as she came towards me, and was gone before she had a chance to get a proper look at me.'

He blew a fresh stream of smoke. She would never know the story was a lie, and he would never enlighten her.

'You are sure it was Carys? It could not have been any-one else?'

Laying the cheroot in the saucer that stood beside the match box, he turned to Maria, pushing her gently back to the mattress.

'There was no one else in sight. I watched from a safe distance. She picked up the letter and put it in her pocket.'

Lifting her arms to his shoulders, Maria smiled. It should

be over within days. The amount of thallium the paper had absorbed was not as great as that which could have been added to food or drink. That being so it would take longer to achieve its results, but those results would be equally deadly. In a few days the threat of losing Meshac's money and Ryder Tempal would be gone.

'What did you write in the letter?'

'Never you mind.' He bent his head, pressing his mouth to her throat. 'It was nothing like this.' Trailing his mouth to her breast, he tongued her nipple, drawing it erect. 'Or this.' Coursing his mouth languidly over her body, he pressed a line of kisses down over her stomach to the crop of dark hair at its base. 'Or this.' Pushing her legs apart, he rolled on to her.

Feeling the hardness of him drive into her, Maria gave herself up completely to the pleasure of the moment. From now on there would be nothing but pleasure for Maria Beddows.

'Be you feeling poorly, girl?' Martha Bates cast a glance at Alice's untouched plate. 'It don't be like you to leave your food.'

'I'm all right, just a bit tired.'

'That ain't like you neither, you ain't never said you was tired afore. I 'opes you two ain't been sitting up nattering half the night?'

Carys met the housekeeper's accusing stare. 'No, Mrs Bates, we did not talk at all last night, Alice went straight to her own room.'

'Hmm!' Martha rose from the table, touching a hand to Alice's brow. 'Don't seem to have no fever,' she said after a moment, 'skin be cool enough. Be there a pain any-where?'

'Some.' Alice touched a hand to her stomach.

''Ave you been at them gooseberries?' Martha crossed to a cupboard, unlocking it with a key taken from the drawer of a chest that stood beneath it.

'I ain't never touched a single one.' Alice groaned as a fresh twinge of pain caught her.

'Then what could 'ave given you the gripe? Can't be nothing I've cooked or we would all be feeling bad.'

'Alice was in the town yesterday.' Carys went to stand beside the other girl. 'Do you think she could have picked something up from there?'

Taking a spoon from the drawer of the kitchen table, Martha measured a dose of rich-looking brown liquid from the bottle she had extracted from the cupboard.

'It wouldn't surprise me. There always seems to be some illness or another rife in that place. Ain't been but a few years since the cholera took half the town.'

Carys's eyes widened with fear. She remembered the sisters at the convent, how they had worked constantly throughout the cholera epidemic that had swept the surrounding area of Bordesly, tending the sick and comforting the dying. But most of all she remembered the fear in each woman's eyes – fear that she might be the next to be touched by the sickness. And then Sister Luke had fallen sick. For almost a week she lay quarantined in the infirmary tended by two of the sisters, each of them excused attendance at services. The novices had been told this was due to the long hours of nursing but they had known it was a way of reducing risk to the convent. But all the nursing, and all the long hours of prayer, had not saved Sister Luke, nor one of the nuns who had cared for her.

'Don't look so frightened, wench.' Martha held the spoonful of liquid to Alice's mouth. 'There don't be nothing serious amiss. Like as not it be coming up to that time of the month. Some girls suffers quite a bit of pain before the flow starts. You get this drop of Indian Brandy into you and then get you up to bed. Come morning you'll be right as ninepence.'

Alice's chair scraped on the quarry tiles, her shoulder sending spoon and medicine flying from Martha's hand as she fled out through the scullery.

'I ain't never known the wench's time to cause her to be

sick, not never once.' Reaching for a cloth draped over the drying line above the range, Martha dabbed at the drops of brown liquid splashed across the front of her apron. 'We best get her to bed and if 'er be no better come the morning, I'll ask the mistress to send for the doctor.'

An hour later Carys looked at the girl whose face was almost as white as the pillow she lay on. 'Where did you call yesterday when you went into town?'

'Just to the butcher.' Alice smiled wanly. 'I didn't 'ave the time to go visiting nowhere else, not even me mother's. And don't go saying I picked up something nasty from Frank White's butcher's shop, not unless you wants to be the next lump of meat laid out on his block!'

'And you were telling the truth when you said you had not been eating gooseberries from the garden?'

'I hates goosegogs!' Alice grimaced. ''Ave done ever since I was a little kid, ask me mother.'

'Then what?' Carys sat on the side of the bed, the concern she felt still obvious on her face. 'What is causing a pain in your stomach and making you feel sick?'

'Whatever it was, I feels better now. Carys,' Alice glanced towards the door Martha Bates had closed when leaving the bedroom, 'about the letter . . .'

'Letter?' She had forgotten.

'Yes, you remember, the letter that young lad brought this afternoon. I told you about it, in the scullery.'

The tiny frown that had gathered between her eyes cleared as memory brought their conversation flooding back and Carys nodded. 'I remember. But you don't want to talk about that now.'

'Oh, but I do!' Alice loosed the top button of her nightgown, taking out the folded sheet of paper she had worn next to her breast since first reading it. 'You remember I said there was no name on the envelope?'

'Not now, Alice. You should get some sleep. We can talk about your letter tomorrow.'

'Carys Beddows, you be getting as bossy as Martha Bates, telling me what I should and shouldn't be doing!' Alice snapped as a spasm of pain shot through her stomach.

'I'm sorry. Concern caused me to forget my manners.' Carys felt it deepen at the uncharacteristic behaviour of her friend.

'I . . . I'm sorry an' all.' Alice gritted her teeth against the pain. 'But I . . . I 'ave to tell you.'

'I will only listen if you promise to go straight to sleep afterwards?'

'Promise.' The semblance of a grin passed over the girl's mouth. 'That envelope,' the smile faded, 'it bore no name. It had the words "To the girl with the pretty hair" wrote across it, and the lad said quite definite 'e had been told to give it into the hands of the 'ousemaid.'

'I see no mystery there. You are a housemaid and you do have very pretty hair.'

'But I ain't the only one. *You* be a 'ousemaid and *you* 'ave lovely hair. Don't you see? That letter could be for you same as it could be for me. I shouldn't 'ave opened it the way I did, I should 'ave waited and shown it to you first.'

'Nonsense.' Carys touched the other girl's hand. 'I have no one who would write me a letter. It was intended for you, there can be no doubt of that. Now what about keeping your promise and going to sleep?'

'I did promise, didn't I?' Alice's eyes gleamed briefly. 'But you said to do it when I had finished talking about the letter and I ain't got to that yet. I've only spoken about the envelope.'

'Alice Withers, you are a crafty madam.' Carys smiled at the return of Alice's humour.

'So me mother is always telling me. 'Er says that one day me tongue will be so sharp it'll cut me own throat.'

'Then why not give it a rest, at least until morning?'

'Cos if it don't get some exercise it'll flap about in me head all night. Here.' She thrust the paper toward Carys. 'Read it and see if you recognises who might 'ave wrote that.'

'I most certainly will not read it!' Carys withdrew the hand covering Alice's. 'That letter was written to you. Whoever has sent it does not want its contents divulged to another.'

'It be a love letter.' Alice pressed the paper to her throat.

'All the more reason for it to remain private. The words are for you Alice, no one else.'

'It be the first I've ever had, the very first in my whole life, but I don't know who sent it. Why do you think there be no name signed to it? If a man truly feels for a woman, so much that he writes 'er a love letter, then why don't he put his name to it? Why do you think that be, Carys?'

'A man can sometimes be as shy as a woman. He does not know if you will welcome his attentions or be annoyed by them. If you spurn him then it is obvious he would be as embarrassed as he was sad. Leaving his letter unsigned could be his way of protecting his pride.'

'How can I welcome his attentions or otherwise when I don't be knowing who he is?'

'You will.' Carys stood up. 'He will write again, I am sure of it, and next time he will sign his name.'

'Ee, I wonder who it be! Maybe it's Albie Fletcher, I caught him staring in church last Sunday. He turned red right up to his ears when I smiled at him.'

'I should think so too, you saucy thing!' Carys bent to kiss the girl's brow. 'Now if you wish to be in church this Sunday, I suggest you keep your promise and get to sleep.'

'Leave the candle,' Alice said as Carys made to blow it out.

'You've got the pain again?' The worry that had not left Carys since her friend ran from the house to be sick in the privy deepened. 'I shall stay with you tonight.'

'There be no need of that.' Alice smiled weakly. 'I ain't got that pain, I just wants to read my letter one more time.'

'One more time and then sleep. Mrs Bates is sure to look in on you before she retires, and if she catches you reading then your letter will finish up in the fire.' At the door Carys turned to look at the girl in the bed, the girl who had befriended her when her own mother had turned her back. And suddenly a finger of cold fear touched her spine.

Watching the door close, Alice opened the letter, pressing its words to her lips.

'You say the girl was taken poorly yesterday?'

Virginia Mountford looked at her housekeeper. Martha Bates was not one to worry unduly. 'Have you dosed her?'

'I tried to, ma'am. 'Er didn't touch her supper and when 'er showed signs of the gripe, I tried to give her a spoonful of Indian Brandy but 'er vomited afore I could get it into 'er.'

'And you say she is no better this morning?'

'Alice ain't no better, ma'am. In fact, it be my opinion the girl be worse.'

'I will come at once.'

'Begging your pardon, I don't think as that be wise. There be signs of sweating. It . . . it could be fever. I thinks it would be best for you not to go near.'

'The girl is my responsibility.' Virginia Mountford's mouth set in a determined line. 'So long as she is under my roof she will remain so. But what of the other, does she display any symptoms?'

'No, ma'am.' Martha shook her head. 'Carys don't be showing no sign of sickness.'

'And you?'

'No, nor Enoch Fletcher nor the lad who helps out with the gardens neither. Seems to be only Alice be poorly.'

'Then it is likely nothing she has eaten, unless of course she has been in the fruit garden.'

'Says 'er ain't, and Alice be no girl to lie.'

'Then why the pain? You said she was griped?'

'So 'er was, and still be.' Martha followed her mistress along the servants' landing. 'But that could most likely be the girl's monthly, it can sometimes be painful. What be most worrying is 'er asking to be sent home.'

'Sent home!' Virginia's hand halted on the door knob of Alice's room.

'Yes, ma'am.' Martha's face held a worried look. 'When I went in to her this morning, 'er asked to go 'ome. Seems the girl wants her mother.'

'Please, ma'am.' Alice's eyes were ringed by dark pools, their pupils dilated, and her face was bathed in perspiration. 'If it be all right with you, I would like to go 'ome to me mother.'

'I think we should first have the doctor to examine you, Alice.'

'I don't want no doctor, thanking you all the same.' She clamped her teeth, waiting for the spasm of pain that twisted her insides to pass. 'Me mother will know what to do. Me mother always knows what to do.'

'I really think we should keep her here.' Virginia turned to her housekeeper. 'I fear, as you do, she could have a touch of fever. To allow her to leave could worsen things. She needs a doctor and I doubt she will get the proper attention at home.'

'You need 'ave no fears on that score. Letty Withers be a good mother and caring of 'er children. The doctor will be sent for and 'e will go, even if them sons of 'ers 'ave to carry him there.'

Virginia glanced again at the girl. Her eyes, dark with pain, seemed to fill her pale face, and hair damp with perspiration clung to her face. 'Alice, my dear,' she said gently, 'do you really wish to go home today? Would it not be better for you to stay here . . .'

'I want to be with me mother,' Alice intervened, eyes brimming with tears. 'Me mother will get me well, I know 'er will.'

'Very well, my child. If you wish to return home then of course you must go, but I shall insist the doctor be called.' She turned to Martha. 'Make sure she wraps up warmly. I will give instructions to Enoch to drive her to her mother's house. Call me, please, when she is ready to leave.'

'Will she be all right?' Carys shaded her eyes, watching the carriage with Alice inside it, round the bend of the drive and out of sight.

''Course 'er will.' Martha turned back indoors. 'The mistress give me two sovereigns to send to her mother, enough to pay a doctor's bill and more beside. 'Er said there was more should it be needed, and that I was to keep 'er well informed of Alice's progress.'

'Can I go to visit her this evening?'

'Best give the wench time.' Martha gave a negative shake of her head. 'A couple of days will be soon enough for that. Letty Withers has enough bodies under her feet in that house without you adding another. Leave Alice to her mother, that be the best help we can give. A mother's love be the strongest cure of all. Two days, that be all it'll take, two days and it'll all be over.'

Following Martha into the house, Carys once more felt the icy touch of fear upon her spine.

Chapter Sixteen

Caine took a rabbit from the snare then reset it, covering it loosely with bracken and ferns. The rabbit had died quick and clean, he thought, picking it up and fastening it on a string about his waist. Not for animals in the wild the agony of living a half life, a life with half a face. Not like him, Caine Lazic, scarred and blinded by a woman.

He had been so sure. It was a short time only since the blood in him had told him this would be the year he would drink the sweet wine of revenge. And now? He walked to the edge of the flooded mine shaft and stood staring into the ebony water. Now he was not sure. The certainty had left him, leaving his mind like an open sore, festering with thoughts of what might be, what should be.

Had his Romany blood told him wrong? Was this to be another year of frustration, one more year he would leave Wednesbury with the aloes of disappointment bitter on his tongue?

On the surface of the black water a woman dressed in velvet the colour of moss rushed towards a boy who stroked his hand along the soft brown flank of her mare. The woman's arm was raised, and as the boy turned it came down, bringing a whip hard across his face.

Kicking viciously at the loose earth, Caine sent a shower of earth into the pool and the picture dispersed with the ripples. Turning away, he stared into the distance. He had dispersed the vision memory had recreated, but he had not destroyed it. It was there still, deep within him, waiting to rise again, to torment him as it had for sixteen years. No, it was not destroyed, nor would it be until that woman was destroyed. An eye for an eye? For Caine Lazic that would not be enough. He wanted more, much more.

From the steps of the caravan, sheltered by the fringe of trees, Bethesda watched her son turn away from the pool and knew the thoughts that twisted his mind, as that woman's whip had twisted his face.

'Was the snare full?' Removing the briar pipe from between her teeth, she spat on the ground, spitting in the face of the evil that dogged her son.

'It was full.' Caine removed the rabbit from the string, dropping it at his mother's feet. 'It will feed the two of us well.'

She descended the two remaining steps of the caravan and picked up the plump rabbit. 'That it will, and some left for the morrow.'

'We move on tomorrow.'

Bethesda showed no surprise. Placing the rabbit in a box strung to the side of the wagon, she returned to the fire. 'There be tay should you be ready, and a bit o' bacon I got for a mixture o' herbs.'

'Bacon will be well.' Taking a large enamel cup, Caine carried it to the log, nursing it between his hands as his mother cooked bacon in a smoke-blackened pan.

'I'd thought to camp here through the summer,' he said, accepting the tin plate criss-crossed with strips of well-fried bacon. 'But the rabbiting be poor and the stream holds few fish.'

'Where be you thinking to make for?' Bethesda refilled the ancient pipe.

'We will go the old way, up along the Sandwell Valley where we will camp for some days, and then down to Worcester for the winter.'

'Why come up 'ere along of Moxley then?'

Caine put the last of the bacon in his mouth, chewing and swallowing before he answered.

'I had thought to spend the winter out along Shrewsbury way, but it seems more practical to go where you be known. Not all villages welcome gypsies.'

'True.' Bethesda held a burning stick to the bowl of her pipe, sucking hard on the stem. 'There be many only too ready to set the dogs on the like o' we.'

'We'll have little trouble if we keep to our regular route.' Caine laid aside the tin plate, picking up the mug of tea. He was no coward. Taking new routes held no fear for him but Bethesda was getting old, she could do without the worry of snarling dogs and men set on breaking bones.

'There be many along of Smethwick and Netherton as well as Lickey End welcome my medicines.'

'That be so.' Caine drank from the mug. 'You saves folk a deal of pennies in doctor's takings, and your herbs often do them a sight more good. And the waters of Droitwich great pool will ease your own bones.'

'Arrh, they be good, the waters.' Bethesda blew a stream of smoke. 'But they will keep, and my bones will take no harm from the waiting of a week or two.'

'No sense in waiting!' Caine flung away the dregs of his tea, setting the mug down hard on the log. 'There be nothing for we here.'

'There be nothing here?' Bethesda watched him through the haze of tobacco smoke. 'Nothing but what you desire most, what your heart be crying out for, and that which will leave you no peace till it be settled. You don't be wanting to leave here for reasons of rabbiting or fish, you be wanting to be away because of what your mind be telling you.

'It says that this year will be the same as all the others, that

you will not taste vengeance. You are feared the blood that
runs in your veins has told you wrong when it said this was
the year. But that blood is of the Romany, it has surged in the
veins of your family for generations past and it speaks truth
to them as knows how to listen. My mother and hers afore
her had the sight that is given to few, and I carry the same
sight. It has never told me false, and it does not lie when it
says that before summer fades, you will make your reckoning.
The debt will be paid in full.'

Maria glanced at the packages beside her on the seat of the
small governess cart. She had enjoyed the choosing of the
materials they held: taffeta and chiffon, silk and lace, whose
colours had glowed like jewels against her skin. Wearing
black irritated her, it was a colour that gave her no pleasure.
She would have the beautiful cloth made into gowns and the
minute the mourning period was over she would burn every
stitch of black she possessed.

Stretching out a hand, she fondled the paper-wrapped cloth.
If only that time were now! And why not? Why not take the
materials to her dressmaker today? That way they would be
ready for her the moment she could wear them.

Guiding the cart along Union Street, she hesitated. The
house that Ryder rented was only a few minutes from here.
She could so easily call. Who was to guess the identity of a
woman sheathed so heavily in her mourning dress, and who
would guess the reason for her visit?

Calling softly to the horse she crossed the Five Ways and on
along Church Street. The Hawthorns stood a little way below
the parish church of Wednesbury.

Touching her hand to the door, her first tap sent it moving.
Ryder must speak to his staff! Maria stepped into the hall.
So this was what her money was paying for! She glanced
around. Well brushed carpet, furniture that gleamed. The
Hawthorns, it seemed, was not the drab little house Ryder
had said it was.

He had asked her for two hundred pounds before they had left that hotel in Needless Alley. The annual rent had to be paid, he said, or he would lose his tenancy. Two hundred! Maria glanced towards the staircase; a huge newel post carved and crowned with a miniature hawthorn bush stood at its base. Seemingly the place was worth the price.

About to cross to what she guessed would be a sitting room, Maria halted. Ryder's laughter rang out from a room above. She could call out to him, or go in search of a servant to announce her.

The laughter came again, lower this time, coming from the back of his throat in the way she had come to know so well. Gathering her skirts in her hands, she climbed the stairs, her tread soundless on thick Axminster. Following the sound of his voice, she turned along a corridor. Whoever he had with him he could get rid of. An hour or so of his love making would be an added fillip to her day.

'But, Ryder darling . . .'

Maria stood perfectly still. Ryder darling! Who would address him in such terms? He had no female kin; in fact, if he were to be believed, he had no relatives at all. If he were to be believed . . . Maria forced herself to remain calm even as once more the high-pitched voice floated to her.

'. . . we shouldn't, your housekeeper . . .'

'I have given her the day off,' Ryder's deeper tones answered. 'We are alone, my sweet.'

Alone! Maria moved in the direction of the sound. His housekeeper dismissed for the day. The front door not secured on the latch. The signs of the hasty admittance of someone whom he wished to remain unseen. Must the visitor remain unknown to any but Ryder? Why? Cold anger rose in her. There could be only one answer.

Now keeping her steps deliberately light, she moved to where she knew them to be, Ryder and his friend.

'Ryder, be patient, only naughty boys grab.' A high-pitched feminine laugh emanated through a doorway a little along the corridor. The door, Maria saw, had again been left open. Careless, she thought, walking quietly towards it.

'Open your mouth.' The voice, half laughing, half commanding, was followed by a moan, the sort of pleasured sound Maria was so very used to hearing.

'That's enough.' The laughter held a domineering tone. 'You must share. You will have more later but now it is my turn.'

Stepping to the open doorway, Maria looked in then stood immediately to one side, using the wall to hide her presence.

It was as she'd thought. The softer voice *was* that of a woman. Anger turning to bile in her throat, she peered around the edge of the door, seeing the rounded buttocks and narrow waist of the figure astride the naked body of Ryder.

So this was what he needed money for! Maria bit back the scream of anger pushing against her teeth. He was playing her for a fool. No wonder he could not find so much time for visits to Birmingham any more. She listened to the soft moans, to the creaking of the bed. How long? How long had he been playing his double game? One year . . . two? Had he known the woman before knowing Maria or was it only since her money had become available that he could afford this pleasure?

Was it someone she knew? Someone who knew her? Did the two of them laugh together at her gullibility, or was that strictly Ryder's preserve? Anger sat, hard and cold, in her chest. Perhaps it had been, and it could go on being so, but not for long.

Carefully, she peeped again into the bedroom. She must see the woman's face, she had to know if Ryder's whore was an acquaintance of hers.

Ryder lay spread-eagled across blue silk sheets, his blond hair tousled across his brow, his eyes closed. The figure now beside him was lying at an angle, auburn head pressed to his crotch.

Maria watched his body jerk in time with his moans, the movement of a puppet in the hands of a master. Then, as he gasped like a drowning man, the head lifted from him and Maria caught a glimpse of smooth creamy skin, the line of a finely curved eyebrow over a straight nose, and along the chin a neatly clipped auburn beard . . .

He was indeed playing a double game! Maria snatched at the reins, slapping them across the horse's flank, sending the cart back down the road towards the town. He was playing it in every sense of the word. What a fool he must think her! How clever to have his cake and eat it too! But that could not go on. Maria Beddows was not a woman to be fooled with. Ryder Tempal would not laugh for long.

'I have decided to take Reuben Fereday up on his offer, I have a fancy to see that gallery of his.'

Maria's smile held none of the anger of yesterday as she looked at her lover.

'That is, of course, if you will accompany me, my dear? It would not be fitting for me to visit alone.'

'I shall be happy to take you there,' Ryder's answering smile was wide. 'When do you have in mind?'

Maria tugged the embroidered bell pull that hung beside the graceful Adam fireplace. 'Now, at once. Unless you have something else to do?'

Ryder glanced sharply at the woman whose goodwill he depended upon, catching a hint of something in her voice. Maria had acted pleasantly enough since his arrival at Holyhead House, but he had sensed a change in her, an underlying ambiguity, a tone in her voice that sounded almost like menace.

'I never have anything to do I would not willingly put aside for you.'

How willing would you be to put aside your interesting diversions? Maria continued to smile despite the thought. The infidelity she had seen yesterday in his house had not been so much of a surprise, but the fact that his companion had been a man had disgusted her. To think he had done those same things with her!

'Then we will go. There is a train at noon.' Maria turned as a maid answered her summons, ordering her carriage.

'Oh!' Swaying as she stepped down from the carriage, Maria leaned heavily on Ryder's arm.

'What is it?' He was aware of heads turning towards them in the street. 'Are you unwell?'

'Will I be taking you back to the 'ouse, ma'am?'

'No! No, thank you, Simms.' Maria glanced at her coachman who had jumped from the driving seat on seeing her sway against Ryder's arm. 'It was just a touch of dizziness, nothing more. I will be perfectly all right.'

'We can easily visit Fereday's gallery another day. Perhaps you should return home?'

Return so you may enjoy another afternoon in the manner of yesterday? Maria smiled beneath the tulle veil. She had left that house as silently as she had entered; he had no idea she had seen him, no idea she knew of his making love with someone else, and that someone a man.

What would happen to him if she let it be known, not only to him but to others in his circle? Tongues wagged in Bilston, wagged long and loud. One word from her and Ryder Tempal would be finished in the Midlands. And it would be worth the risk to her own reputation – worth it had she not something else in mind for her handsome consort.

'I won't hear of it.' Maria too was aware of the interested stares of passers-by. 'Perhaps I might rest in the waiting room until the train arrives.'

Resting her hand on Ryder's arm, she walked into the station.

'There be folk in the waiting room.' The station master, his green uniform resplendent with brass buttons and yellow braid, touched a finger to his peaked cap. 'The lady might be more at ease in private, sir. If I might suggest my office?'

'That is most kind.' Maria swayed again and the portly railway official stepped quickly to the other side of her.

'If you will allow me, ma'am?' Tentatively taking her other arm, he led the way to a room at the end of the platform. 'Sit her in there, sir.' He looked up at Ryder. 'I'll go and get a glass of water.'

'I still think you should return home, Maria,' Ryder said after the station master had brought the water and left them alone in his office. 'It is foolish to continue on to Birmingham when you are obviously feeling unwell.'

'Why let a small dizzy spell spoil a whole day?' She handed him the glass of water, leaning back in a horsehair sofa.

'The Birmingham train is due in two minutes, sir.' The station master tapped politely before entering the office.

Ryder nodded, holding out his arm as Maria rose from the sofa, following the man on to the platform.

A little way from its furthest end the approaching train emitted the piercing shriek of a steam whistle. Uttering a small frightened cry, she shrank a little closer to Ryder. 'I do so fear these dreadful machines,' she said to the station master, still hovering in their vicinity. 'They are so frightening to a woman.'

'They be all right, ma'am, supposing you stands back from the edge of the platform.'

Beneath her veil, Maria smiled at his slightly superior tone.

'If I might suggest your wife stand behind you, sir?'

Ryder nodded, puzzled by Maria's professed fear of trains. She had travelled on them before, and alone. But he stepped in front of her.

'Not too close, Ryder,' Maria cautioned in a small faint voice.

Reaching the start of the short wooden platform, the train emitted a second screech of its whistle while grey-black smoke belched out in regular blasts, shrouding its carriages, the engine appearing like some nightmare monster from among the mist.

Beneath the shelter of her veil, Maria watched the train lumbering onward

Ryder really should have remembered, he really should have thought of the depth of truth contained in the adage: 'Hell hath no fury like a woman scorned.' Nor did it have that which Maria still felt at finding him making love to a man: a cold determined desire for revenge. A woman she might just have accepted, but a man . . . Ryder should have remembered how closely akin was love to hate. She had been so enamoured of him, so filled with a desire that she had mistaken for love. But that had been last week! She would make no more mistakes.

Two short sharp blasts of the whistle signalled the train's drawing to a halt, wheels adding to the screeching sounds as they ground against the brake.

One second. Maria smiled. Ryder really *should* have known. Love and hate. How quickly one turned to the other. Two seconds. He really should have known. Mistakes were so easily rectified for a woman as beautiful as she, and lovers so easily replaced.

From the fog of coal smoke and steam a spine-tingling blare erupted.

'Ohhh!' Giving a startled cry, Maria lifted a hand to her brow, her legs folding beneath her, her body falling against Ryder, sending him toppling to the ground. She heard one piercing scream as his body hit the platform then rolled over the edge, disappearing beneath the engine's huge iron wheels.

Hidden by her veil, the smile deepened. Poor Ryder, he really should have known.

Two hours later Maria lay in her own bed, eyes closed as they had been for most of the drive home, a doctor beside her in the hansom.

'She must be kept very quiet.' Maria listened to the man's voice. 'I fear the losses you have told me of can wreak havoc on the feminine nervous system. Your mistress parting with her only child and then the sudden death of her husband have proved too much. A woman can hide sorrow from her neighbour but she cannot hide it from her body. Your mistress's illness is a result of that sorrow. You will admit no visitor for a week. I will call tomorrow morning.'

The rest of what he said was lost to Maria as together with her housekeeper he left the room.

Ryder had got what he deserved. Her eyes remained closed. He had thought to play her for a fool, but he had lost. I told you, my love, I told you I would share your body with no woman. Bitterness sharp in her throat, she saw painted on her mind's eye two figures sprawled on blue silk sheets.

'No woman, Ryder,' she whispered, 'And no man either.'

Chapter Seventeen

Virginia read once more through the letter she had received from her nephew. Why had he made such a request? Was it truly for the sake of art, or was it something deeper?

She glanced across her sitting room to where the charcoal drawing of her husband hung on the wall.

Reuben had paid more than passing attention to the sketch. He had examined it in detail and when he had turned back to her his face had held a sadness she could not define.

He wanted to mount an exhibition of unknown artists, his letter said. To bring hitherto unknown talent to the notice of the art world. But how many of those words were true? She folded the letter, replacing it in its envelope. Was his motive truly one of enriching the world of art? Was it the talent of many unknown artists that he was interested in, or would it be more honest to say it was only one? She thought again of the look on his face at seeing that sketch. This was only one unknown artist her nephew wished to discover, she was sure.

Virginia pulled the cord that would summon Carys to her.

'You visited Alice yesterday evening?' she asked as the girl entered the room.

'Yes, ma'am.'

'Did you find her any more recovered?'

Carys shook her head, feeling tears prick her eyelids.

'Try not to be sad, child. Mrs Bates tells me the doctor is certain it is not the cholera. We must thank the Lord for sparing us that.'

'Alice is so pale, and she is constantly soaked in perspiration. Her mother is afraid it could be fever of another kind.'

'Letty Withers is a sensible woman,' Virginia replied. 'But when a beloved child is sick much of our common sense flies out of the window. Rest assured, my dear, if the doctor feared that Alice had fever of any kind he would have had her admitted to the isolation hospital. We must trust to his judgement.' And pray God it is sound, she added silently.

'May I ask if I might visit Alice again this evening? I don't think Mrs Bates has anything special she requires to be done. I could be there and back in little more than an hour or so if I take the tram both ways.'

Virginia looked at the girl who had insisted on serving as a maid in her household – at the lovely face, taut with worry, the amber eyes dark with fear – and her own heart twisted. She had hesitated after reading the letter from her nephew; now she knew she had made the right decision. If Reuben and this child of Meshac Beddows *had* met before then, instinct told her, he had not abused her.

'Of course you may visit Alice, and tell Letty I will go myself after church on Sunday. And now, child, I have a request to make of you. My nephew has written to ask for the loan of the drawing you made of my husband. He wishes to give an exhibition of the work of unknown artists and feels that sketch would be a considerable addition.'

'The drawing is yours, ma'am.' Carys maintained the polite form of address she had adopted from their first meeting. Her birth made her the social equal of this woman, but circumstances made her Virginia's employee and as such she would address her. 'You have no need to ask me what you may do with it.'

Virginia's neatly dressed grey hair took on a silver sheen as a beam of sunlight swept through the high window at her back.

'As you say, Carys, that drawing is mine to do with as I wish, but my request is not for that drawing, it is for those you have in your room.' Virginia caught the look that flashed rapidly over the girl's face. 'You have not destroyed them, have you?'

Carys's thoughts ran wildly through her mind. She could not lie, she could not say she no longer had her sketches, yet how could she let them be seen by others? Her mother had called them obscene and labelled her lustful and wicked for drawing them. How would other people think of her?

'Have you destroyed them?' Virginia repeated her question when Carys did not answer.

'No.' She shook her head, a faint trace of pink rising to her cheeks. 'I have not destroyed them.'

'Then would you allow my nephew to borrow them? I give you my word they will be returned to you, and none but myself shall know the name of the artist unless you wish it.'

'I will fetch them for you.' Carys turned towards the door.

'One thing more, my dear,' Virginia called. 'Would you agree to my having them framed before sending them to Birmingham?' She smiled as Carys nodded. 'And try not to worry over Alice. God holds the girl in His hands.'

Closing the door of the sitting room, Carys pressed her hands to her mouth. Yes, God held Alice in His hands, but would He let her go?

Maria fastened the buttons of her black taffeta dress, this time exulting in its colour. She had paid Ryder two hundred pounds . . . how much of that had gone on his fancy man? She had supplied him so often with money, which he had probably spent on deceiving her. Thirty pieces of silver! Ryder Tempal had taken all of that. 'Ryder!' She spat the word. 'Judas would be a better name.'

Now she had paid him in full. She glanced at her reflection in the long walnut-framed dressing-mirror, admiring what she saw. She was cured of her infatuation with her lover. Maria Beddows would enjoy new conquests.

'Do you really ought to be going, ma'am? A funeral, even in early summer, be a dismal affair, and the doctor said you was to be kept in bed a week or two more yet.'

'How can I not go?' Maria turned to the plain girl whose tap on her bedroom door had warned her to wipe the smile of triumph from her face. 'Mr Tempal was a friend of my husband's. I must pay my respects.'

He was even more of a friend to you! Chrissy Williams knew as much of her mistress's carryings on as the dismissed Mary Bartlett. She turned to a drawer, selecting a pair of heavy lace gloves which she handed to Maria. Yes, that handsome Ryder Tempal had been more than a friend to this woman, much more.

'The wreath you ordered be ready in the kitchen, ma'am.'

Maria drew on the gloves, smoothing them slowly down each finger. 'Have it placed in the carriage,' she said, lowering her veil over her face.

Seated in her carriage as the cortège of mourners filed into Woodgreen Cemetery, Maria instructed her coachman to add her own tribute of white Madonna lilies to the carpet of flowers surrounding the newly dug grave. Then, as the priest began his long peroration, she signalled she should be driven away.

She had given Ryder all the respect he deserved, she was well rid of him. As she was rid of Meshac's daughter.

She smiled behind the veil.

There was one good thing Ryder had done: he had ensured she was now sole inheritor of all her husband's wealth. He, Ryder, had mixed the poison. His was the hand that had written the letter, and he the one who had delivered it. Carys had died by his hand. The evidence lay at the bottom of some mine shaft. There was no way in which she could be linked with that death, no blame could be attached to her as could none for Ryder's death.

Maria leaned back in the comfort of her carriage. It had been an accident. So many observers had seen the spells of dizziness attack her in the street – she had taken care they should. And the station master had given her the privacy of his office, even fetching her a glass of water. It had worked exactly as she had planned. A sick and frightened woman fainting on a station platform. Who could lay any blame on her for that? Who could say Ryder's falling beneath a train was anything other than a tragic accident?

A few more months was all that was needed to bring her mourning to a suitable conclusion. A few months only and then she would be able to dress in the jewel-bright colours that so suited her colouring; could dispense with the misery of her widow's garb and be free to enjoy her wealth.

And who would she choose to enjoy along with it? Which young man would share her money and her bed? For a brief moment she thought of Reuben Fereday and the smile returned to her mouth. He had not yet succumbed to her charm, but then she had not as yet fully exerted it. She would visit his gallery alone, and who could tell? Perhaps the handsome Mr Fereday would be the next thing she would buy.

The smile still on her face, Maria watched the drab line of shops and even drabber houses, each packed tight against the other, each as dreary as its neighbour. The Black Country deserved the title its workshops and steel mills had earned, their smoke covering every brick and stone with soot. Maybe she would sell Holyhead House, maybe she would move to Birmingham or London.

Happy with the dream of a fine house set far enough away from the dirt of smelting steel and the smell of factories and workshops, Maria gave only a passing glance at the figure of a young girl turning left off the main highway towards a square of shabby houses.

A faded blue coat, too tight for comfort . . . Subconsciously memory stirred. A brown dress, equally faded, short of her feet by several inches . . . Suddenly the floodgates of memory opened. Those were the clothes Carys had worn the day Maria had taken her to the convent; the same ones she had worn the day she had left it.

Her attention caught, Maria leaned forward, watching the girl walking along a narrow alley that disappeared into the warren of houses. She had the same rich chestnut hair. Then the girl turned to look behind her and Maria gasped. Even from this distance there could be no mistake: the girl she watched was her daughter, the daughter she had thought dead.

Hearing the clip of horses' hooves and the rumble of carriage wheels, Bethesda looked towards the road. Squinting against the sun she watched it come and with it came the quickening. Low in her stomach a surging heat began to throb and blood pounded like a tidal wave, threatening to burst her very veins. Behind her eyes a mist the colour of the setting sun began to swirl, lowering a veil across her sight, cutting off the picture of heath and carriage. Then it lifted, leaving Bethesda with the clearer pictures of her second sight.

From a small governess cart a figure wreathed in black called to Caine and as he answered the summons Bethesda saw a glint of gold move against the blackness. Like seeing figures on a stage, she watched Caine nod his head then point in the direction of the town they had left days before. Replying, the figure lifted one hand. Raising each black-clad finger slowly until all five stood erect the hand closed, then equally slowly repeated the action until each had lifted as many times as Bethesda had fingers on both hands. Caine nodded. Then the hand reached for the whip, and as it was lifted above the veiled head of the figure two uniformed men ran to Caine, seizing both of his arms. As he struggled for freedom, Bethesda again caught the gleam of gold on the breast of the driver of the carriage. But now the gold began to expand and to move, crowding in upon her, twisting and writhing like some living creature, filling the whole of her vision. Then it was gone.

Watching the carriage with her living eyes, Bethesda clenched her briar pipe between her teeth, the memory of the policemen seizing her son vivid still. Caine was in danger from the woman that carriage concealed – mortal danger. She watched the carriage disappear in the curve of the road. The sight did not lie. Tomorrow she would come. Staring into the fire, Bethesda knew the end had begun.

Carys turned into the square of houses. She had ridden the tram to the junction at Dudley Street then walked on along the Holyhead Road, not wanting to follow the Portway on her own. In the quiet streets grouped about St James' church silence seemed to hang heavy. Whenever she had come here with Alice there had been the laughter of children and the occasional greeting from a woman passer-by. But today there was nothing; no one watched her turn into Brick Kiln Street to enter the Witherses' house.

'Mrs Bates allowed me to leave early. She said it would be better to come while the sun was on the streets.'

'Martha Bates has sense.' Letty smiled at the girl who had visited each day since her daughter had returned home.

'Mrs Mountford sends her regards and asked me to tell you she will call to see Alice on Sunday after church. If you will permit it, of course?'

'Arrh, her can come and welcome, and pleased we'll be to see her. Alice always says what a good mistress Virginia Mountford be, though my Alice be a good wench and a hard worker. The mistress ain't never had no call . . .'

The words trailed away and Letty buried her face in her hands, her shoulders heaving as she sobbed.

'Oh, Mrs Withers, don't cry! Please don't cry!' Carys threw her arms about Alice's mother, holding her while the tears poured.

'My wench,' Letty sobbed, ''er don't seem to be getting any better.'

'She will,' Carys soothed. 'It is early days yet. We must give her time. The doctor has said it is not the cholera so you have nothing to fear.'

'I know.' Letty allowed herself to be seated, dabbing her eyes with the hem of her apron. 'But to see my girl just lying there, as pale as if the life had already left her.' She lifted the apron, holding it against her face. 'It fair breaks my heart.'

The months spent in the kitchen of Ridge House had taught Carys the salve for many ills. Unasked she set about making a pot of tea. If only Alice's illness could be cured so easily, she thought, when minutes later she handed the quietly sobbing Letty a cup of the strong sweet liquid.

'I be sorry to go on like that.' She tried to smile. 'You ain't come all that way to listen to me blarting.'

'You cry all you want to, Mrs Withers. Mrs Bates says it does us all good to cry sometimes.'

'I reckon her be right.' Letty smoothed the damp edges of her apron down over her skirts. 'But that don't give me leave to go upsetting visitors with my tears.'

'I am not upset,' Carys lied, feeling the sting of her own tears prick behind her eyelids.

'You be a good wench, Carys, same as my own.'

'How is Alice today?' she asked, having to fight hard against the emotion the other woman's words stirred in her.

Letty took the thick platter cup in her hands, staring into it. ''Er don't seem no better, for all the medicine the doctor says to dose 'er with. Not that her can keep it inside her. I no sooner holds the spoon against 'er mouth than 'er be heaving fit to bring up her stomach.'

'Has she eaten anything?'

'Not a crumb. Not a bite since entering this house. The doctor says not to worry too much on account of that, but how can a mother not worry?'

'I know how hard it must be for you, but Alice will recover, she will get well soon, I am sure of it.'

'Arrh, we must all think that.' Letty smiled through a film of tears. 'We must put our faith in the Lord. Now you drink up that tea and then I'll take you up to see her.'

Alice lay in a narrow iron-framed bed which despite its size almost filled the tiny bedroom. A two-paned window let in a stream of afternoon sunlight that played over a small table set beneath, and Alice's dress hung from a nail knocked into the wall, a dark smudge against the whitewash.

'You 'ave a visitor, me wench.' Letty bent over the bed, lifting her higher on the pillows. 'You two 'ave yourselves a natter. I'll be up later with some broth.'

'Hello.' Carys smiled at her friend as Letty left them. 'How are you?'

'I be all right.'

Alice's voice was little more than a whisper and her face creased with the strain of speaking.

'Mrs Bates sends her love, and Mrs Mountford said to tell you she will come to see you on Sunday, after church.'

Alice tried to smile. 'How be you managing up there? It must be awful hard on you, doing the work of two.'

'I am not doing the work of two.' Carys sat on the edge of the bed. 'Mrs Bates insists I do no more in a day than I did before. She says what does not get done today will bide until tomorrow.'

'Sounds like Mrs B.' Eyes that seemed to have lost their colour stared up from dark hollows. 'Carys, have . . . have there been any other letters?'

Her heart twisting at the hope she saw flare in those faded depths, Carys knew she could not bring herself to answer truthfully. If lies brought damnation to her soul then hers was damned, and she would give it gladly.

'There was no letter.' Carys smiled at the pallid face. 'But a man came yesterday to Ridge House. He stood beneath the trees that edge grounds to the rear, where you say the boy brought that letter a few days ago. He stood there several minutes but when I went towards him he left.'

'What did he look like?'

'He was tall.' Carys paused as if recalling the appearance of the invented figure. Trying desperately to sound convincing, she went on, 'He had fair hair and wore a brown jacket. He was very handsome and as I went towards him he smiled but once I got close turned away.'

'Did he say his name?'

Carys forced a smile to hover about her own lips though her throat felt tight. Was she merely storing up disappointment for her friend? Would her lies have to be faced, or would the man who had written to Alice come some day to speak to her? And if he did, would he in any way resemble the picture she was painting?

'No,' she said, holding the faded eyes with her own. 'He did not say his name. But when I called to him he said I was not the one he came to see, I was not Alice. I asked if he had a message I could give you and he said to tell you he would come again soon. That was as good as a letter, don't you think? This time he came himself, he did not send a boy to bring his message.'

'He come to see me.' The girl's voice was like the whisper of dry leaves. 'He truly came? To see me?'

'He truly came.' Carys pushed the lie past the barrier of her throat. 'It was clear I was not the one he wanted to see. "You don't be Alice", were the words he spoke, neither would he stay to talk. I was not the girl he had written a letter to and therefore he had nothing to say to me.'

'The letter.' The movement tired, almost listless, Alice reached beneath her nightgown to where the letter lay open on her breast. 'I read it often. I know every word that be written on it.' She pressed the paper to her lips before letting her hand fall across her chest. 'You says he was handsome?'

'Very handsome. I could not see the colour of his eyes but he had fair hair and his skin was bronzed by the sun.'

'He . . . he'll come again, won't he, Carys?'

'Yes.' She leaned forward, kissing the other girl's brow. 'He will come again, but now I think you ought to rest. I don't want to make your mother cross by tiring you.'

'Carys!' Her eyes suddenly enormous, Alice clutched at her hand. 'I . . . I don't think I'll be coming back to Ridge House.'

'So you plan to marry your handsome beau as soon as you are well!'

The answer was light but Carys felt a heaviness creep over her as she looked at the girl, lying now with closed eyes, the letter held once more to her mouth.

'She is sleeping,' Carys met the enquiring gaze of Alice's mother.

'She be doing more and more of that, but how did you find her?'

'She seemed little changed from yesterday.' Carys could lie no more but at the expression on Letty's face, added: 'But that will alter soon. Mrs Bates thinks it is too early to expect signs of recovery yet, but it will come.'

'That be what the doctor tells me, but I finds the wait all too worrying none the same.'

'Has he given any intimation of what is wrong with Alice?'

'Like I told you, he has ruled out the cholera. Says the sweating and the aching in her joints be down to something he calls the influenza. Says it seems like fever when it first starts and that we 'ave to guard against it turning to pneumonia. That be why I keep a fire burning in her room even though the days be warm.'

'May I please come again tomorrow?'

'Arrh, me wench.' Letty nodded, accompanying Carys to the door. 'Supposing the mistress allows it.'

Watching Carys until her slight figure turned the corner into St James's Street, Letty closed the door and went upstairs to Alice's room.

She had been reading that letter again. It was all she had done these past days, pressing the paper to her lips as if they touched the mouth of the sender then placing it beneath her nightgown, sleeping with it spread over her heart.

Letty smiled. She knew the thrill of the very first words said in love. Her girl had not heard those words from a man's lips but she had them from his hand, and the thrill they gave was the same.

Bending, she pressed her lips to the girl's brow, then to each of the closed eyes. Tears filling her own, she turned towards the window, towards the brightness spilling through. Slowly she walked across and stood staring out on to the maze of tiny houses, and across to where the spire of the church rose above them. Then, grasping a curtain in each hand, she drew them together. The room was dim now as she turned from the window but the bed could still be clearly seen. Letty crossed to it, staring down at the figure lying there, the letter held to her mouth.

'That be your letter,' she whispered. 'It will be seen by none but you.' Easing the paper from Alice's hand, she flung it into the fire, watching the edges brown and curl, seeing the blue and purple of the flames that consumed it. Then turning back to the bed, Letty Withers drew the sheet over her daughter's face.

Chapter Eighteen

'My mother asked me to come, ma'am.'

Davey Withers showed none of the discomfiture he felt at being in Virginia Mountford's elegantly furnished sitting room.

'I am happy to see you. Davey, isn't it?'

'That do be my name, ma'am.'

'Well.' Virginia's smile was pleasant and genuine. 'Please sit down, Davey. Would you take something to drink? Tea, or perhaps a glass of ale.'

'Thank you kindly, but no. This don't be . . .' He paused, mouth twitching as he sought to keep a hold on his emotions.

'Carys tells me your mother has been kind enough to agree to my calling to see Alice on Sunday.' Virginia covered the awkward moment. 'Please give her my thanks when you return home.'

Davey swallowed visibly, and his eyes as they met Virginia's were moist. 'That be what my mother sent me to tell you. It won't be any use your calling, not to see our Alice anyway. You see, ma'am, my sister died yesterday.'

'What!' Virginia was stunned by what he had said. 'But yesterday . . . Carys said she still looked quite poorly but that the doctor saw no reason to be overly concerned?'

'Miss Beddows told you right, the doctor did tell us that, but it seems he was wrong.'

'I . . . I can't believe it! Only a few days ago Alice was as chirpy as a sparrow.'

'We can't believe it neither.' Davey glanced at the carpet, unwilling for his brimming eyes to be seen.

'Your mother, Davey, how is your mother?'

'Taking it badly, ma'am, as you might expect. Her hasn't showed it by weeping and wailing, and her hasn't said much, but you can see in her face it has torn the heart from her.'

I know the feeling, Virginia thought, the anguish of never having a child could in no way match that of losing one yet the old agony rose in her as she thought of Alice's mother. The woman had been given heartache and sorrow that would be with her for the rest of her life; no amount of tears could wash them away, nor any number of years erase them.

'Give your mother my very deepest condolences,' she said gently. 'And if I may, I would like to be allowed to attend the service?'

'Arrh, ma'am.' Davey could not look up. 'I know my mother would like that you be with the following. I will come myself to tell you when the funeral is to be held.'

'Thank you, Davey.'

Virginia watched him leave. She had wanted to offer financial help but knew this was not the time. They were proud people and would prefer to take care of their own. But Virginia would not forget Alice or her family.

Below stairs, Martha Bates's eyes held the same incredulity as that of her mistress as Davey imparted his mother's message.

'But when?' She dropped heavily into her chair beside the range. 'Carys was only there yesterday and Alice were all right then.'

'It must have been just after she left.' Davey glanced at the girl standing beside the freshly scrubbed table, eyes huge with disbelief. 'Mother says her watched Carys turn the corner into

St James's Street then went straight back upstairs to Alice. Her were lying with her eyes closed and me mother thought as her was sleeping, until her kissed her, and then her knew it were more than sleep.'

'Oh my good God!' Martha murmured. 'Oh, your poor mother! How be her bearing up?'

'It has hit her badly, finding our Alice like that after the doctor saying there were no need for worry.'

Alice dead! Carys felt the breath desert her lungs. It was not true. It was all a lie. She had seen her only yesterday, held her hand, told her of an admirer come to call.

'No!' Her eyes dark with pain, she stared at Davey. 'It is not true, it is not! Alice is not dead, she is not . . . she is not!' Holding a hand to her mouth, she ran from the kitchen.

'Carys.' Davey came to where she stood, staring out across the open heath towards the town sprawled at the bottom of the hill. 'Carys, I be sorry to be the one to hurt you.'

'Oh, Davey.' Tears spilling down her cheeks, she turned to him, sobbing as he took her in his arms. 'Davey, why, why?' Her face buried against his shoulders she repeated the question again and again, grief shaking her slender body.

Holding her close against him, he pressed his lips to her head as he stroked the rich curls of her hair, even in his grief knowing another heavier sorrow. The sorrow of knowing the girl he held so close in his arms did not love him as he loved her. That her being in his arms was through grief and not through love. Above Carys's head his eyes swam with tears.

Reuben Fereday touched his heels to the flanks of the horse he had hired from the livery stables close to Wednesbury railway station. He had received the sketches he had sought to borrow from Virginia and others besides, unmistakably drawn in the same hand: the one that had painted the design on the box purchased from Meshac Beddows, the hand of his daughter. But how? That girl had entered a convent, had taken vows that would keep her apart from the world for the rest of her life.

But that sketch of Virginia's husband . . . there was no mistaking the style. He had examined it minutely, comparing it with one which Virginia assured him in her accompanying letter had been drawn five years ago; the sketch of a man rising from a pool, head thrown back, exultant in his superiority over the dark satiny water. A man he knew to be himself.

The wind playing through his dark hair, Reuben laughed from sheer happiness. It had to be her! It had to be the girl on the heath. God only knew how, but it had to be. The girl who had filled his thoughts for so long must have left her convent, and God willing he would find her.

Cresting the rise, he followed the track that led to the grounds of his aunt's house. He had chosen to come this way rather than drive up Holloway Bank even though riding across the heath meant his approaching Ridge House from the rear.

Still some yards from the wall that protected the gardens from the rough winds that could sometimes rise with devastating force from the flat heathland, he reined in the horse, his eyes on the two figures that stood in its lee.

A man, tall and broad-shouldered, held a girl in his arms, his fair head bent close to hers, hand stroking the rich chestnut of her hair.

The girl on Moxley Heath had had chestnut hair. Suddenly Reuben felt cold. She too had been of slender build, as was the girl in this man's arms. Tightening the reins as his mount tossed its head, the coldness turned to a kind of fear – fear of what he might see. He watched the girl release herself from the man's arms and as she lifted her face to his, Reuben saw clearly the one that had remained indelibly printed on his mind. The girl the man had been holding, the girl he had kissed, whose hair he had stroked, was the girl on the heath.

Disappointment striking him like a hammer blow, Reuben jerked on the rein, whipping the horse about, digging his heels sharply into its soft flesh as he raced back down the rise and across the heath.

He ought to have known. It was nothing short of idiocy to think she would even remember him, much less think she would harbour any love for a man she had spoken to just once, and then for moments only.

Drawing into the yard of the White Horse Hotel, he swung from the saddle. Giving a shilling to the ostler in charge who agreed to return the horse to its owner, Reuben strode into the building. Ordering a gill of brandy he strode into the smoking room.

From her stool beside the fire Bethesda watched the sky turn to crimson as the distant steel works opened their furnaces. She watched as the trails spread like blood oozing from some gigantic wound. Usually the sight so magnificent in its awesome majesty impressed her as did a beautiful sunset, but this evening she watched with eyes blind to its grandeur.

All day she had willed the sight to return, to show her again what she felt she had missed, to tell her what she needed to know. But it had not returned and in its absence cold fear had settled in her heart.

That carriage had held a figure robed in the colour of death, and the figure was a woman's. She had raised a whip. The carmine glow of the sky reflected on Bethesda's face, etching the wrinkles about her eyes and mouth, shadow filling them, showing minuscule ravines whose depths held the secrets of a thousand lifetimes.

Though the face was veiled, the sight told her that the woman was the same one. The same who once before had raised a whip that had cut the eye from a boy's face. That time she had blighted a life; this time she would destroy it. This time Caine would die.

'The Peel men come for him,' Bethesda muttered. 'That much the sight give me. 'Tis the Peel men will take Caine and the Gorgio will 'ang him.'

Overhead the brilliance of the sky muted into gold-fringed purple and then to pearl as the furnace flames were once

261

more closed behind steel barriers, but their beauty was lost to Bethesda. Only the inner world of her mind was real and desperately she probed its corners for the answer she had sought all that day. An answer that would not come to her call.

Tomorrow would be too late. Wrapped in her shawl, she rocked endlessly on her stool. The sight had shown her the danger and her Romany blood told her just as clearly that danger would come with the new dawn, as it told her she, and she alone, could protect her son.

But how? Across the shadowed heath a roosting bird called to its mate whose wide black wings filled her vision as it swooped in answer across the sky.

Its answer was hers.

Pulling the shawl tighter, passing the corners around her back before knotting them beneath her flat breasts, Bethesda spat into the fire. The ways of the earth were ancient beyond time, their mysteries lost to those who had forgotten how to look and listen, how to read the signs. But she had not forgotten. She carried within her the wisdom of her grandmother and many grandmothers before her, taught to her through the years of her growing. A wisdom that surpassed the Gorgio's, a knowledge that caused them fear. But Bethesda did not fear it.

The black wings of the bird had told her, giving her the answer in its swoop to earth. She must seek among the old ways, travel the dark paths, ask the help of the old gods.

Going across to the caravan, she unhooked the tarred leather water jack, pouring a little of its contents into her tin cup before replacing it. Beneath the waistband of her dark flounced skirts a knife touched against her bones. Taking the tin cup in her hand, Bethesda left the camp and headed towards the trees.

Evening had already closed over the sky and as yet no moon rode its dark infinity. The soft sounds of moving animals and the rustling of breeze-touched leaves filled the darkness that closed about her as she entered the small wood. These were sounds that brought trepidation to those who did not have the knowledge, but to Bethesda they sang a song of welcome. Here she would be given what she asked, here the dark ones would answer.

Coming upon a small clearing she halted, listening to the call of her soul. This was the place. It was here she must honour the old ways. Waiting for the light she knew would come, she looked about the clearing, and as the moon broke cover, bathing it in clear silver, saw a flat-topped stone. Crossing to it, she knelt, placing the cup beside her on the ground together with the knife. Reaching beneath her shawl, she brought out the leaves of a rowan tree and tiny twigs of oak she had gathered that morning, grouping them in a heap on the stone.

'Let thy flesh be my flesh. Let thy bones be my bones.'

The words quivered on the silver-traced night as Bethesda picked up the knife. Holding her hand over the cup, she drew the blade across her palm.

'Let thy blood be my blood,' she intoned as droplets of red fell into the water. Then, holding her hand above the stone, dripped several spots on to the dried twigs. Setting the knife aside, she took her box of matches from the pocket of her skirt and struck one. Holding it to the piled leaves and twigs, waiting while smoke began to spiral upward, she leaned her head into it.

'Let thy wisdom be my wisdom. Give me that which the sight did not.'

Sitting back on her heels, Bethesda watched the smoke rise from the stone, drifting into two separate lines. Her mouth tight, old eyes sharp as a hawk's, she watched and waited. Above the stone smoke showed clear in the moonlight, the two columns curling and writhing like twin serpents, their grey bodies twisting in and out of each other, forming and melting only to form again until they hung in the air, two shapes, one interlocked with the other. A perfect 'M', its body joined to an equally perfect 'B'. Below them the last flames spewed from the leaves and sticks, bathing the letters in red-hued gold.

The old ways had revealed what the sight had kept hidden, but Bethesda was not yet finished. She had to know how her son was to be avenged.

Scraping up a handful of loose earth, she mixed it with a few drops of the water. Moulding it into the rough shape of a human figure, she laid it on the stone beside the ashes of the leaves. Then, taking up the cup, she held it between both hands.

'My blood mixes with thy blood,' she whispered, 'let thy wisdom be mixed with mine.' Pouring the water on the ground about the stone she felt her pulses quicken. From the trees circling the glade came a rustling. Like the sound of many voices it rushed towards her, circling the stone, the breath of its coming lifting the ashes of the dead fire, sucking them into itself.

Breath caught in her lungs, Bethesda waited. Then it was gone, leaving the mud figure speckled with dots of grey ash. Gathering cup, matches and knife, she rose to her feet, making a sign of gratitude. Leaving the remnants of her asking upon the stone, she turned away. The old ways had not failed her. Caine would not die. But the woman who had maimed him would often long for death.

Alice had been buried.

In her little bedroom on the top floor of Ridge House, Carys buried her face in the pink cotton of her friend's one walking out dress. She would never see her again, never huddle with her as they laughed over some silly happening.

It had all happened so very quickly, and now Alice was gone.

Sobs dry in her throat, Carys folded the pink-sprigged dress, putting it with the rest of Alice's things in the brown hessian bag Mrs Bates had supplied.

Everything must be returned to Alice's mother. Carys stared

at the few possessions, hardly filling the small bag. Was that all there was to show for a life? Was there no more remaining of the bright bubbly girl than a few clothes?

Bitterness and sorrow merged in Carys as she picked up the bag. Alice had been more like a sister than a friend, always laughing away a problem, always eager to share a confidence.

'Is that everything?' Martha Bates eyed the bag Carys set on a chair in the kitchen.

'Yes.' Her voice was choked. 'That is everything.'

'I be sorry over having to ask you to do what rightly be my duty. Perhaps we should send a message to Letty explaining that I be laid up with the rheumatics and that I will go to see her when they be gone?'

'I really do not mind taking Alice's belongings to her mother. In fact I want to go. Mrs Withers and her family were so very kind to me, and . . . and I feel somehow Alice would want me to be the one to be with her mother when her things are returned.'

Martha touched a hand to her hip in an attempt to ease the painful joint. 'If that be the way you feel then I won't be the one to tell you no. But be sure to explain to Letty. That woman be going through enough heartbreak without feeling I be turning me back on her now.'

'Mrs Withers will not think badly of you if return Alice's property. She knows you well enough to realise you would not forgo your duty lightly.'

'You be right.' Martha nodded. 'Tell her I'll be along just as quick as these 'ere rheumatics be cleared.'

The afternoon sun was warm as Carys followed the Holloway Road towards town, but she felt nothing but the bag in her hand that held so many memories: the beads bought from a pack man who had called at the house, cheap glass that Alice had worn with the pride of a queen bedecked in diamonds; the china shepherdess Eddie had won at the Wakes – sadly tawdry but all Letty had left of her daughter.

Turning into Brick Kiln Road, Carys glanced at the line of cramped houses, each so like the other in their drabness. The curtains that had been closed in respect on the day of the funeral were now open, except in Letty's house. There the merest fraction of a parting allowed in the light of day, a fraction that she knew would increase little by little over the next ten days.

'Sit you down, wench.' Letty Withers tried to smile as she opened the door to Carys but her eyes were averted from the bag. 'It was thoughtful of you to call,' she added, hearing Martha Bates's message.

Placing the bag in a corner alongside the dresser, Carys turned as Letty's sobs filled the little room. Her own eyes filling with tears, she cradled the woman in her arms, holding her while the grief poured out like a stream released from a dam.

Passing into St James's Street later, Carys glanced at a sky that was purple with evening. Letty Withers had cried until she could cry no more, and then she had talked – talked of her daughter, reliving memories of her childhood. And Carys had held her and listened, understanding her need, and though she had never been in the situation before, recognising the healing of the soul her speaking of Alice would bring. The whole of the afternoon had been spent comforting the girl's mother and now it was growing dark.

Drawing level with the church, Carys glanced into the churchyard. She ought to go straight back to Ridge House, she had promised Letty she would when declining the woman's suggestion that she wait for Davey to come in from work so he could see her home. But it would only take a moment to slip around the back of the church to where Alice lay and say a goodbye it had been too difficult to say on the day of her burial.

Glancing along the street, she saw it was deserted. If she went in no one would see and speak of it to Letty. In the gathering darkness her eyes searched for the still bright flowers that had been heaped upon the grave. Here there were few tombstones to mark a person's passing; the inhabitants of this part of Wednesbury did not boast the money to spend on stone.

Picking her way along the narrow paths worn among the grass, she knelt beside the new mound.

'I wanted to be with you once more, Alice,' she whispered, hot tears finding their way down her cheeks. 'I wanted to tell you so much but you were gone before I had the time. The letter came and you were so happy, and now . . . But you had that happiness, you knew the feeling of having a man love you. And you have my love, Alice. I will never forget your kindness to me. I love you, Alice, as much as I could love a sister. I won't ever forget, I will never . . .'

The rest of the sentence was lost as a heavy cloth fell over her head and a pair of strong arms hauled her roughly to her feet.

Chapter Nineteen

She had come that morning, the woman veiled in black. She had come as Bethesda had known she would, as the sight had shown.

'Do you know Ridge House at Hill Top?' she had enquired after calling Caine to the small trap in which she drove herself.

'There is a young woman serving there as housemaid, a girl with hair the colour of ripe chestnuts. A girl I would rather were not there, or any other place. Would you, for a price, be willing to see that she . . . leaves?'

'How much be you willing to pay the gypsies for doing what you ask?'

'A hundred guineas, in gold.'

Bethesda's heart had turned over when Caine had told her of the offer. It was more money than ever they could hope to see in a lifetime, but it was money her son would not live to spend should he accept it.

'What is it you be wanting done with this girl?'

Caine's question had caused no surprise but seemed expected.

'She would make a pretty companion for your bed.' Behind the black tulle Caine had seen the woman's mouth curve into a smile. 'Or if you have no fancy for her then a bed could easily be found in a ditch. I am sure you have enough knowledge of the country to know a suitable place, one where a body could easily be lost.'

'When do you want the girl taken?'

Bethesda had watched her son as he talked, seen the scar that ran along his cheek like a crucifix as he turned his head in the direction of the smoke-shrouded town, and in her heart she saw again the blow of the whip that had taken his eye.

'Today. I want her gone by morning.'

Caine had nodded, sunlight dancing on his hair.

'Do I be getting the guineas now?'

'I am not a fool!'

The woman had jerked in annoyance as she spoke and Bethesda's hand had closed over the knife at her waist. The woman would strike Caine no second blow.

'You will be paid when I have proof the job is done.'

She leaned forward then, the sun catching the gleam of the gold pendant at her breast.

He had told his mother all that the woman had said and listened as Bethesda in her turn related what the sight and the dark ones had shown. Caine was not a follower of the old ways but he respected them.

Slipping her hand into her pocket, she drew out a slender gold chain with its pendant holding an intertwined monogram. The letters of smoke had curved and twisted in just the same way, coiling and circling, joining until they formed the letters 'M' and 'B'. The letters that now glinted on the pendant in her hand.

This was what the dark ones had told her. This was the payment Caine must ask for doing the woman's bidding.

She had been reluctant to part with the trinket, but as Caine had made as if to turn away, had lifted it from her neck.

Returning the pendant to her pocket, Bethesda fetched a rabbit from the box strung against the caravan. Once more seated on her stool she sank the knife into the soft fur, stripping it away from the flesh.

Her son was not a follower of the old ways but he listened when they spoke, just as he listened to his mother. Taking the gutted rabbit to the pool, she bent to wash it in the water . . . Caine would do as she had told him.

He had watched the house from the shelter of the trees, waiting for a chance to strike, yet when the girl had left the house she had gone by the road. It had been too risky to approach her there, with passing carts and trams. But he had followed her along the heath, staying just out of sight, his Romany knowledge telling him always where she was.

It had been almost dark when she had turned into that churchyard. Even had she looked about her she would not have seen him follow. He had dropped the horse blanket over her head before she could utter a single cry, then half dragging, half carrying her, had disappeared into the black shadows of the surrounding heath.

She had struggled as she was struggling now. Caine tightened his grip, pulling the girl's slight body close against his own.

Fifty guineas in gold the woman had promised. Put into his hands this very night. He quickened his pace to a run as Bethesda's words returned to his mind, her warning not to go against the old ways. But he did not fear the old ways, and fifty guineas was fifty guineas.

'I be going to set you down.'

Beneath the rough blanket Carys heard the quietly spoken words. 'If you know what be good for you then you will raise no scream, do you understand?'

The cloth pressed tight against her mouth, Carys could only hope that whoever held her understood her muffled reply.

Still holding her with one arm he pulled the bandanna from his neck, then whipping away the blanket he quickly wrapped the scarf about Carys's eyes, knotting it at the back of her head.

'Why are you doing this?' Fear almost closing her throat,

271

Carys stood waiting for what might happen next. 'What do you hope to gain?' she asked again. 'I have no money I can give you, and no family who will pay for my release. Please,' she cried as a hand grabbed her arm, propelling her forward, 'please let me go.'

Silence answered her cry. Carys stumbled along, only a strong hand preventing her from falling as her feet caught against clumps of rough ground.

Why had this man attacked her? That it was a man she could tell from the deep quality of his voice when he had spoken. Where was he taking her? What was it he intended to do?

Terror pounding in her veins she could only stumble along beside him, hoping he would soon let her go. How long would Mrs Bates expect her to take visiting Alice's mother? How long before she sent someone to the house to enquire after her? However long, it would be too late. Carys whimpered at the thought and a hand clamped over her mouth.

'I told you not to raise a scream!' The hand pressed against her lips, adding painful emphasis to the words muttered against her ear. 'One more sound from you, just so much as a whisper, and I'll do for you right now. You hear what I be saying . . . you hear?'

Releasing her mouth, the hand grabbed the collar of her coat, shaking her with a violence that rattled her teeth then releasing her so she fell sprawling on to her knees.

'Mark me, my pretty one . . .'

The voice, close to her ear again, held more than a hint of a threat as she felt herself once more hauled savagely to her feet.

'. . . you be doing just like I say or I kill you right here. There be none as will see, ain't no moon to light up what I be about. Won't be none will find you for a long time, so just you stay quiet . . . very quiet.'

How long he dragged her with him Carys had no way of reckoning, nor in which direction they travelled. She knew only that they kept to the heath.

'Stand you still.'

The order came after what seemed to her to be hours of jolting and stumbling over uneven ground. Swaying from terror and fatigue, she obeyed. Unbuckling the belt from his trousers, Caine drew the length of it through his hands.

Swallowing the horror that spread through her, giving only a tiny sob of panic, Carys shuddered as her arms were pinioned behind her back, shivers of ice touching her spine as she felt the strip of leather fastened about her wrists. Then she was lifted bodily, slung face down over the man's shoulder.

Pain lancing through her ribs, shooting the breath from between her lips with every step he took, Carys tried to fathom the reason behind her abduction. She had no money, she had told him that, and even if he disbelieved her there could be no denying the truth of it illustrated in her worn out clothes. And if the motive were not the hope of gaining money, then what? If it were to kill her, why had he not done that already? Why drag her miles across the heath before fulfilling his threat?

Questions racing through her brain, Carys felt herself tipped from his shoulder and as her head hit something hard, fell away into unconsciousness.

'Where is she, Aunt?'

Reuben Fereday strode into Virginia's sitting room. He had unpacked the pictures she had loaned him for display in his gallery and among them had been another. A charcoal sketch, tastefully mounted in a simple frame that did not detract the eye from the subject: the body of a man rising through the surface of a fern-fringed pool, a man with his dark head thrown back lifting his face to the sky – a face that was Reuben's.

Virginia smiled, holding up her own face to be kissed. 'Where is who, dear?'

'Aunt, please!' Reuben paced to the window then back again, tension in every line of him. 'Don't torment me. I know it was a woman who drew that sketch of Uncle Oliver, and that the same woman drew the sketch of me swimming in that pool.'

'So it *was* you.' Virginia looked up into the face of her nephew. 'Have you no shame to go bathing in such a public place!'

'It was indiscreet of me.' He acknowledged the reproof. 'I can only say the day was warm and I could not resist the temptation.'

Virginia continued to watch him, seeing the play of emotions across his handsome face. She had ignored her better judgement in including that sketch in the ones she sent to him, telling herself that whatever demon haunted her nephew was best exorcised by facing up to it.

'Was that your only indiscretion that day?' she asked quietly. 'Was swimming the only pleasure you could not resist, or did you avail yourself of another?'

'Such as what?' Reuben stopped pacing.

'You may not forgive what I am about to ask, Reuben, but nevertheless I will ask. Believe me, my dear, when I say I ask it because of my love for you and because I am convinced of what the answer will be. That day you went swimming, did you force your attentions on a young girl?'

The blood drained from Reuben's face and his eyes hardened to black stone. If any man had asked that question he would have knocked him senseless.

'I have never forced myself on any woman, either that day or any other,' he said through clenched teeth.

Virginia felt relief sweep through her but allowed no trace of it to show on her face.

Too distracted to sit, Reuben walked about the room. 'I was returning from Bilston,' he said, 'and decided to bathe in a pool in an old mine shaft. It is somewhat sheltered from the roadway and I thought I would remain unseen, but then I saw a movement among the ferns. When I called out, a girl stood up. She had obviously been watching but on my seeing her she fled. I guessed if I were quick about it I would catch up with her before she reached her home, the nearest houses being some distance away.'

'And did you catch up with her?'

'Yes, I did. And from that day I have never stopped searching for her. I thought once that maybe I had found her. That was in Meshac Beddows's house. I admired several pieces he told me had been painted by his daughter, and the girl on the heath had said she was returning to Holyhead House. But when I asked Meshac's wife about her she told me her daughter had taken the veil. From then it seemed my search was over. Until, that is, saw the portrait of Uncle Oliver.'

'But why be so persistent in your search for this girl if you owe her nothing?'

Reuben sank at last in to a chair, cradling his head in his hands. 'I have asked myself the same question over and over again.'

'And the answer,' Virginia prodded gently, 'was that the same over and over again?'

For several moments silence hung between them. A silence in which neither of them moved. Then Reuben looked up.

'Always, right from the first, I searched for her because I had to know. I had to be certain of what I felt. I have not been free of her since that day.'

He looked up and Virginia felt a jolt in her heart at the look on his face: the sadness, the frustration, the not knowing.

'Aunt,' he asked, 'is it possible to love a woman you have spoken to only once?'

'I think perhaps it might be. But thinking you love a person is not enough, Reuben, you must be sure.'

'I know that.' He gave a half smile. 'I feel I would be sure if I spoke to her. I *must* talk to her, Aunt, before she marries.'

'Marries?' Virginia's brows met. 'Why do you suppose her to be getting married?'

'I saw her.' As if suddenly he could bear the inactivity no longer he got to his feet, resuming his pacing of the room.

'I was in Wednesbury last week and decided to call here at Ridge House. I hired a horse and rode by way of Millfield Heath. I was almost at the house when I saw her. I was not sure at first, many girls have chestnut-coloured hair, but then I saw her face.'

'So why did you not speak to her then?'

'I was about to but she was with a man, one who took her in his arms and held her. A girl only allows the man she is to marry to hold her so close.'

For the first time since his abruptly entering her sitting room, Virginia felt herself want to laugh. Stifling the desire, she simply smiled. 'It is not always love that drives a girl into a man's arms, Reuben. Sometimes it is sorrow and the need for comfort. It is my guess that you called the same day as Davey Withers brought us the news of his sister's death. Alice Withers had been my housemaid for several years. Carys and she were very close friends, and when she heard what had happened she was heartbroken. Davey tried to comfort her. Martha Bates told me of it. That does not mean to say that Carys is to marry the fellow.'

'Carys?'

Virginia nodded. 'The woman who drew the sketches I sent you is, I believe, the same one you have hoped so long to meet again. Her name is Carys Beddows, daughter of Meshac Beddows, and she is here in this house where she has been since leaving the Convent of the Holy Child a year ago.'

'Then it *was* her!' Sinking to his knees beside his aunt's chair, he took her hands, his eyes holding a brilliance she had thought lost. 'May I see her?'

'Not on your knees, my lad.'

Allowing her laughter to escape, Virginia pulled the embroidered bell cord, but when she returned her glance to her nephew her face was solemn once more.

'The girl is still very young and she has been hurt far more than any girl deserves. If it should be she does not wish to see you, or to speak to you, then I will not allow you to press her, Reuben. Carys is under my protection so long as she chooses to be in my house, and though you have always been as a son to me I will not see you, or anyone else, cause her more grief.'

She broke off as Martha Bates limped into the room and her voice took on a note of concern.

'Martha, you should not be hobbling around on that leg. Why are you not resting it as you were told to do?'

'You rang the bell, ma'am. Somebody had to answer it.'

'But that somebody did not have to be you!' Concern for the woman who had been part of her household since the first days of her marriage to Oliver gave Virginia's reply a sharp edge that was not intended.

'Well, somebody had to, begging your pardon, ma'am. There be only me and Carys in the 'ouse, and seeing her don't be back yet then it were me had to answer.'

'I'm sorry, Martha, I was not aware Carys had not returned or we would have come to you. I do not want you walking about the house while you are in pain.'

'The rheumatism be easing.' Martha touched her hip. 'I reckon it'll be well cleared by morning.'

'Then sit down.' Seeing the hesitation on her housekeeper's face, Virginia nodded to Reuben then waited while he helped Martha to a chair.

'That's better.' Virginia smiled. 'Martha, you say Carys is not yet returned from visiting Letty Withers?'

'No, ma'am, she ain't.'

'Is it usual for her to be gone so long?'

'Not usual at all, not for Carys. If her says her will be back by a certain time, then that be the time her keeps to.'

'So when are you expecting her return?'

'I thought her would be here some three hours since.' Martha glanced at the carriage clock on the mantelpiece. 'It don't be like her to be late.'

'She might have waited for Davey to get home from his work so he could escort her. The heath is not a place for a young woman to be alone in the dark, there are so many disused mine shafts dotted all over it.'

'That be worrying me, ma'am. I know Letty would have had the girl home hours ago if one of her lads had been sent along with her. I be feared something might be amiss.'

'We must send and enquire of Mrs Withers. Martha, will you see the trap is made ready?'

'No!' Reuben was on his feet. 'I will go. You cannot take a trap across the heath in the dark. Just tell me how I can find this house.'

'It be close to the church.'

'The one on the hill?'

'No.' Virginia shook her head. 'Martha does not mean the parish church. She is speaking of the church of St James. It is a quarter of a mile from The White Horse. Follow the Holyhead Road in a straight line and you will come to it. Letty Withers's house is opposite to the right.'

Back in the kitchen, Martha started as a heavy knock on the door was repeated several times.

'This be Ridge House?'

Martha stared at the powerfully built man. His hair reached to his collar; a white scar like a crucifix ran the length of his cheek, the empty eye socket staring like a black hole. 'I wants to speak to the mistress.'

'Well, 'er won't be wanting to talk to no gypsy!' Martha made to slam the door but the man moved quickly, the strength of his raised hand throwing the door from Martha's grasp banging it back against a large wall cupboard.

'You tell 'er, missis.' Caine Lazic brought his scarred face close to Martha's. 'You tell that mistress o' yourn, that if 'er be wanting to see that maid o' hers alive then 'er best talk to Caine Lazic.'

'Carys!' Martha gasped. 'You have Carys?'

'If that be the name o' the maid with chestnut hair and a pretty way o' talking, then yes, I've got her.'

'Oh, my good God!' Martha shrank against the door.

'You best be telling your mistress what I say, I don't be intending to stay all night.'

'Yes, the mistress. You come in. No . . . stay there!' Flustered by his sudden appearance and even more bothered by what he had said, Martha stared into his swarthy face.

'You need have no fear for your knick-knacks, missis.' He swept a cold look about the kitchen. 'Caine Lazic takes nothing he has not earned.'

'You've taken Carys!' Martha retorted sharply. 'Gypsies be all the same: liars, thieves and murderers. I wouldn't trust a gypsy no further than I could throw one.'

'That be your choice. But remember it were a gypsy came to tell you of a young woman's whereabouts; that it were a gypsy brought you news of her. Think on that if your mistress asks of her.'

'Wait!' The discomfort in her hip forgotten, Martha almost ran from the kitchen.

'What is it, Mrs Bates?'

Halfway across the hall, Reuben turned as the housekeeper hurried in from the kitchen.

'It . . . it be a gypsy, Reuben. He be in the kitchen, and says as 'ow he has Carys.'

'A gypsy has Carys?'

Virginia's startled exclamation followed instantly on her nephew's query but already he was disappearing through the door that led to the servants' quarters.

'Her be safe enough, but her won't be much longer lessen you come with me.'

Virginia heard the words as she preceded Martha into the kitchen.

'If you have harmed her in any way . . .'

'I done the girl no harm.' Caine did not flinch from the rage in the other man's face. 'Had I wanted I could have done that and been long gone, but I be here.'

'The man is right, Reuben.' Virginia stepped forward, placing a restraining hand on her nephew's arm. 'Had he

279

intended doing Carys harm he would not be here to speak of his taking her.' Her eyes frank, mouth unsmiling, she looked at Caine. 'Forgive my forthrightness but yours is a face we would be unlikely to forget and one the police would have no great difficulty in locating. To me that is a strong reason for believing in what you have said. Now if you will tell us what ransom you are seeking, we can bring this matter to an end?'

'I want no money.' Caine looked from one face to the other, seeing rage on the young man's and calm common sense on the woman's.

'Then why take her?' Reuben's fists tightened ominously and anger sparked from his dark eyes, but again Caine did not flinch.

'I took her to keep her safe.'

'Safe?' Virginia held on to her nephew's arm, feeling the tremor of rage coursing through him. A display of fisticuffs would do no good, and should this man choose to leave . . . 'Are you saying Carys is in danger in my house?'

'Not while she be in your 'ouse, but every minute 'er be outside of it.' He spoke quietly, his tone, while polite, showing no deference to the wealthy gentry. 'Does a woman veiled in black, a woman whose initials be "M" and "B", mean anything to you?'

Virginia's hand dropped from Reuben's arm. '"M" and "B",' she murmured. 'Maria Beddows – Carys's mother!'

Chapter Twenty

Maria slid her arms into a silken négligée, drawing the soft eau-de-nil folds together across her breasts. She had thought to hear from that gypsy before retiring for the night – hear that he had done what she had asked, and promised to pay fifty guineas for.

Fifty guineas! Maria laughed, shaking her hair to fall loosely about her shoulders. The man had been a fool to believe her when she had said she would pay such a sum! He would get nothing. Oh, she knew why he had demanded the necklace that bore her initials. He would threaten to use it against her, threaten to show it to the police, claiming he took it in payment for doing away with her daughter.

Maria laughed again. Let him go to the police, let him say what he would! She would claim that she had lost the necklace weeks ago and that he must have found it. She had been grateful for its promised return, for it had been a present from her husband, but when she had refused to pay fifty guineas . . . She walked to the cheval mirror practising the disappointed, hurt expression she had used many times before and found it impossible for a man to ignore. Then, she would murmur, the gypsy had threatened to concoct the story he told now.

Reaching for her hair brush, she pulled it through her mass of brown curls, mouth curving in a confident smile. But he would not go to the police; gypsies and police did not accord well together. No, the man would cut his losses and leave, but not without returning her necklace. A distraught woman with a torn veil; a beautiful woman, sobbing out the story of her attack by a scar-faced gypsy!

Maria pulled the brush through her hair, smile widening on her mouth. Maria Beddows would not be the one to lose; hers would be the winning hand as it had been with Ryder Tempal.

Oh, he had played well. Making love to her and professing to love while at the same time playing the field. The one she had caught him with would not have been his only sideline. Ryder Tempal would always have had more than one lover. *They* might have been able to turn a blind eye, to accept his carryings on, but she would not.

Anger rising like a newly kindled flame burned in Maria and she threw the heavy silver-backed brush hard on to her dressing table, smashing a dainty painted porcelain powder bowl and a crystal bottle filled with French perfume.

She would have married him! Given him everything Meshac had acquired. She had thought herself in love with him. Then she had found him with his lover and the last of her self-delusion had vanished. Ryder Tempal was taking money from her, money he was spending not on rent or keeping his household as he'd told her, but on keeping his prostitutes. What he had been doing then he would have continued to do after marriage to her, only then he would have had no need to ask for her money.

'Poor Ryder.' Maria turned back to the mirror. 'Poor foolish Ryder. You should have known, you should have known Maria Beddows would be no second string to any man's bow. You could have had all of this.' Opening the silk night coat she stared at her own nakedness reflected in the glass, admiring the swell of her breasts, the curving waist above hips that swelled like a newly opening rose. 'All of this, Ryder,' she murmured, 'but you chose to gamble and you lost.'

Refastening the gown, she crossed to the bed and draped herself across its silken cover.

'And now, my dear . . .' She smiled up at the ceiling. 'Now you are gone and soon will be joined by my daughter.' That had been a shock, she thought, her good humour fading. Ryder was so adamant he had delivered that letter, placed it in Carys's own hands. But if so how come Maria had seen her walking along the street? And it *had* been her, of that at least Maria was certain.

Damn him!

She sat up sharply. Damn Ryder Tempal for a fool! She had thought at first he had lied about sending the letter, but then common sense told her he'd had nothing to gain by not doing so; nothing to gain and everything to lose. Yet she had *seen* the girl. Had the powder she had taken from the office at Bilston lost its potency? She had thought that must be the answer, until she had taken a little from the amount she had kept and fed it to one of the cats. No, the powder was as lethal as Meshac had claimed.

So how?

Staring into the shadows gathered beyond the reach of the lamp beside her bed, Maria twisted the ribbons of the night coat between restless fingers.

The cat had died almost at once, so why not the girl? Unless . . . that must be it! There were at least two housemaids at Ridge House. The one who had shown her in, and Carys. What if somehow the letter had gone to the wrong one? Ryder had said he had given it to Carys herself, but then he had lied before. But it made no difference now. *She* had taken matters into her own hands. It had been a puzzle at the beginning, wondering if it were necessary after all to dispose of the girl, now Ryder was dead.

She smiled again at the thought of how she had trembled and wept, almost fainting into the arms of an attentive constable as she had given evidence at the magistrates' enquiry into the accident. She had lifted her veil back from her face, showing it so pale and beautiful, her wide eyes brimming with tears as she blamed herself. But she must not blame herself, the magistrate had said. A sick woman who had fainted was in no way responsible for what had been a tragic accident.

Tragic? Yes, for Ryder Tempal. But accident? Maria laughed softly.

And now Ryder was dead. He could not blackmail her with threats of exposing that letter, so perhaps she had not needed to employ the gypsy to carry out what should already have been done. Then she remembered the way Ryder had looked at Carys, remembered the beauty that surpassed her own with its fresh softness. He had wanted that softness, and where he led others would follow, and that she could not face.

Rising from the bed, she slipped off the night coat and slid naked between the cool sheets.

The last time she had lain like this had been in that back street hotel. Beneath the sheets, she ran her hands over her breasts and down to her waist. She missed Ryder, missed his lovemaking, but what he had done for her many another man could do. Ryder Tempal had been amusing, but in no way irreplaceable.

Turning off the lamp, she stared into the darkness. Tomorrow he would come, the scar-faced gypsy. Tomorrow there would be no child of Meshac's left alive.

Her head throbbing, Carys tried to open her eyes but they were covered. Behind her back a cord bit into her wrists. She had been kneeling beside Alice's grave. The mists rolled away with blinding speed, the memory of what had happened washing in on her in sickening waves.

He had dropped a cloth over her head, the man with a deep voice, then had dragged her across the heath. To where? She tried to push herself into a sitting position but succeeded only in pressing the crown of her head against something hard. Where was she . . . why had he taken her . . . did he intend other things for her before killing her? Questions tormenting her, she tried again to move, to ease the aching that tortured her every bone.

Would she be missed yet? Was Martha wondering at her absence? How long before someone was sent to enquire of Letty?

She had asked herself these same questions as she was being dragged along by her abductor, and now, as then, the answers afforded her no comfort.

How long did he intend to keep her here, blindfolded, her hands fastened together? Perhaps he had already abandoned her, left her helpless to die in the dark!

Panic filling every part of her, Carys screamed.

'Stop that!'

The voice was not the same. This was softer, a hint of sympathy beneath its curtness, a voice Carys recognised. It was the voice of the old gypsy woman.

'You knows who I be!' Bethesda saw her recognition by the way the girl stopped shrinking and held her head up.

'Now listen to me carefully. I will remove your bindings if you give your word to sit quiet while I 'ave my say. Do you promise, wench?'

At Carys's nod Bethesda loosened first the scarf from her eyes then the belt that held her wrists.

'Why am I here?' Carys rubbed her wrists, her arms painful as the blood began to circulate more freely. 'Why have I been kidnapped? It was him, wasn't it, it was your son?'

'You promised you would listen. You promised to sit quiet while I had my say.'

Carys struggled to her feet, a little of her fear abating. This woman had shown her only kindness, they had sat together at her campfire; surely she would not harm her now?

'Then please tell me what it is has made your son bring me

here in the manner he has? I would have come willingly had he asked me.'

'Which is just what we both of us thought.' Bethesda pointed to the stool she had brought inside the wagon for the night, waiting until Carys was seated. 'We knowed you would come if you thought it was me who bade you, whether the message be brought by Caine or the mouth of another. Tell me, girl, know you this?' Dipping her hand into the pocket of her skirt, she drew out the gold pendant, holding it so Carys could see.

'That belongs to Maria!' She looked from the pendant to the eyes that watched her with the sharpness of a knife.

'Your mother.' Bethesda returned the pendant to her pocket.

'How do you know she is my mother?'

'Bethesda Lazic knows many things.' Placing the briar pipe between her darkened teeth, Bethesda held a fine sliver of wood to the fire burning in the stove. Holding the glowing twig to the pipe, she sucked it into life. 'Things like a young girl nigh on raped in her own garden; like the same girl entered into a convent then abandoned when 'er chose to leave it; like a young woman who even now be grievin' for a friend newly taken from this life.' Bethesda sucked on the pipe, watching the surprise on Carys's face. The sight had shown her this girl's past as clearly as pictures in a book. 'Believe you these things?' she puffed. 'Believe you when I tell you I know many things?'

Carys nodded. 'I believe you, though I do not understand.'

'A Gorgio does not know the ways of the Romany.' Bethesda blew out several tiny clouds of tobacco smoke that rose then hung suspended in the air like lavender baubles. 'He does not have the knowledge. He lost it long ago when he gave up the travelling and chose to live out his life in one place. But Bethesda Lazic knows.' A fresh stream of smoke joined that hovering over her head. 'She sees what others cannot, and she saw the hand of your mother raised against you.'

'You must be mistaken!'

Bethesda's bird-bright eyes peered through the dim light of the candle lamp suspended from the ceiling of the caravan. 'Did 'er not seek to harm you when 'er called at your place of work to tell your mistress of a drawing on a paper beneath the bed you sleep in? Arrh.' Bethesda nodded at Carys's gasp. 'Did I not tell you, wench, I knows many things? And this also do I know. Had my son not taken you then another would have been paid to do it, and it could have been one who would not baulk at the killing of a woman. Oh, yes!' Bethesda met her startled gaze. 'Caine was promised payment if he killed you, but he be no murderer, though there do be one he would do for and gladly, but that one don't be you. 'Twas me told him to take you, me who told him to handle you roughly but do you no real harm. Did my son listen to *all* I said?'

Recognising the meaning behind the question, Carys nodded.

'I said he was to frighten you,' Bethesda went on then. 'You was to learn what will surely happen, for that woman will strike and strike again till 'er be rid of you.'

'But I cannot be any threat to her!'

'While you live you be a threat to the woman who wore that pendant.' Bethesda drew heavily on the briar pipe. 'One day you will know why, but for now it is enough to know that what I and my son have done was for your own good. You must never answer a message that comes from that woman.'

'But could Caine not simply have told me?' Carys rubbed her stinging arms.

'And what attention would you have paid? Words be like leaves in winter, they fall away and are forgotten. But fear, real fear, lives on. It can be hidden in the mind but never truly dies. The fear we have caused you was meant as a lesson, one hard learned 'tis true, but a lesson you will not forget. One that could mean the difference between life and death.'

'But what do you intend to do with me now? You have proved you wish me no harm. Do you intend I should go with you?'

'The travelling be no life for you.' Bethesda shifted the pipe with her teeth. 'Caine be fetching your mistress to take you back. 'Er must see for 'erself how easy it be for that woman to strike at you, just as 'er must choose whether or not my son be given over to the Peelers for taking you. It be a chance he be taking by fetching 'er, but it be one he is prepared for if it means the woman who took his eye and laid that mark upon his face will be paid for the evil 'er has already wrought, and prevented from doing more. But this much I vow. The gaoling of my son will not keep that woman safe, for 'tis the mother of Caine will take vengeance in full!'

'You know the woman I be speaking of.' Caine caught the look that flashed across Virginia Mountford's eyes at his description of Maria Beddows. 'Then you will know I speak true when I say her be offering a hundred guineas for the death of that girl.'

'And you took it?' Reuben tried to shake off his aunt's restraining hand but Virginia clung on.

'I took no money from her as I'll take none from you.' Caine watched as fear and anger chased across the other man's face. He could be no brother to the girl, not dressed in the fine clothes he wore and her nobbut a serving maid in this house. Then what feeling, if not a brother's love, gave rise to the fury that burned in his eyes? 'I came here to ask the mistress to come with me, learn for herself the true extent of the danger that young woman be prey to.'

'My aunt will certainly not go anywhere. And you . . . You will be serving life along the line – that is, unless they hang you!'

'The thought of hanging 'olds no terrors for me.' Caine touched a finger to his scar, tracing the line that ran to his chin. 'I died sixteen years ago, the day Maria Beddows took a horsewhip to a young lad and left him like this.'

'I will go with you.' Virginia held up a hand, silencing her nephew's protest. 'Please wait until my carriage can be made ready then we will go. You, Reuben, may come if you wish.'

'Follow the Holyhead Road toward Bilston,' Caine said as Reuben helped his aunt into the carriage then hauled himself into the driving seat. 'You will see me when you get to the place you be going to.' Before Reuben could answer he'd slipped silently into the shadowed blackness of the garden, swallowed up by the night.

'I will see you in a place other than that,' Reuben murmured, picking up the reins, urging the horse to a sharp trot. 'I will see you in hell!'

She should have known Maria Beddows would not give up with just one attempt to have Carys dismissed her post. Virginia stared out into the darkness. But the girl could not be kept confined to the house, held inside its four walls for a lifetime. She might just as well have remained in the convent if she were to live like that. Nevertheless Virginia could not dismiss altogether the feeling that somehow the blame for Carys's abduction lay with her.

The lighted windows of the Globe Inn came and went, as did those of The White Horse. Then they were passing the constabulary house and a few moments later the spire of St James's church stood like a sentinel against the night sky. Then the huddled shapes of the houses of the Portway, seeming to cower beneath the dark threat of night, were slipping away and no landmark alleviated the black emptiness of the heathland. How far must they travel? Just where had that gypsy taken Carys? To the left of the road the toll house reared darkly but no voice demanded they should halt and the carriage rolled on, the horse's hooves loud in the silent stillness.

Was the girl harmed? Had the man spoken the truth when he said he had not hurt her? Impatient with herself, Virginia forced the thoughts away. It would do no good to harbour doubt.

The sudden halting of the carriage threw her forward in her seat and when she pushed herself upright it was to hear a voice command them to follow: 'But slowly, the heath be rough just above the pool.'

Looking out through the window she caught her breath at the silver beauty of moon-bathed water nestling in a hollow at the foot of a gently sloping rise, trees and ferns etched in black silhouette about its edge.

Was this the pool where her nephew had bathed, and this the place where Carys had made that sketch?

'This be where you'll find the girl.' Caine made to open the door of the carriage but Reuben was there, pushing him aside.

Alighting from the carriage, Virginia looked over to where the caravan stood beneath the sheltering trees. Its colours were lost in the darkness but its bowed roof stood clear and proud against the sky.

'You brought Carys here?' Reuben's voice was strangled with an unnamed fear.

'I brought 'er here.' In the moonlight Caine's face held a cold challenge but in his heart he could understand what it was the other man felt, for kin or not he held a deep love for the girl they had come to fetch. ''Er be in the wagon with my mother. There be only room for one more,' he added as Reuben turned toward it.

'I know your feelings, Reuben, you don't hide them very well.' Virginia looked up at his taut face. 'But *I* must be the one to go inside. Carys could well be in shock, she should first see someone she knows well.'

'Of course, Aunt.' He continued to stare at the caravan. 'I will wait here beside the carriage. You have only to call if you need me.'

Escorting Virginia to the steps of the caravan, Caine waited till she had entered then crossed the clearing to where the horse stood tethered. Tomorrow he would confront the woman who had hired him for a killer. Tomorrow he would tell her that her plan had failed. After that the Peelers could take him, for in the eyes of the law he was guilty of abduction.

Across the clearing the two animals whickered to each other in the soft darkness.

Inside the caravan Virginia sat with Carys's hands held between her own as she listened to all that Bethesda had to say.

'Your motives were good,' she said as the gypsy woman finished speaking, 'though the implementation of them was less so.'

'If by them fancy words you means my son and me acted wrongly then that be your opinion, though I says again, who learns by words alone? Doing is understanding. Only by experience, by living through the fear, would that wench truly come to appreciate the danger that follows 'er. A thing half learned be not learned at all. For all the good it does it might just as well not be done. What I 'ad done this night was meant for a girl's well-being but if you sees it any other way then you send him that come with you along to get the Peelers. Me and my son will still be here when they come.'

'There will be no policemen called,' Carys said quickly. 'I am unhurt. Had the intention been otherwise then there has been ample opportunity for it to have been done before tonight.' She glanced at Virginia. 'This is not the first time we have met. I rode on the caravan the day I came to visit my father's grave, and afterward Bethesda was kind enough to give me tea. So, you see, there *was* opportunity had that been what was intended.'

'I do see, my dear.' Virginia rose to her feet but her hands still held Carys's protectively. 'It shall be as you wish, we shall not involve the constables. Now I think we should get you home to Ridge House.'

'And what of that woman?' Bethesda stood with her back to the door of the caravan, her thin body partly blocking the exit. 'What be 'er reward? What be you going to do about her?'

'There will be time to think about that tomorrow,' Virginia answered. Even in the sallow light of the lamp she saw Carys's mouth quiver and felt the shudder that coursed through the girl's body.

'No, not tomorrow! There 'ave already been too many tomorrows for that one.' Bethesda pulled the patterned shawl more closely across her flat breasts, her eyes glittering with determination. 'There must be a reckoning!'

'She did not mean me real harm.' Carys still tried to block the truth from her mind. Tears she had managed to subdue now streaming down her cheeks, Carys sobbed against Virginia's shoulder. 'She didn't . . . I know she didn't. We were happy until . . . until *he* came. Maria was kind to me in . . . in her way. It was only when Ryder Tempal came along that . . . that she changed. She seemed to think I wanted him, but it was not true. I disliked the man though she did not seem to believe that.'

'That is sometimes the way of things, child,' Virginia said gently. 'A woman can become so infatuated with a man she can see no wrong in him. For her he does right in all things, even when she knows the opposite is true. One day Maria Beddows will see it was so with her, she will know the full depth of her own foolishness. But she must be made to realise that her behaviour towards you has been abominable. She must be brought to justice.'

'No!' Carys pushed away from the older woman, wiping the tears from her cheeks with the flat of her palms. 'No. I will not have her brought before the justice. That will not right the wrong she has done, and she . . . she is my mother, she did what she has because of her feelings for Ryder Tempal. I cannot take vengeance on her. Promise me you will take no action against her?'

'Very well, my dear. It shall be as you wish.' Glancing past the still tearful girl, Virginia saw the tightening of the gypsy woman's mouth.

'And what about this?' Bethesda drew the chain from her

pocket, dangling its pendant from her fingers. 'Will you be wanting to take it with you for proof of what you've been told this night?'

Wiping the remaining tears from her face, Carys glanced at the golden letters. 'Will you ask Caine to return it, please?'

'That 'e'll do.' Bethesda stood aside.

'I must thank you for what you have done, both for Carys and for myself. I know the wisdom behind your actions. It is true when I say that though I myself would have listened to a warning, I would not have treated it with the seriousness it so obviously deserved.' Virginia met the gipsy woman's eyes. 'I would like to repay your kindness to my friend.'

Bethesda's mouth stretched into a smile that showed black gaps between her yellowed teeth. 'Your words be payment enough for Bethesda Lazic.'

'Thank you, Bethesda.'

Beneath Carys's kiss Bethesda's arms ached to hold her as she might have done a grandchild, though she knew that now one would never come.

At the edge of the clearing Caine watched the little group of women come down the steps of the caravan. Would they send for the Peelers tonight, or would they wait for morning? Either way would not bother him were it not for his mother. He would only be arrested after he had taken his revenge.

'Caine!' Her eyes accustomed to the night, Carys ran over to where he stood, his hand still gentling the horse. 'Caine, I know now what my mother did to you and I'm sorry, I am so very sorry.'

Looking into her upturned face, seeing the moonlight reflecting in her eyes, Caine's heart swelled with pain. He had felt something of the kind before when seeing a gypsy girl laugh up at her man, or caught the quiet look of companionship that passed between a man and his wife, but here, looking into those brilliant eyes, he knew for the first time the real extent of what Maria Beddows had robbed him of.

'Thank you, Caine. Thank you for helping me.' Reaching one hand to his cheek, Carys traced a fingertip over the livid scar, then pulling his head towards her, kissed him.

Standing beside the carriage Reuben saw the caress, and though his mind told him it was the caress of a woman for a friend, his heart lurched. Was there someone for whom such a touch would be made from love rather than gratitude? Had the girl he had searched for so long given her heart to a man? He would know soon enough. He watched the slight figure turn and walk back to his aunt then together they came to the carriage.

He would know soon enough. But did he *want* to know?

In the shadows of the carriage he watched his aunt place a protective arm about the younger woman, coming with her towards the place where he stood.

This was the moment he had thought of constantly for five years. At last he was to meet her again, to speak to her, the girl who had captured not just his likeness but his heart.

'Are you all right, Miss Beddows?'

His mouth dry with tension, he strode the last few yards that separated them, the shadowed light etching the planes of his face in gaunt lines.

Carys gasped as he grabbed her hand, but it was a sound of pleasure. She had wondered so many times whether she would recognise him again, but even in the half light there could be no mistake. This was the man she had seen swimming in the pool; the man who had accosted her, his mouth and eyes mocking; the man who had lived on in her mind and heart from that day.

'Oh, my dear, I should have told you someone waited outside for us.' Virginia misconstrued the gasp as one of fear. 'Allow me to introduce my nephew, Reuben Fereday.'

Murmuring a reply, Carys tried to withdraw her hand but he held it fast, staring at her face which moonlight seemed to have turned to white marble.

Urged by Virginia to assist Carys into the carriage, Reuben

reluctantly let go of her, but as he closed the door he looked again into the face of the girl he had wanted to find so badly.

'You will never be in danger again,' he said softly. 'Never, so long as I live.'

Chapter Twenty-one

'Promise me, promise me, you will take no action against her!' The words echoing in her mind, Bethesda lay in her narrow bed, eyes staring out at the patch of dark sky that showed through the bowed window.

The Gorgio woman had promised but Bethesda Lazic had given no such promise. Her tongue had stayed still, shaping no reply to the girl's request. Maybe *she* wanted no retribution, felt no burning inside her for revenge, maybe the girl could forgive, but Bethseda could not, and neither would her son. 'An eye for an eye,' she whispered. 'A life for a life. As you stole from my son so will I take from you. Payment in kind be the Romany way, and you will pay, Maria Beddows. *You will pay in full!*'

Caine had been hard to convince. He wanted the woman arrested, brought before a magistrate to answer for what she had done. But Bethesda knew that without the word of the girl and her mistress they had no real case. The word of the wife of a wealthy man, albeit a dead one, would carry far more weight than the word of a gypsy. No, Caine's way was not the right one. Maria Beddows would answer to a far higher power than any magistrate. But how long could his mother hold back the hand of Caine? He had listened to her

297

tonight, had gone quietly to his blanket beneath the wagon, but the same Romany blood coursed in his veins as coursed in her own. It made the same demand, uttered the same cry for vengeance. A cry that would not be stilled until he had what he sought.

As the sky lightened to a pearly pink dawn Bethesda rose from her bed. She had followed the old ways there in the heart of those trees, followed the ways practised by countless generations of her kind, and the dark ones had answered. They had told her the meaning of the sight, given her what had been left unshown. They would give her the way, but she must wait, wait until all was ready. But could she hold back her son?

Caine was gone. Bethesda picked up the folded blanket laid on the top step of the wagon and placed it inside on a chest. She would lay it across a bush when heat was in the sun. Laying thin sticks in a criss-cross pattern she set light to them before filling the kettle from the water barrel.

'He must not strike,' she muttered, eyes straying towards the copse, words directed to the forces she had conjured there. 'Stay the hand of my son.'

Sipping from her third brew of the day, Bethesda watched a figure advance across the heath, coming out of the midday sun. Putting the tin mug on the ground beside her stool, she replaced the pipe between her teeth.

It was not her son who came towards her. With a swiftness that snatched the breath from her throat, her blood turned to flame in her veins, burning with a fierceness that rocked her, cleansing her mind with the purity of fire. Then came the quiet, almost tranquil state, the less becalming of her mind that preceded the coming of the sight.

With inward eyes Bethesda watched a figure approach, halting a little way from the fire. Turning back a corner of the shawl that wrapped its upper body it revealed a child lying in its arms, a child with hair that lay like a halo about its head, a child that wore the mark of death.

As suddenly as it came so the sight left her. Drawing in a deep breath Bethesda remembered the tiny figure fashioned from mud and water into which she had dripped her own blood, remembered the rush of wind that had scooped up ash from the tiny fire of leaves, scattering silver spots over the effigy. The dark ones had sent her her answer.

The briar pipe gripped between her teeth, she stared at the approaching figure. It was not Caine who came towards her out of the sun. It was the vengeance of Caine.

'They told me you would help my babby.' The woman halted a little beyond the fire. 'The folk over along Bull Lane said as you 'ave a way with herbs, that you would cure my boy.'

Bethesda rose, laying her pipe behind her on the stool. 'I don't be the one to cure, you must ask the Almighty for that blessing, though if I can bring comfort I will.'

Stepping closer she watched the woman turn back her shawl to reveal a golden-haired child of about two years. The eyes were closed and the pale face marked with small florid spots.

This was the sprinkling of the ash. The spots covering the figure of mud. This was the way of revenge.

'The child has been poorly these many days.'

It was not a question. Silently the woman nodded.

''E be sick, very sick.' Bethesda glanced again at the sleeping child. ''T'would be wrong to tell you other. I 'ave herbs that will ease his body, take away some of the heat that burns in him, but the curing of him lies not in my hands. Maybe you should take him to a doctor.' She turned back towards her stool. The woman could take the child to a doctor but it would not save him. She had seen the smallpox too many times not to recognise what it was lay on this woman's son; she had nursed her own child through it, but no medicine or care, however loving, would save this boy.

'Parish won't pay a doctor for one that don't be its own. I

299

don't be of this parish. They will help only if I go into the workhouse.'

The woman's voice was toneless, stripped of all hope. Bethesda turned again, her glance taking in the ragged clothing, the thin face and arms that held the child with a fierce protectiveness.

'I will make you a potion.'

'No.' The woman covered the child again with her shawl. 'Tell me what plants to gather and I will make it myself.'

Bethesda saw the brief flash of pride in the tired eyes. '"Tis a skill must be learned,' she said. 'A body must know the right amounts to balance one with the other, what will poison and what will not. It don't be a thing you can turn your hand to lightly.'

'Please.' The woman bent her face to the child as it began to whimper, then looked again at Bethesda. 'I 'ave to try. I . . . I 'ave no money to pay.'

'A gypsy seeks no payment for the helping of a child.'

'But I can't be taking from you and give nothing back for it.'

Bethesda slid her hand into the pocket of her skirts, feeling the pendant, winding the chain about her fingers. 'You can pay me if that be your choice.' At the woman's nod she went on, 'There be a place a bit further along the road, a house that carries the name Holyhead. Take a package there for me. Give it into the hands of the mistress, only into her hands and no other. That will be payment enough.'

'I'll go straight away.'

The sad empty eyes pulled at Bethesda. If only it were within her skill to cure the child, but she knew it was not. He would not live beyond a week.

Going into the caravan, she took the knife from her belt. Cutting a snippet of the precious white linen she stored as dressings for wounds, she wrapped the pendant in it.

'Take you good care of this.' Outside once more she held the tiny parcel towards the woman.

Taking it in her hand, the woman made to slip it into her skirt then paused. 'I'll let the babby take care of it.' She flashed Bethesda a weary smile. 'That way he can thank you same as me.' Turning back the shawl, she slid the small package beneath the child's clothing, tucking it against his skin.

'The potion be best made fresh.' Bethesda watched the woman close the shawl about the child. 'It be taking near two hours to bring it ready for drinking.'

'I can be back in that time.'

'Should it be the mistress be not home then bring that packet back to me. Leave it with nobody other than her.'

Watching the woman walk in the direction she had pointed Bethesda felt no regret for what she had done. The disease the child carried would be taken by Maria Beddows, a disease Bethesda knew in her heart would not kill her but would take from her as she had taken from Caine.

Maria Beddows would rise from her sick-bed to find her beauty gone. A face pitted with the mark of the pox would stare back at her every time she looked into a mirror. Payment in kind was the Romany way. This then was Bethesda Lazic's vengeance. The reckoning was made. The taking of it was hers.

'I still can't believe it! It still seems unreal.'

In the garden of Ridge House, Reuben smiled at the girl he loved. He had not lived a fantasy for five years. He had searched for the seemingly impossible, not truly knowing what drove him, then he had found it. Looking at her now, so soft and radiant, he knew his heart had not misled him. He loved this girl with a depth he had not believed possible and a passion he longed to share.

'What seems so unreal?' Carys smiled.

'You.' His black eyes deepened as emotions he had to fight to control swept over him. 'Your not being a figment of my imagination, my finding you after so long. God, there were times when I thought I would go mad! I went back to Moxley on any pretence, hoping I might see you by that pool. Then I saw a box at your father's Bilston works. The foreman there told me it had been painted by you.'

'Thomas Blakeway?' Carys's glance strayed shyly to a bed of full-blown roses. 'He was always so kind to me. He would find time to help me get a design right or to blend oxides to give the colour I wanted, no matter how busy he was. He was an extremely good enameller. My father always had plenty of demand for Mr Blakeway's work.'

'He is a very good artist. I have asked him to work for me once your mother has sold up.'

'My mother is selling the business?' Carys returned her glance from the roses to him.

'I went to see her after buying your box. Thomas Blakeway said it was one of six and I wished to purchase the other five. He told me the business was being wound up, everything sold off, and I was afraid that someone else might buy those boxes so I went to Holyhead House. Maria promised to have them sent to my gallery in Birmingham but they never arrived. But that does not matter now. I have found the artist. Carys!'

Taking her shoulders in his hands, he turned her to face him. 'There were times I thought I would never find you, times I almost gave up hope – as when Maria said you had taken final vows and would never leave the convent. But even then something drove me on, forced me to keep searching. Carys, these weeks since finding you in the gypsy caravan, I have wanted to tell you: I love you. I love you so much it's killing me.'

Looking up at him, her lovely amber eyes sparkling mischievously, Carys smiled. 'Don't die yet, Reuben,' she murmured. 'Not until I tell you I love you too.'

Holding her in his arms, his mouth finding hers, Reuben felt the first sweet touch of content settle in his heart.

'I knew it was not his old aunt brought him here from Birmingham every day.' Virginia smiled on hearing Carys had consented to become Reuben's wife. 'But nothing can give me greater pleasure than your news. Now I absolutely insist you take your proper place in this house. I will no longer suffer your being a housemaid, and if you protest I will dismiss you without a reference!'

'Then where would I find a position?' Carys joined in the laughter.

'There is only one position you are ever going to hold.' Reuben took her hand, pressing it to his lips, his eyes melting. 'The position of Mrs Reuben Fereday.'

Carys stared at the little houses grouped in squares about a communal yard. Alice had lived in one of these. The sadness that filled her each time she thought of the smiling, good-natured girl welled up again. Alice had never found out who her admirer had been, who it was had written her that letter. It had given her so much pleasure, Carys thought, remembering the last time she had seen her friend, remembering how she'd pressed the sheet of paper to her lips, how she had held it against her breast as if the very feel of it somehow brought the sender to life before her eyes. Why had everything been snatched so cruelly away? Why could Alice never know the sort of love she and Reuben shared?

Blinking away the tears that misted her eyes, Carys watched the houses until they disappeared. Reuben loved her. The wonder of it, of their coming together after so long, still left her breathless. In two months she would be his wife, the loneliness of her life a part of the past.

'Be this the place, miss?'

It still felt strange, riding in Virginia Mountford's carriage, and Carys smiled shyly as the coachman helped her alight.

'I'll be close by, miss, should you 'ave need of me.'

Her thanks as shy as her smile, Carys turned into the little cemetery skirting Moxley Church of All Saints. Going to her father's grave she stared at the two tiny posies of wild flowers. Mary Bartlett still placed offerings beside those Carys left.

'I came to tell you, Father,' she whispered, replacing her

wilted posy with the spray of summer flowers Virginia had asked her to take from the garden of Ridge House. 'I am going to be married. You knew the man, and liked him. His name is Reuben Fereday.' Carys lifted her glance to the marble headstone, tears stinging her eyes, her whisper barely disturbing the silence of the warm afternoon. 'If only you could have been here to share my happiness. I love you, Father, I love you very much.'

'I thought it would be you.'

Startled, Carys turned from placing the dead flowers on the compost heap behind the church.

'When I saw them fresh flowers on the grave I knew it 'ad to be you as put them there. Ee, Miss Carys! But you look different to the last time I seen you 'ere, all them lovely clothes an' all.'

'Mary! Oh, how wonderful to see you.' Carys smiled, the pleasure clear in her eyes. 'I see your flowers whenever I come here but I have not seen you since . . .'

'No, miss.' Mary Bartlett threw her own wilted posy on to the heap. 'I don't get to visit Mr Beddows's grave as often since I don't work at the 'ouse no more, but I comes when I can.'

'You have left Holyhead House?'

'Not so much left as been chucked out.' Mary's grin was rueful. 'I was given me ticket the day after seeing you 'ere. The mistress up and told me she no longer required my services and that I was to get meself out of 'er 'ouse that same day.'

'But why?' Carys asked astonished.

'Didn't say, miss. Just said "out" and I *was* out. Maria Beddows ain't one for giving reasons. 'Er says jump and the likes of me jumps, we don't ask how high. But 'er ain't telling folk to jump now. Like as not 'er won't tell anybody anything ever again.'

'What do you mean!' Carys felt a sudden fear cold against her spine.

'You ain't heard? No, you wouldn't 'ave, living away over

at Hill Top. Maria Beddows be sick of the pox. It's said by Chrissy Williams that 'er won't live, 'specially seeing as there be nobody to look after 'er except the cook.'

'No one to look after her!'

Mary turned as Carys came to a halt.

'Like I say, there be just Kate Walker – everybody else left when they found out it was the smallpox. Chrissy Williams, the girl who took my place as maid, said the doctor didn't hold out much hope.'

'How long has she been ill?' Carys's voice trembled.

'Can't say for sure. Must 'ave been a couple of weeks, could be longer, Chrissy didn't say. All 'er did say was the medicine they was giving 'er didn't seem to be doing much good, but then 'er didn't really wait long enough to find out.'

'Thank you, Mary.' Carys walked swiftly to the carriage waiting beyond the churchyard. 'Tell Mrs Mountford I have gone to my mother's house,' she instructed the coachman. 'Tell her I say she is not to call there and neither is her nephew.'

'Eh, miss! You can't go to that house,' Mary intervened. 'Smallpox be a terrible thing, it be an awful risk. More often than not folk die of it.'

'I can't not go there,' Carys answered. 'She is my mother, I cannot leave her to the care of just one woman.'

'Well, you know my view, miss, but if you must go then I'll come with you.'

'No.' Carys shook her head. 'Thank you, Mary, but I can't take the risk of your taking the sickness. I will manage.' She turned again to the coachman, repeating her instruction, and as the carriage rolled away her glance wandered to the hollow that sheltered the pool where Reuben had bathed, then to the fringe of trees that had sheltered the gypsy camp. The caravan was gone.

'Ee, Miss Carys, I be glad they found you.' Kate Walker's round face broke into a smile that showed more than a little relief.

'You are glad who found me, Mrs Walker?'

'Why, them solicitors, o' course!'

'I have spoken to no solicitor.'

Kate's smile faded. 'I . . . I thought you be 'ere because of them solicitors?'

'No, Mrs Walker.' Carys shook her head, a little perplexed by the woman's greeting. Why should Kate think she had been in contact with solicitors? 'I am here to see my mother.'

'Then you don't know?' Kate stared at the young woman she had known from birth.

'If you mean I did not know of my mother's sickness then you are correct, at least I did not know until a little while ago. I met Mary Bartlett in the cemetery.'

'A good wench is Mary.' Kate shuffled her feet, fingers twitching a corner of her wide apron. 'It were a shame when her was given the sack from this 'ouse, but her tongue were loose in the wrong place. Gossip be best left unsaid if you don't want it to come back at you. Just what was it 'er told you, Miss Carys?'

Carys glanced about her, at a house she had known so well and which now seemed almost foreign in its quietness. Was it the same house where her father's laughter had rung out as he scooped her into his arms? Had the quiet stillness that now lay over everything always been there? Had she simply imagined Maria's bright, elegant presence, the sound of people talking?

'What did Mary Bartlett tell you, miss?'

Carys looked back at the cook, remembering how the woman had ruled the kitchen, how at a look from that round face maids would scatter like wind-blown leaves, yet at the same time she had been kind and caring, especially to a little girl.

'She told me my mother had taken the smallpox, and that you were nursing her here alone.'

'That be right.' Kate nodded. 'Be that all?'

'Yes, Mrs Walker, that is all that Mary told me. Now, I will go up to my mother's room.'

'Won't do no good. Your mother don't be in that room, nor any other in this 'ouse.'

Her brow creasing, Carys glanced at the well-polished staircase. 'Then where is she?'

'Mary Bartlett didn't tell you the all of it.' Kate led the way to the sitting room. 'Sit you in here while I brew you some tea and I'll tell you what I know.'

'No,' Carys said as the woman's hand fastened on the door knob. 'I . . . I would prefer to sit in the kitchen. That is, if you don't mind?'

'I never minded you being there when you was a child, and I've no objection now you be growed.'

'Mrs Walker, if my mother is not here, then where is she?' Carys had held the question while the other woman had bustled about her task of making tea. Now, seated at the large table with its blue cloth, a cup of tea untouched in front of her, she broke her silence.

'Best I start at the front end.' Kate twisted her own cup in her plump hands. 'Were not long after the funeral of that Mr Tempal . . .'

'Ryder Tempal is dead?' Carys asked, astounded at what she heard.

'Some weeks since.' Kate did not look up. She had said before that gossip was best left unsaid and there was gossip enough about Ryder Tempal's going under that train, and how Maria had shown no sign of any fainting turns afore going off to Bilston station that morning.

'Did . . . did he have the pox?'

'No, miss.' Kate answered the query without meeting Carys's eyes. ''E died of an accident. Then, like I say, your mother were took sick some time after. At first we thought it were nothing more than a chill, but when 'er got worse we sent for the doctor. When he said it were the smallpox the others panicked and left. It be a vicious thing the smallpox, nearly always it kills, and if not that then chances be that them who gets it be marked by it for life, so you can't blame folk for getting out.'

'But you?' Carys asked. 'Why did you not go with them?'

Kate twisted her teacup. 'There be a few who somehow be safe from the pox, don't ask me how for I don't be knowing. All I know is I be one of them, though my father and my two brothers didn't be.'

'I'm sorry, Mrs Walker.'

'Arrh, well, miss, that time be long past.' Kate took a sip from her cup, using the moment to subdue the sorrow that still rose whenever she thought of that period of her life.

'But how did my mother contract the illness?'

'Who knows?' Kate's head moved in a slow shake. 'It strikes at whoever it wishes, comes out of the blue, smallpox. It don't send no visiting card.'

'If I had only known!' Carys breathed.

'Thank God you didn't.' Kate Walker's glance shot upward. 'That at least be one blessing to come out of all this. Anyway there were little to do once the doctor had her moved to the fever 'ospital.'

Of course. Carys remembered the small isolation hospital in Bull Lane. All cases of infectious disease were sent there.

'Be no use your going to that 'ospital neither,' Kate said as Carys made to rise. 'Truth be, Miss Carys, your mother died a week gone yesterday.'

'Died!' She stared disbelievingly. 'But . . . but Mary said she was here?'

'I told you Mary Bartlett didn't know it all.' Kate's tone held sombre sympathy. 'Maria did come 'ome, but in a couple of days she was sick again, this time of the pneumonia. Seems 'er didn't 'ave the strength left to fight off another illness and 'er went. It were quick, wench, you 'ave that consolation at least. There were no suffering the second time.'

It was not true. Kate inwardly sought her maker's forgiveness for the lie. But 'Sufficient unto the day was the evil thereof' was the motto she lived by, and this girl had had enough sorrow for one day. Kate Walker would not be the one to add to it. She would not tell her of the screams that had rent this house when Maria Beddows had looked in her mirror and seen the marks that pitted her face like tiny craters. She wouldn't tell this girl of hearing her mother pace her bedroom day and night, nor would she mention a tiny pouch that held white powder or finding the woman who had swallowed some of it dead on her bed. She had burned the pouch and washed Maria's scarred face, leaving no visible sign of what had happened. She alone knew, the doctor saying Maria's lungs had collapsed and she had died of the new infection. But her suicide had come as no surprise to Kate. Maria Beddows had been a woman too proud of her own beauty to live with scarring, and though she had also been bitter and spiteful in her dealings with her own daughter, the Lord would inflict His own punishment for that. Kate would not have it known she had died by her own hand.

'I be sorry, Miss Carys.' She watched the girl push the cup about the saucer. 'I would 'ave sent word but I had no idea where to send to. Besides, I was told everything would be handled by the solicitors, that's why I thought they had told you.'

'No.' Carys forced the words past the tears welling in her throat. 'I had no word.'

Walking slowly through the silent rooms she let the tears fall unhindered. Both her father and her mother were dead and she had not been there to comfort either of them.

Chapter Twenty-two

Why had Virginia not sent for him? It had been a week since Carys had gone to visit her father's grave. A week since his aunt had received that message to say she had gone to her mother's house. Clearing the busy area around The White Horse, Reuben urged the carriage on, feeling the same panic that had swept over him when he had at last wrung the truth from Virginia.

Smallpox! The word rang like a death knell in his brain. Maria Beddows was ill of the smallpox and Carys had gone to her. Virginia had not sent him word, knowing he would go to that house; she had wanted to protect him from possible contagion. He could not be angry with her for that, but what use was his life if Carys should lose hers? If he had found her only to lose her now?

'*You will never be in danger again. Never, so long as I live.*' Those were the words he had said to her that night at the gypsies' camp. But what use had they proved? Why had he not been with her, to put actions to those words?

Flinging a coin to the keeper of the toll house, Reuben kept the carriage moving. Maybe he would be in time. Please God, let him be in time! He would bring Carys from that house even if he had to carry her out.

Kate answered the insistent ringing of the doorbell, almost falling backward as Reuben rushed into the hall, blinking at his curt, 'Where is she?'

'The mistress be . . .'

'I do not mean your mistress.' Strain showed deep on his face. 'I refer to her daughter, to Miss Beddows, where is she?'

'Miss Carys be outside, sir, in the garden.'

'Is she all right . . . is she ill?'

'No, sir.' Kate watched relief flood his face. 'Miss Carys isn't sick. Who will I tell 'er be calling?'

Reuben released the fear that had held him, letting it drift away in a long, slow, silent breath.

'I will tell her myself.'

Following the way the plump woman pointed, Reuben stepped into the garden, immediately recognising anew the scenes he had seen painted on boxes bought from Meshac and sold in his gallery. A shaded walk overhung with jasmine, a small water garden where a Grecian goddess poured water from one urn on to a surface studded with deep pink water lilies, but it was for a white-painted summerhouse his eyes searched.

Locating it deep with in the garden, it took every vestige of his will-power to walk quietly towards it. He wanted only to rush up to her, to take her in his arms, to kiss away her fears and his.

'Carys.' He called her name softly, then spoke it again louder as she ran into his arms. The questions he wanted to ask became lost; fear he thought had left him caused him to hold her in a fierce embrace.

'Reuben.' Carys tried to speak but the repeated pressure of his mouth on hers prevented her doing so and she lifted her arms to him, giving herself up to the joy of having him hold her.

'Why, my darling?' Lifting his head just enough to see into her eyes, Reuben at last asked the questions that had plagued him all the way from Ridge House. 'Why did you come here? Why put yourself in so much danger?'

Laying her head against his chest, Carys answered softly: 'Because she was my mother, Reuben. Would you not have done the same had it been Virginia who was sick?'

Reuben held her silently, knowing he had no argument against what she said, and only too thankful she had taken no harm in coming to this house.

'My mother is dead.' Carys released herself from his arms. Lifting a face wet with tears, she added: 'I came too late to speak to her, to tell her I did not blame her for what happened between us. Oh, Reuben, can't you see? It was her feeling for Ryder Tempal that caused her to act as she did.'

The sob in her throat catching at his heart, Reuben drew her again into his arms, holding her tight against him as she sobbed out her beliefs – beliefs that would be her comfort in the days to come.

'Love can do strange things to a woman and she was in love with Ryder Tempal. That can be the only reason for her placing me in that convent and then refusing to allow me to return to Holyhead House.'

Was it the only reason? Reuben touched her hair gently with his lips. Maria might once have thought herself in love with Tempal, but would it not be nearer the truth to say Maria Beddows's one true love was herself? That she would have suffered no rival even though the opposition be her own daughter.

'If only I could have been with her, Reuben, told her I understood. Told my mother I knew what drove her to do the things she did.'

From the garden the perfume of full-blown roses drifted across the golden afternoon. The girl he loved had risked her life in coming to this house, but in doing so had eased her heart, had found a kind of peace. Tilting her face with

313

his hand, he looked into her lovely eyes, his own melting with love, and as his mouth closed over hers Reuben knew his own happiness was complete.

He had found his girl on the heath.